Deception Island

A Novel of Suspense

James Boyle

Thanks -
for your bookshelf

James Boyle

Edited by Heidi Connolly

First published by Dog Ear Publishing
4011 Vincennes Rd
Indianapolis, IN 46268
www.dogearpublishing.net

ISBN: 978-1-4575-3726-4

This book is printed on acid-free paper.

This book is a work of fiction. Places, events, and situations in this book are purely fictional and any resemblance to actual persons, living or dead, is coincidental.

Printed in the United States of America

Also by James Boyle:

Ni'il: The Awakening

Ni'il: The War Within

Ni'il: Waking Turtle

For

Daniel P. Boyle

September 11, 1939—July 8, 2014

And

Robert Gatlin

September 19, 1950—July 1, 2014

Acknowledgements

As always, a project as complex as writing a novel is never truly a one-person job. I wish now to thank all those who helped with various stages of this work's creation. Thanks to Mr. Everett Dial, District Attorney of Curry County, Oregon for his invaluable help with some of the legal issues the story raised. I'd also like to thank my critique group who gladly offered their advice and insights on many scenes as I worked on them. All my beta readers who read various versions and helped improve the next, particularly Candace Callen, Melissa Dunn, Stefanie Freele, and Bob and Sandra Gatlin. Of course, my editor Heidi Connolly, whose suggestions have always been invaluable.

And, as always, a huge thank you to my family for their unwavering support.

PART ONE

Death Notice

CHAPTER 1

The memory was clear and sharp, as if it had only happened yesterday.

It was Labor Day weekend. Jason was twelve.

He and Jeremy sat in the captain's chairs at the stern of his father's boat, *The Lady L*, each of them gripping their rods as if expecting a salmon to jerk them overboard at any second. Their dad sat behind them, at the wheel, maneuvering around the other fishermen on the Sound and keeping the boat at good trolling speed.

The late summer sun was warm on Jason's face and flashed in a zillion tiny jewels among the waves. The sky was cloudless. A light westerly breeze cooled the air just enough to make a sweatshirt comfortable. The air smelled of cedar from the nearby islands, sea salt, and diesel exhaust. *The Lady L*'s engine grumbled like a tiger purring.

It was perfect.

"Hey Jason?" his dad called from his seat at the wheel.

Jason turned back toward his father, who would never look more relaxed, more at home, than sitting there in faded jeans and a flannel shirt, his feet shoved into rubber boots, one hand comfortably minding the boat's wheel, and watching his sons work their rods. This was where his father was meant to be, not in a shirt and tie in some office above the cannery floor.

"Yeah?"

His dad nodded at something off the stern on the starboard quarter. "See that twenty-foot Bayliner a hundred-fifty yards out?"

Jason quickly spotted the boat. It was a big, open cockpit number with only a windscreen as protection from the elements; what his dad called a "fair weather" boat. A figure straightened up with a fishing rod and cast his bait out over the stern. His yellow plaid shirt looked unnaturally bright against the white of the boat.

"I see it," Jason said.

"What's he doing wrong?"

It was a test.

Jason glanced to his brother for help, but Jeremy, four years older and a veteran of many such tests, had suddenly grown gravely concerned about the action of his reel.

Jason was on his own.

What was the guy doing wrong? Jason bought a little time by reeling in some line while he scrambled for an answer. For the correct answer. His dad was looking for one in particular. But what was it?

"It ain't that hard a question, son," his dad prodded. "Watch him. What's he doing wrong?"

Jason watched the man settle back in a captain's chair and pour something from a bright silver thermos into a cup. Coffee probably, though something harder wasn't out of the question. Many fisherman spent the afternoon getting wasted out here. His dad said it was fine as long as they weren't piloting the boat. Piloting a boat drunk was just as stupid as driving a car drunk; both could get everybody killed. It was one of THE RULES.

Like someone had flipped a switch, he had the answer.

"He doesn't have a buddy with him."

"Give the man a cigar!" his dad said. "Naw, you're too young. But I'm not."

He fished a cigar out of a shirt pocket, then lit it with his lucky Zippo. Jeremy, who had been paying attention after all, playfully slugged Jason on the shoulder. Jason slugged him back.

"Now, remind me, son. Why should he have a buddy with him?"

"Because there's no one there to help him if he gets hurt or falls overboard."

"Exactly. Rule number one is—?"

Both boys answered together. "Never take a boat out alone farther than you can swim back."

"And how far can you swim?"

"Not far with a busted head," Jeremy said.

His dad's laughter echoed over the blue waters of the Sound.

CHAPTER 2

It being Monday morning and all, a multi-car accident on I-5 just south of 40th Street had transformed all four southbound lanes into a parking lot. Seattle's notorious rush hour had just become a nightmare. According to local news radio, traffic was backed up as far as Everett. Highway 99, the other major north/south route, was nearly as bad because of the overflow.

Jason turned east on 45th Street, away from the Interstate, cruised through light traffic for a mile and a half, then turned south on Mountlake Boulevard toward the University. Lisa had probably steered her little Civic on the exact same route thirty minutes before. Maybe she'd missed the worst of the traffic.

Within a block and a half he was back in bumper to bumper traffic, but that was normal. Like most colleges, the University of Washington had been designed for foot, not auto, traffic. Jason usually avoided the area if he could. But at least traffic was moving. He could probably walk faster, but it was moving.

No sooner had he formed the thought than both lanes of traffic ground to a halt. To their left the massive facade of Husky Stadium hulked across barren parking lots. To the right, students in raincoats or under umbrellas scurried around red brick buildings toward their morning classes. The overcast seemed to have lowered and grown darker. In the distance, he could just see the steel gray surface of Lake Washington.

Jason glanced over at the powder blue minivan idling beside him. A woman with long dark hair was talking on her cell phone and gesturing with her free hand. Behind him, a man with a mustache that matched the dark color of his SUV grimly sipped coffee from a Starbucks cup.

One afternoon, several years before, while sitting at a traffic light just like this, Jason had glanced over to the car next to him and recognized the prominent leader of an area mega church. The good Pastor was spending his down time at the traffic light getting friendly with a blond woman in the passenger seat. Jason suspected the blond was not his wife. He'd snapped a quick photo with his cell phone and done some investigating. The minister had indeed been breaking the Seventh Commandment.

Jason's story had ended up on the front page. Below the fold, but the front page. You never knew where the next story would come from.

But not today.

His cell chirped that he'd received a text. He fished the phone from his jacket pocket and glanced at the display. Lisa. He opened the phone and the message.

CU 2nite? she'd written. *Luv u.*

His phone asked him if he wanted to reply.

He wasn't sure.

He wasn't sure about a lot of things when it came to Lisa. Oh, he liked her. He liked her a lot. No doubt about that. She was kind and smart and funny in a goofy sort of way. She was working on her masters in American history at the University and could instantly go from discussing the nuances of the Nineteenth Century political climate to wrestling with Hector, her Pomeranian, like a little girl.

She collected teddy bears, for God's sake.

Jason truly enjoyed being with Lisa. That wasn't the problem. The problem was that she was beginning to make long term plans. As in lifetime plans. He wasn't sure he was ready for that. He didn't want to break up; he didn't want to see other people. He just wanted to slow down.

They had to have a serious talk. But how to do it without hurting her escaped him.

He avoided the whole issue for now, saved her text, and instead called the newsroom. Marcia, the receptionist, answered on the second ring, only a touch of frazzle to her voice. He told her about the traffic situation and that he'd be late.

"Oh we've heard," she told him. "Believe me, we've heard. Half the newsroom is running late. Miles is not a happy man."

Miles Condiff was city editor and Jason's boss.

"Miles wouldn't be happy if Jesus came down to personally hand him a Pulitzer."

Marcia laughed. She had a nice throaty laugh.

"Besides, it's Seattle," Jason added. "He ought to be used to it by now."

"You know Miles. 'We've got a paper to get out!'"

"Tell him not to have a coronary. I'm on my way."

Marcia said she would relay the message. "By the way, I really liked your story yesterday."

Jason smiled. It still made his heart glow when someone liked his writing.

He thanked her and ended the call.

His car radio was already tuned to one of the all-news channels, such as it was. He viewed most of his colleagues in broadcasting with barely concealed contempt. How could you take seriously a medium in which an in-depth report lasted two minutes? But he wanted to hear whether anyone else had picked up his story.

With the help of an inside source, he had uncovered a scam involving a contractor who was providing inferior asphalt to the City Roads Department, but charging for top-of-the line product. It was no wonder the city's streets were in such sad shape. Not only was the contractor essentially doubling his profits at taxpayer expense, but he'd been doing it for nearly ten years. And that was almost exactly how long the contractor's father, Harold Stevenson, had been on the City Council.

There was no mention of it on the radio, but it was late in the rotation and they were talking about the Huskies win over Cal last Saturday and whether they had a shot at upsetting the Oregon Ducks next weekend. (Jason wouldn't bet on it. The Ducks were very good.) The headlines would come at the hour and half-hour. He checked his watch. Ten more minutes.

The double column of vehicles ahead of him began to inch forward. He slipped his car into gear and followed the taillights of the Camry in front of him for about a hundred yards before the procession again came to a stop. Now though, he could see the traffic signals ahead. With luck, he'd get through the intersection on the next cycle.

A few raindrops splattered against his windshield, then thickened to a light rain.

"Perfect."

He opened his cell phone again and dialed his home phone number. No one was there, of course. No one had been there since Friday morning, which is why he needed to check his messages. When it switched over to voice mail, he punched in the access code and waited as the computers did their thing.

The spooky computerized woman told him he had twelve new messages.

He told the computer to play the messages.

The first three were computer-generated sales pitches offering to refinance his mortgage (he rented) eliminate his credit card debt (it was reasonable, thank you) and save him money on his auto insurance. He quickly erased all three. Next up was a man's voice: "Hey, it's Charlie. Listen, I met this gorgeous woman, but she won't go out unless I find a guy to go out with her roommate. What are you doing tonight?" Jason had no idea who the guy was. Charlie? He didn't know anyone named Charlie. Besides, the message had been left on Friday night, so it was too late now. He deleted the message.

He quickly deleted five more sales calls and hang-ups, then a man's voice caught his attention. The voice had an unusual tone, somber. "This is Detective (the name was unclear), of the King County Sheriff's Department. I'm trying to reach Mr. Jason Reynolds. It is very important that I speak to him as soon as possible." He repeated that it was very important and left a call-back number. The message had been left Saturday afternoon.

Jason frowned. What was that all about? He hit the button to save the message.

*

Fifteen minutes later, Jason hitched the strap of his laptop case back onto his shoulder and stepped off the curb with the crowd of other late arrivals crossing John Street. On the south side, he ducked between two umbrellas, hung a right, and headed up the block toward The *Seattle News* building. The rain had paused for the moment, but the clouds still hung low and pregnant with moisture. The air was cool and smelled of the Sound.

As always, he found himself gazing in simple admiration as he approached the *News* building. Something about the edifice awoke in him the kind of awe a cathedral might inspire in others.

The *Seattle News* building had been built in 1925 by the newspaper's founder and the paper still occupied the first five of its seven stories. The top two housed a CPA and a law firm. It's facade was weathered red brick, darkened now by the rain, with limestone cornices and elegantly arched windows. Every doorknob in the place was polished brass; every door solid wood; every floor tongue and groove oak. It felt solid and eternal, beyond the dirt and decay of the everyday world.

Jason climbed the steps to the arched entrance and pushed through the heavy glass door with the paper's name etched across it.

Pink granite floors and mahogany paneling dominated the lobby. Tropical plants lurked in the corners and ornate brass chandeliers hung from the ceiling. It looked like a genteel hotel.

Jason strode past the elevators and took the stairs. He was only heading up one floor.

The newsroom wasn't anything like in the movies: something of a cross between the floor of the stock exchange and a smoky bar, with a hundred phones ringing, reporters and editors screaming at each other while copy boys darted in and out of the chaos like street urchins.

In reality, the newsroom could have been the workspace at any large company. First, it was smoke-free like every other business in the state. Second, the newsroom only got really intense when a story broke late enough to crowd their deadline. Right now, the deadline was fifteen hours away and the atmosphere was almost serene. Phones chirped, laser printers whirred, people talked. All very business-like.

For some reason he'd never quite figured out, it always smelled dusty.

Marcia sat at her desk across from the elevators, the telephone pressed to one ear. Jason waved at her as he passed. She lifted a hand and smiled. Then he was past her and making his way through the warren of desks to his work station. About two-thirds of the paper's reporters were already there, catching up from the weekend, answering emails, or working on new assignments. He exchanged greetings with a half dozen before reaching his own desk, setting his laptop and briefcase on the floor and booting up his computer.

Debbie looked over from her desk immediately to his right and flashed a smile. She'd woven her dark hair into a French braid that fell between her shoulder blades. Her makeup was almost invisible. Like most of the reporters, she dressed simply: a teal sweater over a white button-down shirt, khakis, and flats. A hooded waterproof jacket hung over the back of her desk chair. Jason liked Debbie and respected her work. More people should. Her sweet, wholesome, girl-next-door look hid a mind like a tiger shark.

"Hey," she said.

"I-5 was a zoo today."

"So I heard. Must be Monday."

"All over," he said. "You talk to Miles yet?"

She shook her head. "Stevenson issued a statement this morning. Did you see it?"

"Not yet, but I heard about it on the radio. It sounded like the usual 'I have nothing to hide' crap."

"Pretty much. It should be in your email."

Both knew that the real victory lay not in what the Councilman said or didn't say in his press release, but in the fact that he'd felt a need to respond to their charges so quickly. It meant they'd struck close to the bone. It meant he was worried.

It's what every reporter lives for, blood in the water.

"Anything from the construction company yet?"

"Not a peep."

No sooner had he sat down than Jason's desk phone chirped. He picked it up. "Reynolds."

"Can I see you in my office?" He recognized Miles' gravelly voice.

"Be right there."

He looked at Debbie. "Miles wants to see me."

"Probably wants to give you a gold star."

"Probably two."

Miles wasn't really the feel-good, positive feedback type.

Jason made his way across the newsroom to the city editor's corner office. More likely, Miles wanted to discuss a follow-up to yesterday's article about everyone's favorite city councilman. Fortunately, Jason already had an article sketched out profiling Stevenson and Debbie was working on a similar story about the son-in-law's construction company. He also had been gathering material about the history of graft in city government, particularly the Public Works Department.

He'd let Miles make the final decision on what to run. He was the editor; he would anyway.

Mile's door stood open when Jason arrived. He tapped on the door and poked his head in. "You wanted to see me?"

Miles sat at his cluttered desk, but he wasn't alone. Two men sat in the client chairs facing the editor's desk. Both were in their mid to late forties; both wore wool suits in earth tones, comfortable shoes and conservative ties. The one to Jason's right was a little taller and heavier, with dark hair graying at the temples. The other had sandy-colored hair buzzed so short it was merely a shadow on his pink scalp.

Cops.

"Excuse me. I'll come back later."

"No, come in, Jason. Please, have a seat," Miles said, his tone unusually mild-mannered. "These gentlemen would like to talk to you."

Jason stepped into the room, all his defenses on high alert. Was Stevenson retaliating already? It seemed a little heavy-handed, even for him.

The dark-haired cop heaved himself to his feet and extended a hand. He was about four inches taller than Jason and fifty pounds heavier. Jason could see the mark where he'd nicked himself shaving this morning. "Detective Kyle Peterson, King County Sheriff's Office. This is my partner, Detective Ron Dahl." The other man had also gotten to his feet and offered his hand.

Jason shook hands with both men, keeping his face neutral. "What can I do for you?"

Peterson took the lead. "Why don't we have a seat?"

Jason glanced at Miles for a clue where this was headed, but his boss's expression was unreadable.

Jason pulled over another client chair and sat to the right of the two detectives. With Miles, the four men formed a small, irregular circle. Like a group therapy session.

Det. Peterson took a deep breath and gathered himself.

"We have been asked to contact you on behalf of the San Juan County Sheriff's Department. Normally, we wouldn't bother you at work, but we tried to reach you several times at your apartment over the weekend and weren't able to catch you."

San Juan County? So this had nothing to do with Stevenson.

"I spent the weekend at a friend's."

Peterson nodded as though he'd suspected as much.

"What's going on? What does the Sheriff want with me?"

Peterson took a deep breath. "There's been an accident involving your father."

One of the detectives was wearing Old Spice cologne. The hard drive in Miles' computer whirred.

"My Dad? Is he okay?" Jason asked.

Peterson shook his head. "I'm sorry."

"What happened?"

The voice sounded like his own, but he was somewhere else, watching it unfold. Disconnected.

"Sorry, we don't know any of the details. You'll have to call the San Juan Sheriff's Office for that. "

The detective handed Jason a business card with a phone number and extension hand-written in ink on the back. Above the number was the scribbled name Sgt. Daniel Hayden.

"When did it happen?"

"Again, I don't know any specifics, but we received the call from San Juan Saturday morning."

Saturday morning. Two days ago. His dad had died two days ago and he hadn't even known.

"I'm terribly sorry," the detective said. "Is there anyone we can call? Any family in the area? A minister maybe?"

Jason shook his head. He couldn't shake the image of his dad lying alone in a morgue for two days while the authorities tried to track his son down. His brother and mother had both died years ago; there was no one else to be there for him. No other family. Two days.

"We'll make sure he gets home safely," Miles said. "Thank you, detectives."

The men rose in unison, and slipped quietly out the door.

Jason ignored them.

Two days.

*

Jason looked down at the card the detectives had left with him. He had to look somewhere. The phone number was still there, written in blue ink, the handwriting firm, but sloppy, like it was jotted by someone used to taking quick notes. A reporter—or a cop. He turned it over and looked again at the print: Det. Kyle Peterson, King County Sheriff's Office and a phone number. The detective seemed a righteous guy. Might be worth trying to develop into a contact.

He flipped it once more and took in the handwritten number on the back. It hadn't changed.

"I suppose I should make a phone call," he finally said.

Miles was watching him closely from his seat behind his desk. His chin rested in his right hand. "You can use my phone, if you'd like."

"Thanks anyway," Jason said. He rose to his feet, the card still held in front of him. "I'll call from my desk and find out what's going on. I'll probably need to go up there."

Miles peered at him. "You going to be okay?"

Jason nodded.

"I'll talk to HR and get you some time off. You have some vacation coming, don't you?"

"I think so."

"I'll take care of it. If there's anything else I can do to help, just let me know."

Jason thanked him and headed for the door.

"And Jason?"

He turned back.

"I'm very sorry about your father."

He made his way back to his desk, feeling as if his mind was on a two second delay. His body acted on its own. It was his body that returned a "*morning*" to Rick Coburg as they passed outside Miles' office, that told his legs to move across the carpet and maintain balance, that avoided running into desks and dividers.

Then he was at his desk, sitting in his chair.

After a moment, he picked up his desk phone and punched in the number written on the card. Sgt. Daniel Hayden.

It picked up on the first ring.

"Sgt. Hayden."

The voice was female. Brusque and business-like, but definitely female.

It threw him for a moment.

"Hello?" she asked again.

"Um," Jason hesitated. His mind seemed to be working with the speed of Jello. "I'm trying to reach Sgt. Daniel Hayden...?"

A pause on the other end. "I'm Danielle Hayden."

Now he was embarrassed. "I'm sorry. The note I have is hand-written; it looks like 'Daniel.'"

"Happens all the time," Sgt. Hayden told him. "Is there something I can help you with?"

"Yes. I think so. This is Jason Reynolds," he managed. "I'm supposed to call you regarding my father, Lee Reynolds."

"Mr. Reynolds," her voice softened a bit. "You're a hard man to track down."

"I wasn't home this weekend," he told her. "I just talked to a couple of Sheriff's detectives down here. They gave me your number."

"Yes. We asked them to. Some news shouldn't come over the phone."

"Can you tell me what happened? Was it a heart attack? He'd had some heart troubles a couple of years ago."

But the medications were working. And he'd changed his diet, quit smoking, drinking, all the stuff the doctors told him to do. He'd been doing fine. At least he'd said he was. How long ago had that been? Two weeks ? Three?

"We're still investigating," Sgt. Hayden said. "But it looks like he had a boating accident."

"A boating accident? What kind of boating accident?" Jason frowned. There were a lot of things that could go wrong out on the water.

"All indications are he fell overboard and drowned."

The sensation of unreality, that the entire morning had to be some kind of twisted dream, grew stronger. "There's got to be something else you're not telling me."

"I'm sorry?" she sounded genuinely puzzled. "What do you mean?"

"My dad practically grew up on the Sound, Sergeant. He spent his whole life on boats, both working and for pleasure. Falling overboard and drowning? That's about as likely as you or me running head on into a parked car on the drive home tonight."

The pause on the other end stretched into discomfort. When she spoke again, Sgt. Hayden's tone had lost its friendly sympathy. "Like I said, Mr. Reynolds, we're still investigating. It's possible something like a heart attack caused him to fall overboard."

Jason closed his eyes, took a deep breath, and forced himself to relax. The woman probably wasn't even involved in the investigation. Probably just some poor slob assigned to notify the next of kin. Pissing her off wouldn't help.

"I'm sorry," he told her and he was. "I didn't mean to be rude. I guess I'm more upset than I thought."

"That's understandable. You've just had a shock." But the sergeant's voice stayed formal.

"Do I need to come up and make an identification?"

"That won't be necessary. But you will have to arrange for the funeral and such things. It's nothing that can't wait though; the medical examiner over in Friday Harbor should be finished by tomorrow."

Jason closed his eyes. A post-mortem. Of course they were doing a post-mortem. They did one on every unusual death. Standard procedure.

"The ferry runs every twelve hours. 7:00 am and 7:00 pm from Anacortes."

Jason thanked her.

"And Mr. Reynolds? I am sorry for your loss. Your father was very well liked in this town."

"Thank you. And again, I'm sorry if I offended you earlier; I'm sure you're covering every base."

Again, a pause on Hayden's end, but shorter this time. "Let me know when you get to town, Mr. Reynolds."

He told her he would, set the phone back on its base and leaned back in his chair. For a few seconds he just sat there, not really thinking about anything, his eyes idly following the geometric patterns cycling through computer's screen saver.

Dad was dead.

His father was dead. Deceased. Passed away.

Dead.

No matter how often he repeated it to himself, it still refused to be real. His dad was too big, too tough, and too strong to let something as flimsy as age or heart disease do him in. The man never saw a doctor the entire time Jason was growing up. It was as if someone told him that Mt. Rainier had crumbled to dust overnight. He'd have to see it with his own eyes.

Tomorrow. He would be able to see it with his own eyes tomorrow.

But first, there were things he needed to do. Preparations to be made, both for the trip back to his home town and for once he got there. He needed to pack some clothes, enough to last for a week, maybe more. He had to arrange for a funeral. Jesus. A funeral. Did Port Salish even have a funeral home? He needed to settle his father's affairs, pay bills, file life insurance claims, figure out what to do with the house, the boat, the truck. Probably a dozen other things he hadn't even thought of yet.

He just needed to start.

Instead, he stared at the screen saver playing across his computer monitor.

"Hey." Debbie looked over at him. "You okay?"

Jason attempted to fake a smile, but didn't quite pull it off. "Sure."

"What did Miles say in there? You look like you got the ass-chewing of the century."

He shook his head. "My dad died."

"Oh my god." Debbie's hand touched his forearm. Gave it a squeeze. "I'm so sorry. Had he been sick?"

Not sick enough to keep him from going out on his boat.

Debbie withdrew her hand as Miles strode out of his office toward Jason's desk.

"I just got off the phone with HR," Miles told Jason. "You're officially on vacation through Friday. I don't expect to see you at this desk until next Monday. If you need more time than that, let me know. We'll work something out."

"What about the Road Department stories?" They had to follow up. It was the only way to keep the pressure on Stevenson.

"Debbie can handle it. Copy her on your notes and make sure she has a way of contacting you if any questions come up. Okay?"

Jason and Debbie exchanged a quick glance. Both nodded. That would work.

"Copy those notes and get out of here," Miles told him. "The paper will survive. Go take care of yourself and your family."

If only he'd had one left to care for.

CHAPTER 3

It took almost two hours for Jason to explain his notes to Debbie, the article he had sketched out on Stevenson, and his ideas for what they should do next. All subject, of course, to Miles' approval. Debbie was more than capable of filling Jason's shoes for a few days and had the advantage of already being familiar with the story. Still, he'd kept most of his ideas in his head, not on paper. That, and the fact that you needed some kind of Rosetta Stone to understand the notes he did have, made Debbie the only practical choice. Anyone else would have taken too long to bring up to speed.

The nuts and bolts mechanics of working a story seemed to dispel the surrealism he'd been struggling with. By the time Debbie and Miles forced him out of the newsroom, Debbie assuring him that she would call if she had any questions at all and Miles insisting the paper could survive for seven days without him, Jason almost felt normal.

At least his mind seemed to be functioning properly and he no longer felt he was standing off to the side watching himself like some kind of puppet. Now he could handle the things he needed to do before leaving.

The tasks he'd face in Port Salish were another story, but he'd deal with that when he got there.

One big problem remained unresolved though. His relationship with Lisa. This new development wouldn't help. She would want to drop everything and come with him. Unfortunately, that wasn't what he wanted. He couldn't explain why, even to himself. It was just something he needed to deal with on his own. At least at first. Now, if he could only find a way to tell her without making it seem like a total rejection.

*

The drive home was uneventful. The accident this morning had been to the north; he was heading east and most of the traffic was still heading into the city, not out. His apartment was part of a large complex on the southwestern edge of Bellevue, across Lake Washington from the city proper.

Jason gathered his accumulated mail, let himself into the apartment, deposited the mail on a dusty kitchen counter and his laptop and briefcase on the floor. For a moment, he stood looking around his small one-bedroom. He hadn't been home since Friday morning, three days ago, and he felt like he had to reacquaint himself with the place. He walked through the living room and into the bedroom and bath. Everything was exactly as he'd left it, frozen in place three days ago.

Back in the living room, he checked his land line answering machine for new messages. There weren't any.

He could put it off no longer. He pulled out his cell and sent Lisa a text asking her to call him when she had a minute. Her class would end in about ten minutes.

Time to start packing.

*

"Jason!"

"In the laundry."

He pulled a soggy mass of wet denim from the washer and tossed it into the dryer. One of the first things he'd realized was he couldn't pack for seven days without doing laundry first. He simply didn't own that much clothing. The first load had just finished washing and he was making room for the second.

Lisa swept into the kitchen, tossed her bag on the counter, scattering pieces of mail to the floor, and headed straight for him, her arms already extended. She looked ready to burst into tears.

He straightened up and accepted her hug.

"I'm so sorry," she murmured into his chest. "Are you okay?"

"I'm okay" he assured her.

Lisa stepped back and looked up at him, her hands still holding his. "Really, how are you doing?"

"I'm okay. Really. I don't think it's sunk in yet."

"It'll take a while, I'm sure."

Jason let go of her hands and returned to moving laundry from the washer to the dryer. "For now, I'm just trying to keep busy."

Lisa looked down at the dirty clothes piled around their feet. "Don't waste much time sorting, do you?"

"Never have." Jason finished loading the dryer and turned it on. "I just wash everything in cold water."

Lisa rolled her eyes. "That's probably why all your white socks are actually light gray. Clothes come with washing instructions, you know."

He shrugged.

"Here, let me do it."

Jason didn't protest as Lisa edged him aside and began sorting his clothes into piles of whites, darks, and colors, explaining the differing water temperatures for each as she went. Jason let her go. It made her feel useful, he supposed, and he had no burning desire to do the laundry himself. The fact that he'd probably never sort his clothes, didn't mean he'd stop her from doing it.

Lisa scooped up the pile of whites and dropped them in the washer. "Bleach?"

"Nope."

She shook her head, added detergent, set the water temperature to hot and started the washer. "Well, hot water's better than nothing." She wiped her hands on the thighs of her jeans and turned to him. "What else do we need to do?"

"I don't know. Not much. I need to pack once the laundry's finished," he told her. "When the Benson's get home, I'll ask them to pick up my mail. I can gas up the car in the morning. I think that's about it."

"You're not leaving tonight?"

He shook his head. "First thing in the morning. Early. I need to be on the road by 5:00." That would get him to Anacortes by 6:30 in plenty of time to catch the 7:00 ferry. Better to be early and have to kill some time, than risk being late. It would be twelve hours before the next ferry.

Lisa looked up at him, her expression a mixture of concern and something else he couldn't quite identify. "I'm sure I could get a few days off. I'd just have to call a couple of professors."

There it was.

Jason had gone over this conversation countless times in his head, searching for the perfect words. He'd never found them. And none of the scenarios had them standing in his tiny laundry room, dirty clothes piled around their feet. Or accounted for the living, breathing Lisa standing right in front of him.

So he punted.

"You want some coffee? I made a fresh pot when I got home."

Something passed over her face. "Sure."

Jason led her into the kitchen. He gathered the mail she'd knocked off the counter, then grabbed two mugs and filled them with coffee. Lisa leaned back against the counter, facing him.

"All I have is non-dairy creamer," he said as he set a mug beside her. "Hope that's okay."

"It's fine." Lisa added some of the powder to her coffee and stirred it in. "You're avoiding my question."

Jason sipped his coffee. "I know."

"You don't want me to go with you."

"It's not that," he paused. The perfect words still eluded him. "I don't think it makes sense right now."

Again, something passed over her face, like a flinch, then was gone. She studied her coffee as if the secrets to the universe were hidden in the dark liquid.

"There wouldn't be much for you to do up there, other than give me moral support," he told her.

"That's kind of the point."

"I know, but school is too important. It makes more sense for you to go to your classes and come up on the weekend. That's when I'll need you the most."

Lisa nodded, but didn't look at him. "You shouldn't have to deal with this alone."

"That's why God invented telephones."

She didn't even smile.

"I really think this makes the most sense. "

Lisa still wouldn't look at him.

This wasn't going the way he'd hoped. "Please, don't be mad."

"I just don't understand," she said, finally looking up at him, her eyes bright with tears. "If my folks died I'd be a blubbering wreck. I'd want you with me because I couldn't function on my own."

"I don't know that it's really sunk in yet," he told her again. "It won't be real until I get to the house. Maybe not even then."

The truth was he hadn't yet shed a tear for his father. It was still just a bunch of words. Shocking, yes, tragic even, but it wasn't truly real. He didn't know when it would make that transition. When he saw the body? When he stood in his father's empty house? At the funeral? He didn't know. With his brother, it had been during the funeral, but when his mother died it had been immediate. Then, the sense of loss had hit him like a giant wave, nearly drowning him in grief.

So far, Lisa had shed more tears for his father than he had.

What did that say about him?

She reached over now and took his hand in her own. "That's what I'm worried about; when it does hit you, you're going to be all alone."

He squeezed her hand and shrugged. "It's just something I'll have to deal with. And I know where you are."

Lisa shook her head and looked down at her coffee. "This creamer sucks."

*

Jason ran down to the deli a few blocks away to get a couple of sandwiches while Lisa started another load in the washer and folded his dried jeans. Lisa had a 2:30 seminar she needed to attend, but until then she would help Jason with his laundry.

When he returned, they unwrapped the sandwiches—a pastrami on sourdough for himself, a turkey on wheat for Lisa and two bags of chips—on the coffee table and sat on the couch to eat. For a few minutes they concentrated on their lunch.

"Tell me about your dad," Lisa said, pausing between halves of her sandwich. "What was he like?"

Jason wiped his fingers on one of the flimsy deli napkins and thought about how to answer to her question. "He was a man."

"Well, I kind of assumed that."

"No." Jason shook his head. "Not just an adult male, but a *man*. There's a difference."

Lisa looked intrigued. "I'm listening..."

"He was strong and tough as anyone. I don't think he got sick the entire time I was growing up. He was a commercial fisherman until us kids came along, then, because Mom thought fishing was too dangerous, managed the cannery until he retired. Both are tough jobs that employ tough people."

Lisa nodded and took a bite of the second half of her sandwich.

"But the same tough guy never raised a hand against his wife, never belittled us kids when we screwed up, never made us feel stupid. Life wasn't perfect, by any means, but growing up I never doubted my parents' love for each other or us kids." He looked at her. "There's an awful lot of people who can't say that."

Lisa hooked an errant lock of hair behind her ear. Her own parents had divorced when she was in grade school. Both remarried within a few years and she'd spent her childhood bouncing back and forth between the households.

"You've never talked about him much."

"Dad and I were never that close," he said. "Not as close as I think either of us wanted."

"Why's that?" Lisa pinched off a corner of her sandwich and slipped the tidbit into her mouth.

"I don't know. We just never had all that much in common. I think if my dad and I were just two men, unrelated, we'd be acquaintances, but not really friends." He looked at her. "Know what I mean?"

"Sure."

"Jeremy was the one who took after Dad. He was the football and basketball star, the hunter, the soldier. I was the artsy one, the one who took after Mom. I sometimes think Dad couldn't quite figure me out."

"'Figure you out'?"

He paused for a moment, searching for a good example. "It's easy to support your kid when they're on the football team. You go to the games. You celebrate their touchdowns. You save their clippings from the paper. That's easy. How do you show the same support for your other kid? The one who was editor of the school newspaper? Then editor of the yearbook? There's no cheering section for that." Jason shrugged. "I don't think he ever really figured that out."

The dryer buzzed.

Lisa was on her feet before Jason could react. "I'll get it."

"I can do my own laundry, you know."

She leaned over to kiss his cheek. "It makes me feel like I'm helping. Besides, I'm going to have to head to my seminar soon. You're on your own after that."

She hugged him, kissed him again, and went off to fold clothing. Jason remained on the sofa, staring at the remains of their sandwiches on the coffee table. After a moment, he reached over and began to re-wrap his sandwich. He was no longer hungry.

*

After Lisa left to attend her seminar, Jason finished his laundry, then packed the clean and folded clothing into a suitcase, then another suitcase. He was going to be gone for several days, possibly a week or more, and the weather could be anything from sunny days in the eighties, to wind and rain, and even an outside chance of snow. In addition to underwear, jeans, slacks, various shirts and sweaters, he also packed a set of thermal underwear, a pair of wool socks, and a knit watch cap.

Finally, he pulled his only dark suit from its spot at the side of his closet and brushed the dust off the shoulders. He was more of a sport coat kind of guy, but during his senior year of college his father had insisted that a new graduate needed a suit. They'd spent a Saturday afternoon shopping the city's menswear shops before deciding on this particular suit. Despite Jason's protests, his dad had insisted on paying for the whole thing, including the alterations. He'd called it an early graduation gift.

The afternoon had been wonderful, just himself and his dad, wandering around downtown; lunching on burgers and a beer at a hole-in-the-wall pub near Pike Street, then another beer; watching the fishing boats coming in on the waterfront. It had been the first time they'd spent any serious time together simply as two men sharing an afternoon.

He slipped the suit into a garment bag along with a couple of ties that seemed appropriate and added that to the pile of luggage near the door. For a moment, he stood there and scanned the apartment, trying to think of anything else he might need. Nothing immediately came to mind.

Lisa had insisted he spend the night at her place. She'd even offered to cook him dinner. As a result, he'd be leaving from there in the morning, so he needed to make sure he didn't forget anything.

He smiled to himself. You'd think he was going across the country, not just a couple of hours upstate. It wasn't like he couldn't come back and get anything he forgot.

Still, he wandered from room to room, double checking his mental list as he went.

He came to his desk and stood looking at his laptop and briefcase, lying among the piles of paper and file folders. The tools of his trade. He hadn't planned to take them because he wasn't working; he was burying his father. Now he was having second thoughts. He'd never let them out of his sight for more than a few hours at a time. Now he was going to leave them in his empty apartment for a week?

What if Debbie called with a question about the Road Department story? He added his briefcase and his laptop to the pile of luggage at the door.

He already felt better, more complete.

Jason stood there for a moment, wondering what to do with himself for the hour until he'd head over to Lisa's. His eyes fell on the pile of unopened mail on the kitchen counter. He began to sort through it, pitching the junk into the trash, saving the bills to deal with later, and concentrating his attention on the few interesting items.

One envelope in particular drew his interest. It was a 9x6 manila, with his name and address handwritten in blue ink on the front. There was no return address. The postmark, though smeared, looked like Port Salish. His hometown. His dad's hometown.

Jason opened the envelope and pulled out a photograph. A young Asian man stood at the stern of a boat. He wore faded jeans, a coat, and knit cap and squinted unsmiling into the camera. Behind him on the left lay blue water bordered by dark ridges of forested land. To the right were the crowded boats and tangled masts of a marina. Port Salish harbor.

It was the standard souvenir photo his dad took for all his charter customers. But they were usually given to the customer. Why did he send it to Jason? He flipped the photo over, but nothing was written on the back. Nothing written on it at all, no name, no date, nothing.

He returned to the envelope, shook it, then peered inside. Nothing. He'd hoped for a note, something to maybe identify the man in the photo. But it was empty. Just the photo of an unidentified Asian man.

So why had his dad sent it? He must have thought the photo itself important enough to make a note unnecessary.

Muffled voices sounded in the corridor outside Jason's door. A second later he heard the unmistakable giggle of Trudy Benson. Her husband, Don, wouldn't be far away. The two were nearly inseparable. He needed to ask if they would collect his mail while he was gone.

Jason slipped the photograph into his jacket pocket and went to talk to his neighbors.

CHAPTER 4

Taylor Smith wasn't actually bald. You just couldn't tell by looking at him. He'd picked up the habit of shaving his scalp as a young man in the Marines, continued in his time as a cop, and now it was part of his daily routine, like shaving his beard. Trouble was, sometimes he missed a spot, like just above and behind his right ear.

And it drove him batty.

He self-consciously touched the line of stubble now as he took one of the chairs in front of the director's desk. It was full dark, well past normal office hours and the lights of Seattle's business district lit up the windows of the office. It was dazzling.

"Anything to report?"

"Not much," Smith answered, willing his hand down to his lap. "He appears to be in for the night. He's probably going up to Port Salish in the morning."

"I assume there will be nothing to find when he gets there." The old man sipped from a tumbler of scotch, his preferred refreshment this time of night. He had not offered any to Smith and Smith hadn't expected him to.

"Of course."

The old man nodded, seemed to consider his next question for a moment.

"Do we think he's going to be a problem?"

"It's too early to tell. So far, he's done nothing a grieving son wouldn't do, but it's early."

"How big a problem could this be?"

"Worst case scenario? He has the potential to be a disaster."

"He's that good?"

Smith nodded and touched the line of stubble behind his ear again. "You read the paper. You've seen his file. He's very good at what he does. He also has the medium to reach a wide audience and a reputation that will make that audience listen. Ask Councilman Stevenson."

The old man snorted. "Stevenson is a moron."

"A moron who's won five straight elections."

The old man downed the rest of his whiskey in a single swallow and set the tumbler on his polished desktop with a thud. "I assume we have contingency plans to deal with this if it does become a problem?"

"Of course. That's what you pay me for."

"Really?" The old man peered at Smith. It was like meeting the gaze of a rattlesnake. "Seems to me you were supposed to take care of this problem a couple of weeks ago. Yet here we are."

Smith refused to be intimidated, but he lowered his hand into his lap again. "It is what it is. We deal with it. This is the wrong business if you're expecting perfection."

The old man nodded. Just barely. "So what is your recommendation?"

"We sit tight and continue to watch him. We should know in the next few days how big a threat he's going to be."

"Either way," the old man told him. "I want this problem eliminated by the end of the week. Understood?"

Smith nodded. "Understood."

CHAPTER 5

The islands appeared on the horizon like a smudge of charcoal in the crease of a gray canvas. The rain had stopped earlier this morning, but it had left the sky hidden behind a curtain of ink-washed cloud. Below it, running to meet the clouds at the horizon, the Sound glistened in the weak light like greased steel, its surface only slightly warped by a gentle swell. It was in the subtle crease where the Sound met the sky that the islands now grew.

Jason leaned against the railing just behind the ferry's starboard bow, his hands shoved deep in his coat pockets against the chill, and watched the islands grow as the ferry plowed toward them. It was peaceful. The only sounds the splashing of water under the bow, the raucous scream of gulls, and the steady thrumming of the boat's powerful engines as they pushed across the water.

He had the exterior deck all to himself this morning. It was well past tourist season. His fellow travelers were all regulars, people whose jobs demanded they ride this ferry early on Tuesday morning. They'd seen the view countless times before and would countless times again; they chose to spend their time in the warmth of the cabin with coffee and the morning paper.

Jason had seen the view before himself, but was too restless to sit inside and wait.

He had read the *News* this morning. The story about Stevenson he'd briefed Debbie on yesterday ran on the lower part of the front page, under a byline crediting both himself and Debbie. The story was good. Debbie had kept to the outline he'd already sketched out, but added some nice quotes that really fleshed it out.

He sent Debbie a text. *Nice job on the story.*

The reply came within a minute. *Thanks. I had help. How are you?*

Okay. On ferry now.

Let me know if I can do anything.

I will. Thanks.

The islands were now close enough that Jason could begin to make out individual features: the blunt point of Mt. Shaw, the highest spot on Ebey Island at a whole 450 feet, the whitewater marking the shoreline of Deception Island to the right, the occasional flash of color marking a house among the forest. They were still too far away to see any real detail.

Jason pulled the photo from his coat pocket and looked at it again. He'd probably looked at the mysterious man's face two hundred times since opening the envelope yesterday afternoon. He still had no idea who the man was or why his dad sent it to him.

The man's identity would be the second question he intended to answer. The first was what had really happened to his dad. Jason had even looked up the weather conditions for Friday and Saturday. It had been mild on the Sound around Ebey Island, with temperatures in the low fifties, a steady rain, and winds barely breaking ten knots. Certainly nothing his dad couldn't handle.

And, of course, there was the rule his dad had drummed into both his boys: never go out on the Sound alone. Had his father broken his own rule the day he died?

Jason sensed, rather than heard, the cabin door open and close behind him. He glanced over as a tall, powerfully-built man in a black overcoat paused to light up a cigarette. He was absolutely bald, not even a shadow of stubble. The man got his cigarette going, nodded at Jason, and leaned back against the cabin wall.

No smoking was allowed in the cabin, of course.

Jason returned the nod, slipped the photo back into his pocket and turned back toward the islands.

His cell phone chirped an incoming text. He fished the phone out of his pocket. Lisa. She would be getting ready for school right now.

How's it going?

On ferry now. Be there in 10.

Good luck. Miss you already.

Me too. Call you tonight.

He ended the call.

The timbre of the thrumming engines changed under his feet. The ferry's bow began turning as if the captain intended to pass to the left of the island. But Jason knew it was merely the maneuver that would begin their approach to the landing at Port Salish. He had watched countless times as his dad had made the same maneuver heading back from a day of fishing.

The islands were now close enough to make out details: the ornate Victorian roof and towers of the Lundgren house high above the bay; the baby blue rectangle of the water tower on the upper slopes of Mt. Shaw. Jason could even pick out the colored jewels that were cars moving along Shoreline Road.

He could not see the town itself yet because the body of Deception Island was in the way. Early explorers had thought it was part of the main island. Only when the area was fully charted was it determined that a narrow channel actually separated the two bodies. Thus its name.

The ferry completed its maneuver, turned to starboard and headed into the channel between the islands.

The smoker coughed behind him. Jason glanced back in time to see him light a second cigarette and drop the first onto the deck. The man caught his eye and shrugged through the cigarette smoke.

Jason turned back to the islands. Now he could clearly see the Victorian castle Lars Lundgren had built on the heights of Lundgren Point where he could keep an eye on his domain. As far as Jason knew, his descendants still lived there. The yellow paint certainly looked fresh. A long set of white wooden stairs led from the house to a dock where a launch was tied.

The ferry passed a shoulder of land on the left and began the turn into Salish Bay. Ahead lay the little town, clustered on a shelf of land and the adjoining slopes at the head of the bay.

The Captain announced their arrival at Port Salish.

Home.

Jason turned away from the rail and started back toward the cabin.

The smoker was already gone.

*

Jason's first stop in Port Salish would be the sheriff's substation. He needed to formally introduce himself to Sgt. Hayden and find out exactly what was going on with the investigation. After he'd picked her brains he'd go up to his dad's house and start there.

Jason drove past the cluster of buildings housing fishing guides, past the boxy building that used to be the cannery, now tourist shops, and turned left on 1st Street heading into the town center. If his memory was right, the sheriff's substation was located about a block west of City Hall.

In Old Town.

He drove into the neighborhood of weathered red-brick buildings left over from the town's glory days: the Evergreen Bank building on his left; beside it, the old Lundgren Company Headquarters, now a museum; the Mercantile on the right; the old Lutheran Church; Schroeder and Sons Funeral Home. All were massive, timeless red brick with white limestone trim, and looked pretty much the same as they did when he was a kid.

It was almost like driving back in time.

He passed City Hall, and spotted the substation on the next block, to his right. It was a low brick building, much newer than the others in the area, fronted by a neatly trimmed lawn and planters filled with juniper. A modest parking lot to one side held a handful of civilian cars and two sheriff's patrol cars.

Other than the patrol cars and the sign out front, it could have passed for a dentist's office.

Jason pulled into the parking lot and parked in a slot marked Visitors. After a moment's hesitation, he locked his car. Probably the only person in town who did.

He walked into the sheriff's office.

A stocky deputy with male pattern baldness looked up from behind his plexiglass barrier as Jason walked in. "Can I help you?"

"I'd like to speak to Sgt. Hayden, please."

"Is she expecting you?"

"I believe so," he said and handed the deputy his business card.

The deputy's eyebrows went up. "A reporter?"

Jason smiled. His card often brought that kind of response. "I'm not working. It's just easier than fishing out my driver's license."

The deputy looked him over, then picked the receiver off the phone console on the side of his desk. He punched in a number, said something, listened, spoke again. He looked up at Jason. "She'll be right out."

"Thanks."

Jason stepped away from the window and occupied himself with reading the public service posters decorating the walls of the anteroom.

Less than a minute later, he turned as an electronic lock snapped open. A slim brunette nearly his height in a sheriff deputy's uniform pushed the door open. Her hair, still wet from the shower, was pinned back in a tight French braid. "Mr. Reynolds?"

"Yes."

"Danielle Hayden. You must have come straight from the ferry."

"I did." Jason shook her hand. "Thanks for seeing me."

"I wish it could have been under better circumstances. I'm terribly sorry about your dad."

Jason thanked her.

"Come on back," she said. "We can talk in what passes for my office."

She held the door open as he stepped into a small squad room holding a handful of empty desks. Computers whirred quietly and a printer somewhere shot a document into the "finished" tray.

"This way." She led him to the right and down a carpeted corridor to a little office. A wood-grained sign on the door read Sgt. Hayden, but no job title. In keeping with the dentist's office motif, this would have been one of the exam rooms. "Would you like some coffee? It isn't too bad by cop-shop standards."

"Sure. Thanks."

"Make yourself at home. I'll be right back. Cream and sugar?"

He shook his head. "Black's fine."

Her office was small, holding a standard gray metal desk with a computer, a file cabinet, two chairs and little else. There wasn't room for much else. An aerial photograph of the island covered one wall. Several framed awards and certificates hung on another. The only personal touch he could see were a pair of bright floral drapes that covered the window.

He could see no portraits of a family, no children, no husband or boyfriend. She wasn't wearing a wedding ring.

Sgt. Hayden returned with white mugs bearing the sheriff's seal, handed one to Jason and sat behind her desk with her own. Jason tasted the coffee. She was right. For cop-shop coffee, it wasn't bad.

For a few beats she gazed at him, smiling.

"What?" he asked.

"You don't remember me, do you?"

He shook his head. He didn't have a clue. "I'm sorry."

Her smile deepened. "There's no reason you should, I suppose. We went to high school together. But I was just a freshman; you were a senior."

"Oh. Sorry. I think, as a rule, seniors don't really see freshmen," he told her. "If you know what I mean."

She nodded. "Pecking order."

"Pretty stupid, wasn't it?"

"Yeah. But I'm sure I did the same thing to the freshmen when I was a senior."

"We all did a lot of stupid things in high school."

She shook her head, and set her coffee mug on her desk top. "But you didn't travel all the way from Seattle to relive high school, did you?"

Jason shook his head.

He watched her select a file folder from the stack on one side of her desk, open it and pull out a bundled sheaf of paper. He sipped his coffee while she scanned the report, flipping from page to page looking for a particular passage.

Danielle Hayden had a habit of pursing her lips as she read which made her look younger, almost girlish. She wore almost no makeup, just the subtlest hint of eyeliner to set off her green eyes.

She glanced up at him. "Sorry. This is the report from the medical examiner up in Friday Harbor. He faxed it over just before you got here, so I really haven't had a chance to go over it very thoroughly."

The post-mortem. On his dad.

"In short," she told him. "He's determined that your father died by drowning, just as we suspected. He's ruled the manner of death was accidental."

Jason started to protest, but her raised hand stopped him. "Before you go ballistic, two things. First, the Sheriff's Department has nothing to do with the medical examiner's findings. They are exactly what they say they are: *his* findings."

Jason nodded.

"Second, he did find other injuries that occurred at or immediately prior to your father's drowning. Most notably—" she sought and found a passage in the report. "an area of contusion including a minor skull fracture to the back of the skull." She looked back up at Jason. "He speculates that your father slipped, hit his head, lost consciousness, and fell overboard."

Jason was already shaking his head.

"What?"

"I'm not buying it. What did he hit his head on? Everything moveable or with an edge is inside the gunwales. If he'd knocked himself out, he would have fallen inside the boat, not overboard."

"Okay. Maybe he fell overboard first, then hit his head. Either way, we have absolutely no evidence to suggest anything other than a tragic accident."

"So that's it?" he said. "You're not even going to investigate it?"

"Unless you have some evidence I'm not aware of, I'm afraid there's nothing to investigate."

He didn't say anything.

"Do you have some evidence for me?"

Jason had to shake his head. He had nothing. "But I knew my father. Something just isn't right. He was a professional out on the water and extremely safety conscious. He wouldn't *accidentally* fall overboard."

Sgt. Hayden nodded thoughtfully, pursing her lips again. "Let me ask you a question. You think your father's death was suspicious. Right?"

"I think it's a possibility."

"Do you have a suspect? Did he have any enemies?"

Jason shook his head. "Not that I know of."

"What about a motive? Why would someone want your father dead?"

"I don't know. That's why I want an investigation. To find out."

She leaned forward, folding her hands on the desktop. "You're an intelligent man. I've been reading your articles in the *News* for years and I've always been impressed, not only with your writing talent, but with your insights into human nature. Both our jobs require a certain understanding of human nature and psychology, don't they?"

Jason nodded.

"So, honestly now, how much of your thinking that your father's death wasn't an accident is because you don't want to believe it was?"

Jason dropped his gaze to his hands on his lap. She was right, the first stage of grief was denial. If he were in her shoes, he'd be asking the very same question. Many people refused to believe their family member was even dead until they'd physically seen the body. A few denied it even then. He had nothing but a feeling that something wasn't right. Why should she believe him?

"Okay." He took a deep breath, looked back up. "You could be right. Maybe I don't want to believe it was just an accident. Maybe I can't believe it. But our jobs have something else in common."

"What's that?"

"Have you ever walked onto a crime scene, heard the witnesses, looked around and knew that something wasn't right? You have no evidence to prove it, but something just didn't add up?"

The sergeant nodded. "Sure."

"Well, we reporters get the same feeling. We call it 'smelling a story.' And I smell a story here."

"I know you do."

"So help me out."

"I have rules I have to live by. My hands are tied," she told him. "But bring me some hard evidence and I'll help type the story up for you. Deal?"

"Are you giving me permission to snoop around?"

"As if you needed my permission." Sgt. Hayden smiled and sipped her coffee. "Just try to not be a nuisance. Remember, this is a small town and word travels fast."

He didn't need her permission to investigate anything, of course, either personally or officially. Nobody did. It just made a life a lot easier if the local authorities weren't opposed to what you were doing.

Almost as an afterthought, Jason slipped the photograph from his pocket and handed it across the desk to her. "Do you know who this is?"

She took the photo from him and studied it for a good minute before shaking her head. "I don't think so. Why?"

"My dad mailed this to me. I got it last Friday."

"Last Friday?" She looked again at the photo. "Curious."

"That's what I thought. There was no note, no explanation with it. Just the photograph."

"I don't think he's a local. I would have seen him around." She handed the photo back to Jason. He returned it to his pocket. "Maybe he was one of your dad's clients."

"It looks like one of the souvenir shots he takes for them. But why would he send it to me?"

She couldn't answer that.

*

The house where Jason and his brother had grown up was a '30s-era Victorian farmhouse in a neighborhood of similar houses on the lower slopes of Beacon Hill. Back in the boom days the homes had been built by the prospering fishermen, cannery managers, and merchants who called Port Salish home. By the time Jason was born the boom was long over, the neighborhood was no longer upscale, and many of the houses were losing their battle with time and the elements. But they'd still been captivating, especially to a young boy with imagination.

Now, as Jason drove down Salmon Berry Lane, he noticed that Port Salish's reincarnation as a retirement and tourist community had been good to the neighborhood. Many of the stately old houses had been restored to their former glory and he counted two that were in the middle of major work. The shrill of power saws filled the air.

Even the house on the south side of his dad's had a dumpster parked in front.

Jason pulled into the drive sloping up the left side of his father's house, beside the neighbor's dumpster.

His dad's pickup wasn't in its usual spot. But it wouldn't be, would it? It'd either still be down at the Port, or in the police impound yard.

He parked beside the house, removed his briefcase and laptop from the car and climbed the half dozen steps to the front porch. Jason still half expected the front door to open and his dad emerge to greet him. To welcome him home. He didn't, of course. No one did. No one was there.

Jason took a deep breath and tried the front door. To his surprise, it was locked. His dad never locked the house unless he was going out of town. When Jason had pointed this out, his dad had shrugged. "Port Salish is a small town," he'd said. "On an island. No burglar worth his salt is going to bother with us."

But today it was locked.

Fortunately, his dad had given Jason a key years ago. He unlocked the door and stepped into the living room. It was exactly as he remembered it. His father hadn't changed the decor since the day his mother died. He'd never seen a need to.

Jason set his briefcase and laptop on an armchair and just stood there for a moment taking in the atmosphere. The place simply oozed his father. There were hints of his mother, of course. Everything from the art on the walls to the patterns on the furniture were his mother's choice, but her choice of over twenty years ago. It didn't so much show a woman's touch as the memory of one. It was now all his dad's.

It was also a cave. All the window blinds were drawn.

He opened the blinds, letting the living room fill with light.

It looked like his dad had just stepped out for a beer or to grab something from the market. In the kitchen, dishes still soaked in the sink; the coffee maker held half a pot of cold coffee. A fishing magazine lay on the dining room table folded open as if he'd intended to finish the article later.

Jason found his dad's answering machine. To his surprise, there were no messages. There should have been a few, he thought. Word traveled fast in a small town, but it wasn't perfect. Somebody would have called, not knowing he was dead. Somebody would have tried to reach Jason. A telemarketer would have called. Somebody would have called.

But no one had.

He left the kitchen, glanced in the downstairs bathroom, saw nothing of interest, then moved into the den at the back of the house. Or what used to be the den. His father had pretty much turned it into his office years ago. But it had always been "the den" to Jason; he just couldn't bring himself to call it anything else.

His dad had updated the television to a fifty-inch flat screen, but the room was dominated by a desk, a PC, a printer/fax combo and a two drawer steel file cabinet. It was his office, study, and living room. And again, it looked like he'd just stepped out for a few minutes. An empty beer bottle and a partial can of peanuts sat next to the keyboard. So did the remote for the TV. The air was scented with the memory of cigar smoke.

Jason sat at the desk and turned on the computer. While it booted up, he began looking through the desk drawers. He wasn't sure exactly what he was looking for. Something labeled in bright orange "CLUE"? He didn't know. At some point he'd need to go through all his dad's files, business and personal, but right now he was just glancing around, orienting himself.

And looking for clues.

He found his father's checkbook and scanned the register, but nothing looked out of the ordinary. Most everything else in the desk drawers were what he'd expect: office supplies, copies of the fish and game regulations, and odd correspondence. Nothing of interest.

He turned his attention to the computer. He saw all the usual programs, Microsoft Office, Outlook Express, Internet Explorer, Photoshop. Nothing attracted his attention. He briefly opened his dad's accounting program, but found nothing interesting there, either by its presence or by its absence. He then tried Internet Explorer. It successfully opened to his dad's homepage, Yahoo News, so he had internet access.

He leaned back in the chair, thinking. Something was wrong, he was sure of it. Deep in his gut he knew he was missing something significant, something right in front of him. He just couldn't put his finger on what it was. It was as if he'd blanked out the name of some familiar movie star.

The answer was to walk away. Quit thinking about it.

His cell phone rang. A local number. The only person in town who knew his cell number was Sgt. Hayden.

He answered it.

"Mr. Reynolds?"

"Jason," he told her.

She paused. "The medical examiner has released your father's remains. They'll be on the evening ferry. I took the liberty of calling Schroeder and Sons, the local funeral home."

"Thanks."

"No problem, but you'll still need to call them to arrange the funeral and everything."

"Of course."

"Got a pen and paper?"

He was a reporter. He always had a pen. He pulled a pad of notepaper closer and told her he was ready. She gave him the name of Lindsey Schroeder and a local number. He scribbled it in an unused corner of the page, just below a note reading "strawberry fields."

Odd. He didn't think his dad had ever voluntarily listened to a Beatles song. He was more of a Johnny Cash man.

"Mr. Reynolds? Jason?"

"Yeah. Yeah. I'm here."

"Everything okay?"

"Yeah, fine," he said. "Sorry, something distracted me."

"Anything I should know about?"

He smiled. "Are you a Beatles fan?"

"Excuse me?"

"Never mind."

"One other thing: the Department will release your father's boat to you tomorrow morning. Do you know where the sheriff's dock is at the port?"

He told her he thought so.

"A deputy will be there between 8:00 and 9:00. You just need to bring some ID and sign a couple of release forms."

He told her he would be there.

"That's all I've got. Is there anything else you need?" Sgt. Hayden asked.

"No. No, I think that's it. And thanks."

"Happy to help," she told him.

They disconnected.

He immediately called the funeral home and set up an appointment with Mr. Schroeder for 3:00, two hours from now. The woman he'd talked to said Mr. Schroeder would explain all the options then. She'd had an extremely soothing telephone voice. Jason wondered whether they trained for that at mortuary school, or did it come naturally?

He put down his phone.

Again, he had the annoying feeling that something important was lying there just beyond his grasp, taunting him.

The musical *ding-dong* of the doorbell echoed through the house.

"Coming!"

He opened the front door just as the bell began its second chime. An older couple stood on the front porch, smiling uneasily. They looked to be somewhere in their mid-sixties, he a foot or so taller than she, and both wearing the pudginess that develops where less activity meets a growing income. The woman held a casserole dish in front of her, her hands protected by stylish oven mitts.

"You must be Jason," the woman said. "We're the Stockton's, from next door. I'm Emma and this is my husband, Tom."

Jason shook Tom's hand. It was strong and dry.

"We wanted to give you our condolences," she continued. "Your father was a very nice man."

"Thank you," Jason said. "Would you like to come in? I have to be at the funeral home in a little bit, but I've got a few minutes."

Tom was already shaking his head.

"We don't want to intrude." Emma exchanged a glance with her husband. "But we thought with everything you're going through, you probably hadn't even thought about feeding yourself, so I made a little something for tonight." She indicated the casserole dish.

"That was very thoughtful of you," he told her and meant it. He hadn't eaten anything but a bagel all day. Until now, he hadn't even thought about it.

"It's a tuna casserole. Nothing special. But it will fill you up."

"I'm sure it's very good. Thank you."

She smiled. "Just point me toward your fridge..."

He showed her the way to the kitchen. Jason turned to Tom. "You were friends with my dad?"

The older man peered at him. "We were friendly. Went fishing a few times. Had him over for barbecue a couple times. Wouldn't call us best buddies, or anything."

Jason understood.

"What did you want to know?"

"How he seemed last week. Was he acting different, like something was bothering him?"

"I don't know." Mr. Thomas frowned. "Didn't really talk to him last week."

"You tell him about what happened at the post office?" Mrs. Stockton said, returning from the kitchen.

Her husband shook his head.

Jason looked from one to the other, waiting for an explanation. "What happened at the post office?"

"It was nothing really," Emma told him. "Last Thursday, I think it was." She glanced at her husband for confirmation. He nodded. "I was down at the post office getting our mail. There's no mail delivery in town, you know."

Jason nodded. It had been that way when he was growing up too.

"Anyway, I spotted your dad walking out right ahead of me. So I said 'Hi, Lee' and he just about jumped out of his skin. I apologized for startling him, of course, and he recovered quickly, kind of laughed it off, you know."

Jason nodded.

"I can't get over the look in his eyes," she told him. "He looked really scared."

*

"I was giving you until 6:00," Lisa told him when she answered the phone. "Then I was going to be really pissed off."

Jason had purposely waited until after 5:30 to call. By then, he figured Lisa would be finished with her classes, whatever errands she'd needed to run, and be safely home. One of their issues was Lisa's habit of talking on her cell phone while driving. For him, it was a matter of safety, not to mention the law; she thought the subject a silly waste of time. So he avoided calling when he thought she would be driving.

"I wanted to make sure you were home."

"I know."

He could hear Hector in the background, barking and barking.

Lisa covered the phone to say something to the dog. "Hector says hi."

"Hi, Hector."

"How are you doing up there?" she asked. He could almost see her as he listened. She'd be in her purple Huskies sweats, sitting crossed-legged on the sofa as they talked, Hector on her lap greedily soaking up attention.

"About what I expected." He briefly told her of his meeting that morning at the sheriff's office and the longer, darker meeting with Charles Schroeder at the funeral home. The funeral director had been quite nice, the consummate professional, but it was a business and he was selling products and services. The business of death. How much was he willing to pay to say goodbye to his father? How much for a final disposition of the body?

"That sounds horrible," Lisa told him. "I wish you'd have let me come. You shouldn't have had to do that all alone."

Jason ignored her last remark. "I decided to have him cremated and sprinkle his ashes in the Sound. I think he would have liked that."

"Sounds beautiful."

"The service will be Saturday at two in the afternoon."

"You know I'll be there. I'd be there tomorrow if you wanted."

"I know you would. But no," he told her. "It would be nice, but now I've just got to go through his papers and stuff, find insurance forms, a will if he had one, bank documents, that sort of thing. Come up Friday. That's when I'll really need you."

"Okay, but I miss you, Jason. So does Hector. He keeps lying down in front of the door, waiting for you to come back."

Jason smiled. "I'd have thought he'd be happy to have you all to himself."

"Go figure, huh?"

"The beast doesn't know when he's got it good."

For a few seconds Jason listened as Lisa obviously bestowed some of that attention on the little dog. He could hear Hector's satisfied little growls and Lisa's cooing.

For the first time, he felt a pang of missing out.

"So how about the other thing?" Lisa asked. "Your questions about what happened? Have you found any answers?"

"No. Not yet. Just more questions. Something doesn't smell right, but so far I seem to be the only one that thinks so."

"Maybe you're the only one that's paying attention."

He hadn't really thought of it in quite those terms before. "I guess I'll just have to get their attention, won't I?"

*

He spent the rest of the evening going through his dad's files, looking for financial information and that sort of thing: bank and investment accounts, insurance policies, outstanding loans, mortgages, et cetera. In short, he needed to start the process of settling his dad's estate.

He warmed a plate of the Stocktons' tuna casserole in the microwave, grabbed a Coors from the partial six pack in the fridge, and carried both into the den to his father's desk. He sat down uncomfortably in the desk chair. It felt like trespassing. He knew he needed to do this and his dad wouldn't have objected, but it still felt wrong.

The quiet made it feel worse, so he turned the television on. It was tuned to ESPN, which would have been fine if there'd been a football game on. But it was Tuesday, so no football. He scrolled through the channels until he found a movie that looked interesting, then set the remote aside.

The funeral director had given him a checklist of things to do to get his father's affairs in order. First thing in the morning, he would have to order copies of his father's death certificate from Vital Statistics and call the Social Security Administration.

In the meantime, he needed to go through his father's files.

Luckily, his dad was a meticulous record keeper. There were separate files for each of his bank accounts, both personal and business, with a year's worth of printed statements arranged in chronological order in each. It made gathering the information easy.

From what he could see, his dad had been in pretty good shape financially. He was not rich, by any stretch, but he wasn't struggling to pay his bills and seemed to have a little left over at the end of each month. An awful lot of people would love to be in that position.

His dad drew his income from Social Security, a pension managed through AG Edwards here in town, and the profits from his guide service.

He also found a life insurance policy for $75,000. He jotted down the policy number and agent's phone number on the legal pad. It was another phone call he'd have to make in the morning.

The fact that he was listed as the beneficiary felt decidedly odd, like he was profiting from his dad's death. He briefly wondered if he could afford to ignore it. Sgt. Hayden had asked who had a motive to kill his dad. One answer was that he, Jason, would make $75,000.

But that was a touch paranoid, wasn't it? People collected on life insurance all the time and his dad wouldn't have named him beneficiary if he hadn't wanted him to have the money. Besides, he hadn't killed his dad, so what was he worried about?

Jason decided to deal with that in the morning.

He did not find a will, a copy of any mortgage, or a title to the house. Maybe his dad had a safe deposit box.

In his dad's business files, Jason found copies of the contract every client had signed for the year, arranged in chronological order. He paged through the last couple of months, but none seemed to be the mysterious man in the photograph. There were no Asian names at all. Even more interesting was the fact that his dad had no clients at all the final week of his life. Nothing.

So why was he out on the Sound when he died? A personal trip? It was possible, but he was still breaking his own safety rules by going out alone. It seemed unlikely.

He paused to stretch his back and rub his eyes. It was nearing midnight and he'd been going virtually nonstop since five in the morning. He reached for his beer bottle but found it empty, as was the plate of tuna casserole. Maybe it was time to call it a night.

Jason returned his father's contracts to their file folder and turned to slip the folder back into the drawer, then stopped in mid-motion. Something was lying on the bottom of the drawer, under all the file folders.

It was a single, business-sized envelope addressed to his father. The return address was Evergreen Bank here in town and the postmark was dated last Tuesday. Inside was a single sheet of heavy bond, bearing Evergreen Bank's letterhead.

Mr. Reynolds:

It has come to my attention that recently you have engaged in activities that have been in direct violation of the terms for the lease of the property at 2310 Salmon Berry Road. Specifically, your actions have been in violation of paragraph 3 "The Leasee shall engage in no activity that is in direct competition with the leaser, damages the leaser's business interests, prospects, or reputation in any way."

This letter is your first and only warning. Any further violations of the lease agreement on your part will render the agreement invalid and the owner will begin eviction proceedings immediately.

The letter was signed by Martin Haislip III, Vice President.

Jason wasn't sleepy anymore.

CHAPTER 6

The rain was back Wednesday morning as Jason drove down to the sheriff's dock. It was the dreary drizzle Puget Sound was famous for, heavy enough to keep everything wet and dripping, but barely enough to warrant windshield wipers. Jason didn't even bother to bring a raincoat.

He parked in the nearly empty lot above the docks, pulled his watch cap over his head, and headed down toward the docks. It was cool and still, but not cold, the only sounds the distant murmur of traffic building downtown and the screams of seagulls.

Most of the boats in the marina were still in their berths. The weather was keeping the fishermen at home.

A young deputy with bright red hair and county rain gear waited for him near the gate across the sheriff's dock. A sign behind him read: "No trespassing. Authorized personnel only." Beyond the fence, the sheriff's launch and inflatable were tied up, as well as three other boats. One of them was Jason's dad's, the *Lady L.*

"Mr. Reynolds?" the deputy asked.

Jason admitted he was and the two men shook hands.

"Sorry about your dad," the deputy told him. "He was a good man."

"You knew him?"

The deputy, his name tag identified him as Berger, shook his head. "Just to wave at, small talk, that sort of thing, but he was always friendly. That counts for a lot."

Jason smiled. "Yes, it does."

"Let's go down to the boat. I need you to look it over and sign a release before you can take possession of it."

"Have to keep the lawyers happy."

Deputy Berger chuckled. "Exactly."

Jason followed the deputy through the gate and down the dock to where the *Lady L* was tied, port side to the dock. At first glance, she seemed to be in good shape. The hull looked intact; the interior didn't seem to be shipping any water.

"Can I get in and look around?"

"Please do."

Jason gingerly climbed down into the boat. It had been a while since he'd been boating and he no longer had the instinctive feel for the shifting of the vessel. But he got down safely and began to look around.

"Where did you find it?" he asked.

"The Coasties found it adrift up near Rosario Strait."

Jason nodded. That was where the currents off the east side of the islands would take it. Probably.

The first thing he noticed was the absence of fishing gear on board: no poles, no tackle or lures, no bait.

"Did you guys remove anything? Clean it up?"

Deputy Berger shook his head. "Just looked around a bit to see if there was anything to explain what happened." He shrugged.

Jason lifted the hatch and glanced in the engine compartment. It too was dry. The engine looked perfectly normal, but he wasn't a mechanic. He closed the hatch and moved into the boat's modest cabin. It was just big enough to shelter four people from the weather, if, as his dad used to say, "all four really liked each other".

He could see nothing in the cabin that seemed damaged or missing, but that really didn't mean much. He hadn't been on the boat in more than a year.

Something crunched under his feet. He glanced down, then squatted to have a closer look. It was dirt. Or, to be more specific, clumps of dried mud someone had tracked into the cabin. Clumps and smears of it were scattered across the cabin floor.

Interesting.

Jason returned to the deputy. "What's with all the dirt in the cabin?"

Deputy Berger shook his head. "Like that when we found it. Somebody had muddy shoes, that's for sure. Maybe they went clamming."

Jason nodded and signed the release form.

*

A half hour later, Jason had managed to move the *Lady L* from the sheriff's dock to her slip in the public marina. Fortunately there hadn't been any other boat traffic because he wasn't much good behind the wheel anymore. He just went very, very slow and hoped no one was watching.

With the boat securely tied off, he shoved the keys in his pocket and started up the dock toward the parking area.

Naturally, the sheriff's dock and his car were at the far end of the Marina. The rain had grown heavier, falling steadily now straight down from a featureless overcast. Jason turned up his coat collar, pulled the watch cap down and began to trudge across the empty parking lot.

As he walked, he mulled over the matter of the dried mud in the *Lady L*'s wheelhouse. Despite what the deputy had suggested, he didn't believe his dad had stopped to dig up some steamers that last day. For one thing, where were the tools? You needed a shovel and some sort of bucket to hold the clams. Neither were on the boat.

Even more telling, the mud he'd found had been nearly odorless. As anyone who has ever been near a harbor at low tide knows, the mud in tidal flats is anything but odorless. It stinks. Badly. Wherever that mud had come from, it hadn't been picked up clamming.

Tires hissed across the wet pavement behind him.

Jason turned just as a fifteen-year-old Chevy pickup spotted with gray primer coasted to a stop beside him. A rifle hung in the cab's back window.

"Heard you'd be down here," the driver said. "We need to talk."

Jason peered at the man in the truck. His hair was longer and worn loose, instead of in a ponytail, but the face was the same. "Sonny? Sonny Adams?"

Sonny's dad had worked for years with Jason's, both at the cannery, then as a deck hand on the boat. Sonny was three years younger than Jason, but they had spent many a summer day together, hanging out, helping where they could.

"Hey, Sonny, good to see you," Jason said. "How's your dad?"

"Better than yours." Sonny didn't smile. "We need to talk, but not here, not now. The walls have ears, if you know what I mean."

Jason wasn't sure he did, but nodded. "When and where?"

"Know the Port and Starboard?"

Jason thought he did. If he remembered right it was a hole-in-the-wall tavern on the edge of Old Town. Many of the guides and commercial fishermen liked to hang out there. Or they used to.

"Come by at 1:00," Sonny said. "I'll buy you a beer."

Jason told him he'd be there.

Sonny nodded and shifted his truck into gear. "Watch your back, my friend."

Jason watched as Sonny drove away. What did he mean by that?

*

Somewhat to his surprise, Jason was able to get an appointment with Martin Haislip, III that morning. The money factory must be slow this time of year. Or maybe he remembered Jason from school and wanted to catch up, though that didn't seem likely. Martin and he hadn't exactly operated in the same social circles back then. Martin was a rich kid and knew it. Jason was not. In the twelve years they spent together in the Port Salish school system, they'd probably exchanged fewer than a dozen words.

Whatever the reason, Jason arrived at Haislip's office on the second floor of the Evergreen Bank building ten minutes before his 11:00 appointment and introduced himself to Rebecca, the lovely secretary guarding Haislip's office. She invited him to sit in the waiting area. Mr. Haislip would be right out.

Jason did as he was told.

Fifteen minutes later and five minutes after his appointment was scheduled, Jason heard a door open and looked up as Martin Haislip, III walked past his secretary toward him.

Jason stood as the banker approached.

Haislip hadn't changed that much since his high school days. He still strutted when he walked, still seemed athletic, still wore ostentatious rings on each hand and a Rolex watch. The only damage the years seemed to have caused was an extra two inches of forehead under his hairline. He'd also grown a goatee that was not only trimmed to the exact length of his head hair, but was also the exact same shade of brown.

It had to be the work of a professional stylist.

"Sorry to keep you waiting." The banker smiled politely and extended his hand. "I'm Martin Haislip."

That was a change. In their school days, he'd always tacked on "the Third," like royalty.

Jason shook the man's hand and introduced himself.

"Terribly sorry to hear about your father. Such a tragedy."

Jason thanked him.

"Come into my office and we'll get this process started. I promise we'll make it as painless as possible."

Jason followed him past the secretary and into his inner office. He had purposely failed to mention the letter or the lease when he'd set up the appointment. It was probably the oldest interview technique in the world: surprise.

Martin's office wasn't terribly large, but it was luxurious.

Jason sat in a leather chair that probably cost more than his car and waited while Martin settled in behind his desk and called up something on his computer.

"I've taken the liberty of looking up your father's accounts with us," he said, looking at the computer screen. "It looks like he has several, both personal and business."

Jason knew all that.

"So, if I could just have a copy of your father's death certificate, we can get started."

"I don't have it yet," Jason said. "Probably by the end of the week."

Martin looked confused, then annoyed. "I don't understand. Legally, I can't give you any information about your father's accounts without either a death certificate or a power of attorney. Rebecca should have explained that when you called."

Jason slipped the letter out of its envelope and set it on the desk in front of Haislip. "Can you explain this to me?"

Martin picked up the letter and began to read. Jason watched his eyes. They stopped moving side to side a full fifteen seconds before he looked back up.

"It seems pretty self-explanatory to me," Martin said.

"I was under the impression my dad owned that house. He inherited it from his father, my grandfather."

"You were mistaken. Your father inherited the lease from your grandfather. Perhaps you misunderstood."

It was possible. Jason shrugged. "Maybe."

"I shouldn't even tell you this because, strictly speaking, the bank has no documentation of your father's death, but because of the circumstances I'm going to bend the rules."

Jason smiled. "Thanks."

"As your father's only surviving heir, you will inherit the same lease, providing certain conditions are met."

"Such as those in the letter?"

Martin nodded. "And others. All the conditions will be spelled out in detail when the lease offer is made. Unfortunately, that won't happen until we have proof the current lease holder is deceased."

"Of course," Jason said. "Like I said, I should have the death certificate by Friday."

"Good. We can discuss it in detail then. Just set up another appointment with my secretary."

He was being dismissed.

"I'd like the letter back. Please?"

Martin started, like he'd forgotten about it, then folded the letter and handed it to Jason, who carefully returned it to its envelope.

"Just one more question before I let you get back to work."

Martin raised his eyebrows. "Yes?"

"Who's the landlord? Who actually owns the house?"

The banker hesitated.

"Come on, it's public record. I could go look it up in Friday Harbor. You're just saving me a ferry trip."

"It's owned by The Lundgren Corporation. We just administer the leases."

Leases. Plural.

Jason thanked him and let the banker usher him from the office.

*

Jason drove back to the house after his meeting with Haislip. Could he really even call it home anymore? It was where he'd grown up, where his family had lived and loved, but his family was gone and the house had become more a souvenir than the home it had been. Now, with the lease thrown in, the house itself seemed tainted even more.

He parked in the driveway and hurried through steady rain to the house. He had about an hour before he was supposed to meet Sonny at the tavern and at the very least he needed to change clothes. Slacks, dress shoes and a dress shirt wouldn't exactly blend in in a fisherman's bar. But his mind was racing.

He tossed his jacket over the back of a dining room chair and headed upstairs.

Once he'd changed into worn jeans, athletic shoes, and an old sweatshirt, he sat down and wrote up what he'd learned from Martin Haislip, III. First of all, Martin didn't want him to know about that letter. Why? And even more questions. What kind of real estate lease gets passed from father to son like an inheritance? And where was his father's copy of the lease? Jason couldn't see him throwing away a document like that. What had his father been doing to make the bank threaten the home he'd lived in for decades? And how was the Lundgren Corporation involved?

Something else nibbled at his consciousness, but again, he couldn't quite put his finger on it. He closed his eyes and mentally replayed the meeting with Haislip; he still couldn't come up with it. He tried again, this time replaying every detail he could remember from the moment he entered the building to the moment he left the office.

He stopped.

When they'd paused at Martin's secretary's desk to set up the new appointment, she had consulted her computer to see what was available. He'd had a choice of thirty minutes at 10:30 or a full hour at 1:00 in the afternoon. Rebecca had suggested the hour would be better and Jason had agreed.

She had consulted a scheduling program. Most computers had them now. Heck, most cell phones had them. And if you didn't have access to a computer, there were old-fashioned paper appointment books at every office supply store. It was a basic time management tool. Every business had one.

But he hadn't seen one at his dad's.

He all but ran to the den and woke up the computer. A quick glance through the list of installed programs showed no scheduling or calendar application. He then went through the desk drawers again. Nothing. If his dad had used a scheduler to manage his guide service, it wasn't here now.

Maybe it was with his copy of the lease and the last few fishing contracts.

He picked up the land line phone and dialed an in-house number for the *News*. At the prompt, he entered the extension for the Archives Department. It rang and was answered almost immediately.

"Archives. This is Adrienne."

"Hi, Adrienne. This is Jason Reynolds. I need you to do me a favor."

"Jason? How are you doing? I heard you were on personal leave."

"I am, but you know how it is. Reporters never sleep."

Adrienne chuckled. "What do you need?"

"Could you pull everything you can find on the Lundgren Corporation and email it to me?"

"Sure. It might take a little while. Your company address?"

He thought for a moment. Whoever was behind this might hesitate to hack into the email network of a major newspaper. A lot more than a personal email. "Yes," he told her. "My company account."

"Consider it done."

*

The Port and Starboard occupied the ground floor of an aging red brick building in a row of similar buildings on the eastern edge of Old Town. Whatever the building's original purpose, it had been a tavern for as long as Jason could remember, catering to the local fishermen and, when it was operating, the cannery workers. Both his dad and grandpa had been known to spend an occasional hour here after work.

Jason parked on the street around the corner on Marina Way, locked the car and walked to the tavern entrance. The rain had stopped, though the sky remained heavily overcast and the air damp and cool and tainted by the foul odor of low tide.

He pushed open the door and stepped into the tavern just before 1:00. Inside, it was dim to the point of darkness. He could smell stale beer, dust, and ancient cigarette smoke. As his eyes adjusted, he made out an ornate bar on the right manned by an older man with white hair and a pot belly. Two men in plaid flannel coats sat at the bar, while two others stood beside a pool table in the back. A bank of empty booths lined the wall to Jason's left, opposite the bar.

A jukebox played Kenny Rogers singing about a gambler.

Every single face in the place was looking at him, the stranger.

The bartender caught his eye, then nodded toward one of the booths.

Jason followed his gaze and realized the booths weren't all empty as he'd first thought. He walked over and slid in opposite Sonny, who was already pouring him a beer from the pitcher on the table.

"Friendly place," Jason said.

Sonny shrugged. "Sometimes when you got to be nice to strangers at work, you don't want to be nice when you're off the clock."

Jason could understand that.

"Don't worry about it. They know who you are; your dad was their friend."

Jason nodded. There didn't seem anything to say.

"It's been a long time, old friend," Sonny said.

"Yes, it has. Five years?"

Sonny nodded. "Since Jeremy's funeral. You only seem to come home when someone dies."

"Seems that way, doesn't it?"

"You got the hell out of Dodge and never looked back. Making a name for yourself in the big city."

"As they say, 'it's where the action is'." Jason shrugged. "And the jobs."

Sonny nodded and sipped his beer.

"How're Linda and the girls?" Jason asked.

"Good, good. Emily's eight and Becca's five now, just started kindergarten. My three girls. They're the best thing that ever happened to me."

Jason smiled. "Being a family man suits you."

Sonny smiled briefly and sipped his beer. "It changes how you look at things. It changes your priorities."

Jason could only imagine having a family, but he was sure it would change things. You would no longer be the most important person in your world.

"I should have been out there with him, man," Sonny said, his voice just above a whisper. "I was his deck hand. I should have been there. If I was, maybe he'd still be alive."

"Or maybe you'd be dead too. Then what would your girls do?"

Sonny's mouth twisted into a half smile. "That's what your dad said."

Jason frowned. "When?"

"When he sent me home, gave me the rest of the week off. He said what he was doing was dangerous, too dangerous for a family man. He told me to go home and be my girls' daddy."

Jason sipped his beer.

"I couldn't talk him out of it," Sonny said. "I never saw him again."

"There was nothing you could do."

"Don't make me feel much better though." He poured himself another beer, then offered the pitcher to Jason, who declined. The last thing he needed was to get drunk.

"What was Dad doing that was so dangerous?"

Sonny shook his head. "He wouldn't tell me. It had something to do with that Jap guy who'd hired him."

Jason perked up. "Jap guy?"

Sonny shook his head. "He was American, but with Jap blood, know what I mean?"

Jason nodded, fighting the urge to hurry his friend along.

"So he hires us one day, I think it was Monday last week, your dad's schedule would say for sure."

"I can't find Dad's appointment book. I can't find any business records from last week at all."

Sonny looked at him. "For real?"

"For real."

"Shit. They're covering their tracks."

"Who is?"

"I don't know, Jason." Sonny just shook his head. "But they killed your dad and got away with it. Probably this Jap guy too. Nobody's seen him around either."

Jason pulled the photo his dad had sent him from his pocket and handed it across the table. "Is this the guy?"

Sonny had barely glanced at it before he started nodding. "Yeah, this is the guy. Greg, or Craig, something like that. I never got his last name. It should be in your dad's..." His eyes closed. "Damn it."

"Don't worry about it. You'd be surprised how many ways there are to identify someone."

Sonny handed the photo back to Jason, who returned it to his pocket. The photo was showing damage from too much handling. He needed to make some copies.

"I don't know what he got your dad into," Sonny said. "But I know what we did that first day. The weirdest fishing trip I've ever been on."

"Why's that?"

"The guy couldn't have cared less about fishing. All he wanted us to do was cruise around Deception Island while he watched it with binoculars."

*

All in all, Jason spent a little over two hours talking with Sonny. By that time, Sonny was drunk enough to be a little unsteady on his feet. He wasn't exactly staggering, but he definitely shouldn't be driving. It had begun to rain again, which would only make things worse.

On the sidewalk outside the tavern, Jason offered to give him a ride.

"No, thanks," Sonny said. "I live just a couple blocks away. The walk will help clear my head. Maybe I won't be in too much hot water when I get home."

Jason smiled. "Good luck with that."

"I'll probably need it." His face grew serious. "And you be careful. These people don't fuck around."

Jason nodded. "I will."

"Let me know if I can do anything."

Sonny waved and crossed the street, heading north into the newer part of town. Jason watched him for a few moments and then walked around the corner toward his car. He needed to get his thoughts about what Sonny had told him on paper and organize the new questions he now had. He also needed to check his email and see what Adrienne had been able to find on the Lundgren Corporation.

He could tell something was wrong when he was still thirty feet from his car.

He slowed and approached warily.

Someone had written "Go Home!" in neon yellow across his windshield. They'd also slashed all four of his tires.

CHAPTER 7

Apparently, he'd ruffled someone's feathers.

Jason scanned the streets and buildings around him in case the messenger was still around, but saw no one. Other than the parked cars, the street was deserted. He would actually have been surprised if it had been otherwise. He was not dealing with a bunch of teenagers pulling pranks.

The next thing that came to mind was to make sure Sonny was all right. If they'd targeted his car, what was to keep them from targeting the guy he'd been talking to? They'd exchanged cell numbers before leaving the bar, so Jason opened his cell and punched in the number.

Sonny answered on the second ring. "Wow. Miss me already?"

He sounded fine.

"Are you home?"

"I'm about a block away. What's up?"

"Someone slashed my tires and left a love note on my windshield. I just wanted to make sure you're okay."

"I'm good. But I think I'm going to hurry now."

"Lock your doors."

"You too. Jesus."

They disconnected.

"Damn," he said out loud. He should have asked Sonny for the name of a good tire shop in town. He was pretty sure his insurance covered vandalism, but he'd need a police report. Meanwhile, he was standing there in the rain, getting soaked.

It probably wasn't her jurisdiction, but he pulled Danielle Hayden's card from his wallet and placed the call.

*

The city police squad car arrived five minutes later and parked in a vacant spot across the street. It was not using its flashers, which was fine. This was hardly an emergency. Jason probably wouldn't have involved the police at all, but he needed to establish a paper trail for the insurance company.

The officer who emerged was middle-aged, stocky, and wore the weary expression nearly every veteran cop eventually shared. He'd seen the worst of human nature and moved on. He had dark hair streaked with gray and a neatly trimmed mustache. He also had the beginnings of a double chin.

He looked now at the ruins of Jacob's tires, at the message on the windshield, and shook his head. "Looks like you pissed somebody off."

"Yeah, and I don't even live here."

The officer pulled his notebook from his breast pocket. "Any idea who could have done this?"

"Not a clue."

For the next ten minutes, they played the cop-and-victim game of information, the police officer asking questions, him answering, and the policeman noting his answers. As the rain grew heavier, they moved into the shelter of a nearby doorway. The occasional passing pedestrian glanced at them from under their umbrellas, so did the odd motorist, but none looked to Jason like anything but curious citizens.

The officer, whose name was Riley, was actually pretty nice. He made a point of letting Jason know that the odds were against law enforcement ever catching the vandals unless they stumbled upon them doing the same thing to another car. Jason understood.

When Jason asked him about a good tire place, Officer Riley called a local shop and arranged for a tow truck. A flatbed arrived a few minutes later and, after dealing with the work order, began the process of easing Jason's car out of its parking spot.

Two minutes later, a white sheriff's car pulled up behind the tow truck, double parked and turned on its flashers. It had to be Danielle. Sgt. Hayden.

She rolled down the driver's window as he walked up. "Looks like you need a ride."

*

"You do realize you've barely been here twenty-four hours?" Sgt. Hayden asked as they followed the tow truck north on Ferry Street toward the tire shop. "Barely twenty-four hours and you've already got someone vandalizing your car?"

Jason shrugged. "It's a gift."

"Any chance it was random, or a case of mistaken identity?"

"Sure. Been having a rash of slit tires in Port Salish lately?"

Sgt. Hayden shot him a sharp look, then smiled and turned back to the road, shaking her head. "So, have anyone special in mind as a suspect?"

Jason shook his head. "The only person I rattled today was Martin Haislip and slashing tires doesn't seem like his style."

"The Turd?"

Jason smiled. He hadn't heard that nickname since he was a kid. *Martin Haislip, the Turd.*

"You're right, that isn't his style," she said. "Haislip would rather pull up beside you at a stop light in a Bentley so you'd feel grossly inadequate."

Jason laughed.

They quickly moved out of the antique charm of Old Town, through an area of older residences and then into the modern town. As they moved north, small retail and office buildings gave way to used car dealerships, body shops, and mini storage lots. Chain-link fence became the dominant decor and the houses were all either modest ranch styles, or mobile homes.

"Welcome to the bad side of town," Sgt. Hayden said.

"Whatever." Most of his friends when he was growing up lived on the north side. It wasn't bad. It just wasn't rich. People like Haislip didn't understand the difference.

Ahead of them, the tow truck signaled for a left turn, then drifted to a stop, waiting for a break in traffic. Sgt. Hayden eased her squad car to a stop behind it and, after one more swipe, turned off the wipers. The rain had stopped again. Now they were mainly dealing with the spray from other vehicles.

About a half block ahead of them, on the right, Jason noticed a bright scarlet billboard with yellow script reading: Strawberry Fields Organic Fruit, 7.5 mi. Smaller script in the same yellow announced that the retail stand was open from April 1 to Labor Day.

"Strawberry Fields?" Jason asked. It had been the phrase he'd found on the scratch paper on his dad's desk. At the time, all he could think of was the Beatles' song.

Sgt. Hayden glanced over at him. "It's the big strawberry farm the Morgan family owns up in the Salle Valley."

Jason remembered. They'd been pretty big when he was a kid too. A lot of kids had worked summer jobs there, picking berries.

"Where's 'Strawberry Fields' come from?" he asked.

She shrugged. "Joe Morgan, the head of the company now, rebranded it, went organic, and started marketing in Seattle and Portland. They're one of the biggest growers in the Northwest."

"A real success story, huh?"

She shrugged. "I guess so."

The tow truck released its air brakes with a hiss and pulled into the tire shop. Sgt. Hayden paused to let another car pass, then followed the tow truck, turning aside at the last minute to park in front of the office.

Jason was still thinking about a local berry farm and why his dad had been interested in them.

*

It took fifteen minutes for Jason to select the replacement tires, fill out the paperwork and get the job rolling. The man behind the counter assured him the job would be finished well before they closed at 6:00.

Jason turned to Sgt. Hayden, who'd come in with him. "Looks like my wheels will be available, after all. You don't have to stick around if you don't want to."

"I'm okay." She shrugged. "When's the last time you ate?"

He thought for a moment. "Breakfast."

"That's what I thought," she smiled. "Let's get something to eat while they're working on your car. You can update me on who you've been pissing off over the last twenty-four hours."

Ten minutes later, Sgt. Hayden pulled into a half-full parking lot on 3rd Street on the edge of Old Town and parked. They were in front of yet another old red brick building with expansive windows. *Mary Lou's Old Fashioned* was painted across the front.

Jason broke into a smile.

"We used to come here all the time," he said. "I can't believe it's still here."

Sgt. Hayden returned his smile and released her seat belt. "Still run by Mary Lou too. And still the best burgers in town."

They walked in to find the restaurant not even half full. It was the afternoon lull between lunch and dinner. Sgt. Hayden and Jason were shown to one of the booths with a window looking out into the street and settled in while the waitress went to get their coffee. Jason was still marveling at how little the place had changed over the years. It had been remodeled, of course, and refurbished, but the overall look had not changed. The booths were red vinyl arranged around the three walls opposite the kitchen. The tables were wood-grained Formica. A matching counter with attached stools ran the length of the room opposite the booths and a few tables were scattered about the middle of the linoleum tile floor. Soft country music filled the air and antique photos of the town and local industry hung from the walls.

"You okay?" Sgt. Hayden asked, just a hint of a smile on her lips.

"Fine. Just wallowing in nostalgia."

A lithe young waitress strode up to the table, set their coffees in front of them and passed out menus. She had auburn hair clipped to the back of her head and a beautiful smile. Her name tag read: Amber.

"Hey, Danny. You going to have your usual?"

"Of course." Sgt. Hayden unfolded her napkin across her lap. "Extra onions, please."

Jason smiled up at the waitress and opened his menu. "I don't have a 'usual' yet."

"What's taking you so long?"

"Just slow, I guess."

"Amber," Sgt. Hayden nodded toward Jason. "This is Jason Reynolds. He's a reporter for the *News* in Seattle and a local alum."

Amber shook his hand, a surprisingly dry, firm shake for a woman. "An honest-to-god reporter, huh? I guess I'd better watch what I say when you're around."

Jason smiled. "I'm off duty."

"Lee Reynolds was Jason's dad," Hayden said.

The waitress's demeanor abruptly changed. She reached over to gently touch his wrist. "I'm so sorry. Your dad was a great guy. Everybody around here is really, really going to miss him."

"He was a regular?"

"Yeah," Amber said. "He'd eat here two or three times a week, sometimes with a client, sometimes just by himself. He was always very nice. And a good tipper."

Jason glanced at Sgt. Hayden, slipped the photograph out of his pocket and handed it to waitress. "He ever have dinner with this guy?"

Amber glanced at the photo, nodded her head. "Oh, yeah. What was his name? A tourist. I never saw them together, but they could have come in on my days off."

Sgt. Hayden looked up at her. "He and Jason's dad knew each other?"

Amber seemed to take a mental step back. "What's this all about, anyway?"

She handed the photograph back to Jason.

"It's nothing to get excited about," Jason assured her with his best smile. "He might have been my dad's last client, that's all."

Amber nodded. "He'd been coming in for dinner every night for a week. I guess he was researching a book, or something. One night, he asked me if I knew where he could rent a boat. Go figure, we live on an island and I didn't know of any boat rentals, but I recommended your dad to him."

"Thanks," Jason told her. "That helps."

Amber smiled.

Jason closed the menu and handed it back to the waitress. He hadn't even looked at its listings. "Just give me the same thing Sgt. Hayden is having."

Amber scribbled the order on her pad and left to submit it to the kitchen.

When they were alone again, Jason looked over at Sgt. Hayden. "It all boils down to this mystery man. Who is he and what did he get my dad involved in?"

Sgt. Hayden eyed him over the rim of her coffee mug.

"What?"

"You do realize that even if you nail down this mystery man, it still doesn't mean your dad's death was anything but an accident. In fact, if he talked your dad into doing something dangerous, it could be evidence that it really was an accident."

He hadn't really thought of that. But he almost immediately rejected the possibility because it was too inconsistent with the rest of the evidence. If it had been just a tragic accident, for instance, why the destruction of his tires and scribbled warning? And where was the mystery man? No, something else was at work here. Something larger.

And he was making someone nervous.

"It's not that simple," he told her.

"It never is. So tell me what you've found so far."

Jason filled her in on what he had discovered up to that point: the missing business files, the missing appointment book, the neighbor lady's feeling he was afraid of something, and finally, Sonny's layoff because what Jason's dad was doing was "too dangerous for a family man."

"Is it possible he just hadn't gotten around to completing the files yet? Maybe he was busy."

"This time of year?" Jason shrugged, then shook his head. "You didn't see those files. They were perfect. Meticulous. No, somebody went through and purged them."

Amber reappeared at their table with their burgers. She set a platter in front of each, a wire caddy of condiments between them, and left again to get some coffee. Jason planted his face in the scented steam rising from the plate and wallowed in the aroma. Until this very second, he hadn't realized how hungry he was.

His dinner partner was already cutting her burger in half.

"What exactly am I about to eat?" he asked her. "Because I will probably want to order it again."

"A fajita burger," she told him. "It's the bomb."

For the next few minutes, they concentrated on their burgers. What little conversation they had was limited to the food and how it had been prepared. Amber returned to refill their coffees and check on the food. Neither could talk because their mouths were full.

Around them, the restaurant began to slowly fill as the afternoon wore on.

His initial hunger sated, Jason leaned back and wiped his mouth with his napkin. Half his burger was gone. It had all but evaporated.

"Was I right, or what?" Hayden asked.

"Oh, man."

She smiled and took another bite of her burger.

Amber swung by and refreshed their coffees, then moved off again.

"So tell me about this letter that got Haislip so upset," Sgt. Hayden said, grabbing another fry and pushing it through a puddle of ketchup.

He briefly described the letter to her and Haislip's assertion that it referred to a lease.

Sgt. Hayden looked at him. "You're telling me your family doesn't own the house you grew up in?"

He shook his head. "Apparently not."

"Can I see the letter?"

Jason checked his coat pockets, then realized he'd left it in the sports coat he'd worn to the meeting with Haislip.

"I don't have it with me," he told her.

"You can bring it by the office in the morning," she suggested. "Or even better, make a copy and bring that by."

"Or," he suggested. "You can swing by the house tonight, see the letter, and see what I mean about his files."

She thought for a moment, then nodded.

*

Jason's car was ready by the time they returned to the tire shop. It had four brand-new tires that could physically hold air and, courtesy of the store manager, a windshield without a scrawled warning. Jason handed over his credit card and retrieved the keys.

"Be careful now," the manager warned him as he was leaving. "Someone who's willing to trash your car is usually just as willing to do it to you."

Jason slipped the folded receipt into his wallet. "I'll keep that in mind."

Hayden waited in the parking lot in her squad car and fell in behind him for the drive across town. By now it was nearing full dark. The streetlights were lit and the cars and trucks that formed Port Salish's tepid rush hour all ran with their headlights on. The rain had stopped again, but traffic still kicked up enough spray to require windshield wipers.

Everything seemed to hiss through Old Town.

He led Hayden up through the neighborhood and pulled in to park in his usual spot. Hayden parked her squad car on the street and met him on the front porch.

The house stood dark and quiet, silently dripping old rain from the eaves.

"It's so hard to believe your family doesn't own this place."

"Surreal, isn't it?"

He unlocked the front door and walked ahead to flip on lights in the living room and kitchen. That seemed to bring a little life to the old building. His sport coat still hung draped over the back of one of the dining room chairs. Right where he'd left it.

"Interesting," Sgt. Hayden said as she looked around.

"What?"

"It's a bachelor pad for a sixty-year-old."

Jason smiled. That was exactly what it was.

He reached into the breast pocket of the sport coat, then stopped. The pocket was empty. The letter wasn't there.

"What's the matter?"

"It's gone."

"What do you mean 'gone'?"

"I mean they took it, the letter. Someone came in here, and took it."

"Who did?"

"I don't know," he told her. "Whoever's behind all this."

Hayden shook her head and used the tips of her fingers to briefly examine the jacket. "You sure you didn't leave it somewhere else?"

He shook his head. He had placed it in his coat pocket as he was leaving Haislip's office. He'd come straight home and taken off the coat to change into something more appropriate for the Port and Starboard. It had never occurred to him to hide it. The house had been locked. He'd kept it locked since he'd gotten here.

"Anything else missing?" Hayden asked. "Anything tampered with?"

Jason took a quick look around, but could find nothing amiss. The most valuable items, his laptop, camera, and the household electronics were all in place. This was no normal burglary.

"Anything?" Hayden asked.

He shook his head.

She returned to the front door, opened and examined it, then shook her head and closed the door. A quick exam of the back door and ground floor windows also uncovered no sign of forced entry.

"Now what?" Jason asked when they'd regrouped in the living room.

"Well, first thing in the morning, I'd get the locks changed. In the meantime, you might want to think about spending the night at a motel."

Jason was already shaking his head. They were trying to intimidate him; he wasn't going to let them.

Hayden nodded, as if expecting his response.

"Still think my dad's death was just an accident?"

She looked up at him, her eyes serious and steady. "Let's just say I'm beginning to have my doubts."

PART TWO

Port Salish

CHAPTER 8

Sgt. Hayden—Danny—she'd agreed they'd moved beyond a formal police officer/citizen relationship by this point, left a few minutes later. Jason had walked her to her squad car, then she'd waited until he had safely returned to the house before pulling away from the curb. Once she was gone, he'd locked both locks on the front door, then went to the back of the house and made sure all the locks were engaged on the back door, too. It wasn't really much of a defense if the bad guys had copies of the house keys, but it made him feel better.

Believe it or not, in all the years he'd lived in the city he'd never been the victim of a burglary. He'd had his car broken into a couple of times, but never his home. His home had always been inviolate.

Violated. He'd heard that term used many times to describe how a burglary victim felt, like someone had posted your private diary online. Even worse, was the feeling of insecurity. If, despite the locks, someone could walk into the house while he was gone, what was to prevent them from walking in while he was asleep, or in the shower? Absolutely nothing.

It was creepy.

He returned to the dining room, grabbed his laptop, and carried it into the den/study to set it up on his father's desk. He should have some emails waiting for him from Adrienne in Archives, probably a lot of them. The Lundgren Corporation had been around quite a while, so he assumed they'd received their share of press. Somehow, Lundgren was mixed up in his father's death; he needed to know everything he could about them. Besides, he needed to be doing something to keep his mind off every little creak and groan the old house made.

Now that his senses were tuned into it, the house generated an amazing number of little creaks and pops, snaps, sighs, and groans. A million. He felt like a scared little kid, jumping at every shadow after watching a horror movie. Every few seconds he'd hear the front door ease open or stealthy footsteps in another room. A couple of times, he even got up and walked around the lower level to check for intruders. He never found any, of course, and always returned to the den feeling foolish.

Once the computer had finished booting, he logged into the News' network and checked his email. There were dozens waiting for him, mostly from friends and colleagues offering their condolences. There was a short note from Miles asking how it was going. Debbie had also given him a brief update on the Stevenson story.

He paused to listen as he thought he heard something in the front room. But it was just another random creak.

Adrienne in archives had also sent an email. It read: *Might as well have asked me to send you half the paper. I assumed you weren't interested in financial reports, so I kept it to the company's legal issues and other shenanigans. Hope it helps.* Attached was a sizable zip file.

He was just about to download the file when his cell rang. He nearly jumped out of his skin.

It was Lisa.

"You scared the shit out of me," he told her, as his heart rate slowly returned to normal.

"I'm sorry. It was getting late and you hadn't called. I was starting to worry."

He glanced at his watch. It was already after 6:00, so yes, he was a little late, but not that much.

"Sorry. It's been kind of crazy this afternoon."

He briefly told her of the vandalism to his car and the break-in at the house. "So I'm feeling just a tad paranoid right now."

"My God! Are you okay? Who would do something like that?"

He assured her he was fine, just a little spooked.

"Did you call the cops?"

"Of course. They left maybe fifteen minutes ago. Not that there's a whole lot they're going to be able to do about it."

"There must be something they can do."

"Lisa, other than the vandalism, I can't even prove a crime happened."

She grudgingly admitted he had a point, but was still worried about him. She was particularly concerned about what the bad guys, whoever they were, would do once it became clear he wasn't going to be scared off that easily.

"Maybe you should stay at a motel," she suggested. "At least until you can get the locks changed."

That's what Danny had suggested.

"I'm not going to let them chase me out of this house. Once I do that, I might as well pack up and head home. They've won."

She knew better than to argue the point further. "I don't know how you'll be able to sleep knowing someone could walk in on you at any time. At least I have Hector."

Jason wasn't thinking he'd get much sleep tonight either, but he had plenty of work to keep him busy. Thanks to Adrienne, he had a ton of old newspaper articles to go through. Maybe there would be something in there that would let him know just who or what he might be dealing with.

That reminded him: Lisa was writing her thesis on Northwest history. "What can you tell me about the Lundgren Corporation?"

She hesitated. He could picture her frowning as she concentrated. "Um, not much of anything off the top of my head. Do you think they're the guys behind this?"

"I don't know. Right now I'm just doing basic research. I've got a bunch of articles from the paper to go through tonight. "

"The only thing I can think of was that one of the owners ran for governor a couple of times back in the thirties. He was extremely conservative, like KKK, John Birch Society conservative."

"I assume he lost."

"Yeah, but I think he had a bigger following than you'd expect," she told him. "The KKK was huge in the Northwest in the twenties and thirties, as big as in the south."

He admitted he had not known that.

"Look, I can check with a couple people and have more for you tomorrow. Derek would definitely know something."

"There's no huge hurry. I just thought I'd see what you knew."

"I want to do it. It makes me feel like I'm doing something other than just worrying about you."

He decided to change the subject.

"How's Hector?"

"Sleeping," she said. "He falls asleep watching the front door like he's expecting you to step through at any time."

Aw....

"Are you planning on bringing him with you on Friday?"

"No. Hector likes his routines. Suzie's going to watch him for me."

That was a good idea.

They chatted a while longer about school and the ongoing soap operas of her friends' lives, then said goodbye.

Jason checked the locks one more time, then turned to his laptop. It was time to go through the archived newspaper stories Adrienne had sent him.

*

Adrienne had sent him well over fifty news articles, all having to do with the Lundgren Corporation and some sort of legal or ethical problem. Just the fact that there were that many accusations raised red flags, but he tried to reserve judgment until he'd read the stories. Accusations did not mean actual crimes and every successful enterprise was bound to make some enemies along the way.

Still. Fifty?

So he began to read, taking notes on a legal pad as he went.

Within minutes, he was fully immersed in research mode. It was comfortable territory, familiar, and he was good at it. Many of his colleagues hated researching background, but Jason had always liked it. He'd actually met Lisa while doing research at the University library. And he knew background was an essential part of his job. Just like a good attorney, a good reporter will never ask a witness a question if he doesn't already know the answer. It was how you caught people in lies.

So he read. The stories were in chronological order with the oldest dated July 1915 with gaps of several years early on and the stories occurring with more regularity as they grew more recent. Some articles he read word for word, others he merely skimmed. The most important points and questions he noted on his legal pad. Within three or four hours he had twice that many pages of notes.

He broke once to go to the bathroom, twice to get something to drink and once to reheat a plate of the tuna casserole the Stocktons had given him. He never heard the creaks and groans of the house settling in the night and never gave a thought to any possible intruders. He was in a different world now and they didn't matter.

Finally, just after two in the morning, Jason finished the last article and let his tired computer go to sleep. He leaned back in his chair and rubbed his eyes.

He now had a pretty good idea of what kind of business the Lundgren Corporation was and it wasn't pretty.

The first and oldest story Adrienne had sent him was typical. It was dated July 17, 1915.

> **Shootout on Skagit Bay**
>
> Several fishing boats from the Bellingham salmon fleet engaged in a short, but fierce gun battle with fisherman from the San Juan Islands on the waters of Sammish Bay. The Bellingham fisherman have complained that their equipment has been systematically sabotaged by fisherman from Lars Lundgren's San Juan Island fleet, something Mr. Lundgren denies. Today, the Bellingham fleet confronted their rivals, and shots were fired by both sides in a running twenty minute gun battle. Three fisherman from Bellingham suffered minor gunshot wounds. As of this date, no arrests have been made.

Another story, from several years later, during the height of Prohibition :

Fed's Raid is a Bust

In a coordinated raid, Federal Agents from several agencies descended on a warehouse owned by Lars Lundgren and Son on remote Deception Island in Puget Sound, looking for illegal Canadian liquor. Unfortunately, when they arrived, the warehouse was empty. Special Agent Donald Minor tells this reporter that he believes the smugglers were tipped off about the raid and moved the contraband. Federal Agencies have long suspected Lundgren and Son of using cargo ships and their fleet of salmon boats to move liquor from Vancouver to the San Juan Islands, but have been unable to prove it.

The other stories held to a similar pattern. A competitor, private citizen, or government agency would file a complaint against the company for some unethical or illegal behavior, but before anything could be done the evidence would disappear, the witnesses would recant, or disappear. Nothing ever stuck. Nothing. Meanwhile, Lars Lundgren, his son Nils, and grandsons became very wealthy.

Jason's overall impression was of a company run much like organized crime. If so, and if they were the ones behind all this, they would prove to be a very dangerous opponent.

He got up to check the locks one more time before he went to bed.

*

Taylor Smith eased his car to the curb a block from the observation post, cut the lights and engine, and stepped out into the damp evening. To his mild surprise, the overcast seemed to be breaking up, allowing the moon to peek through occasionally. Maybe there'd even be sunshine tomorrow. Hallelujah!

He lifted the collar of his overcoat against the chill and followed the sidewalk toward the house that held the OP. It was well after midnight and he was the only being moving. The neighborhood was dark. All the good citizens in bed and resting up for tomorrow's workday. The only lights burning were in the Reynolds' house, where Jason was doubtlessly scheming to make Taylor's life more complicated.

Somewhere in the darkness an owl hooted.

At the house next to the Reynolds' he turned up the driveway beside the dumpster and entered the open garage. Fortunately, he was gifted with excellent night vision and able to navigate the construction mess without mishap and nearly without a sound. The house was having its interior completely reworked and the demolition had left nothing but bare studs inside the outer walls. Except for one, well-equipped, light-proofed room.

Taylor tapped lightly on the door.

A few seconds later, time enough to extinguish the interior lights, the door opened and Taylor stepped inside.

Todd Baxter closed the door behind him, flipped on the dim working light and returned to his seat in front of the surveillance monitors. His partner, Benny Jackson, was stretched out on a small cot on the other side of the room. Other than the cot and the listening station, the only other furnishing in the room was a card table holding a coffee maker and an assortment of fast food and snack wrappers.

"There's coffee, if you want it," Baxter told him. "No promises about the quality."

Taylor passed. At some point he would need to get some sleep tonight. "What's our boy up to?"

"He's spent the last few hours in the back room, working on his laptop," Baxter told him. "That's about it."

Taylor pulled up a battered wooden chair, dusted off the seat and sat down. "You said you had something I should hear."

"Yeah." Baxter cued up something on the computer and handed a set of earphones to Taylor.

Taylor listened as the digital recording played Jason's conversation with his girlfriend. It was telling because of the reporter's attitude after the events of the day. Even after the warning, he was still requesting information about the company from his girlfriend and planned to read the articles from the newspaper archives.

He was reading the articles on his laptop now.

Taylor handed the headphones back to Baxter.

"It looks like our warning didn't work," Baxter said, just to be saying something.

"I never really thought it would, did you? The guy's a professional reporter. He won't be intimidated that easily."

Though it would have made his life so much easier if he had.

Taylor ran a palm over his shaved head, feeling the stubble already beginning to grow back after this morning's shave. He was tired. He was tired of cleaning up other people's messes. But that was what he'd done for most of his adult life. It was a little late to become a librarian.

Jackson stirred on his cot. "Why don't we just put a couple of bullets in his brain and be done with it?"

Subtlety was not Jackson's strong suit.

"It may come to that," Taylor said. "But not yet."

He stood up and adjusted his overcoat. "I'm heading back to the condo. Let me know if anything else breaks."

Baxter nodded. "What about the lady cop?"

"She's already been taken care of."

*

Apparently, Thursdays were slow for the locksmith business in Port Salish. Jason called him at 8:00 and by 8:30 the man was switching out the locks on both the front and back doors. The locksmith worked quickly and efficiently and by 9:15, Jason had the new keys in his hands and knew the house was as secure as he could make it.

Once the locksmith had left, Jason found an envelope, dropped one set of keys inside and addressed it to himself at his Seattle address. The other set went on his key ring.

*

Jason's first stop was at the post office in Old Town. He mailed the envelope containing the keys and checked his dad's box. He had a lot of mail but it all seemed to be routine or junk mailers. Most important, Jason found no package from County Records in Friday Harbor containing the copies of his dad's death certificate. Then again, he hadn't really been expecting them this quickly. A one day turn around was expecting a lot from any government agency.

That done, he set about his real project for the day: finding out who the Mystery Man was.

His plan was simple. This morning, while the locksmith worked on his doors, he'd plotted the locations of every motel in town, paying close attention to those within easy walking distance of Mary Lou's restaurant. If the Mystery Man had eaten there nearly every day as the waitress said last night, odds are he wasn't staying too far away.

Three seemed most likely. Not only were they close to the restaurant, but they were relatively inexpensive. The man had been researching a book; he'd be on a budget. He wouldn't be staying at a hundred-dollar-a-night resort.

Jason's tactics would also be simple. He would produce his business card, introduce himself to the person in charge as a reporter for the *Seattle News,* and ask for their help. In his experience, the average person was so flattered by the possibility of being part of the news that they were overjoyed to help. Even more so if they thought their name might appear in the paper.

It added a touch of glamor to their routine.

He wore his standard reporter uniform: a light sport coat over a polo shirt, blue jeans, and white sneakers. He had to look the part. He even had a little notebook, though, like most reporters now, he usually used the digital recorder on his smart phone.

The day had turned out beautiful for wandering around town. The overcast had disintegrated into scattered white clouds. The sun was bright and warm and working hard to dry everything out. A little autumn chilled the air, but it was more refreshing than uncomfortable. Off to the northeast, the ghostlike cone of Mt. Baker floated above the horizon.

Jason checked his rearview mirror as he pulled out of the post office parking lot, but could see no suspicious car tailing him. He hadn't been able to spot one on the drive down from the house either, but he wasn't sure that really meant anything. If they were good, and they wouldn't have been successful this long if they weren't, he probably wouldn't be able to spot them anyway.

He parked on 2nd Street near the City Center Motel, his first stop, and walked up to the office. The desk clerk was bored, duly impressed by his business card, but had never seen the Mystery Man. They also hadn't had any guest stay longer than two nights since the summer.

Jason thanked her for her help and walked the four blocks east to his next stop, the Restwood Inn. There, he got the same result, an assistant manager more than willing to help, but knowing nothing. The Mystery Man had not stayed there.

This was why the cops called it "legwork."

The next motel on his list was called the Salishan. He cut down Coho Avenue, then turned east on 1st Street. As he walked, he did his best to keep an eye on his surroundings, especially people who might be paying undo attention to him, but was unable to spot anyone. One man in a business suit across the street drew his suspicion, but then disappeared into a CPA office like an ordinary person.

Maybe he was just being paranoid after all.

The Salishan was larger and somewhat nicer than the other two motels, but still a step below the resorts closer to the bay and along Ferry Street. It featured two decks of rooms with exterior walkways arranged around a central courtyard that held a mostly empty parking lot and a modest pool. A maintenance man was in the process of brushing the pool.

The office stood at the east end of the complex under a portico to protect cars from the weather.

Jason walked up under the portico, opened the door and stepped into the office.

The desk was directly across the room from him, manned by a very pretty and very young girl in a red blazer. To his right was a breakfast area/lounge that was empty save for one man sitting at a table, reading the newspaper. Everything about him screamed ex-military.

"May I help you?" the young woman asked with a smile. Her name tag read Brittany, Assistant Manager. She looked young enough to be in high school.

"I hope so." He handed her one of his business cards, introduced himself, and gave his little speech. "I'm working a story and need to establish a person's identity. I think he may have been a guest here a week or two ago. Could you take a look at his photo and see if you recognize him?"

"I guess so," Brittany said.

Jason pulled the photo from his pocket and laid it on the desk, never taking his eyes from the young woman's face. He was rewarded with a quick flash of recognition, followed by something like fear before she regained control and shook her head. "He doesn't look familiar."

Why was she afraid?

"Are you sure? He would have stayed here for several days."

This time she glanced over at the man reading the paper before returning to Jason and shaking her head. "I'm sorry. I can't help you."

"Look," Jason lowered his voice and leaned into the desk, cutting the space between them. "I don't want to get you in trouble, or anything, but I'm at a loss here. All I need is his name. I can do the rest on my own. No one needs to know how I got it. Your name need never come up."

She looked trapped, almost to the point of panicking.

"You can call the newspaper, if you'd like, talk to my editor," he told her. "They'll verify who I am. Honestly, I just want to find this guy so I can ask him a few questions."

If possible, she looked even more distressed. He thought she might burst into tears. "They said I wasn't supposed to talk about it." Her voice was little more than a whisper.

"Who did?"

"The FBI."

The FBI? The feds were involved with this? This was the first hint of that.

"Why were they here?"

"I don't know. They just hauled away all his stuff, made sure his bill was paid and told me to pretend they were never here."

Jason had worked with the Feds on a few occasions. He had never known them to care one way or another whether a subject's bills were paid.

"Did you see their ID?"

She looked offended. "Of course."

As calmly as he could, he ripped a blank page from his notebook and slid it across the desk to her. "Don't talk about it. Just write down a name for me. Please?"

Brittany hesitated a moment, then turned to her computer and hit a few keys. A second later, she scribbled something on the notebook paper and slid it back to Jason. He glanced at the name, Gregory Takashi, before sliding it and the photograph back into his pocket.

"Thanks," he told her. "We've never met, have we?"

Brittany shook her head and turned away.

The man in the lounge noisily folded his paper.

*

Taylor Smith checked the display on his cell phone. It was Anderson; he and Jackson were watching Reynolds today.

"Them?" Melissa asked from her seat across the coffee table.

Smith nodded and opened the phone. "Yes?"

"Reynolds was just at the motel," Anderson said. "He was talking to the girl behind the desk but I couldn't get close enough to hear what was said."

That wasn't good.

"He's gone now?"

"Yeah. I'm tailing him on foot."

"How does he seem?"

"Happy as hell."

Okay. Taylor had to assume Reynolds had found what he was looking for: Takashi's name. It was the only reason the reporter would be canvassing motels. Obviously, their hint had not kept him from his investigation. Taylor had never really believed it would.

He returned to Anderson on the phone. "What's he doing now?"

"Seems to be heading back to his car."

"Let me know where he goes next."

He closed his phone.

Melissa eyed him. "Reynolds not cooperating?"

"We need to become a bit more persuasive."

"We can do that," Melissa smiled. "Much more persuasive."

*

It was all Jason could do to keep from skipping down the sidewalk like a schoolgirl. He had the Mystery Man's name. With that and a photograph, he had the resources to find out just about everything he wanted to know. All he needed was his computer and an internet connection.

Once he reached the public sidewalk and had started back toward his car, he gave up all pretense of professional detachment and pulled out his cell phone. He loaded his web browser, then plugged "Gregory Takashi" into Google and hit search.

As usual, Google returned thousands of results. On top was Greg Takashi's Facebook page, second and third were links to a paper he'd co-authored on the assimilation of the Japanese immigrant community in Northern California. The fourth was a newspaper article about his disappearance.

Jason didn't have time to read the article right now, so he went to Takashi's Facebook page. It was a little difficult to read on a cell phone screen, but he learned that Takashi was a graduate student at San Jose State University, engaged to a woman named Tricia, and that no one had seen or heard from him in almost two weeks.

In fact, the last four posts on his Facebook wall were pleas from family and friends to contact them.

Jason logged off the web and shut down his phone.

It wasn't exactly a smoking gun, but he was close enough now to smell the cordite.

Then there was the issue of the FBI. He still doubted that the actual FBI would give a flip about Takashi's motel bill. It would be like rushing in to arrest a Mafia boss in his favorite restaurant, then stopping to pay for the linguini on the way out. It wasn't how they operated.

No, his bet was that the men Brittany encountered at the motel were impersonating FBI agents, which was a major crime in itself. So why would they risk it?

He'd stopped walking as he read the web results off his phone. Now he forced himself to walk in the direction of his car while he punched in Hayden's phone number.

She answered on the third ring, sounding brusque and harried. "Hayden."

"It's Jason. Guess what? I've got the Mystery Man's name."

"Great," she interrupted him. "I'm in the middle of something right now. Could I call you back in about ten minutes?"

"Sure."

She disconnected without another word.

Well, that was odd.

He closed his phone and continued walking back to his car, thinking this new information through.

Greg Takashi, a graduate student from California, in town to research a book, hires his dad's boat for some reason not related to fishing. They do something that gets mud all over the inside of the boat's cabin, then Takashi disappears and Jason's dad is found dead. Was Takashi another victim? It seemed more likely than being a killer.

So why? What did he find in his research that could result in two possible murders?

That would be relatively easy to find out. Jason just needed to duplicate Takashi's research. And the most likely places to start? If Jason were researching anything in Port Salish, he would start with the Historical Society and the local newspaper.

His cell phone rang. The display showed a cell number he didn't know.

He answered it anyway.

"Jason? It's Danny." Her voice was so low she was almost whispering. "Can you meet me in fifteen minutes at Mary Lou's?"

"Sure. Is everything okay?"

"I'll explain over lunch."

*

Mary Lou's parking lot was absolutely packed when Jason arrived. Either the restaurant was even more popular for lunch than dinner, or the nice weather had lured everyone out of their offices. And it was very nice. The sun had even warmed away the little chill from this morning. It felt like spring.

Jason found a spot to park at the curb on the next block. He took off his sport coat, locked it in the car and started walking to the restaurant.

He'd just turned the corner and started up toward Mary Lou's door, when movement in the street caught his eye. He turned as Danny's squad car stopped, then expertly parallel parked at the curb across the street. He strolled back down the walk to meet her.

She strode across the street to where he waited and forced a smile.

"Bad day?"

She made a face. "You have no idea."

They made their way inside and rather than wait ten to fifteen minutes for a table to open up, decided to sit at the counter. When the waitress appeared to take their orders, both ordered the same burger they'd had last night.

"I keep eating here every day," Danny muttered, "My butt's going to get too big for my car."

Jason smiled. "You've got a ways to go."

"Such a gentleman."

"So tell me what ruined your day."

"Oh, I got my ass chewed by my Lieutenant. Get this, for coming out to help you yesterday."

Jason frowned. "Isn't that what the police are supposed to do? Help the public?"

"Apparently not when it isn't our jurisdiction and not when the subject is actively investigating a case the department closed." She sighed heavily and shook her head.

"Sorry."

"It's not the end of the world. I've just got to tiptoe for a while."

"How?"

"Basically, anything I do to help you needs to be on my own time."

"Look, I don't want you to jeopardize your career for my sake."

"You're not the problem." She shook her head. "The problem is Lt. Marks. He's always had a problem with women officers, especially in leadership positions."

"A good ole boy."

She nodded. "He thinks women should be limited to dispatch and giving safety talks in the schools. He doesn't come right out and say it, of course, but we all know what he wants."

Jason shook his head. "The sheriff lets him get away with this?"

"Oh, he's one of the sheriff's golden boys," she told him. "I just have to keep a low profile for a while. It's part of the game."

Jason frowned as something occurred to him. "Does Marks work out of your office?"

"No," She said. "Headquarters in Friday Harbor. He made a special trip down this morning just to chew me out."

"So how did he know you helped me yesterday?"

Danny stopped still for a beat. "Good question."

"Did you tell anybody at the office where you were going?"

She shook her head. "There was only one deputy in the squad room when I left. I just told him I'd see him tomorrow."

"Then somebody else must have told him. Like someone who was watching me."

"Oh, shit," she said under her breath.

The waitress brought their burgers and set them in front of them, then left to attend to her next customer. For a minute neither of them said anything, neither touched their food. They just sat there, thinking.

"There's something else," he told her.

"What's that?"

He told her about looking at Greg Takashi's Facebook page and the newspaper articles on the internet. "Now, if his friends and family have declared him missing and are actively searching for him, shouldn't your office have been contacted? Wouldn't you at least have seen a missing person's report?"

She frowned. "I should have. Yes."

"But you'd never seen, or heard of him until I showed you his photo."

She shook her head.

"So why not?"

"Because somebody buried it before it got to me."

"That's what I was thinking."

Danny stared down at her plate without touching it. "Oh, God."

The waitress returned, looking worriedly at their untouched plates. "Is everything okay?"

Jason assured her the burgers were fine. "We've been busy talking."

"You're sure?"

"As a matter of fact," Danny said. "Something's come up. Do you think we could get to-go boxes?"

The waitress retrieved two carry-out boxes and left them, still worried that she or the kitchen had screwed something up.

Danny carefully transferred her burger from the plate to the box, then dumped in the fries. Jason did the same with his burger and was deciding whether the fries would be any good cold when a subtle wave of perfume washed over him.

A young woman appeared at his elbow.

"Jason Reynolds?"

"Yeah?" He nodded, confused.

On closer inspection, the woman wasn't that young, just well-maintained.

"This is for you." She set a plain manila envelope on the counter beside his burger and walked away.

"Excuse me?"

But she was already out the door.

Jason felt like he'd been served a summons.

"Friend of yours?" Danny asked.

"Never seen her before." Jason opened the envelope. There were four photographs, all full 8x11 in size, all candid shots taken with a good camera and lens, and all of Lisa. The first showed her walking out of her apartment building, cell phone pressed to her ear, apparently on her way to class. The second was taken the same day through an open doorway and showed her explaining some point to a room full of students.

Danny looked over at him.

The third photograph showed her sitting at a table with Suzie, Markus, and another of her friends. They seemed to be having lunch and enjoying it. Her clothing had changed, so he assumed it was a different day.

"Everything all right?"

The last photo showed her in jeans and a sweat-shirt standing quietly in line at a grocery store, the basket holding her selections hanging in front of her hips. A crosshairs had been drawn over this image, centered on the bridge of Lisa's nose.

"Jason?"

Jason just sat there staring at the photographs and trying not to throw up.

"What's wrong?" Danny asked.

He turned to show her the photos and the computer-printed note that came with them. The message read: "If you want to see her alive again, go to your father's house. Go now. Stay there and await instructions."

CHAPTER 9

"What are you going to do?" Danny asked as they headed down the walk from the restaurant.

"Exactly what they want me to do until Lisa's safe," he told her. He was typing a text message on his cell as they walked. *Can you talk?*

He sent it to Lisa.

"You're just going to give up?"

He shook his head. "I didn't say that. I said I was going to make sure Lisa's safe."

His cell signaled an incoming text. *No,* it read. *Library.*

Call me ASAP, he replied, then added *911* for emphasis.

?K

"Watch out," Danny pulled him aside to allow a group of four business people to pass. They all looked happy and content, whether from having full bellies, or shirtsleeve weather, it was hard to tell. Maybe no one was threatening their loved ones.

Once the business people had passed, Danny looked up at him. "I assume you have some kind of plan in mind?"

"I'm working on it," he told her, more than aware they were probably being watched as they spoke. "First things first, though. We make sure Lisa is safe and you don't lose your job."

"I'm not going to lose my job. I haven't done anything wrong."

"We both know that has nothing to do with it."

She shrugged.

"So go back to work. I'll go back to the house and wait for my instructions."

She didn't look happy about it, but she nodded.

"Call me on my cell when you're done for the day. Hopefully, I'll have something figured out by then."

He sincerely hoped the bad guys hadn't tapped his cell phone. If that were the case, they were screwed.

She still looked skeptical, but nodded. "Be careful."

"You too. Don't trust anyone. Call me when you get off work."

Danny nodded and headed off toward her squad car.

*

Jason's cell phone rang before he took two steps. It was Lisa, calling him back.

"What's wrong?" she asked as soon as he picked up.

"Where are you?"

"On the front steps of the library," she told him. "It's the first place I could call you."

"Listen carefully. Someone has threatened your life," he told her. "We need to change plans."

"You're kidding."

"Dead serious, Lisa."

Lisa paused as this sunk in. "What do you want me to do?"

"You've already arranged for Suzie and Markus to watch Hector this weekend, right?"

"Well, Suzie mostly, but yeah."

"See if they'll let you sleep over tonight. I think the more you're with other people, the safer you are. In fact, see whether Suzie or Markus can take you to get Hector and whatever clothes you need."

"Okay...." She sounded like she thought he was overreacting. "I don't think it will be a problem."

"Good. Use the buddy system. Try not to go anywhere completely by yourself."

"Jesus. They've really got you spooked."

"These guys are scary, Lisa. One person is already dead, maybe two. We can't ignore their threats."

"Shouldn't we call the cops?"

"And tell them what, Lisa? We don't even know who they are."

"I guess you're right."

"One more thing. Instead of coming up here for Dad's funeral on Friday, I want you to go visit your parents."

Lisa's parents lived in Longview, down by the Oregon border and, he hoped, far away from any potential danger. More important, if the bad guys had been listening in to their plans they would not be expecting that. They might even lose track of her.

Silence on the other end of the phone.

"Lisa? You still there?"

"You're scaring me."

Jason reached his car and leaned against it while he talked, trying to spot the people watching him. But they were too good. He could see no one that could be a spy.

"Listen," he told her. "They sent me photos of you outside your apartment, teaching class, even at the grocery store. Different days, different locations. They're watching you. They're probably watching right now. You should be scared. I'm scared."

She paused for just a moment. "What about you?"

"What about me?"

"What's to keep them from hurting you? Maybe you should come back. Let the authorities handle it."

"The authorities don't think there's anything here. I've got to get enough evidence to change their minds. I owe it to my dad."

"Is this the Lundgren Corporation we're talking about?"

"I don't know," he told her. "They're mixed up in it somehow."

"Please be careful. I've been doing some research and these are not nice people. Supposedly Lars Lundgren, the founder of the company got his start by killing the Captain of a fishing boat at sea, then buying the boat cheap from the grieving widow. These guys do business like the Mafia."

"Even more reason why I can't walk away," he told her. "Somebody has to stop them."

"Does it have to be you?"

He didn't answer.

"Get a hold of Suzie, see if she'll help," he told her. "Text me when you're safely there."

Lisa said she would.

They disconnected. After looking around in vain one last time for a surveillance team, Jason unlocked his car, climbed in, and headed for the house.

*

Jason tried his best to come up with a plan on the drive back to the house. He was tired of being two steps behind these guys. He wanted them to react to him for a change. But he had several things working against him. First of all, the drive wasn't long enough. In the early afternoon, it barely took ten minutes to travel from Old Town to his dad's house. More important, he didn't have enough information. It was impossible to form a plan of attack when you didn't know who the enemy was, where they were, or what was motivating them. They knew everything about him and he knew nothing about them.

It was an immense disadvantage.

Jason parked as usual in the driveway beside the neighbor's construction dumpster, unlocked the front door and stepped into the house.

It looked exactly the same as he'd left it.

He'd half expected some mysterious guy in a trench coat to be sitting in the living room, waiting for him. But the room was empty.

"Okay, assholes," he said aloud. "I'm here. What do you want?"

Nothing happened.

Mind games. They were using psychology on him. It was the same strategy that made a lawyer keep a client waiting fifteen minutes even if she wanted the meeting as much as the client. It was why the love-struck teen didn't answer the call from his dream girl on the first ring. It established where the power was, who was in charge.

Nothing he could do but accept it.

He took the carry-out box with his burger to the refrigerator and slipped it inside. What he'd love to do, he thought to himself, was to sit down and eat his burger and make them wait until he was finished to conduct their business.

Unfortunately, everyone involved knew it didn't work that way.

Instead, he decided to tear the house apart and find the devices they were using to keep track of him. He wasn't sure what he'd do once he found them, but it would be nice to know exactly where they were. Maybe they'd left a blind spot. And it would be nice to just know.

The most obvious place for a bug was the house phone, on the counter just five feet from him. Unfortunately, his experience with telephone bugs was limited to movies where they unscrewed the mouthpiece from a princess phone and spotted the device inside. The phone on the kitchen counter was a modern solid state cordless model. He could see no way to get inside, much less plant a bug.

The phone rang in his hand. He jumped a good foot and almost dropped the receiver.

His impulse, naturally, was to answer, but he stopped himself. If they enjoyed mind games so much, he could play with the best of them.

He stood there, looking at the receiver as it rang a second time, then a third, but did nothing. Only when the tone of the fourth ring began, did he punch the "talk" button.

"Hello?"

"Mr. Reynolds." The voice was baritone, confident. The voice of someone used to having people listen. "I was beginning to think you'd misunderstood your instructions."

"No. I was just in the middle of something."

"Well, thank you for making time for me."

"To whom am I speaking?"

"Names are not important. If you wish you can call me Mr. Smith."

Jason carried the phone over to the dining room table and sat down. With his free hand, he pulled a notebook and pen from his briefcase. "Okay, Mr. Smith. What do you want?"

"I want you to do exactly as you're told. Since you're talking to me, I assume our little photo album conveyed what's at stake if you disobey your instructions."

Jason swallowed the anger rising in his chest. Lashing out would do no good. It would only confirm how weak his position was.

"Yeah," he said. "I understand."

"Good. Now your instructions are fairly straightforward, but I want no room for confusion or misunderstanding."

"I'm ready. Go ahead."

"Very well. Instruction number one: you are to stay in your father's house. You will not leave except to conduct tasks related to settling your father's estate. You will not tour the local sights. You will not meet with anybody. You will stay in the house. Watch TV, read a book, take a nap, I don't care, but do not leave the house. Understood?"

"I understand."

"You will receive the copies of your father's death certificate in the mail tomorrow. With them, you can close your father's bank accounts, claim his life insurance and social security. You can do all that with one trip tomorrow afternoon."

How did he know what he'd get in the mail tomorrow? Who was this guy?

"Number two: you will be contacted first thing tomorrow by Mr. Robert Mundelein of Island Estate Sales. He will go through the contents of the house with you. Anything you want to keep, he will place in storage until you can ship it to Seattle. Anything else they will offer at auction to the public. After deducting their fee, the proceeds of the sale will be forwarded to you."

"What if I don't want to sell any of it?"

"Then your storage fee is going to be astronomical. You don't have room in your apartment for everything. I'd suggest you choose a handful of keepsakes with strong memories attached and let the rest go."

Smith knew what would fit in his apartment? "Thanks for the advice. Anything else?"

"Number three: on Saturday, you will attend your father's memorial service like the grieving son you are. You will accept the condolences of his friends, then you will return directly to the house. On Sunday, you will catch the morning ferry and return to your life in Seattle. You will have no further reason to come to Port Salish, no reason to waste any more time or energy here."

"You want me to basically go home and forget this entire week ever happened?"

"Exactly. Go home and live a long, happy, and successful life."

"And I'm under house arrest until Sunday?"

"That's a good way of stating it. Yes."

"And if I refuse?"

"There will be consequences. You will not like the consequences."

The line went dead.

*

After the phone conversation with Mr. Smith, Jason found himself with nothing but time on his hands. It wasn't quite 2:00 now. He didn't expect to hear from either Lisa or Danny until after 5:00 and it wouldn't be a good idea to call either before then. Lisa needed to know that he trusted her and Danny was already in trouble at work because of her association with him. In both cases, the best thing he could do was wait for them to contact him.

After wandering aimlessly around the living room and kitchen for a few minutes, he returned to the idea of figuring out how the bad guys were keeping track of him.

The den/office seemed the logical place to start. If he were trying to listen in on what someone was planning, it's where he would concentrate. He walked into the room and began his search, working systematically from the ceiling down, examining everything that might be out of place, or might be hiding a second purpose. He had no idea what he was looking for. He'd never actually seen a bug before.

He started with the ceiling fixtures, worked down to the shelving, the entertainment center, the computer, desk and chair, and the file cabinets, but found nothing that leaped out at him. He even got down on the carpet and examined the underside of the furnishings. Again, he found nothing.

Which didn't mean a thing. With today's technology and a decent budget, he was fairly sure there were devices so small and so well-disguised an amateur like himself would never spot them.

He needed to approach this from a different angle. Assuming the house was totally wired to listen to and watch him, that still left the logistical problem of what to do with all that information. It did no one any good unless a human was around to analyze it. Which meant they had to have access and the quicker the better.

They had to have some place to receive all the overheard talk, listen to it, and decide what was important. All the devices would probably have wireless transmitters these days; everything else did. The question was where were the receivers?

Just as important, it had to be close enough that when he did leave the house, they could begin tailing him immediately. True, they could and probably had stuck a GPS device on his car, but that would only tell them what roads he took and where he'd stopped. They would have to have human eyes on him to understand what he was doing and who he was talking to.

Which meant they had to be close, as in line-of-sight close.

He wandered out into the kitchen, filled a mug with water and stuck it in the microwave to heat while he finalized the beginnings of a plan. He was going to watch the watchers. When the microwave signaled that the water was hot, he slipped a tea bag into the mug and carried it out onto the front porch.

It was a lovely autumn afternoon, warm with just a hint of a breeze and the porch was a perfect place to enjoy the weather and a mug of tea. If the circumstances had been different, it would have been downright pleasant. Somewhere in the neighborhood a lawnmower droned. A dog barked a few times, then went quiet. It was nice.

Just as important, he wasn't leaving the house. He was sitting there in plain sight for anyone interested. And he could see the length of the street in both directions.

He scanned the neighborhood, property by property, from one end of the street to the other, looking for anything that could serve as a surveillance nest: a van, a panel truck, even a minivan with blacked out windows. A car or pickup would be too small. They would need a certain amount of equipment to monitor the devices and that would require space. They'd also need space for the people to operate it.

Only a handful of vehicles were parked on the street at all. It was early afternoon and most people were still at work. To the far left, a dusty old Buick sedan sat forgotten. A new Toyota pickup was parked kitty-corner across the street, and to the right, in front of the construction site, were a black mid-sized SUV and gray Japanese sedan.

That was it. Nothing else.

Okay.

They weren't watching him from a vehicle, which meant the nest had to be in one of the neighborhood houses. He glanced at a couple of the homes nearby, but quickly ruled them out. They were all occupied, perfectly normal suburban single-family homes. A couple even had a basketball hoop above the garage door. He couldn't see someone allowing a group of strangers to set up shop in the spare bedroom for a couple of weeks.

Just as important, he couldn't see it staying secret for very long, certainly not for several weeks. It went against human nature. People talked. Neighbors snooped. Especially in a small town where everybody knew everybody else.

That left the construction site next door. Now that he thought about it, the location was ideal. It was empty, so they wouldn't have to deal with curious roommates and the neighborhood was used to seeing strangers around. They could set up almost anything inside without anyone growing suspicious.

Though there had always been vehicles parked in front of the house, he couldn't recall ever hearing any of the usual sounds of construction, no whining power saws, no hammering, not even the blaring radio every construction site seemed to have. It had always been dead silent.

He got up now and strolled to the end of the porch nearest the site. He could clearly see the windows nearest him, but nothing inside. They were merely sheets of black glass, reflecting back the yard and the side of his house. But they had a clear line of sight to his house.

The SUV was the vehicle in front parked closest to him.

He pulled out his cell phone and sent a text to Danny:

Do me a favor? Run WA plates 576 AES.

He hoped she could do that without getting in trouble.

While he waited for her reply, he walked into the house and casually strolled through the living room and then the den/office. As he suspected, the windows next door had a fairly clear view through the windows of his father's house. There would be blind spots, but anyone watching would be able to see enough to know what was going on.

Now he knew why his dad had all the blinds drawn when Jason had arrived. He'd been trying to shut out prying eyes.

His cell signaled an incoming text from Danny. Jason hit the button to accept it and read the display:

Registered as part of a fleet to Lundgren Corporation. ???

He quickly replied. *I think I have a plan.*

*

Jason spent the rest of the afternoon rehearsing his plan in his head, while physically going through the house trying to decide what, if any, of his father's possessions he would like to keep. Truth was, it was something he'd needed to do since he'd arrived, but he'd been too occupied with the investigation.

Or maybe he'd simply been avoiding it.

He rejected most of the furniture without second thought. He already had furniture and these were both out of fashion and fairly worn. The one exception was his father's desk. It was much nicer than his own. Maybe he could upgrade.

He saw nothing in the kitchen or either of the baths he couldn't part with and little in the bedrooms. The family photographs were a different story, as were some of his brother's high school trophies and the framed flag from his funeral. He wasn't sure about his father's fishing gear. He hated to part with it, but he hadn't been fishing for years.

Then there was his dad's boat. What would he do with that if he kept it?

His cell phone rang. It was just past 4:30. He checked the display. It was Lisa, a bit earlier than he expected, but maybe she'd decided to cut out of school early.

He quickly walked back out on to the front porch, hoping to avoid most of the listening devices and picked up the call. "Hey," he said. "Everything set with Suzie?"

She replied with a kind of quiet, painful groan.

Something was wrong. His stomach lurched and the muscles across his shoulders tightened.

"Lisa? "

For a moment, he listened to her struggle to control her breathing. Another voice spoke in the background. A woman. It sounded like Suzie.

"Lisa? What's wrong? Are you okay?"

"Oh, God," she finally choked out. "They killed him! The fuckers killed him!"

She broke into full sobs.

He'd never felt so helpless in his life. "What happened? Killed who?"

Lisa sobbed fully out of control. Her words came out in one and two syllable fragments. "Hector. They. Killed. Him. My sweet. My sweetie."

A wave of relief passed over him, then an immediate, second wave of guilt. He had been terrified that one of their friends had been killed, but Hector didn't deserve to die either. He had been a good dog, absolutely devoted to Lisa. And Lisa truly loved the little guy.

"Oh, God. Are you okay?" he asked.

"Oh, yeah," she managed to blend sarcasm with her tears. "Peachy."

He supposed he deserved that.

"Is Suzie with you?"

"Yeah."

"Let me talk to her."

He waited while the women transferred the phone.

"Hold on a minute, Jason," Suzie said. "I'm driving. Let me get off the road."

About a minute and a half later, Suzie came back on. "You still there?"

"What happened?"

"We drove over to her apartment to pick up Hector and some clothes," Suzie told him. "Hector was right in the front room. Jason, it was pretty bad. It looked like the poor guy'd been kicked to death."

"Shit. Sorry you guys had to see that."

"Yeah, me, too."

"But you guys are all right? No one tried to mess with you?"

"No. We grabbed her things and got the hell out of there. We're on our way back to my place now."

"Good. Stay there. Stay inside and don't open the door for anyone you don't know," he told her. "And don't let Lisa go anywhere by herself."

"I will. What—what kind of a person would do this?"

He took a deep breath. "A bad one. A very bad one."

"Hang on, Lisa wants to talk to you again."

He waited while the phone changed hands again.

"Jason?" She had control of her sobbing now, but her breathing still sounded ragged and uneven.

"I'm so sorry about Hector. He didn't deserve that."

"Just promise me we're going to get the heartless fucker who did this."

"We are. We're going to get them all."

*

Danny called his cell at almost twenty minutes after five. This time, he was expecting the call. He was already out on the porch, sipping on iced rather than hot tea and keeping an eye on the construction site. There had been no activity that he'd seen. The same SUV and Japanese sedan were still parked in front, almost like they belonged there.

A few more cars and trucks had been parked on the street since he first looked, but not that many. Most vehicles were stored in driveways or garages.

A handful of boys were playing a pickup game of football in a yard a couple of houses to his left and across the street. He'd been passing the time watching them and remembering similar games he'd played when he'd been their age. In the same yard to be exact.

"So tell me about this plan of yours," Danny asked as soon as he picked up the call.

"First, tell me you still have a job."

After the news about Hector, he really didn't want to be responsible for making another friend's life more difficult. He really felt for Lisa, how bad she was hurting and how it was, indirectly at least, his fault. No, one was plenty, thank you.

She seemed surprised by the question. "Of course I do. It takes more than a tirade from Marks to get rid of me. Besides, he doesn't know it yet, but I've got something on him now."

"What's that?"

"I found the missing person report we sent back to San Jose. It says we interviewed the motel manager and found Takashi'd checked out on Wednesday, October 14th. We believe he took the evening ferry back to Seattle."

"And?"

"It was signed by Marks and filed the same day the office received it from San Jose. I guarantee that the commander of Patrol Division did not hop a boat from Friday Harbor to personally investigate a missing persons case. I also know that no one in this office interviewed anyone about it. Which means Marks invented the whole thing."

"Wow. What are you going to do about it?"

"I haven't decided yet," she sounded almost gleeful. "I have a friend over at the State Police who would just love this. He has a thing about dirty cops."

"It would be interesting to find out why he faked the report."

"Wouldn't it though? Oh, I'm taking tomorrow off, a personal day, so I will be at your service if you want. They have nothing to say about what I do on my own time. Now, tell me about this plan."

He sketched out his idea and her role in the affair. "What do you think? Turn the tables on these bastards for a change."

"It's worth a shot."

"The only hitch would be if they own the local cops," he said. "But that would be obvious pretty quickly."

"Or they have a good cover story."

"Either way, we'll find out in a couple of hours, once it gets dark."

She hesitated a moment. "You know that if it does work, they're not going to be very happy with you."

"But if it works they won't know where I am."

CHAPTER 10

By ten minutes after seven it was fully dark and the neighborhood had grown quiet. The pickup football game had ended thirty minutes ago, called by mothers who insisted it was time to come inside. The decision wasn't popular with the kids, but what could you do? You lived and died by the officials. Jason sat out on the front porch as he had most of the afternoon, a steaming mug of coffee on a patio table beside him. He wore a light coat against the evening chill.

There had been no activity at the construction site next door. No one had come and no one had left, not even for a dinner run. Apparently, they had food and drink on the premises. Bathrooms, too.

At 7:15 he sent a text to Danny. *Ready?*

She replied in seconds. *Yep.*

K. Showtime.

He sent a short, wordless prayer into the cosmos that he not be screwing everything up worse than it already was and punched 911 into his cell phone. When the operator came on, he identified himself and gave her his address. "The house next door to me is under construction, being remodeled, I think. Well, this might be nothing, but I just saw a group of people go inside and I don't think they're construction workers. I don't know if they're trying to steal equipment, or tearing the place up, or what, but I think they're up to no good."

"We'll send an officer to check it out."

"Thank you."

He closed his phone, leaned back in his chair, and waited. If the plan worked as he hoped, the bad guys would not only take a hit in terms of personnel, but lose their surveillance operation, while giving him and his friends some much needed information about just who they were dealing with. That's where Danny came in. She would be his eyes and ears.

That is, if the plan worked like he hoped.

The obvious downside was that even if the plan worked to perfection, "Mr. Smith" would not be very happy with him. Recent history suggested that "Mr. Smith" could be very dangerous when he wasn't happy.

But he couldn't just cave and walk away from this. Somebody had to stop these people.

Headlights flashed off to his right.

He watched the lights draw steadily nearer. The driver was moving decisively, but not rushing. Soon, Jason could make out the black and white paint scheme of a city police squad car. It slowed as it passed the sedan and SUV, then nosed into the driveway behind the dumpster and parked.

An officer in the dark blue uniform of the city police stepped out of the car, paused to speak into his shoulder radio, then pulled the flash from his equipment belt and walked up toward the house.

Jason waited.

Nothing happened. The neighborhood was dead silent around him. Even the crickets had nothing to say. What was going on inside the construction site? Had the bad guys somehow gotten wind of his scheme and made their escape? Or were they and the police on the same side, greeting each other like old friends?

A muffled shout next door, followed by another. Jason couldn't make out what was said, but recognized the command voice cops used when you absolutely had to do what they said. The shout repeated two more times. Then nothing.

Jason's cell phone chirped an incoming text.

It was from Danny. *Bingo.*

Within seconds, emergency strobes lit the trees and houses with flashing blue and red as Danny's squad car pulled to a stop, double parked beside the SUV. She leaped out of her car and hurried into the construction site, sidearm drawn. She looked all business.

Maybe a minute-and-a-half later more emergency lights lit up the night and another sheriff's car pulled in behind Danny's. The second deputy ran into the house. His weapon was also in his hand.

Then all was quiet.

Jason sipped his cooling coffee and watched the strobes paint the houses around him in Christmas tree flashes of blue, red, and white. The plan seemed to be working perfectly. A few of the neighbors had noticed the excitement and come out on to their porches and front yards to see what was happening.

"What's going on?"

Jason glanced over to find Emma Stockton standing on the edge of her front lawn gazing at the activity.

"Your guess is as good as mine," he told her.

"Probably druggies. They like to take over these abandoned houses."

That caught his attention. "It's abandoned?"

She nodded. "The bank foreclosed on it a few months ago. It's just been sitting there until a couple of weeks ago."

"What happened a couple of weeks ago?"

"They started working on it again. Maybe the bank found a buyer."

"Probably." But he was thinking the new activity had nothing to do with a buyer.

Emma complained about the cold and returned to her house.

About fifteen minutes after Danny had arrived another car pulled down the street and parked across the way from the cluster of police vehicles. It had the paint scheme of the city police cars, but no light bar across the roof. Jason guessed this was the watch commander.

A tall man in the dark blue of the city police climbed out of the car, strode across the street, and into the house. He did not draw his firearm.

Jason smiled and sipped his coffee. He felt like he'd just thrown a touchdown pass with time running out, submitted a prize-winning story minutes before the deadline. For once, finally, he'd caught his enemies off-guard and hurt them.

Somewhere, "Mr. Smith" probably wasn't even aware that his surveillance operation had just been blown to smithereens.

"Mess with the people I care about," he murmured into his coffee mug, "And there will be consequences."

He sipped his coffee and tried to control the growing excitement.

Another car meandered down the street, this time coming from his left, instead of the right. It clearly was too small to be a police vehicle and the driver seemed to be either lost or intimidated by the mass of police vehicles and flashing lights on the street.

It came to a hesitant stop in the middle of the street, then swung over to park at the curb right in front of his house.

It probably wasn't the bad guys. They wouldn't show any indecisiveness.

He watched a slim woman with long blond hair streaming from a knit cap step out of the car and pause to get her bearings. She gave a lot of attention to the activity at the construction site, but then stepped around the car and started up the walk toward Jason's porch.

He doubted she could see him. There was no light on in the porch proper, just the spill from the living room windows.

Something about her seemed vaguely familiar.

She reached the porch steps, still unaware of him sitting there and stepped up.

He didn't want to startle her, so as gently as he could he said: "Hi."

She still jumped.

"Sorry. I didn't mean to scare you."

"Jason?"

He knew that voice. It drew him to his feet. "Lisa?"

"Don't be mad. I want to help."

He wasn't mad at all. He rushed over to hug her.

*

"What are you doing here?" he asked, then stopped himself. "That came out wrong. I'm glad to see you. I've been worried all night. But this is the last thing I expected. And the blond hair?"

"Hopefully, it's the last thing those bastards expect, too."

They were both sitting on the porch now, because Jason still didn't feel comfortable talking in the house. He had poured Lisa a mug of coffee and refreshed his own. Now they sipped their coffee, talked, and watched the police activity going on next door. Not that there was a lot to see. Most of the action was inside the building. It was boring enough that most of the gawkers had lost interest and returned to their homes. Watching a patrolman hang crime scene tape wasn't very exciting.

"I just couldn't sit there and do nothing," Lisa told him. "After what they did to—after what they did, I couldn't just hide while you faced them alone."

"I'm sorry about Hector. I really am. I never saw that coming."

"It wasn't your fault."

But indirectly it was and they both knew it.

They looked over as the city cop and a sheriff's deputy led two men in handcuffs out of the construction site and placed one in the back of each officer's car. The officers closed the doors and returned to the house, leaving their prisoners where they sat.

"Who came up with the disguise?" Jason asked.

"Both of us. Me and Suzie. The wig is from her Halloween costume last year. Remember Li'l Bo Peep?"

He did. It had been quite a costume. A nursery rhyme character as re-imagined by Zalman King.

"Once she realized that I wasn't going to run off and hide at my parents, we started getting practical. If someone was watching the apartment—watching me—they were looking for a brunette driving a white Civic, not a blond driving a black Jetta. So I traded cars with Suzie, borrowed her overcoat and wig, and headed up here."

Jason could only shake his head. It was beautiful. So simple it was foolproof. Anyone watching the apartment probably wouldn't even know they'd lost her until Suzie got into the Civic to go to school in the morning.

"So what's the deal next door? I was terrified when I drove up. I thought they'd done something to you."

Jason briefly explained to her his idea about their surveillance operation against him and what he'd done to bring it down.

Lisa smiled. "I like it. So now they're going to jail?"

"It looks like a couple of them are, at least for the night."

"I hope they rot in there."

Jason sipped his coffee. Much as he'd like to see the same thing, he doubted the two men were facing terribly serious charges. In all likelihood, they would be arraigned in the morning and bailed out by afternoon.

"How badly do you think this hurts them? The bad guys?"

"I don't know," he told her. "Not that bad, I think. These are just worker bees, following orders. The guys giving the orders are still out there somewhere. The biggest advantage is it disrupts their information flow. The whole time I've been up here they've been one step ahead because they always knew what I was going to do. It levels the playing field for a little while."

The trick now was to take advantage of the change, hit them again and keep them off balance.

"At least you did something."

"Yeah," he sipped his coffee. "Score one for the good guys—two, counting your escape—that leaves us only behind by a dozen, or so."

"But it's a start."

"It is." Now he had to figure out what to do next. Before he could do that, he really needed to hear from Danny. He was starved for information. Who they were up against, specifically? The Lundgren Corporation was a big organization. More important, why? Why all the spying? Why the violence and intimidation?

Next door, the deputy walked out of the house, climbed into his car and drove away with his prisoner. A few seconds later, the city cop did the same. The officers seemed to be wrapping it up over there.

"What do you think they'll do next?"

"Who?"

"The bad guys. Lundgren, or whoever it is."

He didn't know. But it probably wouldn't be pleasant.

"You know you can't stay here anymore."

"No, that probably wouldn't be a good idea."

Plus, having him out there in parts unknown would maximize the advantage the raid had given him. If they not only lost their surveillance advantage, but had no idea where either he or Lisa was or what they were doing, someone might panic and make a serious mistake.

The question was where to hide. Port Salish was a small town on a small island. There were only so many places.

Lisa smiled. "I have a motel room. I got it as soon as I got off the ferry. If we use Suzie's car instead of yours...."

Damn," he said. "You're good."

*

Fifteen minutes later, Jason interrupted their conversation and pointed next door. "Here comes our inside man."

Danny and the watch commander strolled out of the construction site and stood on the sidewalk for a few minutes, talking quietly.

"The guy?" Lisa asked.

"Nope. The other guy."

Danny and the watch commander continued their conversation. By now, the neighborhood had returned to their televisions. Danny and her colleague had the street to themselves.

"How'd you get her to help?" Lisa asked. "I thought the police weren't interested?"

"I don't know. I guess she believed me. So far, she's the only cop who does."

Danny and the watch commander finished their conversation, shook hands, and the Commander strode across the street, climbed into his car and drove off.

Jason pulled his cell phone from a pocket and sent Danny a text. *All done?*

He watched her pull her cell out and read it. *Kinda. Got to watch the scene until relief gets here. Meet me outside?*

I'm on the porch.

Danny read the text, glanced their direction, then started down the sidewalk toward the house. Either she was still amped by the raid, or something was bothering her. Her pace seemed faster, more driven, than usual.

"Did we do good?" Jason asked as she started up the porch steps, as much to reveal his location as to start the conversation.

"We did good," Danny said. "We've got a lot to talk about, but we shouldn't do it here."

"Because?"

Danny stopped in her tracks. She'd just stepped onto the porch proper and noticed Lisa, sitting quietly beside Jason. She clearly had not been expecting a third person.

Neither had Jason until a few minutes ago.

"Sgt. Danielle Hayden, meet my friend Lisa Martin. She decided she wanted to help."

The women exchanged polite greetings, like diplomats about to negotiate a cease fire.

"In the pictures you were brunette," Danny said.

"It's a wig. I thought they wouldn't be looking for a blond."

"Good idea." Danny said.

That seemed to be the limit of their conversation.

"So why can't we talk now?" Jason asked.

"The guys we arrested are pros. They immediately invoked their Miranda rights and clammed up," Danny told them. "They're being processed right now, but they're going to get their phone calls any minute. I guarantee that one will be to an attorney, the other will be to their boss."

"Crap," Jason said. He hadn't thought of that.

"You think someone will try to retaliate?" Lisa asked.

"I think they'll send someone down to find Jason again. Damage control, more than anything. But I think it's best if they don't find you."

Jason was already getting to his feet. Lisa also stood. "How long are you going to be tied up here?"

"I don't know. There's another city officer on his way, but it might take him a while. He was off duty when his boss called. Besides, I'd kind of like to see who drives through the area in the next hour, or two."

"Okay. We can meet up later. Send me a text when you're ready."

Danny nodded. "You have a place to stay?"

Lisa told her about the motel room. "We could meet there when you're finished."

"It's a plan," Danny said. "Now get your things and get out of here, but leave the lights on and your car where it is. Let them think you're still here."

"Got it," Jason said. "Text me when you're free."

Danny said she would. She turned and went back to the construction site. Jason and Lisa went inside to gather his things.

*

Taylor Smith was settled in for the night. He sat in the living room of his condo, wearing only his boxers, sipping a bourbon while a Jean-Claude Van Damme movie played on the satellite television. He was relaxed. Things seemed to be working out for the time being. In a couple more days, it might be done for good. Finally.

His cell phone rang at five minutes to nine.

He crushed his cigarette in the ashtray, picked up the phone and looked at the display. A local number, but not one he was familiar with. He decided to answer anyway.

"Smith? This is Baxter. We've got a problem."

"What's that?" Smith's mind immediately shifted from idle to problem-solving mode.

As Baxter told him of the raid on their observation post, his mood grew more and more dark. This was bad. This was really bad. Two of his operatives were in jail, facing multiple charges; his observation post was destroyed, all the equipment and recorded information now in police custody; the police were probably preparing a search warrant for the condo next door, where Baxter and Jackson had been staying when they weren't on duty; and the subject of their surveillance was in the wind.

For all he knew Jason Reynolds could be in Timbuktu by now.

He willed himself to remain calm. "You have legal lined up?"

Baxter said that Jackson was making the call.

"Hang tight. We'll get you out as soon as we can. Thanks for the heads up."

Smith disconnected the phone and sat there for a moment, thinking, establishing priorities, making plans and discarding them. Finally, he picked up the phone again and hit a number on speed dial.

"Anderson, we have a situation. The police are going to serve a search warrant on your condo within the hour. I need you to gather your things and move them over to my place. I'll leave the door open. Grab anything that could be incriminating and bring it over here. Got it?"

As soon as his man acknowledged the instructions, Smith disconnected, then hit another number on speed dial.

When it was answered: "Melissa. Get dressed and meet me at my car in ten minutes. We're going to take a ride."

He disconnected again, set aside his drink and went to put some clothes on.

*

"You really think these guys are going to come back tonight?" Officer Joe Barret asked. "That would be pretty ballsy, especially with the car parked right here."

They were sitting in the front seat of Barret's squad car, where they could take advantage of the heater. The night had grown downright cold.

"You didn't see the setup they had in there," Danny told him. "It was like something from a Bourne movie. These guys are pros and they just lost track of their subject. They'll want to see what's going on so they can figure out their options."

Barret shrugged.

So far, the only car to drive by had been a minivan and it had pulled into a driveway down the block before disgorging a woman and two kids. Apparently, an event had run late tonight.

There had been no other traffic at all.

She opened her cell phone to check the time. Almost 9:30. She'd expected them to show fairly quickly. It had already been nearly an hour. Maybe she'd been wrong. Maybe they were skittish about being caught near the spy nest so soon after the raid. Maybe they were going to take an entirely different approach.

Danny hated this, sitting and waiting.

She imagined Jason was going stir-crazy too, sitting in a motel room, wondering what was going on, wondering what she'd learned.

Barret stiffened beside her. "Got something. Pedestrian. One o'clock."

Danny looked up as a woman strolled down the sidewalk toward them. She looked to be somewhere between twenty-five and thirty-five years old, with shoulder-length dark hair under a knit cap. Her hands were shoved deep into the pockets of a dark winter coat.

She looked like she was taking an evening stroll.

"What do you want to do?" Barret asked.

"Nothing. Just see what she does."

For all she knew, this could be nothing more sinister than a local resident out for some fresh air before bed.

The woman glanced at them curiously as she approached, then at the house with the yellow crime scene tape stretched across it. When her eyes returned to the squad car, they briefly met Danny's gaze. The woman flashed a smile, then looked away again and continued past the car.

Danny couldn't swear to it, but she thought it was the woman who'd delivered the threatening photos to Jason at Mary Lou's.

"Stay here," she told Barret as she opened her door and climbed out on to the sidewalk.

The woman—if she was indeed an operative for Lundgren Security—was good. She had to have wondered whether Danny had recognized her and she'd probably heard the car door open, yet her pace remained unchanged as she walked past Jason's house.

Danny watched as the woman glanced over at the house. To the casual observer, she was just idly taking in her surroundings as she walked. Danny, however, noticed she did not look to the other side of the street, just at Jason's house. Then she continued walking down the street.

Clever, Danny thought to herself. A pedestrian, not a car. Nine times out of ten, no one would have given her a second thought.

*

Jason checked his cell phone again, just to make sure the battery hadn't died in the last sixty seconds. It hadn't. But he thought waiting around was going to drive him insane.

It was almost 10:00. He was beginning to worry that Danny had gotten into trouble.

"Would you just try and relax?" Lisa said. She lay on the motel's queen-sized bed, ignoring a sit-com on television while he paced. Her wig now lay on top of the cabinet beside the TV like a sleeping cat. "She'll be here."

"That's not what I'm worried about."

"She's a cop. She's more than capable of taking care of herself."

“I know,” Jason agreed, but continued pacing. “I just wish she’d call and let us know what’s going on.”

Lisa sat up and ran fingers through her loose hair. “So what’s the story with you two anyway?”

“Story?”

“You guys seem to have known each other more than three days.”

“No. Not really.” Jason shook his head. “I guess we went to high school together, but I don’t remember her. I was a senior when she was a freshman. You know how that works.”

“But she remembered you.”

“Yeah. That’s what she said.”

Lisa nodded.

“What?”

“Just wondering.” He couldn’t read the expression on her face.

His cell phone rang. It was Danny.

“Where are you?”

“I’m on my way. I had to change clothes and cars. A cop car parked in front of your room isn’t exactly low profile.”

Jason took a deep breath. That made sense.

“Have you guys eaten tonight?”

“Just some snacks out of the vending machine.” Neither of them had even thought about it earlier. They’d come straight to the motel.

“All the restaurants are closed, but I’ll pick up something at the grocery store. It could be a long night.”

Jason thought that would be a good idea. “Pick up some coffee grounds too. There’s a coffee maker in the room, but only enough coffee for about four cups.”

“Okay. I’ll be there in about fifteen minutes.”

*

Twenty minutes later someone tapped lightly on the motel room door. Jason checked through the peephole, unlocked the door and let Danny in. She had changed out of her uniform and now wore a pair of faded Levi’s and a crimson and gray WSU hoodie. She could have been a college student, except for the gun on her hip.

She set two plastic bags from the grocery store on the room’s small table and glanced at Lisa. “I hope you’re not vegan.”

“Not a chance,” Lisa told her.

They slid the table over so the bed could serve as a third seat then gathered to eat the slightly stale sandwiches Danny had brought. There were two ham and two turkey, with one beef thrown in for good measure. They weren’t exactly gourmet, but they were nourishment. Jason was hungry enough that it didn't really matter what his food tasted like.

"Several things we've learned," Danny told them around a bite of ham sandwich. "First, both men arrested tonight carried employee ID cards from the Lundgren Corporation, Security Division."

"Surprise…surprise."

She nodded. "We also found counterfeit FBI credentials in the room, which means legally speaking, they are in a world of hurt. The Feds don't like people pretending to be them. Of course, neither of the men is talking without a lawyer."

"They wouldn't. They're pros."

Lisa frowned, wiped her mouth with a paper napkin. "But why would Lundgren be so interested in you? Why the Security Division?"

"Because I wouldn't accept my dad's death as an accident," Jason told her. "The real question is why were they after my dad?"

Danny shook her head. "I didn't see anything that pointed to a motive."

"Maybe they're smuggling drugs," Lisa suggested. "From what I've read about the company, I wouldn't put it past them. They were supposed to be heavily into bootlegging during Prohibition."

"Through Port Salish?" Danny shook her head. "I don't think so. We would have seen some sign of it. Believe me, we have a drug problem like everyone, especially meth, but if this town was part of a major pipeline, there's be a lot more drugs around and they'd be a lot cheaper. It's got to be something else."

"Something big and bad enough to have a security team to protect it," Jason added.

"You should have seen the place they had over there," Danny said. "Thousands of dollars just in the technology: computers, digital recorders, GPS feeds, plus however many devices are in your house. It was impressive."

"So whatever they're protecting is either very damaging," Jason said. "Or very lucrative."

"Whatever it is, I still don't think it involves smuggling," Danny insisted. "Remember, this is a small town on an island. People would notice if there were serious shipments of anything moving through the area. Especially this time of year."

She made sense. Smugglers preferred the cover of a lot of activity to hide themselves. That's why they used major ports as entry points, hoping their efforts would be lost in the crowd.

"Get this, though. The men we arrested had keys to a condo down on the waterfront owned by Lundgren. The company probably uses it as a management and client perk," Danny said. "The condos are managed by one Martin Haislip, III at Evergreen Bank."

Jason paused halfway through his second sandwich. "Really?"

Danny nodded. "In a striking coincidence, the property where they built their spy nest was foreclosed last spring. Three guesses who owns and manages it now."

"Evergreen Bank and Martin Haislip, III."

"Give the only man in the room a gold star."

"Sounds like we need to pay Mr. Haislip a visit."

"Who is Haislip?" Lisa asked. She had no idea who they were talking about. "You guys know him?"

"We knew him from school," Jason told her. "He was the rich kid who never let you forget it. You know the type. Thought he was better than everyone else because his dad had lots of money."

"Now he's a vice president of Evergreen Bank," Danny added. "Mainly because his family owns it. Daddy's the president and CEO."

Lisa raised her eyebrows. "And now you can get your revenge?"

Jason glanced at Danny, who seemed to be mulling that point over. He finally shrugged. "It will definitely make the moment sweeter."

Danny agreed. "Definitely."

"Okay." Lisa shrugged.

"So we pay Haislip a visit tomorrow?" Jason asked Danny. "I think under the right pressure he'll fold like a wet noodle."

Danny agreed. "But we're going to have to get him out of his comfort zone, which means away from his office and probably his house, too."

Jason agreed.

"Do you think this Haislip guy knows why they're after us?" Lisa asked.

Danny shrugged. "I don't really see him as a major player. More of a local gopher."

"He's a yes man," Jason agreed. "Haislip does what his dad tells him to do. He'll know a lot of the day-to-day details, but not the whys. The biggest thing he might be able to give us is the names of the security people."

"And the details about that weird lease your dad had," Danny added.

Jason nodded.

"So how do we find out why they're doing this?" Lisa asked.

"It all keys on this Takashi guy," Jason said. "Whatever he was researching seems to have started this whole thing. If we could find out what that was, we'd be way ahead on this."

Danny agreed. "But how do we figure that out?"

He hadn't figured that out yet.

"You guys call yourselves investigators?" Lisa looked at each of them. "Why don't we call the school and ask them? He had a thesis committee and an adviser. They'd know what he was working on."

Jason looked at Danny, who shrugged. Neither of them had thought of it. "Okay. First thing in the morning."

They made a pot of coffee and began to make concrete plans for the next day.

CHAPTER 11

Friday morning, as usual, Danny woke ten minutes before her alarm, set for 7:00. She had been on day shift long enough now that her body woke up between 6:30 and 7:00 no matter what time she'd gotten to sleep. Last night it had been well after 3:00. She had stayed at the motel until 2:30, discussing strategy with Jason and Lisa until they thought they had every angle covered.

She walked out into the kitchen in her pj's, got coffee started, then went to the front window and peered past the drapes to the street outside.

One of the angles discussed last night was the probability that Lundgren would put a tail on her, hoping she'd lead them to Jason. It was what she would do in their shoes.

She peered out at the deserted street of her modest little neighborhood. Most of the houses were smallish one- or two-bedroom cottages, built in the '40's to house the workers at the canneries. Now most of the residents were either retired couples or young ones just starting out. That's how Danny had ended up here. She and her husband had bought the little house because they could afford it and it was plenty big enough for the two of them. When the marriage ended, Danny had kept the house.

Nothing was moving on the street, which wasn't unusual. She was usually one of the first up. The only other lights she saw were in the Rasmussen house across the street. He'd been fighting cancer for the past year and didn't sleep much.

One car parked in the street caught her attention, a nondescript mid-sized sedan. There wasn't enough light to distinguish its color, but the shade was dark: black, blue, maybe dark red. She had never seen it before.

The windows looked steamed up.

Someone was in the car.

She hurried to the hall closet, retrieved a spotting scope her husband had left behind and returned to the window. With as little movement of the drapery as she could manage, she slipped the scope into position and focused on the car. In the shadows, she could just make out a single figure sitting low in the driver's seat.

"Gotcha," she said to herself.

She set the scope aside and returned to the bedroom to take her shower and get dressed. She wanted to be at the bank when her buddy Haislip showed up for work. She'd need to lose her tail before then.

Twenty minutes later, she emerged from her bedroom in jeans, running shoes, and a light flannel shirt. Her wet hair was tied back in a ponytail and her only makeup was eyeliner and a little mascara.

She poured herself a cup of coffee and checked the time. It was almost 8:00.

Time to start the ball rolling.

She found her cell phone and punched in a number from her contact list.

It was answered on the second ring. "Sullivan."

"Hey," Danny said. "Are you busy?"

"God, no. It's been dead. I've given out one warning for a broken taillight and answered one prowler call."

"I've got a favor to ask. There's some guy sitting in a car outside my house for no good reason. Could you swing by and check him out for me?"

"Give me the details and I'll head right over."

Danny gave him the description of the car and its location, thanked him, and hung up.

Ten minutes later, she had her coat on, handbag and keys in her hand, and was waiting by the front door when Sullivan's car pulled in behind the suspect and lit the emergency lights.

Danny immediately went through the door, locked it, and climbed into her Subaru. As she was backing out of the drive, she could see Sullivan talking to the person in the car, probably asking for identification. She didn't wait around for the results. She pointed her car in the other direction and drove.

If the guy in the car was supposed to tail her, he'd just failed. Now she had to deal with the possibility they'd put a GPS device on her car. They seemed to be pretty high-tech. That's why she was driving across town to trade cars with her mother. If they followed the GPS, they'd end up sitting outside her mother's house for hours before they figured out she wasn't there.

That should buy her enough time to do what she needed to do.

She would still be able to get to the bank before Haislip did.

Her cell phone rang just as she was pulling into her mother's driveway. It was Sullivan.

"What can you tell me?" she asked him.

"According to his driver's license, the subject is one Thomas Anderson, from Mountlake Terrace," Sullivan told her. Danny scribbled the name in her notebook next to the names of the two they'd arrested the night before. "His car was a rental. He claimed to have had a fight with his girlfriend last night and driven around until he had to get some sleep."

"You buy it?"

"Not really, but I had nothing to hold him."

"Thanks. You've been a big help."

"Has he been causing you problems?"

"It's complicated."

"It always is," Sullivan said. "Well, his name's going to be in my report, so that's something. Let me know if there's anything I can do to help."

Danny assured him she would, then ended the call. Before closing the phone she sent a text to Jason. *You guys awake?*

The reply came almost immediately. *Not happy about it. Everything a go?*

Everything as planned. See you soon.

Danny ended the call.

*

Wearing jeans and a fuzzy off-white sweater, Lisa plopped down on the edge of the bed beside Jason and planted a kiss on his cheek. She smelled of jasmine and baby powder. He'd forgotten how good she smelled in the morning.

"How are you doing?" she asked.

"Okay," he lied. He was exhausted and stressed. They were risking so much over the next few days. Even he might not appreciate the gravity of the situation.

"Did you get any sleep at all?" Lisa began brushing her wet hair with long, smooth strokes.

"Maybe an hour or two."

That was being generous. They had finally crawled into bed at something like 4:30, too exhausted to do anything but hold each other. Lisa had fallen asleep almost immediately, but Jason's mind had continued to spin at ninety miles an hour, going over their plans for the umpteenth time, searching for flaws and trying to anticipate what Mr. Smith and his cronies would try next to stop them.

It had been largely a waste of energy.

"How long do we have?"

Jason checked the time on the clock radio beside the bed. "Five minutes."

"Just enough for a cup of coffee." She set her brush down and went to fix them each a cup.

They'd taken advantage of the motel's wi-fi last night and accessed the San Jose State University website in order to find the phone number for the history department, and, just in case, the graduate school, though Lisa assured him the history department should have the information they needed.

They'd also decided that the best time to make their call would be shortly after 9:00 in the morning. Then, Lisa assured him, the staff would be fresh and less frustrated than later in the day.

Lisa brought Jason a cup of coffee. He thanked her and sipped it, hoping the caffeine would be enough to overcome the grit in his eyes and heaviness in his limbs. He needed to be alert today, not a zombie.

Lisa touched him on the thigh. "It's time."

He set the coffee on the nightstand and dialed the number on his cell phone.

"History Department," a woman answered. Her voice hid her age. She could have been anything from twenty-five to sixty. "This is Gail. How can I help you?"

Jason identified himself and told her he was a reporter with the *Seattle News*. "I'm working on a story about a missing graduate student and wondered if I could get some information?"

"Oh, yes. That would be Greg Takashi. Everybody's very worried about him. It's like he dropped off the face of the earth."

"So I gathered. My notes say he came up to Washington to do some research for his dissertation."

"That would be his thesis," Gail corrected him. "Dissertations are for doctoral candidates. Greg was working on his master's, so it was a thesis."

"Okay, thanks, I'll change that." He changed nothing. His notebook was open in front of him, but to a blank page. "So he was working on his master's thesis and in Washington to do some research for it. Funny thing is, I can't find any information anywhere about the subject matter he was researching. Could you help me out with that?"

"Well, we should have the title of his thesis on file," she said. "Could you hold for a minute while I look that up?"

He told her that would be no problem. The line abruptly snapped and he was listening to classical music, something with a lot of strings.

"She's looking it up," he told Lisa, who nodded and sipped her coffee. She had finished brushing her hair. It was now twisted into a knot at the back of her head. She would be wearing the blond wig most of the time today. Better to go unrecognized.

Gail came back on the line. "Are you still there?"

"I'm still here."

"Okay. I've got the title of his thesis. You ready?"

Silly question. He was a reporter. His pen and paper had been at the ready since she'd answered the phone. "Ready."

"It's titled," she paused, either for effect, or to get her head around it. "*The Social and Economic Impact on the Japanese-American Community of the Japanese Removal and Internment 1942-1945.*"

Jason jotted it down on his notepad. "Got it. Thank you very much."

"Is there anything else I can do to help?"

"I don't think so, not at this point, but if something turns up I'll certainly give you a call."

He disconnected before the exchange could go any further.

Lisa was reading his note. "The Japanese internment. Not our country's finest hour."

Jason knew a little about it, just the basics: after Pearl Harbor, the military and government decided all people of Japanese descent were potential spies and saboteurs, so they were forced to move from the West Coast to internment camps inland. That was about all he knew.

Lisa, however, was already moving. She slipped into a chair in front of his laptop, set up on the motel's little table. "Let me get some background so I'll know better what we're looking for."

Jason grabbed his coffee off the nightstand and followed her. What about the Japanese internment would have Lundgren killing people seventy years later? He didn't know. They didn't know. But now they knew where to look.

*

Taylor Smith was having a bad day.

Last night's raid on their observation post was only the beginning. Not only had they lost a lot of expensive equipment, and had two of his operatives thrown in jail, but now the authorities had been alerted to their activities. He had information that the state police had sent a team over to examine their equipment and that an FBI team was also on the way. Things could get very hot very quickly.

They also had no idea where Jason Reynolds was or what mischief he was up to. A couple of carefully planned passes by his house overnight had told them that all the lights on and the presence of his car was merely window dressing. The house was empty. No one was there.

Smith tried to rub the fatigue from his eyes. The effort wasn't successful. He got up and walked across the condo to pour himself another cup of coffee, though he didn't think that would help either. The only thing that would really help was to figure out a way to put an end to this mission, once and for all.

Easier said than done.

He returned to his makeshift desk and sat for a minute, sipping his coffee, and listening to the thumps, bangs, and muffled voices coming from the condo next door. The police had shown up at 8:00 this morning, search warrant in hand, and were in the process of tearing the place apart. Smith and Melissa had stayed in their own condos, as invisible as possible, hoping Anderson hadn't missed anything last night.

Unfortunately, Anderson wasn't the brightest bulb in the pack. Hard working, dependable, and loyal to a fault maybe, but he honestly was not good at thinking on his feet, especially under pressure. It was just who he was.

That's why Smith had not been terribly surprised, disappointed, but not surprised, when Anderson called this morning to tell him what happened outside Hayden's house. She'd obviously spotted him and had another deputy roust him while she made her escape. Anderson had been stuck, answering the deputy's questions as she drove off.

Now they had no idea where she was either.

Events were spinning out of his control. He needed to stop it and stop it now.

Much as he hated it, the time had come to pull the trigger. Violence usually caused more problems than it solved, but sometimes he had no other choice. Jason Reynolds only had himself to blame.

He called a number off his contact list.

A baritone voice answered on the second ring. "Crawford."

"Smith," he answered, though he knew the display would have told Crawford exactly who was calling. "Our subject needs to be shown we're serious. Rough her up. Scare the shit out of her, but nothing permanent. Understand?"

Crawford didn't respond.

Smith had a sinking feeling that was becoming much too familiar. "What?"

"Um," Crawford sounded like a little kid caught in the cookie jar. "We have a small problem."

Smith pinched the bridge of his nose. Crawford was six feet tall, two hundred forty pounds of muscle, and not a lick of conscience. He had no problem with violence; Smith didn't think he'd hesitate to beat a baby to death if those were his orders. So the problem was something else.

Next door, something slammed against the wall hard enough to rattle the cheesy art prints on his wall. Were they searching the place, or destroying it?

"What problem is that?" he finally asked.

"We, um, don't know where she is."

How could a twenty-three-year-old coed shake the tail of two seasoned professionals? He decided he didn't want to know.

"Okay," he told Crawford. "Change of plans. Get up here to Port Salish. The ferry leaves Anacortes at 7:00."

"Both of us?"

"Both of you."

He was bringing in reinforcements.

*

Lisa dropped Jason off on the sidewalk two blocks from the bank and sped off in Suzie's Volkswagen. She was heading to the local paper, to go through back issues looking for what had led Greg Takashi to hire Jason's dad. She wore the blond wig and had prepared a story about some paper she was writing on how the war changed life in small-town Washington.

They hoped no one on the newspaper staff would notice that they were retracing Takashi's research.

Jason walked down the street, bundled up in a winter coat and with a knit hat pulled low over his eyes. It had clouded up overnight and a cool breeze was blowing in from the south. The weatherman this morning had mentioned rain by the afternoon. If the weather had been like yesterday, he would have looked ridiculous, but this morning he fit right in.

He pulled out his cell and sent Danny Hayden a text. *Where are you?*

Side street n of the bank parking lot. Blue Buick sedan.

He was already on the north side of the street, opposite the bank, so he continued walking at an unhurried pace until he was across from the parking lot, then glanced up the first side street. A very anonymous looking blue sedan flashed its parking lights. Jason nodded, crossed the street at the corner and walked up to the car.

As nonchalantly as humanly possible, he opened the passenger door and slipped into the seat beside Danny. "Nice ride."

"Shut up," she said, but with a smile. "It's my mother's. Besides, it's practically invisible."

She was right. It was about as invisible as a car could be. Which was to say it was a perfectly ordinary American sedan, with paint that had probably started as royal blue, but had faded over the years to just blue. It was perfectly ordinary. No one would give it a second glance.

"Haislip has been hard at work all morning," Danny told him. "He hasn't left the building anyway."

"Good."

"You'll never guess which car is his."

Jason peered across the street to the bank's employee parking. Only two cars were in the running. One was a Jag. That probably was Daddy's. Too much luxury and not enough sport for Martin's playboy image.

"The Turbo Carrera."

"Give the man another gold star."

The Porsche fit Martin's style: high cost, high performance, and high profile. The exact opposite of the car they were sitting in. The Porsche was painted a bright apple red, polished to a mirror-finish, and guaranteed to turn heads.

"It should be easy to follow him in traffic," Jason said.

"Unless he takes it out of second gear."

Jason couldn't dispute that.

"So were you two able to find out anything from the school?"

"We were," Jason said. "But I don't know quite what it means."

He told her what the title of Takashi's thesis was and what Lisa's general background research had found about the Japanese internment.

"Japanese internment?" Danny frowned, thinking. "I remember something about it from school, but just barely. History was never my thing. But that was a long time ago, right?"

"During World War II. 1942. More than seventy years ago."

"So what does that have to do with what Lundgren is doing today? And what does it have to do with you or your dad?"

Jason shook his head. "I have no idea."

*

"There he is." Danny straightened up in her seat.

Jason snapped out of his daydream and concentrated on the bank's employee entrance. Martin Haislip, III had just opened an umbrella against the misty rain that had begun about thirty minutes ago. He waited a beat for his female companion to join him, then walked her across the parking lot to the passenger door of his Porsche.

"Any idea who the bimbo is?" Danny asked.

Jason knew exactly who she was. "His secretary."

"Sheesh, his secretary? How cliché."

Jason smiled.

Martin closed the passenger door, strode around the car, collapsed the umbrella, and climbed in behind the wheel.

Danny started the engine and shifted the Buick into drive but kept her foot on the brake.

"Where does a playboy wannabe take his mistress for lunch in Port Salish?" Jason asked.

Danny shrugged as the Porsche pulled across the bank parking lot and paused at the entrance to wait for a break in traffic. His turn signal indicated he was heading to their right, which meant they wouldn't need to try and make a left turn to follow him. A break for the good guys. Danny pulled away from the curb, then waited at the intersection.

"Most of the better dinner houses aren't open for lunch. A couple of them close down completely during the winter," she said, thinking aloud. "My bet would be one of the resorts on the waterfront. Most of them have bars, too and I'd bet he drinks part of his lunch."

Jason certainly wouldn't bet against her.

The Porsche pulled into the street. Danny waited for another car to pass, then pulled out behind both.

"He's heading the wrong direction for the resorts."

Danny shrugged. "Unless he's going to take Ferry Street. Maybe they're just going to get a motel room and take their lunch in bed."

"Even better."

Danny smiled.

As she'd predicted, Haislip turned south on Ferry Street, then took Harbor Way across town before finally pulling into the lot at the Marina Resort and Yacht Club.

Danny found a spot to park on the street nearby. The Marina was definitely high end. Their aging Buick would stand out among the Beamers and Mercedes in the lot as much as it was invisible on the streets.

"How do we want to handle this?" Jason asked. "We're not exactly dressed for this style establishment."

"You've been in the city too long," she told him. "It may call itself a yacht club, but you don't see many yachts in the marina, do you?"

No, he had to admit, he didn't.

"It's Port Salish in the off-season. As long as we don't look homeless we're fine."

Neither looked homeless. What they looked like was middle class locals.

They got out of the car and headed up the walkway through the thickening rain. It also seemed to be getting colder and Jason briefly wondered whether there might be snow in the near future, though the weatherman hadn't mentioned any this morning.

They pushed through the glass doors of the resort entrance, then turned left in the lobby to enter the restaurant.

Jason followed Danny. She seemed to know what she was doing.

A young hostess smiled as they approached her station. "Two for lunch today?" She already had two menus pulled out of the stack, as though her question was rhetorical.

"Actually we're supposed to be meeting someone here," Danny said, as innocently as could be. "Martin Haislip?"

"Oh, yes," the hostess, her name tag read Heather, said, still smiling. "They're at table four." She pointed toward the bank of windows overlooking the boat basin. "It's the second one on your right."

"Thank you."

"My pleasure. Would you like to start with something to drink?"

"Coffee would be perfect."

Jason nodded. "Make that two."

Heather said she'd bring them to the table. Jason thanked her again and joined Danny as she walked toward the windows and Haislip's table.

"You have a plan?"

"Yep," Danny nodded. "Just follow my lead."

Haislip and his secretary were sitting on the same side of the table like a couple of high school sweethearts, and so wrapped in each other, they had no idea what was going on around them.

"Oh, this is perfect," Danny whispered to Jason as she pulled out her cell phone and activated the camera.

Haislip and his friend didn't even look up until the shutter sounded on Danny's camera.

"Hey!" the secretary protested as she pushed Haislip's hand from her breast.

Jason slipped into the chair across from the secretary. Danny took the one across from Haislip.

"What do you think you're doing?" Haislip made a grab for Danny's phone, but wasn't nearly quick enough.

"What a cute couple," Danny told Jason. "And a lovely photograph. Do you think the missus will like it too?"

"She'll love it," Jason agreed. "I think she'll have it framed and hang it on the wall. Right above the divorce decree."

"You know, Marty." Danny turned her attention to Haislip. "The one that gives her half of everything you own?"

"You wouldn't dare!" The secretary glared at Danny.

Danny kept her eyes on Haislip, her tone level and menacing. "Try me."

Haislip closed his eyes as if fighting through pain.

"Martin!"

"Shut up, Rebecca. Why don't you go powder your nose, or something?"

Rebecca looked like she wanted to scratch his eyes out. Instead, she pushed her chair back from the table. "Fine."

She stalked away.

"Hate to tell you this, Marty," Jason said. "But you might have just lost that one."

Haislip ignored him. "Who are you and what do you want?"

"That depends," Danny pulled her badge and ID from a pocket and showed it to him. "You're about to find yourself neck deep in some serious legal shit."

"Real serious." Jason agreed. "Did you know there's no such thing as time off for good behavior in the federal system? You serve every day of your sentence."

"And then they bring you back to serve your state time," Danny shook her head. "It's not a nice situation."

"And then, of course, there's the civil lawsuits against both you, personally, and your bank." Jason told him. "Probably millions and millions of dollars."

Haislip looked from one of them to the other. Jason thought he detected the first twinge of panic in his eyes. "What are you talking about?"

"We're talking conspiracy to violate the civil rights of at least two people and two more counts each of conspiracy to commit kidnapping and murder," Danny said. "Your only hope of avoiding real jail time is if we can convince the DA that you cooperated fully with the investigation."

"You guys are full of shit," Haislip shook his head, suddenly brave. "I didn't conspire with anybody to do anything. I don't know anything about any murders."

"Really?" Danny leaned across the table toward him, just a little, but enough to make him back into his chair. "I have three words that say you're a liar: The. Lundgren. Corporation."

Haislip blanched slightly.

"I don't know if you've heard about it yet, but the police discovered a high-tech surveillance operation last night on Salmon Berry Lane. The men running it were employees of Lundgren's Security Division. Funny thing is, the house they were working in is a bank-owned property managed by you. The men were also living in a condo managed by you. The person they were spying on was Lee Reynolds, a murder victim, who also received a letter from you threatening to cancel his lease." Danny shook her head. "It sure looks to me like you've been working hand-in-hand with these people from the beginning."

"I'm pretty sure a jury will see it that way too." Jason said.

"You're not even a cop." Haislip spat at him. "You're his son."

"But I *am* a cop," Danny told him. "And the state police are retrieving the bugs from his father's house right now and going through the seized computers. The city police served a search warrant on the condo this morning too. An FBI team is on the way over from the mainland. I'm guessing someone will show up at the bank, oh, probably no later than tomorrow morning with a lot of pointed questions."

Haislip was looking uncomfortable. "What do you want from me?"

Rebecca returned from the rest room. She looked more than a little unhappy as she pulled her chair back from the table.

"Go powder your nose again," Danny said without even looking at her.

"What?"

"You heard me," Danny said.

"Give us fifteen minutes," Jason told her.

She looked at Haislip. "Martin?"

He simply waved her away.

She looked like he'd hit her, turned, and stormed off.

"What do you want?" Haislip asked again.

"Everything you know about Lundgren security in Port Salish," Danny told him. "From the beginning."

Jason pointedly opened a digital recorder app on his cell, turned it on and set it on the table in front of Haislip.

"You're recording this?" Haislip hissed.

"Damn right we are," Jason told him. "So if you lie to us, we'll have everything we need to hang you right there."

Danny snapped her fingers in front of Haislip's face. He jumped. "Now. Lundgren. Everything you know."

Haislip nodded. "There isn't much to tell. About a month ago, I had a short meeting with the bank president."

"Your dad."

"Yes." Haislip closed his eyes. "My father. He told me some men from Lundgren were coming over to do some work and would stay in the condos. I was to offer any assistance they needed, no questions asked."

"Do you often offer services with 'no questions asked'?" Danny asked.

Haislip shrugged, then shook his head. "Lundgren has a special relationship with our bank. My grandfather was partners with Lars Lundgren."

Danny nodded. "Go on."

"A week, maybe ten days later, I get a call from the Lundgren guy asking about the property on Salmon Berry. He wants unfettered access to the house and the electricity and sewer turned on."

Jason stopped the narrative. "That didn't strike you as odd? What could they possibly want with a hollowed-out shell of a house?"

Haislip shrugged. "No questions, remember?"

Jason sighed.

"Go on," Danny prompted Haislip.

"A few days later, I get another call from the lead Lundgren man."

"What was his name?" Danny asked.

"Smith. Taylor Smith."

Jason and Danny exchanged a subtle look. Their "Mr. Smith" of the threatening phone call was really named Mr. Smith?

"Smith calls and tells me that Lee Reynolds is acting outside the terms of his lease. He asked me to write him a warning letter. Which I did."

"Explain the lease to us," Jason told him. "We're having a hard time understanding it."

Haislip took a deep breath. "They're pretty simple, really. Each lease gives the holder rights to the property for one year at the cost of one dollar. As long as all the conditions are met, the lease is automatically renewed each year and as long as the family continuously occupies the property, the lease can be transferred from generation to generation."

Jason glanced at Danny to see if she'd registered his use of the plural. There were multiple leases, not just his dad's. Her face remained neutral.

"Wow," Danny said to Haislip. "You're talking essentially free housing. Forever."

"Basically. As long as the terms are met."

"Which are?"

"The property must be occupied by the leaser. It cannot be used as a vacation home or a rental property, for example. And the leaser must not do or say anything that would interfere with or damage the Lundgren Corporation's business interests, profitability, or reputation in any way."

Jason did some quick math in his head. At today's rates, it was costing Lundgren something like $12,000 a year in lost revenue for each lease. That was a lot of money.

"You told me these leases were given out as a kind of bonus or reward to certain employees?" he said.

"That's my understanding," Haislip said. "The leases were all set up years ago, even before my father joined the company. I believe there were originally about a dozen, but over the years the number has fallen to only three or four still in effect."

"No new leases have been set up since then?" Jason asked.

"Not that I know of."

Jason was having trouble wrapping his head around the figures involved. Twelve leases at $12,000 a year per lease for twenty years totaled something like three million dollars virtually given away.

"What did a Lundgren employee have to do to get free housing for himself and his family for eternity?"

"I have no idea."

It had to be very big and very bad to justify Lundgren paying that much money to keep people quiet.

CHAPTER 12

They asked Martin Haislip a few more questions, but he knew little else of substance. He was not part of the operation's brain trust. Jason turned off his recorder app, shoved the phone back into his pocket and dropped a five on the table for their coffees. Even letting Haislip buy their coffee would have left him wanting a shower.

"Hey, I cooperated," Haislip looked up at them as they got to their feet. "I told you what I know. You're going to help me out, right?"

"We'll tell them you helped," Danny told him.

"I'd still hire myself a good attorney, if I were you," Jason added.

Haislip's face fell, but he nodded.

They walked out of the restaurant, told the confused hostess that they'd left money for their coffee on the table, and entered the resort lobby.

Rebecca, Haislip's secretary/mistress, was sitting on one of the love seats scattered strategically around the lobby. She sprang to her feet as they approached.

"Do you think I could get a ride back to the bank?" she said. Most of the fiery anger from earlier had gone from her eyes. "I don't want to ride back with him."

Danny hesitated. Jason could tell by her body language that she really wanted to say "you picked him, you're stuck with him," but something made her stop. Maybe she'd seen enough domestic abuse cases that started out with something like this to give her second thoughts.

"Please," Rebecca added. "I didn't even bring a coat."

Danny looked to Jason, who shrugged, then nodded. He saw no harm in it.

"Come on," Danny said and started out the door.

Rebecca smiled with visible relief.

"Is Martin really in serious trouble?" she asked when they were all buckled into the car, Danny behind the wheel, Jason beside her in the passenger seat, with Rebecca in the back seat behind Jason.

Danny didn't answer. She started the car and pulled out into the traffic of Harbor Way.

"Pretty serious," Jason told her.

"Good. I hope they throw his ass in jail."

Danny's eyes flicked to the rearview mirror for a second before returning to the road.

Jason couldn't let the remark go. "Because he was rude to you at lunch?"

"Martin's a slimeball," Rebecca said. "And his dad's a snake. No one at the bank would shed a tear if both of them went to jail."

Danny's eyes again went to the rearview mirror. "That slimeball had his hands all over you when we walked in."

Rebecca met her eyes in the mirror. "You don't like me much do you?"

"I don't know you," Danny told her with a shrug. "But no, I don't like your behavior."

Rebecca shrugged and gazed out her window. "Martin has a lot of money and likes to spend it. It was fun. It's not like I was going to marry the guy."

Danny just shook her head.

"I want to help."

Danny and Jason exchanged a look.

"I want to help put him and his dad away."

Jason turned to look at her. "Why would you want to do that?"

"Like I said, they're snakes. You have no idea some of the shit they've pulled, foreclosing on grandma because she missed one house payment, stuff like that. Anything to make money. If I can help them get the punishment they deserve, I will. With pleasure."

Jason glanced at Danny, who seemed to be deep in thought.

"Do you have access to his files?" He asked Rebecca.

"Of course," she said. "I'm his secretary."

He glanced again at Danny, but couldn't read her thoughts. She seemed willing to let him make this decision on his own.

"Tell you what. Are you familiar with the one-dollar-a-year leases Lundgren Corporation gave out?"

"Sure," Rebecca said.

Danny pulled into a parking lot next door to the bank and parked, but left the engine running. "This is as close as I'm going."

Jason glanced over at Danny. She shrugged.

"Get us copies of those leases, the ones still in effect and the ones no longer valid."

"It might take a little while," Rebecca asked.

"That's fine," Jason said. "Don't put yourself in any danger. Just make some copies for us."

"How do I get them to you?"

Jason gave her his cell phone number. "Give me a call when you have the copies. We'll arrange a meeting then."

Rebecca entered the number in her cell phone, thanked them for the ride and got out of the car. They sat there and watched her scurry up the sidewalk through the steady rain and disappear into the bank. Her boss's Porsche was not in the parking lot.

"You don't think that was a good idea?" Jason asked as Danny backed out of the parking spot.

"I don't trust her. What if she makes up with Martin when he gets back from lunch? Does she tell him what we asked her to do?"

Jason shrugged. That was a possibility, he guessed.

"And the cop in me is saying that any documents we receive from her will be no good as evidence because they were stolen."

He knew that. "But it will give us a better idea who is involved in this."

"But if we can't convict them..."

"There is that."

"Besides, she's barely a step above a whore. I don't trust her."

Danny had a point. Rebecca could very well be working for Lundgren in one form or another. If Jason were running an operation, and were forced to use Haislip as part of it—even a minor part—he would certainly want to have someone nearby to keep an eye on him. Who better than his own secretary?

He decided that they would have to be very careful when it came time to set up their next meeting.

*

The call Taylor Smith had been dreading came early Friday afternoon. He signaled to Melissa Deveraux to remain silent, activated his cell phone's speaker and digital voice recorder, then sat back in the loveseat. They were in the living room of his condo, working out the details of their strategy to take care of Reynolds and company.

Actually, the old man's call couldn't have come at a better time.

"Good afternoon, sir."

"What the hell's going on up there, Smith?" Taylor could almost see the spittle spraying from his boss's mouth. "You're supposed to be making this problem go away and now we've got two of our people in jail?"

Smith kept his voice calm and level. "We suffered a minor setback. That's all it is."

"You call this a minor setback? Not only are they in County, but they're facing federal charges! Federal! How long before we have the FBI knocking on our door?"

"All the police have to link them to Lundgren is their employee identification," Smith told him. "There is nothing to prove they weren't over here on their own. The FBI will probably want to ask someone some questions, but all you have to tell them is you have no idea what they were doing. Plausible deniability. They can't prove otherwise."

"And the men in jail?"

"Are trained professionals. They'll keep their mouths shut."

"Your job is to *eliminate* the problem. Not only is the problem still there, now our visibility is higher than ever. Do you even know where your subject is right now?"

Smith wondered where his boss was getting his information. It was awfully accurate. Was one of his operatives also reporting directly to the old man? He glanced over at Deveraux, by far his most capable agent, but she was staring out the window, lost in thought.

"We're confident he hasn't left the island. The area isn't that big. We'll find him."

"What do you mean by that?"

"Life is about to become very difficult for our Mr. Reynolds. Monitor the local news this evening and you'll see what I mean. Our problem, as you call it, could disappear by tonight."

"Tonight?"

"There are no guarantees, but it is possible," Smith said. "If not, we'll go to Plan B tomorrow."

"If you can't get the job done, we'll send someone over there who can."

"Of course."

The line went abruptly dead.

Smith turned off the recorder and his phone.

"Asshole," Melissa said without a drop of emotion.

Taylor Smith smiled.

*

Lisa wasn't at the motel room when they got back, but that wasn't really a surprise. The only reason she would have been was if, for some reason, she'd been unable to do what she wanted at the newspaper office. Her mission was a little more time consuming than theirs.

Jason texted her anyway. *How's it going?*

It took nearly five minutes for her to reply. Again, that wasn't unusual. Her ability to focus was one of the reasons she was such a successful student. *Good. Almost done. Good stuff.*

Bad guys?

Don't think so. See you in about an hour.

In other words leave her alone so she could finish what she was doing.

"She okay?" Danny asked.

"Fine. Just hip deep in research, her natural element. She says she'll be done in about an hour."

"So what do we do in the meantime?"

There wasn't much they could do. They didn't have enough information at this point to make a move. They knew Lundgren was after them just as it had been after his dad. They knew it was about something his dad and/or Takashi had uncovered, but they didn't know what that something was. Only that it was bad enough to give a number of people free housing in exchange for keeping their mouths shut.

And to kill if they didn't.

"All we can do is wait for Lisa," he said and stretched out on the bed, suddenly bone-tired. "Maybe she'll uncover something in the newspapers that will point us in the right direction."

"I hate not being able to do anything."

"Me, too."

Danny found the remote and turned the television to a cop show rerun. "Have you thought about what you're going to do about tomorrow?"

"What about tomorrow?" he asked without opening his eyes.

"The funeral. Your dad's memorial service. You know Lundgren's people are going to be there."

"I know. And no, I haven't decided what I'm going to do about it."

Danny was quiet. Jason opened his eyes and found her sitting in one of the two chairs at the table, seemingly engrossed by the television show. Two detectives were doing the good cop/bad cop routine with a scruffy-looking suspect.

"I think my dad would understand, under the circumstances, if I didn't go to his memorial service."

"The ones who won't understand are the family and friends. They don't know what's going on. They'll just think you didn't bother to show up."

Jason thought he could probably live with that for a while. Once the truth got out, they would understand.

"Even if Lundgren was there," he said, the thought just occurring to him, "What could they really do? I'd be in a crowd of my dad's friends, most of whom are commercial fishermen. Tough guys. Lundgren could hardly assassinate me right there; they'd never get out of the building alive."

Danny shook her head. "But they could get you on the front steps as you're leaving."

"Good point." He closed his eyes again.

*

He must have fallen asleep because the next thing he knew, Lisa was shaking his shoulder. "Come on, sleepyhead, wake up. You need to hear what I found."

"I'm awake. I'm awake." He sat up and tried to rub focus back into his eyes.

Danny was watching him, grinning.

"How long was I out?"

"Not long," she said. "Maybe thirty minutes. You sure were snoring though."

"Snoring?"

"Like a longshoreman."

Lisa was organizing her notes on the table. "You do," she said without looking up. "Especially when you're really tired."

"Learn something new every day," he said, then looked up at Lisa. "Tell me you found something."

She smiled, pulled out the chair across from Danny, and sat down. Jason realized she was no longer wearing the blond wig, then spotted it on the bureau beside the TV. She must have taken it off as soon as she'd come in.

"Actually, I think it's what I didn't find that's most interesting," Lisa told them.

"Hang on," Danny said and used the remote to shut down the TV.

"What didn't you find?"

"Let me start at the beginning," she told them. "You'll understand what I mean better if you know the whole story."

Jason nodded. "Go on."

"Okay," she said. "I did a little research before I went and found out that the military issued Public Proclamation Number One on March 2, 1942, which authorized the Relocation and on May 3, issued Civilian Exclusion Order 34, which basically said all Japanese who hadn't already moved had to report to the removal centers. The entire relocation of the Japanese from the West Coast took only two months."

"Pretty remarkable feat back in 1942," Jason said.

Danny grimaced. "Who says the Government can't be efficient?"

"The local paper is published every Wednesday, so I only looked at those two months, March and April. It was something like nine issues, because there were five Wednesdays in April that year."

Jason mentally asked her to get on with it. This wasn't an academic audience where your methods were as important as your results. But that was her background. She needed to tell the story in her own way.

"The first two editions carried news of the Removal Order and some pretty nasty editorials in favor of it, as well as a minor story that interviewed some local Japanese, who protested that they were as loyal as any other American. Judging by the letters to the editor, no one believed them."

"People were scared and the Japanese were different," Jason said. "It must have been a lot like the attacks on Arab-Americans after 9/11."

"Exactly," Lisa agreed. "Or the anti-illegal immigrant movement. Only much more blatantly racist, especially among the newspapers and government officials. Apparently, a pretty good-sized Japanese community lived here back then, especially in," she consulted her notes. "the Salle Valley."

"Oh, yeah," Danny said. "I remember hearing something about that. They'd cleared some land up there—it's on the northern end of the island—and did some farming. I think that's where Strawberry Fields is now."

"Maybe we should pay the good folks at Strawberry Fields a visit," Jason suggested.

Danny nodded.

Lisa returned to her story. "The first really interesting piece is in the edition of March 25. It says that Lundgren Transport won a contract from the Army to move Japanese residents from the San Juan Islands to an assembly center in Tacoma. To help with that, local men would be hired to convert an old warehouse on Deception Island into a temporary holding camp. Others would be hired to guard the camp."

"Deception Island?" Jason looked at Danny. "Have you ever heard of any kind of camp there?"

Danny shook her head. "Not a word."

"Interesting, huh?" Lisa asked. "Okay, in the edition of April 8, there's a photograph of the preparations at the converted warehouse." She grabbed a copy of a grainy photograph and handed it to Danny.

"They look like horse stalls." She handed the photo to Jason.

They did look like horse stalls. The partitions appeared to be plain plywood over two-by-fours, rising from the floor to maybe seven feet. The area between the partitions looked to be scarcely larger than a jail cell. Significantly, in Jason's mind, none of the partitions had doors. Not only would it be crowded, but there would have been no privacy at all.

"Next," Lisa accepted the photo back from Jason and returned it to her pile of notes. "The edition of April 15 carried a front page copy of the Exclusion Order dated April 13 ordering all Japanese residents of San Juan County to report to their local relocation centers by April 19. All they were allowed to bring with them was clothing, bedding, personal hygiene products, things like that. Everything else they'd either have to sell, rent out, or put into storage."

She handed a copy of the front page to Danny. She looked it over, then handed it to Jason. He scanned it quickly. It aroused a complex mix of emotions. He understood that it was a different time and that most of the West Coast was deathly afraid of a Japanese invasion, but it still seemed horribly cruel. These people were imprisoned without being convicted of anything and everyone was just fine with it.

He handed the photo back to Lisa.

"There were a couple of advertisements in the April 15 edition I thought were interesting, too," Lisa said and handed another sheet of paper to Danny. "The first one is by Evergreen Bank, offering to buy any land the Japanese needed to sell. They claim to offer market rates and a property management service if they didn't want to sell. Internees were urged to talk to Martin Haislip."

Danny read the advertisement, shook her head in disgust, and handed it to Jason. "Market rates, my ass. They probably offered pennies on the dollar."

"Martin's grandpa," Jason said.

He didn't even look at the advertisement. He just handed it back to Lisa.

"The other one," Lisa continued. "Is from the Lundgren Corporation, offering to store any property the Japanese were unable or unwilling to sell in a safe facility for a low, monthly fee until they could return."

She handed another copy to Danny, who glanced at it, then handed it to Jason, who did the same.

"In other words," he said as he handed the sheet back to Lisa, "certain people saw a chance to make a profit and jumped at it."

Lisa nodded and fished another sheet of paper from her notes and handed it to Danny. "This was also in the April 15 paper. It's a photograph of the men hired to guard the camp."

Something in the photograph made Danny blanch a little. She looked up at Jason, then passed it to him.

The photograph was grainy black and white, clearly enlarged from a faded newspaper print. It showed a group of young men standing in a row against the wall of a building. Each wore what looked like some kind of uniform shirt and work pants and each carried a rifle. According to the caption, the third one from the right was Joseph Reynolds, Jason's grandfather.

"Did your grandfather ever say anything about being a guard at the camp?" Lisa asked.

Jason shook his head. "I've never even heard about the camp until now."

He looked at the photograph again and the list of names under it. He didn't recognize most of them; they were his grandfather's age, after all. But he recognized several family names. Some of them were prominent, like Morgan.

"It would be interesting to compare these names to the names on the leases Rebecca's supposed to get for us."

"Wouldn't it, though?" Danny agreed.

Lisa frowned and glanced from Jason to Danny. "Who's Rebecca?"

They quickly described their meeting with Haislip and the offer from his secretary.

"That would be good, if she can get those copies for us."

"It would be very good," Jason agreed. "I'd love to see who got all those leases."

They all agreed; it would be very interesting.

"Go on," Danny told Lisa. "What else did you find?"

"That's just it," she said. "I didn't find anything else."

"What do you mean?"

Lisa shook her head. "I looked through the next four editions and there isn't another word about the camp, Lundgren, or the Japanese. The subject is never mentioned again."

"Nothing?" Jason asked. "What about the ads?"

"Nothing." Lisa shook her head. "It's like the whole thing never happened."

"Or," Danny said, almost in a whisper. "No one wanted to talk about it."

"That's what I meant about what I didn't find being the most interesting."

It would also explain why Takashi had hired his father. He'd found the same void in the newspaper accounts and wanted to investigate. To do that he'd needed someone with a boat to take him out to Deception Island. Jason's dad had agreed. And if Takashi had decided to do some digging around out there, it would also explain the mud in the boat's cabin.

What had happened out there that the local paper refused to cover?

*

"I think we need to take a trip out to Deception Island."

"We could use my dad's boat," he told the others. "There's just a couple of problems."

"You don't know how to drive it?" Lisa volunteered.

"Sarcasm, nice," he told her. "No, I'm not as good as my dad, but I can get us there and back without killing anyone."

"So, what are the problems?" Danny asked.

"I don't have the key. It's on my dad's key ring and that's back at the house."

"Which Lundgren is probably watching."

Jason nodded. "And if whatever happened on Deception Island is truly at the core of this whole thing, they'll probably be watching the boat too, in case we try to go out there."

"There are a couple others too." Danny said. "Deception Island is owned by the Lundgren Corporation. Our setting foot on the island will constitute trespassing and they could have us arrested. I believe they also have a full-time caretaker out there to enforce the no trespassing rule."

Jason frowned. "Someone lives out there?"

"There's a cottage just above the boat landing. The reason, supposedly, was that the island was used for bombing and gunnery practice during World War II and there are a lot of unexploded shells around."

Jason smiled. "I was told it was an haunted Indian burial ground."

"Stories to keep people away," Lisa said. "Urban legends. They change as the audience changes. A haunted burial ground will work for little kids, but not as well for teenagers, so they came up with the unexploded shells for them."

"What if we went after dark?" Jason suggested.

Danny looked skeptical. "You said yourself you're not an expert with a boat. You really want to try and do this when you can't see? Not to mention that flashlights will be as good as a marching band to announce our presence to the caretaker."

She was right. He had to admit it was tough enough fighting the currents in the channel when you could see what you were doing. She was right about the lights, too.

But there was something else.

"Everything we've found so far points to something on Deception Island being behind Takashi's disappearance, my dad's death, and everything else, right?"

Lisa and Danny agreed.

"And the mud I found on the boat suggested they'd done some digging, probably on Deception Island, right?"

Again, the women nodded.

"So how'd they get on the island? I assume the caretaker was also there last week. And we know from the spy nest that Lundgren was already watching them. So, like I said, how did they get on the island?"

Danny was frowning as she thought about it.

"There has to be another way on to the island," Lisa said.

Danny was already shaking her head. "The dock at the northwest end is the only spot a boat can land. The rest of the island has cliffs pretty much down to the water."

"But it's the only thing that makes sense," Lisa insisted. "Jason's dad and Takashi would have had the same problem with the watchman we do. They must have found another way."

"My dad's charts," Jason said. "He had charts for all the waters around here. I wonder whether there's something on his chart for Deception Island. A clue to how they got around the caretaker."

"Where are his charts?" Danny asked.

"Either on the boat in the chart drawer, or the same place the key is—back at the house."

"Well," Danny said. "It looks like we're going to have to make a trip back to the house. You're right though, I'd bet my paycheck Lundgren is keeping an eye on it. We're going to have to figure out how to get around that."

Jason broke into a smile. "I have an idea, but we'll have to wait until pretty late at night, probably 10:00 at the earliest."

Danny's cell phone buzzed an incoming call. She checked the display. "It's Lt. Olsen, the watch commander from last night. I'd better take it."

The others nodded, as she answered. "Yes, Lieutenant. I'm at a friend's. I took a personal day today. Yes, of course. I can be there in say, thirty minutes? Okay, see you then."

She disconnected and turned back to the others. "I need to go in and file my report about last night's raid. The district attorney is a bit anal about having all the reports in hand before she does anything. Olsen's sweating about it blowing their case."

"You have to do your job," Jason told her. "Just be careful. Watch your back."

He wasn't thrilled about their being split up like this, but what could they do? She was a cop. Filing reports was part of her job. The last thing they wanted was for the case to go away.

"I will," she assured him. "I shouldn't be more than an hour or two. I didn't have that big a part in it."

Jason smiled. She'd had a huge role in last night's raid. She just couldn't put it into her official report.

Danny's cell phone went off again before she made it to the door. She frowned and looked at the display, then grinned sheepishly. "My mother."

"Checking up on you?"

Danny shrugged and answered the phone. "Hi, Mom. I'm kind of in the middle of something so—they what? Slow down, Mom. Tell me exactly what they said."

No one was moving in the room now. They barely breathed. Both Jason and Lisa were watching Danny, trying to read her for clues. Something bad had happened. They just didn't know what, or how bad.

Danny looked at Jason and pointed at the clock radio on the nightstand. "95.7 FM."

Jason did as she asked.

"...capping today's top story," the smooth baritone of the disc jockey said. "Officers from the Interagency Narcotics Task Force served a search warrant at a house on Sunset Street this afternoon and uncovered evidence of a drug distribution operation. According to source in the San Juan County Sheriff's office, police found a sizable amount of methamphetamine, as well as thousands of dollars in cash.

"No one was home at the time of the raid, but the house is owned by Danielle Hayden, a sergeant with San Juan County Sheriff's Department."

"That son of a bitch," Danny hissed, then into the phone. "Sorry, Mom. No, of course not! It's a set-up. Someone framed me. You know I wouldn't do that."

Jason was focused on the rest of the news report.

"Authorities believe Ms. Hayden is still somewhere on Ebey Island and may be accompanied by a man, identified as Jason Reynolds." An accurate description of each of them followed. "Citizens are urged to call the San Juan County sheriff's office if they have any information regarding the fugitives."

Jason shut the radio off.

"Mom, I'll call you later, okay? Hang tight." She disconnected.

"Shit," Lisa said.

"I was about to walk right into the police station," Danny said. "They would have had me in cuffs before I knew what was happening. Goddamn it!"

Jason was trying to think. They'd been wondering what Lundgren's next move was going to be. Now they knew. And it was a good one. Now they not only had Lundgren's goons looking for them, but every law enforcement officer on the island would be on the hunt.

"Shut off your cell," he told Danny. "Power it down. They can trace it by pings off the cell towers."

He was already doing the same with his own phone.

"Shit!" Danny immediately hit the button to power down her cell. "They'll also know I'm driving my mother's car. There's probably an APB out on it already."

It was parked in the motel parking lot.

"We've got to move," Jason said and started gathering his things. "We need to get out of this motel and we need to do it fast. They could already be on their way."

The two women began packing whatever they could.

"Where are we going to go?" Lisa asked.

"I don't know," he said. "I just know we need to get out of here."

Within minutes, they'd loaded their things into Suzie's Volkswagen, belted themselves in and were pulling out of the parking lot.

They were on the run.

CHAPTER 13

"What do we do now?" Lisa finally voiced the question Jason had been wrestling with since they'd left the motel. Danny was probably thinking the same thing, but remained quiet in the back seat of the little Volkswagen. Or maybe she was in shock over how quickly her career and reputation had been blown into kindling.

They were parked in the lot of the Safeway store on the corner of Nils Lundgren Boulevard, of all things, and Ferry Street, hoping to get overlooked among the minivans and SUV's. It had been barely twenty minutes since they'd left the motel, but seemed longer than that. At first, Jason had just driven, taking streets at random, less worried about where they were going than putting distance between themselves and the motel. That changed after they passed a city police squad car waiting at a stop light. The officer hadn't recognized them, but it had been scary. Once they were able to breathe again, Jason decided driving around aimlessly was too much of a risk. They had a better chance of staying out of jail—or worse—if they just found a spot and stayed there until they could come up with an actual plan.

Now they sat parked between a minivan and a 4x4 pickup as a steady rain drummed on the roof and trickled down the windows. The rain was a blessing. It cut down on visibility and all the shoppers were in too much of a hurry to get out of the weather to pay attention to them.

"We need to find a place to stay," he finally said. "I'm open to ideas."

"We could get another motel room," Lisa suggested. "They aren't looking for me. If we register under my name, we should be okay."

Jason shook his head. "The last room was registered under your name. They'll figure it out sooner or later, then all they'll have to do is call around asking if you're registered."

Lisa bit her lip, nodded.

Jason turned to look at Danny, who was staring out her window at nothing. "How long do you think it will take them to find your mom's car?"

She shrugged without turning from the window. "It depends on how hard they look. Before daylight anyway. It's procedure to go through the motel parking lots."

It was kind of what he'd thought. The Buick wasn't exactly hidden. Then it was just a matter of getting the list of motel guests, talking to them, and running background checks.

"They'll also have the make, model, and plates of this car," Danny told them. "It's on the motel registration."

Lisa groaned. "That's right. It is."

The good thing, if it was one, was that for a few more minutes, the authorities would still be expecting Danny to come walking into police headquarters. They probably wouldn't start the actual search until they were sure she wasn't going to make it easy for them.

That bought them a little more time. Maybe thirty minutes.

"I should make some phone calls," Danny said, as much to herself as to the others. "Somebody on the force has got to see this is bogus. They know me."

"Not with any of our cells though," Jason told her. "Especially not yours."

Danny didn't reply.

Lisa looked over at the facade of the grocery store. "Do they sell any of those prepaid cells here? Tracfone, Cricket, something like that?"

"I don't know. They might."

Lisa looked at Jason. "No one's looking for me. I should go find out. And I don't know about anyone else, but I'm starving."

Jason got some money out of his wallet and told her to get some sandwiches, coffee, and a couple of prepaid cells, if they sold them. Lisa checked her wig in the vanity mirror, then hurried through the rain toward the store.

Jason watched her go, then turned to Danny. "We've got to find a safe place to rest for the night. Do you know anyone who would put us up? Anything?"

"And risk being charged with harboring a fugitive?" she shook her head. "And I wouldn't ask them anyway. I wouldn't put my friends in that position."

Jason admitted she had a point.

"What I should do is turn myself in. That would take the heat off you and Lisa."

"You really believe they can't get to you in jail?"

She turned toward her window.

He understood her feelings, but right now their legal problems weren't his primary concern. They needed a place to hide. Only when they'd had a chance to rest and relax would they be thinking clearly enough to decide their next move.

He toyed with the idea of sneaking everyone into his dad's house. They could probably get in through an upstairs window. The problem with that was if the house was being watched, it would be tough enough sneaking one person through a second floor window, much less three. Then they'd have to live without lights, without making any noise, without walking past a window, without doing anything to give away their presence. It would be almost impossible.

Danny's house would offer the same problems and she wouldn't want to put her mother in a position where she could face criminal charges.

It was beginning to look like they'd be sleeping in the car.

"I don't even have any clean underwear with me," Danny said.

"You can borrow a pair of mine."

Danny just shook her head.

An older black Camry mottled with patches of primer pulled in and parked in the slot directly in front of them. An Indian man in his thirties climbed out and slapped a cowboy hat over his long black hair. For a second, Jason thought it was Sonny, but this guy was older and heavier. And Sonny drove a pickup.

The man headed toward the store.

Sonny.

"I have an idea," he turned on his cell, and called up the contact list. Before he could talk himself out of it, he punched in Sonny's number and sent the call.

Sonny answered on the second ring. "I was wondering if you were going to call. I hear you're a big bad meth dealer now."

"We were set up. We're not dealers."

"Ya think? All the real dealers in town are shaking their heads. Sometimes the cops are dumber than dirt."

"Well, that's good to know. I was wondering if you could do me a favor?"

"Depends."

"Do you know someplace we can stay for a few days while we figure things out? It's a big risk, so feel free to say no."

Sonny laughed. "Believe me, if I thought even a bit of this were true, you'd be on your own, buddy. But I don't, so there. And I know the perfect spot to hide out."

Jason breathed a sigh of relief. "You're a lifesaver."

"Remember me at Christmas. You know Shoreline Drive?"

Jason did. It was the common name for the county road that ran most of the circumference of the island.

"About three miles outside of town on the northwest is a gravel lookout on the Sound side of the road. Meet me there in an hour."

Jason said he would.

"What are you driving? Wait, never mind, I don't want to know. You know my pickup, right?"

Jason did and said he'd be there and disconnected. He immediately shut his phone down again. "I think we have a place."

"Or it's a trap," Danny said. "And we're all going to jail."

Jason shrugged. "We'll find out in an hour."

Five minutes later, Lisa returned, carrying a plastic grocery bag and a fiber tray with three paper coffee cups. Jason reached across and opened the door for her.

"Thanks," she said as Jason took the tray of coffees and she settled into her seat. "I got everyone ham and Swiss on a hoagie. I hope that's okay."

"Did they have phones?" Jason asked.

She smiled and pulled the plastic packages from the grocery bag. "Two prepaid and anonymous cell phones."

Two problems solved. Now they just had to deal with the big ones.

*

"It's right around this next turn," Danny said. "I think."

Jason slowed as he entered a sweeping right turn in the narrow, two-lane road. Shoreline Road, as its name suggested, followed the shoreline of the island pretty closely, which meant the entire three miles had been a ceaseless series of twists and turns. With the road unfamiliar and slick with rain, Jason had seldom dared go over 35, though the posted speed limit was 45.

Just beyond the curve, Jason spotted the turnout and Sonny's big pickup idling near the guard rail.

"That him?" Danny asked.

"That's him."

He pulled up beside the pickup and slipped the Volkswagen's transmission into neutral. A second later, his cell phone rang.

"Who's that?" Lisa frowned.

"It's him." He picked up the call. "You raise laziness to a new level."

"Too wet to go out," Sonny said. "I hope you weren't followed."

"If we were, they were invisible."

"Okay. Follow me. It's about a quarter mile up the road, on the left."

"We'll be right behind you."

Jason let Sonny's truck move out onto the road, then pulled in behind it.

Just past the turnout, the road jogged inland, away from the shore for a distance. Sonny's pickup slowed and its left turn signal flashed, then he pulled into a narrow gravel road that barely fit between the trunks of the native cedars.

Jason followed him on to the road and into a forest so close that branches scraped the sides of the car as they passed and so dense he needed headlights.

"Wow," Lisa said. "We are in the boonies, aren't we?"

"Around here we call it nature," Danny said.

Lisa stuck out her tongue.

About a hundred yards from the road, they emerged into a small gravel clearing right on the edge of the Sound. On the far edge stood a beautiful little log ranch house, complete with a covered porch and cedar shake roof. Behind the house, a floating dock extended a short distance into the Sound.

"It's gorgeous," Lisa said.

"Beautiful," Danny agreed. "And we're trespassing."

Sonny parked his truck in front of the house, hopped out, and was searching his key ring for the front door key when the others caught up with him on the porch.

"This your house?" Lisa asked.

"God, no," Sonny laughed. "It's a vacation rental. I do maintenance and caretaker stuff in the off-season. I take care of a bunch of them."

"You won't get in trouble for letting us stay here?" Jason asked.

"Not if they don't find out about it. So no wild parties and don't run up the electric bill."

He found the right key, took it off the ring, and unlocked the door. "It usually sits empty all winter, so I don't think anyone will even know you're around."

They walked into a small entryway. To the right was a cozy living room decorated in a southwestern motif. A huge window looked out over the Sound and the dock. A kitchen lay to their left. A hallway led toward the back of the house and, Jason supposed, the bedrooms.

"It's freezing in here," Danny said.

"No heat," Sonny said. "It's a summer place, remember. There's a wood stove in the corner and plenty of firewood. Let me get things hooked up and turn on the power."

He walked into the kitchen, quickly plugged in the refrigerator and stove, then flipped circuit breakers to turn on the power.

"There's some canned food in the cabinets, but nothing fresh or frozen."

"That's fine," Jason said. "We don't want to eat all their food. We don't want anyone to even know we were here."

"Is there a phone?" Danny asked. "Internet?"

"There's a land line, but no internet," Sonny said. "I think the point of a vacation place is to get away from all that."

"You clearly haven't met many business people," Danny said.

Lisa grinned. "Or teenagers."

Danny was checking her cell phone for coverage. She looked up at the others. "One bar."

Sonny nodded. "It's better out by the dock."

"I'm sorry," Jason said. "I should have introduced you."

Sonny stopped him. "The less I know, the less I might have to lie about. We can take care of all that stuff after you've beaten those bastards."

Jason nodded. "Fair enough."

*

It took about forty-five minutes for the wood stove to heat the living room to a comfortable level. By then it was dark outside. Dark, as it only gets when you are surrounded by nothing but forest and open stretches of water. They could have been inside a cave. Lisa had rummaged around the kitchen and found a coffee maker and some coffee. It was stale but welcome as they waited for the stove to do its job. They had all the utensils they'd need in the kitchen, but would have to run to the store for some food. The canned goods Sonny had mentioned were odds and ends, mismatched cans of vegetables, soup, and the like. Not enough to make a meal for three adults.

The house also had two bedrooms, so no one would have to sleep on the couch.

Danny and Jason had activated their new cell phones, but hadn't used them other than a quick call by Danny to let her mother know she was okay. Jason convinced her that they needed to have a plan before she contacted any of her colleagues.

They gathered now in the living room, Lisa and Danny on the couch with their coffee mugs, Jason facing them in an easy chair. The window overlooking the Sound was a picture of blackness, streaked with rainwater, simply reflecting them back on themselves. The wood stove ticked as it pumped out heat.

"Okay, let's talk about this," Jason asked Danny. "Who exactly are you going to call?"

"I don't know. The guys I work with, I guess. Maybe a friend of mine who's with the state police. Someone has to believe I'm innocent."

Jason nodded. He understood what she was going through. His life had pretty much come undone the last few days too, but not as badly as hers. Still, he wanted her to think her actions through, to act rationally, not emotionally, hard as that might be. He also wanted her to come to that conclusion herself.

"What are you planning to say to them?"

"That I didn't do it. The whole thing is a set-up."

He nodded again. "I'm pretty sure that your friends already know that. The question is what can they do about it? How can they help you?"

Danny shook her head. "I don't know."

"They probably don't either."

"If the roles were reversed," Lisa asked. "And one of your friends faced charges like this, what would you tell him?"

Danny thought about it for a minute, dropped her eyes. "Hire himself a good defense attorney and turn himself in. If he's truly innocent, the system will prove it. That's why we have trials."

"And innocent people never get sent to prison?" Lisa asked.

"No," Danny shook her head. "Unfortunately it does happen. Most of the time, though, the system gets it right. Most of the time."

To Jason's relief, Lisa accepted this without objection. They did not need a debate right now.

"There's only one problem with the system."

"Really?" Jason had to smile. "Only one?"

Danny shrugged. "Only one that matters."

"What's that?" Lisa asked.

"The system only really works when everybody, from the Supreme Court to the cop on the street, honestly does their job to the best of their ability. That means judges, prosecutors, jurors, defense attorneys, crime lab techs, and cops. All it takes is one lazy, incompetent, or corrupt person to screw the whole thing up."

"Enter Lt. Marks," Jason said.

"Exactly. That sonofabitch."

Lisa looked confused. Danny quickly sketched out her history with her boss, ending with his recent attempt to prevent her from helping Jason and now the driving force behind the frame.

"So he's crooked?"

"He seems to be," Jason said.

Lisa frowned, pondering something.

"What?" Danny asked her.

"Let's see if I've got this straight. Jason calls the city cops and they bust the spies next door. At about the same time, I cleverly lose the people watching me, right?"

Jason and Danny both agreed.

"So Lundgren has two goons in jail and no idea where we are. It gets even worse when Danny loses her own tail the next morning. So Lundgren decides to increase the pressure, calls up this Lt. Marks and has him frame Danny as a meth dealer, getting the entire police force out looking for her and ruining her credibility." Lisa looked at Danny, then Jason. "That pretty much sum it up?"

"Pretty much."

"So where'd they get the meth?"

"What?" Danny asked.

"Where did they get the meth? Surely they don't keep a supply with them just in case they need to frame someone? That seems awfully risky."

Jason looked to Danny. "She's right. And it would have to be a large enough amount to support an 'intent to distribute' charge."

Lisa nodded. "The news report said it was a 'sizable' amount, whatever that means."

Danny had her lips pursed. She was thinking.

"You're familiar with the drug scene around here," Jason said. "Where would they get that much meth on a few hours' notice?"

"I have no idea," Danny shook her head. "All the meth activity I've seen is small time. Port Salish is too little to support that much product. Like Lisa said, you'd have to hold it too long. It's too risky."

"Could Lundgren be in the business? Using their own stock to frame you?"

"Possible," Danny shrugged. "But there's still the same problem. It's not good business to bring that much into Port Salish. There isn't enough demand. And drug dealers are only doing it for one reason. To make money and make it fast."

They thought about the problem for a few moments. Lisa got up, went into the kitchen and brought back the coffee pot. Both Jason and Danny let her refill their mugs.

"I suppose they could have had somebody run it over from the mainland," Jason said, as much to himself as to the others. That scenario had much the same problems, namely Lundgren's ability to find a 'sizable' quantity of meth on a few hours' notice. It seemed unfeasible.

Unless, of course, they kept a supply in storage for precisely such an occasion. From what he was learning about Lundgren, he wouldn't put it past them.

"Oh shit!" Danny suddenly sat up straight. "Shenkle. Devon Shenkle."

"Who's Devon Shenkle?" Lisa asked, returning to her seat.

"He's some numb nut who was cooking meth in an RV up on Orcas Island. He did something wrong and blew up the RV. He should have killed himself, but managed to get away with just some burns. Unfortunately for him, they found enough meth in the main house to put him in prison for years."

"How does this help us?" Jason asked.

Danny smiled at him. "He was just convicted last summer. The case is on appeal."

"And?"

"All the evidence used to convict him would still be in the evidence locker up in Friday Harbor."

Jason looked at her as this sunk in. "They wouldn't have destroyed it?"

She shook her head. "Not while the appeal is still pending. Just in case there has to be a new trial."

"And Marks has access to the evidence locker?"

Her smile broadened. "He was the lead officer on the case."

"But wouldn't someone notice that the stuff is missing?" Lisa asked.

"Not necessarily." Danny shook her head. "It's kept in a storage box in a secure room. Unless someone actually looks in the box, who would know? It's perfect."

*

Jason's cell phone rang, startling them all. It was his old one, not the Tracfone.

"I thought you'd turned it off," Danny said.

"So did I." He picked up the phone and looked at the display.

"Who is it?" Lisa asked.

"I don't know." The display only showed a cell number, local area code, no other information. He seriously considered letting it go to voice mail, just to be safe.

It rang again.

"You going to answer it?" Danny asked.

"Don't." Lisa shook her head.

Jason motioned for quiet from the others and picked up the call. "Hello?"

"Hi, it's Rebecca. From the bank?"

"Oh. Yeah. What's up, Rebecca?"

Neither Lisa nor Danny relaxed noticeably.

"I have what you wanted. Copies of all eleven Lundgren leases."

That surprised him. He didn't know that he'd expected to hear from her at all, much less the very same day. She'd taken one hell of a risk.

Or she was setting them up.

"You want to meet somewhere?" she asked.

He did, but he didn't have a clue where that might be. He hadn't even given it a thought.

"Where are you now?"

"I'm at home. You want to swing by here?"

Not in a million years, but he needed to come up with an alternative.

"Just stay there for now. I'm in the middle of something. I'll call you back in ten minutes."

He scribbled her number in his notebook. "Ten minutes," he told her again and disconnected. This time, he made sure the phone was turned off.

He turned to Lisa and Danny. "She has copies of the leases and wants to meet."

"Already?" Danny was shaking her head. "I don't like it. That was way too quick."

"I know," he admitted. "That's why I'll go alone. If it is a trap, they'll only get me."

Now Lisa was shaking her head. "I can't agree to that. No way."

"I'm with Lisa on this one," Danny said. "Remember what you said about turning myself in? We're in this together. Right?"

Lisa agreed.

Jason hated it when someone used his own argument against him.

"Besides, three pairs of eyes have a better chance to spot a trap before they can spring it. That would be almost impossible by yourself."

Jason wasn't going to win this debate. "Okay, we'll all go. Now we need to decide on the best place to meet her." He checked his watch. "I said I'd call her back."

"How about the supermarket?" Lisa suggested. "There will be lots of people around. We need to get some food anyway. We'll blend right in."

"But so would any cops, or Lundgren thugs," Danny said.

"We have an advantage though," Jason told her. "You know most of the cops in the area."

"Provided they're locals," Danny said.

"Let's hope they are."

Over the next few minutes, they hammered out the basics of a plan, then Jason called Rebecca. It wasn't quite 6:00. "Can you be outside the north entrance to the Safeway store at 7:00?"

"7:00?" Rebecca repeated. "Sure."

"Understand, this won't be a social occasion. I'm just going to take the copies and get out of there. I'd suggest you do the same. These aren't nice people we're dealing with."

"I understand," she said. The sudden seriousness of her tone suggested she did.

"Okay. I'll see you at 7:00."

They would have an hour to get ready.

*

The plan was fairly simple, as the best plans usually were. Danny drove the Volkswagen into town and circled the Safeway parking lot, scanning the parked vehicles for any that belonged to the police. She didn't see any. Once they established that no one was lying in wait, they found a spot that gave them an unobstructed view of the north entrance, where the meeting was to take place.

Danny was to remain in the car and keep an eye on the vehicles and people in the parking lot.

Lisa adjusted her wig, got out, grabbed a shopping cart and went into the store. Her job was to get the groceries they needed, while discretely watching for shoppers who weren't shopping, or store employees paying unusual attention to the entrances.

Jason climbed out of the car with Lisa, but instead of going into the store, pulled the hood of the raincoat over his head and went to slouch against the wall between two vending machines, about fifty feet from the entrance doors. He hoped everyone would see him as just another twenty-something slacker waiting for a ride. He appeared to be fixated with working his cell, but that was just for show. He was actually watching everything and everyone around him.

The store was still pretty busy. But it was the tail end of the dinner rush and most of the customers were lone adults picking up last minute things. A few had kids in tow, but they were outnumbered by men leaving with a gallon of milk and loaf of bread, or tired-looking women in business clothes carrying frozen dinners.

Jason scanned each person as they came within view, but saw no ear buds. No one seemed unusually interested in the store's entryway. No one said a word into their wrists.

It was all perfectly normal.

A text came in from Lisa. *Nothing.*

It was ten minutes to the meeting. If this was indeed a trap, if Rebecca were working for Lundgren or the cops, their people would have to be in place by now.

He sent a quick text to Danny. *Anything?*

All clear.

Another text from Lisa. *Can't stall much more.*

Finish up and head to the car.

K.

Five minutes later, Lisa pushed her shopping cart out of the store and over to the car. Danny didn't get out to help her load the groceries. She had more important things to do, like watch for Rebecca.

Lisa finished loading the groceries into the trunk of the Volkswagen and climbed into the passenger seat. The rain continued to fall in a steady, windless downpour. Jason was beginning to feel the chill in his hands and feet.

"Crap!" Jason turned away from the parking lot. One of the people heading into the store was Mrs. Stockton, the lady of the tuna casserole. His dad's neighbor. He prayed she hadn't seen him.

His Tracfone signaled an incoming text from Danny. *She's here. Your 12 o'clock.*

He glanced up.

Mrs Stockton had disappeared into the store. She hadn't recognized him.

He quickly found the secretary walking across the dark parking lot, an umbrella protecting her from the rain. She had changed into jeans and sneakers since he'd last seen her and wore a camel-colored overcoat against the chill. She held a manila envelope in her right hand. The other clutched the umbrella handle.

Jason watched as she waited for a passing car, then crossed over to the shelter of the entrance portico, closed her umbrella and glanced around, looking for him. Her eyes passed over him without recognition and she turned to face the parking lot, waiting.

The flow of customers into and out of the store had slowed by a few degrees. As far as Jason could tell, none of them took any notice of Rebecca.

He needed to get the leases and leave before Mrs. Stockton made another appearance.

He sent a text to Danny. *Anything?*

Nothing.

I'm going in.

Careful.

Jason took one more look around, saw nothing that aroused his survival instinct, then pushed himself away from the wall.

Rebecca had her back to him, but had shifted a little away from the store's doorway to get out of the traffic.

He approached her from behind. "Rebecca?"

She started, turned, and broke into a nervous smile when she recognized him under the hood. "Oh, hi."

"Hi," he replied and pointedly looked at the manila envelope in her hand. "Those the leases?"

Out of the corner of his eye, he noticed a car pull out of the parking area beyond Rebecca and move toward the exit. It seemed to be going a little fast.

Rebecca handed him the envelope. "All I could find."

"No one knows you did this?"

She shook her head. "I was care—"

Someone set off firecrackers. Rebecca grunted and her eyes went wide, then she fell against him. Jason tried to catch her, but lost his balance and went over backwards with Rebecca draped over him, smacking the back of his head. Now the delinquents threw rocks at them too. They cracked against the concrete around him and the side of the store. Someone screamed. Jason stared up at the underside of the portico as stars whirled before his eyes, wondering why kids would do this? They think it was funny? Didn't they have anything better to do?

Then it went silent.

Someone was sobbing.

Jason tried to push himself up, but his right arm refused to work. No pain. It just wouldn't do what he wanted.

He managed to slide out from under Rebecca. She wasn't moving. She would never move again. A chunk of skull above her left ear was missing. Jason could clearly see the grayish flesh of her brain. He got to his feet, stumbled a bit, then regained his balance. The front of his raincoat was covered with blood. More blood dripped from his right hand and something warm was trickling down his neck.

"Jason!"

He looked over as Lisa leaped from the passenger seat of the Volkswagen, just feet away. "Oh God! Oh God! Are you hurt?"

He shook his head.

"Come on!" Danny yelled through the open car door. "We need to go!"

Lisa tried to help him, but he shook her off, picked up Rebecca's manila envelope and half climbed, half fell into the back seat of the car.

Danny had it moving before the door even closed.

"What the hell happened?" Jason asked.

"Drive-by shooting," Danny said, glancing up at him in the rearview. "They came out of nowhere. There was nothing I could do."

The initial shock was wearing off. His right arm began to throb and hung useless. His hand felt on fire.

He was still in better shape than Rebecca.

"Jason, your hand," Lisa said. Her face was white, her eyes wide and glistening. "Look at your hand."

He did. A neat little hole had been punched through the flesh between his thumb and index finger. It looked as if someone had stabbed him with a pencil. A steady flow of blood ran across his hand and dripped on to the floor boards.

He'd been shot.

CHAPTER 14

The call Taylor Smith had been expecting came just before 7:15.

"Yes?" he answered. Both he and his operative at the other end knew exactly who was speaking. Formalities were pointless.

"It's done," Crawford said, freshly in from Seattle. In the background, Smith could hear the sounds of traffic and some kind of hard rock. ACDC, he thought.

"Good. Confirmation?"

"Negative. Too many witnesses to hang around, but the subject and the woman were both down."

Damn. It figured. Nothing about this case had been easy.

"Okay. Stay out of sight for a while."

"Roger."

Smith disconnected, shaking his head. Military people. Some are never really able to put it behind them, no matter how long ago they quit wearing the uniform. Or what caused them to leave.

He punched another number in from memory. It was not written down anywhere, just in case.

His call was answered on the third ring. "What the hell were you thinking? A drive-by at a supermarket? You're out of your mind!"

Actually, Smith had no idea the shooting had been at a supermarket. His people had just been told to follow the secretary and, if she met up with Reynolds or Hayden, to take them out. The location of the event had been unimportant.

"Can you confirm that our subject has been neutralized?" Smith asked.

"No, damn it, I can't," Marks told him. "But I can confirm that one woman is dead and three other people have been wounded, all innocent civilians."

Judging from the background noise, Marks was at the supermarket right now.

Smith frowned. "You're sure none of them is Reynolds?"

"What do you think?"

Smith was beginning to have a lot of respect for this reporter they were chasing. He was more resourceful than half the trained agents out there.

"What are we supposed to do now?" Marks wanted to know. "This stunt of yours is going to bring down major heat on this town. The chief of police is talking about turning this shooting over to the state troopers. He doesn't think he has the resources."

"So let him."

Marks had no response to that.

"It's a drive-by shooting," Smith told him. "Fairly common when drug operations are fighting over turf. It just shores up our story. I don't see the problem."

"I have no influence over the state troopers."

"I don't care. I want to know where Reynolds is. I was told he went down during the event."

"We're checking the hospital and clinics, but haven't found him. A couple of witnesses saw a man climb into a dark sports car right after the shooting. At least one thought he was wounded. If he gets medical attention, we'll hear about it."

Smith was aware of that. It depended on whether he'd actually been wounded and how badly.

"Let me know if you hear anything," he told Marks and disconnected before the other man could respond.

Smith set the phone down and looked over at Melissa Devereaux, sitting across the condo living room from him. She seemed mildly bored, but she always seemed mildly bored. He'd known her for years. She was one of the most intelligent people he knew and one of the coolest under pressure. That's why she was his number two.

She looked at him now as he lit another cigarette. "He got away again."

"So it seems." Smith said. "He's probably wounded. We just don't know how bad."

"It would have been helpful to have someone there to tail him."

"No time to set it up," he told her. "The shooting was supposed to eliminate the need for a tail anyway."

She nodded.

*

Jason sucked air through gritted teeth as the pain surged again.

"Sorry," Danny murmured. "I'm being as gentle as I can."

"I know," he said. "Do what you've got to do."

He was sitting on the closed toilet lid in the bathroom of the vacation house, stripped down to his boxers and trying very hard to handle the pain as Danny tended to his wounds. He'd been lucky. Only two bullets had hit him directly, the one through his right hand and another through the bicep of his right arm. Neither seemed to have hit a bone, or cut a major blood vessel, though both bled like crazy.

Another bullet had cut a trench across the inside of his left thigh and a fourth had removed half of his right ear lobe. He also had a goose egg on the back of his head, probably from hitting the concrete deck when he fell.

He'd almost fainted when he first saw his reflection in the bathroom mirror. It looked like he'd been through a meat grinder. It was only as Danny and Lisa began cleaning him up that it became apparent that most of the blood had not been his.

"Hold still," Danny told him now as she worked on his upper arm. "I'm almost done."

"Sorry. I've never been shot before."

"That isn't funny," Lisa said. She was standing against the bathroom wall, arms crossed under her breasts, watching Danny work. She looked like she'd aged ten years in the past hour. Her face was pale and drawn, with smudges under her eyes.

"I'm okay," he told her. "We're all okay."

Lisa looked away, blinking back tears.

Danny stripped a length of tape off the roll and wound it around the bandage on his upper arm and fastened it tight. Jason wondered whether it might be too tight, but figured she wanted to keep pressure on the wound. If his arm started to go to sleep they could always adjust it.

"Okay. Let's see to that ear."

The bleeding there had stopped a while ago, so all she did was tape a piece of gauze over the wound and leave it at that.

She sat back and looked over her handiwork. "That's about all I can do. You should really be in the hospital."

"No." Jason shook his head. "No hospitals. No doctors."

"Jason..." Lisa started.

"Do you really think Lundgren won't be able to get to me in the hospital? Is their security that good?"

Neither of the women had an answer.

"I'll be okay. The bleeding has stopped."

"You're going to be pretty sore for a while."

He was pretty sore now. He could only imagine how he'd feel tomorrow.

Danny stood, pulled a bottle of Tylenol from the medicine cabinet, shook four into Jason's good hand, and poured him a glass of water from the tap. "The best we can do."

Jason swallowed the pills and prayed they worked quickly. His hand and arm throbbed in perfect time with his heartbeat.

"Can I put some pants on?"

"I'll get some for you," Lisa said and slipped out the door.

"Be careful," Danny told him. "You lost quite a bit of blood. You're going to be weak."

Jason managed to get jeans and a shirt on and moved out to the living room couch, where he collapsed, exhausted. Lisa sat next to him on his left, good, side. Danny had rekindled the fire and it crackled merrily in the wood stove. She'd also found a bottle of vodka and poured an inch into three glasses, then handed one to each of them.

"I don't know about anyone else," she said. "But after tonight, I could use a drink."

No one objected. Each took a glass and silently drank the straight liquor. Jason normally hated vodka, particularly straight, but tonight the alcohol hit his stomach and turned into a beautiful warmth that spread through his body like spring sunshine.

"You realize, don't you," Danny finally said, gazing down at the liquid left in her glass. "That tonight changes everything?"

Jason looked up at her. "What do you mean?"

"Up to now, everything Lundgren has done has been designed to scare us off, or to ruin our credibility. To stop us. Tonight was different. Now they want us dead. They want us all dead."

Lisa squeezed Jason's good hand. Hard.

"They're panicking," Jason said. "That means we're getting close."

"Probably." Danny agreed. "What's bothering me is that they don't seem to care how many other people might die at the same time. It's bad enough that we're risking our lives in this, but are we putting the lives of everyone in town in danger? I don't know if I can live with more innocents getting hurt."

"What are you suggesting?"

She shook her head. "I'm not suggesting anything. I'm just telling you how I feel."

Jason looked over at Lisa, sitting beside him. "What do you think?"

She took a moment, then shook her head. She was still grasping his hand as though afraid to let go. "I don't know. When the shooting started and you fell, I thought my heart was going to explode. I've never felt anything like that before."

She took a deep breath. "I never want to feel it again."

He squeezed her hand.

Lisa wiped at her eyes with her free hand.

"The problem is I don't think we could quit now, even if we wanted to."

"We can't?" Lisa asked.

"Even if we figured out a way to get off this island," he said, "somehow made Danny's legal problems go away and just went back to our lives in Seattle, it wouldn't be enough. Lundgren would never leave us alone. Not now. We know too much."

"He's right," Danny said.

"I'm a reporter. There's nothing to say I wouldn't write a story about it next year, or five years from now. They won't rest until they're sure I'll never reveal what I know."

For a moment no one said anything.

"So what do we do?" Lisa asked. Her voice was barely audible.

"Our best weapon is the truth," he said. "We need to uncover the truth and make it public. That's the only way we're going to stop them."

Neither woman showed any reaction at all.

"We have to get out and see what's on that island," he said.

"Well, that's going to be difficult without a boat," Danny said. "And you're certainly in no shape to do much of anything for a few days."

She was right, of course. Right now, he didn't think he could get himself off the couch.

Something occurred to him then. It must have shown on his face, because both women were watching him, waiting for him to voice his thought.

"I wonder if we couldn't walk right into the house right now and get the keys and charts without having to sneak through any window."

Lisa frowned. "I thought we'd decided they'd be watching the house."

"I'd be really surprised if every single cop in Port Salish wasn't at the supermarket, trying to figure out what happened there."

"They'd have called in everybody who wasn't out of town," Danny said. "But Lundgren might still be there."

He shook his head. "I don't think so. They'll be expecting us to lie low for a while, especially if I'm wounded. I think we should go right now, while everyone is busy with the shooting."

"You're not going anywhere," Danny told him. "You can barely stand."

Lisa agreed. "You need to rest."

"Besides, I don't like the whole idea," Danny told him. "Town is going to be crawling with cops. About half of them will be pulling over any car that could even possibly be connected to the shooting. We'd be taking a tremendous risk."

Jason hadn't thought of that. Once again, she was right.

"The best thing is to just cool it for now," Lisa suggested. "Get something to eat, clean up the mess, get a good night's sleep and start over when we're fresh."

"I think she's right," Danny said.

Jason knew when he'd been overruled.

*

Lisa and Danny retrieved the groceries from the trunk of the car where they'd been forgotten during the emergency, and started putting together a meal for the three of them. Jason remained on the couch, under strict orders to stay there unless his life depended on it. Truth was, he didn't feel much like moving anyway. His body was perfectly happy doing nothing but hurting. He rested and cat-napped to the sound of his companions bonding over food preparation. Their conversation was subdued, but light enough. They were talking about something other than murder and mayhem.

About thirty minutes into the preparations, Jason realized he didn't have his cell phones.

Lisa emerged from the kitchen in response to his call and quickly found both of them in the pocket of his discarded, bloody jeans.

"Thanks," he told her. "You think you could get me the manila envelope I got from Rebecca? And that photograph of the guards you found in the paper?"

She planted her hands on her hips and stared at him. "You're supposed to be resting."

"I am resting, physically," he told her. "It's my mind that's restless."

"What's going on?" Danny appeared in the kitchen doorway, wiping her hands on a towel.

Lisa told her what Jason wanted and Jason made his case for something besides pain to occupy his mind. She shrugged when they were both finished. "As long as he doesn't leave that couch, what harm could it do?"

She returned to the kitchen.

Lisa wasn't happy about it, but found Rebecca's envelope and the photograph he'd requested and brought them to him on the couch.

He thanked her as sweetly as he could. "One more thing?"

"What?"

"See if you can find a phone book? Maybe we can find out whether any of these guys," he pointed at the envelope containing the leases, "are still around."

She disappeared into the kitchen and returned a moment later with a copy of the slim local directory. "I'd better finish helping Danny."

He thanked her again and she walked out of sight into the kitchen.

Jason woke up his original cell and looked at the missed calls display. A quick look wouldn't be too dangerous. He had two missed calls and one text, which somewhat surprised him. The only people with his cell number were pretty much with him now. He decided to check out the text first. It was from Sonny.

Just heard about the shooting at the Safeway. I figured u had to b involved. Hope all are ok. Let me know if u need anything.

He thought for a minute, then typed out a reply.

All okay. Thanks.

Next, he turned to the missed calls. The first surprised him again. It was from Miles, his editor at the paper. It had gone to voice mail.

He punched in the code to access the voice mail. Within seconds, his boss' familiar voice filled his ear. "Reynolds. What the hell's going on up there? I send you to bury your father and now I'm getting inquiries from other news outlets asking about your involvement in a meth franchise? And then there's a drive-by shooting? What's going on? And why don't I have any stories about it?"

Jason smiled. He wasn't sure which bothered the editor more, that one of his reporters might be in trouble, or that he hadn't received any stories about it. It was probably a tie.

He would have to contact Miles, but not tonight.

The second missed call had been from Debbie, the fellow reporter who had taken over the Stevenson story when he'd left for Port Salish. It too had gone to voice mail.

Her message was short and simple: "We're worried about you. Let us know you're okay."

That was easier to respond to. He found her cell number and sent her a text. *I'm okay. On to something big. Major bad guys.*

He hoped that would reassure her. A little.

As soon as the text had been sent, he shut down his cell again.

The scents of whatever the women were cooking were beginning to fill the little house. Jason could not remember the last time he'd eaten an honest-to-god, freshly-cooked meal and his stomach began to grumble in anticipation.

With a little difficulty, being one-handed and all, he removed the leases from the blood-stained envelope and glanced over them. The wording in each document was exactly the same. Each had been signed and finalized within the first week of May, 1942 by the leaser and Martin Haislip. The first Haislip, Jason presumed, since he didn't have a number after his name.

It only took a few moments to confirm that almost all of the people receiving the leases had been part of the security detail in the photograph. That included his grandfather.

The only exception was George Morgan. He had a lease, but hadn't been in the photograph. However, two Morgans were. His sons maybe?

The property named in the lease was at 199 East Shoreline Drive.

His lease was canceled in 1972.

Strawberry Fields?

Looking the names up in the phone book was a bit more of a chore using only his left hand, but by the time Lisa and Danny brought out plates jammed with baked chicken, mashed potatoes, and green beans, he'd established that none of the original lease holders were still listed. Either they had all died, were in nursing homes somewhere, or had unlisted numbers.

He set the leases and phone book aside and turned his attention to the drumsticks and potatoes on his plate.

"Feel free to eat with your fingers," Danny told him. "It's why we gave you the drumsticks."

"Thanks," he told them and meant it. He'd been trying to figure out how he was going to cut meat using only his left hand.

"Did you learn anything from the leases?" Lisa asked.

He nodded. "We need to get out to Deception Island."

"We already knew that."

"But now I think I know what we're going to find there."

"What's that?"

"A mass grave."

*

By 11:00 that evening, Taylor Smith had to admit that the ambush at the grocery store had been a failure. He had Lt. Marks on the phone again and Marks had just told him that neither the hospital or the smaller urgent care clinic had treated anyone suffering from a gunshot wound.

"Either your target escaped unharmed," Marks told him, "his wounds weren't serious, or he's already dead and Hayden's trying to figure out what to do with his body."

Smith doubted Reynolds was dead. That would be a lucky break and nothing had broken his way so far. Why start now?

"We have made progress though," Marks said. "The locals found the car Hayden's been using, a blue 2002 Buick Regal registered to her mother, abandoned in the parking lot of the Islander Motel. No room was rented out to either Hayden or Reynolds. They're still checking out the registered guests over the past few days, but my guess is it was just a handy place to stash the car."

Taylor was inclined to agree with him. Neither of his opponents were foolish enough to rent out a room under their own name and he really doubted they had access to false ID, especially on such short notice.

"So far, there's been no sign of them at any other motel in town."

"They're not in a motel," Taylor told him. "They either found someone willing to put them up, or an empty house somewhere."

"There's something else you should know about."

"What's that?"

"No one is buying into the whole gang shooting scenario I floated. The locals are sure there isn't anything like that kind of gang activity in the area and they're having a hard time believing Hayden was selling dope," Marks said. "Some of them are getting pretty suspicious."

"Don't try to sell it too hard. In fact, don't try to sell it at all. You've made your point," Taylor suggested. "Let me know if anything else develops."

Lt. Marks said he would and they disconnected.

Melissa was sitting on his sofa. They usually met in the evening to go over the events of the day and plan their strategy for the next. Besides, he enjoyed her company.

"Nothing?" she said now.

He shook his head. "Nothing. They found the car Hayden had been using, abandoned in a parking lot, but there are no leads as to where they might be hiding."

"So we're at stalemate."

Taylor nodded. Stalemate was a good way to put it. Hayden and Reynolds had found a spot to hide where neither his people nor the police could find them. As long as they kept their heads down and didn't run out of food or money, they could stay out of sight indefinitely. They couldn't act against Lundgren without exposing themselves, but Lundgren couldn't act against them until they exposed themselves. It was classic.

"We need to draw them out," he said.

"Why? Time is on our side. Sooner or later, they're going to have to make a move. In the meantime we can be tying up some of the loose ends hanging all over the place."

Taylor assumed she was speaking primarily about Haislip. He had called earlier this evening, nearly hysterical over the death of his secretary. Taylor had pointed out that not only had her death been unintentional, but fortuitous. They'd stopped a damaging leak from his office and probably saved him millions in a potential divorce. Now his wife would never need to know.

Haislip had calmed somewhat, but both Taylor and Melissa knew he'd last about thirty seconds under a police interrogation.

It was just a matter of deciding what to do about it.

"I think it would be a mistake to act rashly, especially now," Melissa said. "After the shooting, town is crawling with cops and the citizens are spooked. Spooked people make better witnesses. I think we'd do better to wait them out and let things cool down a bit."

"I agree with you. Unfortunately, the director does not."

She threw her hands into the air. "I'm going to bed. See you tomorrow."

He watched her leave and a few seconds later heard her moving in her own condo next door. It was getting late and he was exhausted. He'd love to call it a night and hit the sack himself. Instead, he lit another cigarette and tried to figure out the best way to draw Hayden and Reynolds out of hiding.

By 1:00, he thought he had a pretty good idea.

*

Danny was the first to wake on Saturday morning, which suited her just fine. She always liked to have the first few minutes of her day to herself. Even when she was married, she always got up at least half an hour before Patrick to sit alone, sip her first coffee and enjoy the peace and quiet. She used the bathroom, walked out to the kitchen and started a pot of coffee. While the coffee maker chugged and wheezed over the morning brew, she restarted the fire in the wood stove, then returned to the kitchen and threw together some French toast batter so it would be ready when the others got up.

She poured a mug of the fresh coffee and took it and her cell phones out into the living room.

The rain had died off sometime during the night, but the dark cedar boughs outside the window hung dripping wet and the Sound was the color of raw wool under overcast skies. Only the faint ticking of the wood stove heating up and the steady drip of water from the eaves broke the silence.

It was peaceful.

Danny curled her legs under her and sipped her coffee for a bit, contemplating what she was about to do. It was a substantial risk, but she didn't think they had much of a choice anymore. She had been on the other side of too many manhunts and knew the advantage lay with the authorities. It was just a matter of time before the three of them would need to come out of hiding, whether for food, money, or medical supplies. As soon as they did, someone could spot them. And someone always did.

Sometimes you need to go for broke.

She hesitated another moment, then punched the phone number into her "disposable" cell and hit send.

It was answered on the second ring by a smooth male baritone. "Sgt. Decker."

"Hey, Kevin. I figured you might be on duty this morning."

A pause on the other end. She prayed Decker wasn't starting a trace. When he spoke again, Decker's voice had dropped into a secretive hush. "Danny? Where the hell are you?"

"Next question."

"Okay. That wasn't fair," he admitted. "But what are we supposed to think? Why are you running?"

"Because it was a set-up," she told him. "You think the shooting at the Safeway last night was a coincidence? If I turn myself in, I'm dead. So are my friends."

Another pause while Decker absorbed this.

"You're saying someone's dirty?"

"Remember the Shenkle case from last summer? The meth lab?"

"Of course."

"I think it would be very interesting to take a look at the evidence in that case."

He paused again. "Because?"

"Because I think somebody used the Shenkle drugs to frame me. I think all you'll find in evidence is an empty box."

"Those are serious accusations, Danny. Do you know who's supposed to have done this?"

"The answer will be on the log-in sheet, won't it?"

She disconnected the phone before he could answer. Or complete a trace.

*

Jason and Lisa emerged from their bedroom shortly after 9:00. Jason's color looked better than it had last night and he was able to walk unassisted, but he was still weak and held his right arm like he was afraid it would fall off. Lisa didn't look a whole lot better.

Danny poured each of them a cup of coffee and doled out four more Tylenol to Jason, then set about changing the dressing on his wounds.

"We're going to have to get some more bandages," she said when she was finished. "This was the last of the supply from the first aid kit."

"Lisa's still the best one to do that," Jason said. "No one's looking for her."

Danny dumped the soiled bandages into the trash. "I called my friend at the state police this morning."

The others looked at her.

"I suggested he check the evidence locker and see if any meth was missing."

"Do you think he'll do it?" Jason asked.

"I think so. He knows me. He knows something screwy is going on."

"Did you tell him about Marks?"

"No. I thought it would be better that he figure it out for himself. Marks should have been the last one to check out the evidence, so he'll be the obvious suspect."

It would be an immense help if they could get the charges against Danny dropped. It was going to be tough enough to beat Lundgren's thugs without having to worry about the cops too.

"What happens then?" Lisa asked. "I mean is there a procedure, or something, for this kind of thing?"

"All hell breaks loose. Everyone in command from the sheriff and district attorney on down is notified because if the evidence lockup isn't secure it calls into question every case they're working on. It's a defense attorney's dream."

"Cool." Lisa said. "Let's hope."

Danny made a face.

"Anyone hungry? I have French toast batter."

"I'll help," Lisa got to her feet. "I'm starving."

Jason remained on the couch, trying unsuccessfully to find a comfortable position. His arm and hand had come to dominate his being out of all proportion to their size. The throbbing pain had kept him awake most of the night. Whenever he had managed to drift into sleep, he'd moved wrong and the flaring pain had jolted him awake again.

The Tylenol didn't even seem to dent it.

Danny and Lisa stepped out of the kitchen a few minutes later, bearing steaming plates of French toast. One of them had thoughtfully cut Jason's into bite-sized squares. Lisa set his plate on the coffee table and handed him a fork.

"Will that work?" she asked.

"We'll find out," he said and tried to reposition himself so he could reach his breakfast. It wasn't easy. Every movement seemed to light a fresh fire in his arm.

"You going to be okay?" Danny asked.

"I'll be fine."

"We should get him to a doctor," Lisa said.

"No." Jason shook his head. "No doctors. No hospitals. It would be as good as turning myself in to Smith." He stabbed a square of French toast and got it into his mouth. "Very good," he told Danny.

She thanked him.

Lisa shook her head and ate her own breakfast.

"So what are we going to do today?" Danny asked. "Other than keeping Jason tied to the couch and hiding from everyone?"

Jason looked up at her. "We've got to keep going, keep digging. We can't let Lundgren get away with this."

"You're in no shape to do anything," Lisa told him.

"I realize that. You and Danny are going to have to do everything."

"You have something specific in mind?" Danny asked.

"I think a tour of Strawberry Fields could be interesting, don't you?"

*

After making sure Jason had everything he'd need within arm's reach of the couch, Lisa and Danny climbed into the Volkswagen for a trip to the drug store and then Strawberry Fields. Danny, the fugitive, wore Lisa's blond wig; Lisa wore her hair down under a knit cap.

At the drug store, Danny waited in the car while Lisa went in and bought more gauze, bandages, tape, and ibuprofen. They'd been concerned that the clerks might be watching for someone buying similar supplies, but no one seemed to pay her any attention. She returned to the car and they headed toward the north end of the island and Strawberry Fields.

As they passed the Safeway at Nils Lundgren Boulevard and Ferry Street, they grew solemn. The north entrance was still closed to business and even from the street, they could clearly see the yellow crime scene tape around the area. One city police car and a state police van were parked nearby.

"Still investigating," Danny said.

Lisa nodded.

They drove the seven miles north to Strawberry Fields Farm in near silence. Lisa spent most of the time gazing out the window. She seemed to be simply enjoying the scenery of the island.

Shortly before arriving at the farm, Danny finally broke the silence. "We need to talk about what we're going to do once we get there."

Lisa didn't turn from her window. "We're going to be tourists, right? Tourists asking questions."

"Yeah, but we've got to be smart about it, or we're going to make someone suspicious."

Before leaving the house, they had discussed with Jason the key points they were looking to find out: how the Morgan family came into possession of the Salle Valley farmland; when they'd come into possession of it; what had become of the previous owners; who had brokered the transaction. They probably wouldn't be able to get all the information on a tour of the farm, but they hoped to get enough to know where else to look.

"Maybe you should ask all the questions," Lisa suggested.

"I could."

"Good."

Danny looked at her. "Are you okay?"

Lisa shrugged and continued staring out her window.

"Want to talk about it? I hear that helps."

"I don't know."

They drove for a while in silence.

"You really didn't sign up for this, did you?"

Lisa shook her head.

"I'm sorry you got dragged in. I'm sure Jason is too. If we could get you out of it, believe me, we would."

"Oh, I know," Lisa said. "It isn't that."

Danny didn't say anything. Sometimes the best thing was to give someone the space to tell their own story.

Lisa took a deep breath. "Every time I close my eyes, all I see is Jason falling outside that Safeway store."

"Nightmares."

Lisa nodded.

"I don't know what to tell you."

Lisa finally looked over at her. "You've been shot at before?"

"Oh, no. Never." Danny shook her head. "And I've never shot at anyone either. Most cops never even draw their weapons."

"So how do you guys do it?"

"Do what?"

"Keep going like it was nothing."

Danny took a deep breath. "Everybody in this business sees a lot of unpleasant things, from car accidents to little kids beaten so badly they're unrecognizable. They only way you can survive mentally is to compartmentalize."

"Compartmentalize."

Danny nodded. "You acknowledge it's bad, wall it off and store it. You can't let it paralyze you."

"But how do you do that?"

Danny pulled into the parking lot at Strawberry Fields Farm and parked amid the half dozen other cars in the lot. It was the off-season and there were many more empty spaces than cars. But they had known that coming in. When she'd called that morning, asking about tours, the person on the phone told her they were held on the hour, providing enough people were interested.

She switched the engine off and turned to Lisa. "Think of it like this. Have you ever had your heart broken?"

"Well, yeah. Everybody has."

"But some people never recover from it. They're hurt so deeply that they never let anyone get that close again. Right?"

Lisa nodded.

"But that isn't healthy, is it? The healthy response is to suffer the pain, but get on with your life. Get back on the horse as they say. It doesn't mean we've forgotten it, or that it didn't mean anything. It just means we don't allow it to dominate our lives."

Lisa thought about it for a minute, nodded. "I like that. Thanks."

"Let's go see what we can find out about Strawberry Fields."

*

There had to be something Danny detested more than a perky blond.

"Strawberry Fields Farm," their perky guide was saying now. "Or, as it was known before 1972, the Morgan Family Farm, was founded in 1942 by George Morgan, the grandfather of the present owners. Over three generations it has grown from a small, local fruit farm to one of the largest suppliers of strawberries in the nation. It is a true American success story."

Their guide looked barely old enough to drive. She wore her blond hair loose, with bangs cut at her eyebrows, a yellow rubberized raincoat, immaculately faded jeans and hiking boots. Danny doubted she'd ever set foot in the actual fields.

She led her little tour group across the parking lot to a cottage labeled with a brass plaque that read: "Morgan House 1930-1942"

"This is the original house that George Morgan and his family lived in when the farm was founded. As you can see, it was very small. Imagine raising six children with only two bedrooms, no electricity and no indoor plumbing. The family has come a long way since then."

Danny gave the house a quick exam. The house was indeed small and probably looked better now than it had while it had been in use. It was freshly painted and the grounds surrounding it expertly landscaped. And yes, it would have been a pain to raise a family in such a small place, without power or plumbing, but Danny guessed it wasn't all that uncommon back then.

"The story of the Morgan family is truly the story of America. A rags-to-riches story of hard work paying off," their guide continued.

Danny raised her hand like a school girl. "I have a question."

The guide smiled at her, the indulgent teacher. "Yes?"

"You said the farm was founded in 1942, but the sign says the family lived here from 1930. What did George do for a living before founding the farm?"

"A good question," the guide said. "The answer was he had a small farm then, too, just a few acres, mainly raising vegetables to feed his own family. He also worked on neighboring farms to help pay the bills. He was, as the saying goes, dirt poor."

Lisa leaned over to whisper in Danny's ear. "So how'd he get the money to buy all this?"

"Good question."

The Morgan Family Farm, also known as Strawberry Fields, occupied almost the entire Salle Creek Valley. The original house, where Danny, Lisa, and the rest of the tour group now stood was near the top of the valley. As they looked toward the Sound almost two miles away, the valley spread out below them like a narrow green fan, gradually dropping in elevation as it grew wider. Nearly the entire floor of the valley was covered with rows and rows of strawberry plants, while the slopes of the hills to either side held warehouses, outbuildings, and a series of greenhouses.

Granted, much of the development had had been done after George Morgan's time, but Danny couldn't imagine the cost of the land itself. Farmland wasn't cheap.

"It would be interesting to see the foreclosure notices from that summer," she told Lisa.

"Wouldn't it, though?"

*

Jason was sound asleep on the couch when they returned. He stirred when they came in, but did not wake and neither of them was about to do anything to change that. Sleep was the best thing for him right now. It also meant he'd managed to get the pain under control.

The small television was tuned to the Huskies-Ducks football game.

"What's the score?" Danny whispered.

"34-7," Lisa groaned. "Oregon."

"Figures."

They quietly moved into the kitchen and fixed themselves some lunch. They could do nothing about the Morgans until Monday, when the newspaper and County offices reopened. Jason needed his rest and, to tell the truth, they were all running on fumes.

Shortly after finishing her sandwich Lisa excused herself and went back to the bedroom to get some sleep herself.

Danny washed the dishes, checked on Jason one more time, leaving the medical supplies on the coffee table to let him know they were back, then went back to her own bedroom.

CHAPTER 15

Alice Teale woke up Sunday morning worrying about her daughter. She was a mother. A mother worried about her children, and Danny was her only child, so she probably worried more than most. But the last few days had been different. Danny was in serious trouble. Her fellow police officers were hunting for her and now there'd been a horrible shooting. Danny was in trouble and Alice could do absolutely nothing to help her. Absolutely nothing.

She got up, fixed herself a light breakfast and got ready to start her day. It wouldn't do Danny any good to just sit in the house and worry herself sick. She needed to go about her business.

But it was hard.

At least Danny had called last night to let her know she was okay. It was such a relief, even if the entire conversation had lasted less than a minute. Still, after hearing about the shooting at the supermarket, it had eased her fears a little.

Danny had given her the number of her new cell phone, but made her promise to only use it in an emergency. She was afraid the bad guys could trace it and find her.

For the hundredth time, Alice had to talk herself out of dialing the new number, just to hear her daughter's voice again. Instead, she put on a nice floral dress with a contrasting jacket, checked her make-up, and put on her coat. It was Sunday. She would attend services at the small Methodist parish, then run by the grocery store to pick up pork chops for dinner.

A glance outside showed the rain had stopped. She brought an umbrella with her just the same.

She walked out her front door, stopped to lock it, something she'd only begun doing the last couple of days, and climbed behind the wheel of her daughter's Subaru station wagon. Danny still had her car.

It started right up. She was a little uncomfortable driving a stick; she knew how to do it, but was out of practice. Still, she found reverse and backed out of her driveway into the street.

With a crash of tortured metal, the car leapt up and to the side, then dropped into silence. A terrible silence. A silence broken only by the tinkle of broken glass.

Her door creaked open and a young woman with the most beautiful brown hair was beside her. "Oh my God!" she said. "I never saw you. Are you okay?"

Alice heard a voice she faintly recognized as her own saying she was fine.

"No, you're not fine," the woman said. "You're bleeding. I'm calling an ambulance."

Alice heard her talking to the 911 operator and giving them her address.

"They'll be here before you know it," the woman said. "You and I are going to stay right where we are until they get here. Okay?"

Alice nodded. She could already hear the siren starting up. The ambulance. Coming for her.

The young woman took her hand and gave it a gentle squeeze. "You're going to be okay. The paramedics are on their way."

Alice was grateful for the woman's reassurance. "What's..what's your name?"

"Everyone calls me Mandy."

"Thank you, Mandy. Thank you for staying with me."

The siren was growing louder. The ambulance would be here in no time.

"Is there someone I can call for you? A friend? A relative?"

"My daughter, Danny. Danielle."

"Want me to call her for you? Let her know what happened?"

Alice gave her Danny's new cell phone number.

Bingo! Melissa Deveraux thought to herself.

A few seconds later, the ambulance arrived. As the paramedics tended to the injured woman. Melissa stepped back out of their way. A small group of curious and concerned neighbors had gathered on the sidewalk, watching the activity, and she joined them for a few moments. Mrs. Teale had obviously been rear-ended. The two cars still sat in mangled silence. Gradually, she eased over to the edge of the gathering, then walked a short distance up the street and climbed into a car parked at the curb.

"Let's go," she told Anderson.

They pulled away. No one at the scene noticed a thing.

*

Sunday morning, they were gathered in the living room for a breakfast of scrambled eggs, oatmeal, and toast and to discuss whether it was worth the risk to visit the newspaper again to look for foreclosure notices. Jason wasn't sure it would advance their case much, other than proving that George Morgan was a ruthless opportunist. Danny thought it could be valuable to find out who'd held the note on the farm. Lisa seemed to be leaning toward Danny's side.

Then Danny's cell phone rang.

For a moment, they all froze in place like a video on pause. Jason, sitting on the couch, didn't think he even breathed. He knew, as they all did, that Danny's cell phone was "clean." No one knew her number.

Or no one was supposed to.

"It's probably my mother," Danny said a little sheepish and pulled the phone from her pocket. She looked at the display, then tightly shook her head as it rang a second time. "It's not her number. Local. Do I answer it?"

"Lundgren isn't likely to call first," Jason said. "Neither are the cops."

Danny nodded and picked up the call. "Hello?"

She listened for a moment. "Who is this?"

Again, she listened. Her face paled. "Is she okay? Can I talk to her?"

She began to pace, walking to the kitchen entrance, then turning and heading halfway back into the living room. "Okay, thank you. I'll get there as soon as I can."

She disconnected and looked at the others. "That was the hospital. My mom's been in a car accident."

*

"Wait!"

Danny turned on him. "She's my mom, Jason. I don't care if they arrest me. I'm not going to leave her alone in that emergency room!"

"No one expects you to." He found the phone book on the coffee table and tossed it to her. "Call the hospital. Make sure your mother really is there."

Danny looked at him, then down at the directory in her hands. She finally took a deep breath. "You're right."

"If she's really a patient, we'll all go. Lisa and I will protect you as much as we can."

Lisa agreed.

"But we have to make sure it isn't just a ruse to get us out of hiding."

Danny looked up the number and placed the call. "Yes. I wanted to know whether you've admitted a patient named Alice Teale? She would have come into the emergency room just a few minutes ago."

She waited while the person looked up the information, then listened. "Thank you."

Danny disconnected. "She was admitted twenty minutes ago."

Jason pushed himself to his feet. "Let's go."

*

"How do we want to do this?" Jason asked.

"How about I walk in there and ask what room my mother's in?" Danny suggested. She downshifted as the little Volkswagen entered a curve heading back into town. "If they want to arrest me, fine, as long as they let me see Mom first."

"It's not the police I'm worried about."

"Lundgren?"

"What are the odds that your mother would get hurt right now?" he asked.

"It's a heck of a coincidence," Lisa added from the back seat, "you have to admit."

Danny thought about it. "Okay. You think it's a trap."

"I think it's a possibility."

It's how he would do it.

"So, you guys have any suggestions, or just more problems?" Danny asked.

"There are only so many places they can set up an ambush," Jason asked. "Right?"

She nodded.

"So we just need to spot them before they spot us."

"And then what?"

"I haven't gotten that far yet."

*

Salishan General Hospital was a twenty bed facility serving the residents of Ebey Island. The hospital occupied a full city block just on the northern edge of Old Town, between 6th and 7th Streets. The main entrance, open during business hours, was on 6th street, pretty much in the center of the building. The emergency entrance, which doubled as the after-hours entrance, lay on the left end of the building, also facing 6th Street.

The obvious spots to set up an ambush were the two entrances. Danny would have to go through one of them to see her mother. Lundgren would either have a separate team watching each entrance, or a spotter watching both with communication to a nearby team.

"Keep your eyes open," Danny said as she pulled on to 6th Street and headed toward the hospital. "I'm just going to drive through the first time."

"What am I looking for exactly?" Lisa asked.

"Someone paying an awful lot of attention to the hospital," Jason suggested. "Not just waiting for someone, or killing time before an appointment."

"Okay."

Danny had taken the long way around, so they were now approaching the hospital from the west on 6th Street. The hospital stood on their left; a gravel overflow parking lot to their right. Danny kept her speed near the limit and drove without hesitation. The object was to look like they were ordinary citizens passing through, with no interest in the hospital at all.

Jason sat in the passenger seat, adjusted his arm in the sling they'd rigged for him, and scanned the area, trying to spot a trap. Everything looked perfectly normal. There weren't many people walking about, but it had started to drizzle again, so there probably wouldn't be. One man leaned over a woman in a wheelchair under the shelter of the entrance portico, apparently waiting for a ride. A city police squad car and Sheriff's car were parked outside the emergency entrance, though that stood to reason. There had been an injury accident. The police would want the victim's statement.

They would also want to talk with the victim's daughter if she showed up. It was a small town. He had no doubt the police knew exactly who Alice's daughter was.

He paid closer attention to the dozen or so cars and trucks parked in the small lot across from the hospital. Most probably belonged to hospital employees, who would be inside working. The rest would belong to visitors, who had decided to park there and walk across the street to the hospital. Again, there would be no obvious reason to be sitting in one's car.

And no one seemed to be. All the cars and trucks were empty.

"Wait!" Lisa called out from the back. "Someone moved."

*

Melissa Devereux detested surveillance. It was dull. Mind-numbingly boring. You spent hours sitting in a car, watching and waiting for something to happen, someone to show up, someone to leave. Something. But as much as she—as everyone hated it—surveillance was as important a part of security work as making arrests and writing reports. It was information gathering at its most hands-on.

Her radio popped and Crawford's voice came over. "How long are we going to stake the place out? Salazar's getting hungry."

Sure he was. She hit the transmit button. "We'll stay until the mission is complete, or I say otherwise."

Crawford and Salazar sat in a second car out of sight down the street, where they'd have quick access to the road when needed. Their job was even worse than hers. They had absolutely nothing to do but wait for her orders. At least she was actively watching the hospital.

"Just bored," Crawford said.

"Try to stay alert," she told him.

Melissa shifted her position in her seat, trying to keep her butt from going to sleep. She was somewhat surprised Hayden hadn't shown up yet. The woman seemed to be quite close to her mother. But she was also on high alert. She and

Reynolds were being hunted and knew it. She was going to be suspicious. If they had learned anything over the past few days, it was that it didn't do to underestimate either Hayden or Reynolds.

The police cars out front certainly didn't help.

Still, it was the sergeant's mother in the hospital.

Melissa glanced at her watch. They'd been staked out now for more than an hour. How long should she wait before admitting that Hayden had smelled their trap and would be a no-show?

A small black car turned into the hospital's public lot and parked.

Melissa picked a pair of compact field glasses off the console and trained them on the couple getting out of the car. The man and woman were each bundled up against the weather in hats and raincoats. Melissa almost immediately ruled them out. They were too chunky, too old to be their targets.

A second later, she got a good look at the man's face and confirmed he had to be nearly sixty. Just another citizen come to visit Aunt Flo after her gall bladder surgery.

She lowered the field glasses. Another false alarm. To make matters worse, her own bladder signaled that she was going to have a problem soon. One of the disadvantages of being a woman on surveillance: you couldn't pee into a bottle.

Her passenger door swept open.

A man slid into the seat beside her. "Looking for us?"

Jason Reynolds. His right arm and hand were heavily bandaged and supported by a sling, but he seemed to have no trouble gripping the chrome automatic in his hand.

Then her own door swung open and the barrel of another weapon thudded against her skull just above the left ear.

"Just give me a reason," Hayden murmured.

Melissa barely breathed. She had no wish to die today.

*

Danny removed the woman's sidearm, cell phone, and radio and handed them to Lisa, without ever letting her own pistol waver from the woman's head. For her part, their new prisoner didn't resist and kept her mouth shut. Her behavior reminded Jason of a military prisoner-of-war, resigned to the inevitable indignities, but unwilling to volunteer anything of value.

He found her purse, stashed under the front seat and dug out her wallet and her driver's license. "Melissa Deveraux," he read aloud. "From Bellevue. There's also an employee identification card from Lundgren."

"Surprise, surprise," Danny said.

"And a concealed carry permit from the King County sheriff's office."

"Well, Melissa Devereaux," Danny said. "Let me tell you what we're going to do. You and I are going to walk across the street to the hospital so I can make sure my mother's okay. I'm going to have my weapon trained on you the entire time, so if your friends try anything, I will make damn sure you're the first one to go down. Understand?"

The woman nodded.

"I will also be in constant contact with my friends here, so if anyone tries to hurt them, the same rule applies. You go down first. Got it?"

The woman nodded again. "You do realize you're adding kidnapping to the list of charges they have against you?"

"I'll take my chances," Danny said. "Now, out of the car."

Melissa slid slowly out of the car and stood beside Danny, her arms carefully at her sides. Danny slipped her gun hand into her coat pocket and pressed it into the small of the other woman's back. "Remember the rules."

"I remember."

The rain was growing thicker. Danny already had the hood of her raincoat up. Melissa's coat didn't have a hood and the rain quickly began to bead in her dark hair.

"Let's go," Danny said and prodded her captive forward.

Jason watched them walk across 6th Street without incident and enter the hospital's main entrance. Now it was all up to Danny. There were at least two cops in the hospital, probably in or near her mother's room. He hoped she would be able to talk her way out of an immediate arrest.

He slipped Melissa's driver's license and carry permit into a pocket, as much for the hassle replacing them would cause her as anything else, then reached over with his good hand and broke her car key off in the ignition.

He tossed the remaining keys into a patch of tall grass at the edge of the parking lot.

He and Lisa then returned to the Jetta to wait and see if Danny would make it out of the hospital.

*

Taylor Smith was working on his laptop. Specifically, he was updating the file he called "Ejector," which was a collection of interesting audio and print documents, with an occasional video thrown in. Only a fool didn't insure himself.

When his cell rang, it wasn't really a surprise. He'd been expecting a couple of calls. One was from Devereaux reporting on the operation at the hospital. The other call would be from Lt. Marks, who Smith had been unable to reach all day. So far, the cop was neither answering his phone or returning his messages. Smith hoped he had a very good reason.

When he picked up his cell, he was surprised to see neither Devereaux, nor Marks on the display.

Why would Crawford be calling?

He answered the phone. "Yes?"

"Um, Mr. Smith?"

"What is it, Crawford?"

"Ah, I think we've got a problem."

Naturally.

"What problem is that?"

"I'm pretty sure I just saw Miss Devereaux walk into the hospital. She was with some woman."

Smith straightened up. "Are you sure?"

"Like I said, pretty sure, say seventy-five percent positive. We've tried to raise her on the radio several times. She hasn't responded."

"A bathroom break?"

"She would have let us know."

Of course she would. Smith rubbed his forehead, as if the massage would prevent the headache from forming.

"What do you want us to do?"

Smith thought about it for a minute. Unfortunately, both Crawford and Salazar were enforcers, men of action. That's why they'd been teamed with Devereaux. Her judgment, their strength.

"Okay," he finally said. "Stay where you are for another thirty minutes. If you haven't heard from either Devereaux or me by then, stand down and await further orders."

"Will do."

Smith disconnected and immediately dialed Melissa's cell, but he wasn't expecting much. The only reason she would move out of position like that were if she had been compromised.

*

"Were you really going to shoot her?" Lisa asked.

"Me? God, I don't know," Jason told her. "I'm glad I didn't have to find out."

His hands were still shaking.

They were sitting in the Jetta at the rear edge of the parking area across the street from the hospital. The chrome .32 Danny had given him was now safely stashed in the car's glove box, along with the pistol they'd taken from the Devereaux woman. He'd had enough gun play for one day.

Now they were waiting on Danny Hayden.

Jason shifted his injured arm, trying to find a comfortable position. He'd done something during the Lundgren woman's take-down to make it flare up. It hurt worse now than it had all day.

"You okay?" Lisa asked.

He nodded.

A cell phone rang. It wasn't Jason's ring tone. He looked at Lisa, who already had her cell out, looking with mild confusion at its blank display. It wasn't hers either.

It rang again.

"Wait!" She started digging into her coat pockets. "Danny gave me that woman's cell. I just shoved it in a pocket."

She pulled the phone out as it rang a third time and looked at the display. "Taylor Smith?"

Mr. Smith. The enemy.

"Answer it," Jason told her.

"Me? And say what? You answer it."

"Just say 'hello.' Get him to think you're her. I'll handle the rest."

She looked skeptical, but answered the phone. "Hello?"

Lisa immediately passed the phone over to Jason, who pressed it to his ear.

"What's going on over there?" a familiar baritone asked. "I just got a call from Crawford. He said you went into the hospital."

"I'm sorry," Jason said. "Melissa is not available to take your call. Perhaps I can be of some assistance?"

He thought he glimpsed a smile from Lisa.

Over the phone, an icy stillness. "Who is this?"

"Oh, I think you know exactly who I am. We've got Melissa, just so you know, and we're coming for you next."

Smith disconnected.

*

"Keep your mouth shut," Danny murmured to her prisoner, Lundgren's agent, Melissa Devereaux. "Maybe we'll all get to go home tonight."

"Whatever."

They passed through the entrance and into a kind of foyer. To the left was the hospital's small gift shop. To the right, an empty waiting area with a modest flat screen TV playing a sit-com re-run. Directly ahead of them was a small desk labeled "Admissions/Information."

Danny asked the gray-haired woman for her mother's room number, thanked her, and marched Devereaux down the corridor toward the nursing station and the patient rooms.

"You really think they're going to let you walk out of here?" Devereaux asked.

"I really don't care."

No one at the nursing station seemed to pay any attention to them as they walked by. No one asked whether they needed any help, or what they were doing. Certainly no one picked up on any body language between the two women that things were not quite normal.

The corridor beyond was empty. Other than the muffled murmurs of distant televisions, the building could have been deserted.

She saw no sign of law enforcement.

They arrived at room four, Danny's mother's room. The door was propped open and soft voices sounded from inside.

Danny took a deep, steadying breath and pushed her prisoner through the door.

Her mother lay on a hospital bed directly in front of her. She had a splint and bandage across her nose, another small bandage just below her hairline and the beginnings of two black eyes. Her lower left arm also sported a brand new cast.

Two police officers, Perkins of the city police and Deputy Sullivan sat at the foot of her bed, notebooks in hand.

Their eyes grew wide at the sight of Danny.

Alice turned to look at her new visitors and broke into a smile. "Danny!"

"Hi, Mom. How are you feeling?"

"I'm okay. Banged up, but okay." She sounded perfectly normal, if a little nasal. "I wanted to go home, but I have to stay the night because they're worried about a concussion. I broke my nose too."

Danny wanted to hurt someone. Instead, she smiled. "It makes you look tough."

Her mother laughed.

Officer Perkins rose to his feet, his notebook in his hand. Beside him, Deputy Sullivan did the same, his eyes on Danny and Melissa.

"Danny," Sullivan said.

"She's got a gun," Devereaux told them.

The atmosphere abruptly changed. The two officers gently edged apart.

"Easy...," Danny said. She removed her gun hand from her coat pocket and held the weapon in plain view as she removed the magazine and jacked the shell out of the chamber. She then turned the pistol and held it out butt first toward Sullivan. "Just let me visit with my mother first."

Sullivan took the weapon from her.

"I know you," Danny's mother was peering at Devereaux through her glasses. "You're the woman who ran into me."

Both officers were now focused on Melissa.

"You've mistaken me for someone else, ma'am."

"No, I'm sure of it, Alice insisted. "You called 911 and held my hand until the ambulance came."

Sullivan was closer than Officer Perkins. He approached Devereaux. "I think we'd better have a little chat."

Melissa was dumbfounded. She pointed to Danny. "What about her? She's the fugitive! She brought me here at gun point!"

"Oh, yeah." Sullivan turned to Danny. "The APB on you has been canceled and I believe the charges have been dropped."

It was Danny's turn to be dumbfounded. "Really? When?"

"It went out over the radio about thirty minutes ago."

*

Thirty long minutes after Danny disappeared into the hospital, Jason's cell finally rang. It was Danny. The wave of relief was indescribable. If she'd been arrested, she wouldn't be calling.

He accepted the call. "Everything okay?"

"Everything's fine," Danny told him. "No it's better than that. Everything is good."

He gave the thumbs up signal to Lisa.

Lisa audibly sighed.

"Tell me about it."

"First of all, my Mom's okay. She's pretty banged up, but nothing serious. They're keeping her overnight, but she says that's just because she's old and hit her head. "

"Good. I'm glad to hear it."

"Second, they've canceled the APB. We aren't fugitives anymore. They're dropping all charges."

"What? Your phone call worked?"

"It worked, alright. Boy, did it work. Word is that the sheriff himself flew down from Friday Harbor this morning and personally arrested Marks."

"Wow. Very cool."

"I guess the sheriff wants to talk to me about the case, so I'm going to meet him right after I'm finished here."

"What about our friend, Melissa?"

"She's being charged with felony hit-and-run and grand theft auto in connection with my mother's accident this morning, so she'll be cooling her heels in lockup for a while."

Jason smiled. Things finally seemed to be working out. "What do you want us to do?"

"I think you guys should head back to the house. You need to rest and I'd like to see what the sheriff has to say before we decide on our next move."

Jason thought it seemed a reasonable plan. The truth was, he was feeling pretty worn out.

"You'll call us as soon as you know something?"

"The minute I can," she told him. "Imagine what we could do if the sheriff authorizes a full investigation of this thing?"

"I know. But be careful. This isn't over yet. Mr. Smith is still out there somewhere. And we don't know who Lundgren has on their payroll."

Danny paused. "You mean the sheriff?"

"The sheriff, the district attorney, chief of police," he told her. "We just don't know. So watch your back."

"I will." Her voice was more muted now.

Jason disconnected.

"You think she'll be okay?" Lisa asked.

"I think she'll be fine."

Lisa started the car and headed out to the street. As they waited for a minivan to pass, Jason followed activity across the street, in front of the emergency entrance. An officer in the midnight blue uniform of the city police led a handcuffed Melissa from the building and put her in the back of his squad car.

Jason smiled.

CHAPTER 16

Above all, Taylor Smith thought of himself as a realist, a problem solver. His job as project manager in the security division was to gather the facts surrounding a problem, imagine all possible solutions and implement the one with the most realistic chance of success. If that plan didn't work, he would turn to the one with the next most realistic chance of success. Ethics and morality had little to do with his decisions because they weren't real. The bottom line was he was a realist.

Right now, the realist in him told him he was rapidly running out of options. Three of his original four agents were out of action, including Melissa Devereaux, his best. His inside man in the sheriff's department was not returning his calls, so he was probably also in jail.

And the two people who were the source of his problems were running circles around him.

At this point, he really didn't know what to do next. If it were up to him, he'd probably pull the plug, retreat, and live to fight another day. Unfortunately, it wasn't up to him.

Without many options, he'd ordered his three remaining agents to guard the one place he knew Reynolds and Hayden would have to go. It would be the logical target of their investigation, just as it had been for Takashi and the elder Reynolds before them. Deception Island.

He'd also given the only order that made any sense at this point: shoot to kill.

His cell phone rang. The director. He was probably going to suggest they nuke Port Salish.

"Yes, sir," he answered.

"Smith. I understand legal just received a call from another of your agents, one Melissa Devereaux."

"Yes, sir. I suspected as much."

To Smith's surprise, the old man wasn't his usual bundle of rage. "It's time we had a face-to-face to discuss this operation. I will be in Anacortes this evening. The ferry leaves Port Salish at 7:00. Is that correct?"

"I believe so."

"I will have a suite at the Best Western Fidalgo Hotel. I expect to see you at 8:30. Understood?"

"Understood."

The Director disconnected.

Smith slipped the phone into his coat pocket. That certainly changed things. It wasn't unexpected, but it certainly changed things.

It might be time to activate his "Ejector" file.

*

"Turn right," Jason told Lisa as they approached the intersection where 6th Street ended in Coho Avenue. Across Coho lay the stretch of green that was Lundgren Park, deserted now because of the weather.

Lisa frowned but changed the turn signal from left to right. Only when they'd stopped at the sign did she look at him. "I thought we needed to go left to get back to the house."

"We do," he said. "I want to make a stop first."

"Where?"

"My dad's house. We need to get the boat keys and chart of Deception Island."

"We're supposed to go back to the house and wait for Danny," she protested. "You were going to rest." She pointed at the bandage covering his hand. The gauze was stained with blood. "You *need* to rest."

"We will. I will," he assured her. "But I will rest better if we have the information we need to get on to that island and now would be the perfect time to get it. The cops will have dropped their surveillance and Lundgren has to be running short of people. We should be able to get in and out without any trouble. There's no guarantee that will be true tomorrow."

"There's no guarantee that will be true today."

"Just go, Lisa," he told her. "Please. We're holding up traffic."

"Fine." Lisa released the clutch, and turned onto Coho, heading south. "But I still don't understand."

"What don't you understand?"

"Danny's meeting with the sheriff. The charges against both of you have been dropped. It's pretty obvious Lundgren was behind everything. Why don't we just let the authorities handle it from here? It what they get paid for."

"You're assuming that Lt. Marks was the only person Lundgren has on their payroll. What if they own the sheriff too?" he told her. "What if they own the prosecutor? They open an investigation to make us happy, go through the motions, then shut it down. Lundgren gets away with everything. I can't let that happen."

"You're assuming the worst."

"I'm not assuming anything. Even if they're all squeaky clean, law enforcement is limited by the Constitution. We aren't."

"What do you mean?"

"Deception Island is Lundgren's private property. Law enforcement can't set foot on the place without a search warrant. Do we have enough evidence to convince a judge to issue that warrant? I'm not sure we do."

At 2nd Street, Jason had her turn right again, heading west, across town.

"So we sneak onto the island," Lisa continued. "It's still trespassing. We're still breaking the law."

"But any evidence we find there and turn over to the police would be admissible because they weren't the ones who illegally searched the place."

Lisa just shook her head.

"We have to find out what's on that island. Too many people have died to walk away from it now."

"I don't want any of us added to that list," she said quietly.

"Believe me, I don't either. 'Martyr' is not something I want on my resume."

Jason talked her through the series of turns that led to Beacon Hill Drive and the short climb up the hill toward Salmon Berry and his dad's house. The rain had thickened now, making wipers necessary. With no wind to speak of, it fell straight out of the skies like a tropical monsoon. Traffic was heavier than usual, but compared to the madness they were used to in Seattle, not an issue.

Lisa pulled up at the curb in front of his dad's house. There were no suspicious cars in sight, not police, or anything that looked like it might be Lundgren's goons. In fact, because of the rain, there was no activity at all in the quiet neighborhood.

He opened the glove box and slipped Danny's little .32 auto into his coat pocket.

"Jason...?"

"Just playing it safe," he assured her. "I don't think there'll be any trouble. I'll just run in, get the keys and the chart and be right back out. It shouldn't take more than ten minutes."

"I'm coming with you." She unbuckled her seat belt.

"No. I want you to stay out here and keep your eyes open. If anybody comes near, you send me an SOS text. Okay?"

Lisa nodded, but didn't look happy about it.

Jason had her set up the text on her phone so all she'd have to do is hit "send" if something happened, then raised the hood on his rain coat and climbed out of the car.

"Be careful," Lisa told him just before he closed the door.

*

Danny spent a good hour chatting with her mother and the doctor and reassuring herself that other than the broken arm and nose and a few bruises, she really was okay. The doctor told her again that they were only keeping her overnight because of a possible concussion. Danny would be free to take her home late tomorrow morning.

"Did I blow it giving them your number?" her mother asked at one point. "I know it was supposed to be a secret."

"I would have been really pissed if you hadn't called me."

"I didn't know what to do. I was scared."

Danny grasped her mother's hand and gave it a squeeze. "You did just fine."

"Did that young woman really run into me on purpose?"

"It looks that way."

"Just to get to you?"

"They judged, correctly, that I would come out of hiding if you were hurt."

"What kind of people would do that?"

"People who don't care who gets hurt," Danny told her. "That's why we've been trying to put them all in jail. The drug charges and the accident were all about trying to stop us."

Her mother smiled, but her eyes remained serious. "They picked on the wrong girl, didn't they?"

Shortly after 1:00, Danny climbed into the passenger seat of Sullivan's squad car for the short ride down to the substation. For a Sunday afternoon, the parking lot was packed. Nearly every space was occupied by a car, official or private.

"What's going on?" Danny asked. "Some kind of convention?"

"Haven't you heard? Port Salish is in the middle of a crime wave. All personnel are on duty until further notice."

She smiled. "I heard something about it."

Terry Gillespie, one of their reservists, was manning the front desk when they walked through the outer doors. He broke into a grin at the sight of Danny. "Well, welcome back, Sergeant."

"Thanks."

"They're waiting for you in the conference room."

Gillespie disengaged the lock on the sally port and Danny and Sullivan walked into the squad room.

Every deputy and reservist who had been with the local force for the past twenty years was crowded into the squad room. They sat on the edges of desks, leaned against filing cabinets, and stood in clusters of two and three in the narrow aisles.

As Danny walked in, the low buzz of conversation came to a sudden halt. Then someone began slowly clapping. A regular, rhythmic cadence. Others joined in and those lucky enough to have a seat stood and joined the impromptu applause.

Danny felt her face grow hot.

"I missed you too," she managed to say. "Now don't you have work to do?"

This caused a few laughs, more groans, but the gathering did go back to business.

Danny continued toward the conference room at the back of the building. "I've never been so embarrassed in my life."

Sullivan smiled. "No one in this room could ever believe you were a dealer, no matter what the evidence said. For God's sake, you drive a Subaru."

She glanced at him. "What's wrong with a Subaru?"

The conference room door was closed. Danny knocked, and when a voice told her to come in, opened the door and stepped into the room. Sullivan, his delivery complete, closed the door behind her.

Sheriff Schneider sat at the head of the table, his bolo tie in place over a white shirt. His cowboy hat lay on the table in front of his left hand. "Come in, Sergeant. Please, have a seat."

Danny took the chair at the opposite end of the table, directly facing the sheriff.

"First, let me introduce you to everyone," he said. "You probably already know Chief Knudsen of the Port Salish Police Department."

Danny did and exchanged a polite nod with the man sitting to her left.

"You should also be familiar with District Attorney Andrea Meade."

She was. They had worked together on several cases over the years. The DA looked up from the legal pad she was jotting on and lifted a hand in acknowledgment. Danny gave her another polite nod.

"You probably don't know Captain Horace Snider of the state police."

They exchanged greetings.

"Let me be the first to offer my apologies on behalf of the entire department," the sheriff said. "It has become clear over the past few hours that the charges against you were fabricated. I think I can say with confidence that everyone at this table agrees that there is nothing worse than someone knowingly using the system to try and put an innocent person in prison."

Everyone at the table nodded agreement.

"Let me assure you that the person or persons responsible for this act will see no mercy from us."

"I have already drawn up the paperwork to have all pending charges against you dropped without prejudice," the DA said. "However, the courts will not be open until tomorrow morning, so try to avoid getting pulled over until then."

Danny smiled. "I'll do my best."

The sheriff continued. "You have also been reinstated to active duty, with all the rights and privileges that go with it. And again, I offer my apology for any hardship this has caused you and your family."

"Thank you."

"Now, to the second reason we wanted to talk to you today," the district attorney said. "Could you tell us why Lt. Marks would have set you up like that? Because we sure can't figure it out."

"I assume he's not talking."

Sheriff Schneider shook his head. "He lawyered up as soon as he caught a glimpse of the evidence."

"He wanted to stop the investigation I've been conducting with Jason Reynolds."

"The reporter from the *News?*"

Danny nodded. "Jason was also the intended target of the shooting at the Safeway Friday night. It's pure dumb luck he isn't dead right now."

The sheriff exchanged glances with the others around the table. "And what investigation is that?"

"The investigation into the death of Lee Reynolds, a local fishing guide and Jason Reynolds' father," Danny told them. "I think that once you examine Marks' financials, you will find he was on the payroll of the Lundgren Corporation."

This statement caused the exchange of several surprised looks around the table.

"Are you saying that Lundgren Corporation is behind Marks' attempt to frame you?" the sheriff asked.

"I believe the Lundgren Corporation is behind all the major crimes that have occurred in Port Salish the last few weeks." Danny ticked each off on a finger as she stated it. "The disappearance, and I believe murder, of Gregory Takashi, a graduate student from California; the death of Lee Reynolds, who tried to help Mr. Takashi gather information; the electronic surveillance of Jason Reynolds; the planting of evidence to frame me and Jason Reynolds; the shooting at the Safeway; and the hit-and-run car accident that put my mother in the hospital."

She was met by a moment of stunned silence.

"We already have three Lundgren employees sitting in jail for the wiretapping and hit-and-run charges. Surely you don't believe that's just a coincidence?"

Chief Knudsen cleared his throat. "Are we talking about *the* Lundgren Corporation, as in Lundgren Memorial Park, Lundgren High School and the Lundgren Scholarships?"

"The same," Danny said.

Silence filled the room.

At last, DA Meade shifted in her seat. "I think you'd better lay out your case for us with as much detail as you can."

*

As he'd suspected, Jason was able to retrieve the keys to his dad's boat and the chart of Deception Island without any trouble. The entire operation took fifteen minutes, and then only because his ordinarily meticulous father had no system for organizing his charts. They were all merely rolled up and shoved into what amounted to an umbrella stand in a corner of the den. Jason had to go through nearly all of them to find the one he wanted.

Now he sat on the couch in their safe house with the chart rolled out across the coffee table, the sandwich Lisa had made for him slowly drying out on a plate beside him.

He was studying a portion of the southeast end of the island now. It looked like someone—his father obviously—had made some notations in pencil, then had gone back and tried to erase them. The marks were still there, but so faint Jason was having trouble reading them.

"Lisa!" he called toward the kitchen where Lisa was cleaning up. "Could I borrow your eyes for a second?"

She walked out of the kitchen, drying her hands on a towel. "You haven't eaten your sandwich."

"I will, don't worry. I just wanted to look at this first."

"What did you want my eyes for?"

He pointed to the area on the chart. "It looks like something was written there in pencil, then erased. Can you make out what it says?"

"Jeez...you need a magnifying glass."

"Yeah, but all I have is you."

She flashed him a fake smile, then bent down to peer at it closer. "I don't know, Jason. It kind of looks like an 'H' and then two numbers."

"That's what I thought. Like 2340 and 1138?"

She shrugged, "Yeah, I guess. Something like that."

"See this spot?" He pointed to an area on the map. By the contour lines, there seemed to be a small creek or ravine that started some hundred feet inland and ended at the cliffs on the waterline. It looked like his father had drawn a circle around that particular formation.

Lisa nodded.

"This looks like a ravine, or maybe just a crack in the bedrock, eroded by runoff over the years."

"Okay. If you say so."

"I think the notation beside it is talking about the tides. 'H' is for high tide and the numbers are military time. Every high tide is about twelve hours apart."

Lisa's face said she thought his hypothesis was reasonable, but still failed to see the significance.

"I think my father figured out that at high tide a boat could get close enough that someone could climb up that ravine and get on to the island."

Lisa looked at him. "Okay. What happens to the boat?"

"Well, we don't know. Maybe there's something to tie it to. We can't know until we get there."

"What do you mean 'get there'?"

"Want to go for a boat ride?"

"No. No way." Lisa turned and walked away, heading back to the kitchen. "Absolutely not."

"Lisa?"

She stopped at the kitchen doorway, hands on hips. "We're not going anywhere until we hear from Danny. That is non-negotiable. You are to rest and heal. Understand? Now eat your sandwich."

She turned and disappeared into the kitchen.

Jason took a bite of his sandwich.

*

Danny spent the next hour outlining the investigation Jason, and then both of them, had conducted so far. Many of her allegations were necessarily on the vague side, since she did not have the evidence with her, such as the names of the Lundgren guards at the internment camp, but she thought she'd made her point. Lundgren's reaction to their inquiries sure made it look like they were heading in the right direction.

The people around the table interrupted her with questions at various points, either seeking clarification on what she and Jason had found, or why they'd chosen to go that route.

When she was finished, Danny sat back in her chair, tired and hungry, and watched the others digest what she'd told them. And for a few moments, that's all they did, sat in their chairs, staring at their notes, or into space, trying to decide what they needed to do next.

Danny didn't push them. They were all her superiors in the law enforcement community, commanders, and this was a command decision. Pushing them would be counterproductive.

Finally, the sheriff shook his head. "Lundgren Corporation contributed to my last re-election campaign."

"Mine too," DA Meade nodded.

Chief Knudsen didn't look up from his notes. "You might want to return that money."

The sheriff looked up at Danny as if just noticing her presence. "Thank you, Sergeant. I assume you will be making out a full report as soon as possible?"

"Of course."

"Very good."

DA Meade looked up at her. "We'll also need Mr. Reynolds and Ms. Martin to come in and swear out official statements."

"Yes, I assumed that."

"Thank you."

"I'd also like you to be available to brief any other investigators we decide to bring in on this case," the sheriff added.

"With all due respect, sir, however you decide to move forward on this, I would like to be part of the team," Danny said. "It's my case. I know it better than anyone except Jason Reynolds. I'd like to see it through to the end."

Sheriff Schneider nodded. "We'll take that into consideration. And again, you have my apologies for any hardship you and your family have gone through because of the false charges."

"Thank you."

*

Taylor Smith locked his car, and checked that he had everything he needed: his Glock on a holster just above his hip, a six-inch switchblade in his right overcoat pocket, and a can of pepper spray in his sock. To say that he suspected a trap was to put it mildly.

He climbed the stairs from the auto deck to the ferry's main passenger cabin and paused to examine his surroundings. Everything appeared normal. At this time of year, without the summer tourist traffic, the ferry was scarcely half full. The chairs and benches held an eclectic mix of tired parents trying to keep their children occupied, a few couples heading home after a weekend on the island, and a mixture of sales reps and delivery drivers heading home for the day. No one paid particular attention to him. No one seemed out of place.

He walked through the cabin and to the cafe in the back, where he waited in the short line for a few minutes, then ordered a coffee with room for cream.

The elements of a successful trap were the same, whether you were trying to catch a rabbit for dinner or trying to eliminate a national security threat. First, place the target at a particular location, either by baiting them or by determining they will go there anyway. Second, eliminate their means of escape. Third, attack quickly and with enough force to neutralize any defense.

It was very simple.

The way to defeat such a trap was also simple, but often difficult to pull off. You needed to counter as many of the three elements as possible.

Of course, when the site of the trap was a ferry at sea, there wasn't much you could do about the location or means of escape. Which left you with only one way to foil the planned trap.

He received his coffee, paid for it, and walked over to the condiment stand to add cream and sugar. No one sitting around the little cafe gave him more than a glance, nor did anyone in line, though there were a couple of men with military bearings who looked like good candidates.

When he was finished doctoring his coffee, Smith tossed the plastic lid into the trash and carried the full paper cup out onto the exterior deck. The rain had stopped again, but the night was still cool and damp, the metal deck glistening with moisture and the reflected lights from the communities slipping by through the darkness. Only one couple stood out on the deck, near the bow railing. Everyone else had opted for the warmth of the cabin.

The ferry had left the dock a few minutes ago and was just about to make the turn that would bring it around the west end of Deception Island and into the Sound proper. It was once they were out in the Sound that he expected the attack.

He sipped his coffee and moved leisurely away from the couple, toward the stern.

Of course, he could be wrong and the trap was set up somewhere else: the drive from the ferry terminal to the motel, in the motel parking lot, or in the motel room itself. There were a number of possibilities, depending on how much risk the director was willing to take.

He reached the stern railing, turned and leaned back against it as though he was just enjoying the cool evening and the fresh smell of the sea. In actuality, from here he had a clear view of anyone who might try to approach him.

And he waited.

For fifteen minutes, nothing happened. The ferry made the series of turns, one to the right, then another to the left, that pushed it beyond the end of Deception Island and into the open Sound. The powerful thrumming of the boat's diesel engines deepened as it pushed toward cruising speed and the lights of the island receded into the distance. Soon, there was nothing but the thrum of the engines, the sibilant slap of water against the hull and the surrounding darkness.

The couple near the bow decided they'd had enough and walked back toward the cabin doorway. Taylor sipped his coffee and watched them. As they slipped inside, they passed a young woman who stepped out and walked over to the railing amidships. She wore a London Fog-style raincoat, buttoned up tight, and a knit hat out of which flowed blond hair down to her shoulders. Her hands were shoved deep into the coat pockets and her heels clacked noisily on the metal deck.

Taylor watched her without making it obvious.

She stood at the railing for a couple of minutes, staring out into the darkness, hands never leaving the pockets of her coat, then turned and began strolling idly in his direction.

Taylor remained where he was, sipping his coffee, readying himself.

The woman certainly seemed to be in no hurry. She paused every once in a while to watch as some lights on a distant island were revealed by the ferry's progress, then started strolling again. By all outward signs, she was utterly relaxed, whiling away time as the ferry made its crossing. But she was also drawing steadily nearer and nearer to Taylor, the only other person out here.

It took her nearly ten minutes to draw close enough for Taylor to see that she wasn't quite as young as he'd first thought. Instead of college age, she now appeared to be somewhere in her thirties, her face, though still lovely by any definition, beginning to show some of the laugh and worry lines life liked to leave behind.

Something about the way she was holding her left arm struck him as odd. Still, he didn't change his stance, or give her more than the attention a pretty woman would normally receive from a man. He sipped his coffee. It was still warm, but cooling rapidly in the night air.

"Hi," the woman said when she'd drawn within speaking distance. "Nice night, isn't it?"

Taylor nodded. "That it is."

She continued to stroll toward him. She was almost within arm's reach now. He still didn't like the way she held her left arm.

"I love riding the ferry at night," she said. "Flying through the pitch blackness. It's almost like riding an open-air spaceship."

"I guess you could look at it that way."

She turned to face the rail. That was her mistake. It let Taylor see the muzzle poking through the front of her coat.

He threw his coffee at the woman's face and leapt away from the rail. Two pops sounded in the night air as she cried out. Taylor already had his knife out and open. Something burned along his right side, but he ignored it. As she stumbled away, hands at her eyes, he used his weight to pin her against the rail, then plunged the knife into the side of her neck.

She stiffened against him.

"When you get to hell," he whispered in her ear, "Tell the director I said hi."

She moaned quietly.

He reached down, grabbed her rump with one hand and flipped her over the rail. A second later, something splashed into the dark water.

He quickly checked himself over. Warmth trickled down his right side. She'd grazed him. There was also a bit of blood on his right hand and the sleeve of his coat. But that wasn't his blood.

Taylor pulled a handkerchief from a pocket and cleaned up as best he could.

No one was raising an alarm from inside the cabin.

No one had seen anything.

Perfect.

CHAPTER 17

Jason awoke with the unsettling feeling that he'd slept too long. The light coming through the living room windows had faded to watery twilight and great shadows had grown in the corners of the room. He sat up and moved aside the blanket someone had draped over him. Artificial light poured out of the kitchen doorway, along with the scents of what he assumed was going to be dinner.

He groaned, rubbed his eyes, and checked his watch. It was after 5:00. He'd lost the entire afternoon.

"Hello?"

He heard footsteps and Lisa appeared in the kitchen doorway. "Welcome back. Have a good nap?"

"You shouldn't have let me sleep so long."

"You needed it."

He decided to change the subject. "Is Danny here?"

"Danny's here," Danny said, emerging from the kitchen. "Who do you think has been slaving away on this wonderful marinara we're having for dinner?"

Lisa walked over and turned on the table lamps at either end of the couch. The deep shadows hiding in the corners fled.

"Did Lisa tell you I think I figured out how to get on the island?"

"She did." Danny sat on one of the armchairs, facing him. "We need to talk about that."

"Okay." He leaned back against the couch. "Let's talk."

Lisa moved over and took a seat on the other armchair. Jason had to fight the feeling that they were ganging up on him.

"I met with the sheriff this afternoon."

"Yeah, right. How did it go? Are they going to move on this?"

Danny nodded. "They're setting up a task force, with the state police, sheriff, city police and prosecutor's office all involved. The sheriff has assigned me to the group. Our first meeting is going to be tomorrow afternoon."

"Good. It's a good start. Maybe they'll assign enough manpower to get something accomplished."

"I hope so. Of course, we're all going to have to go down and swear out formal statements as soon as possible. Tomorrow afternoon would probably be best."

Jason nodded. "No problem."

"I'm going to have to take all our documents, too. They'll need to be processed as evidence and put in the case file."

His reporter's instinct was to object. It was his story. The documents they had, he and his friends had uncovered themselves. They'd worked hard for them, risked their lives for them. It went against the grain to simply hand them over.

On the other hand, without them the authorities would either have no evidence at all, or have to waste valuable time retracing the investigation the three of them had already completed.

Trust was also an issue. He wasn't quite as quick to believe that Lundgren still couldn't sabotage the police investigation. If they could corrupt Danny's immediate boss in the sheriff's department, what was to keep them from corrupting others?

"Can I keep copies of them for my story?"

"I don't think that would be a problem."

Jason waited for her to move on to her objections over going to the island.

Danny finally looked over at him. "I don't think getting on the island would be a good idea."

"I gathered that."

"First of all, you're in no shape to be climbing up a cliff."

Jason was about to object, but thought better of it. Truth was, he was still weak and his arm throbbed almost constantly. Under normal circumstances, he would be the first to bow out, but these weren't normal circumstances.

"Second, in all likelihood, Lundgren's thugs are out there on the island right now just waiting for us to walk into their trap. And since we'd be trespassing on Lundgren property, they'd be within their rights to shoot us."

Lisa agreed. "And they would."

"And last, but not least," Danny continued. "Since I've been reinstated as a sheriff's officer, anything we found on the island, any evidence we uncovered would be useless. It would be the product of an illegal search and inadmissible in court."

"What if we went without you?"

Danny shook her head. "Since we've worked so closely up to this point, any defense lawyer would argue that, as my partners, you were working as agents of the police. It would get thrown out."

Jason sighed. It made sense, but he still didn't like it.

"Listen to her, Jason," Lisa urged. "We've won. You've won. Despite everything Lundgren's thugs threw at us, we kept going and now the police are taking up the investigation you started. They have more people, more resources, and more tools than we do. It's time to step back and let them do their job."

Jason took a deep breath, released it. He wasn't going to win this argument, so why push it? Everything they'd said made perfect sense. As far as it went. He just didn't think it went far enough. Yes, the police were better trained and equipped to run an investigation than he was, but they were also more limited. By the Constitution and by the rules of evidence. And by the question of whether it would lead to a criminal conviction in a court of law.

Jason, on the other hand, was motivated by one thing only. Finding the truth.

*

As soon as Danny and Lisa moved back into the kitchen to finish the dinner preparations, Jason picked up his cell phone, opened his contact list and punched in a number.

It was answered on the second ring.

"Hey, Jason," Sonny said. "How's life on the run?"

"Old news. They dropped the charges. I have a question for you though."

"What's that?"

"Want to take a boat ride?"

*

Trevor Sanford was, by and large, a wholly unremarkable individual. He was unemployed, but able to live well enough off several well-planned investments that lack of work wasn't an issue. He was licensed to drive in Washington State and had a perfect driving record. He had a U.S. passport, but had never traveled outside the country. He had a Social Security card. He had a VISA, Mastercard, and American Express, all of which he paid in full at the end of the month. He did not subscribe to any magazines or online movie services. He did not have a Facebook, Myspace, or Twitter account. He did have a smart phone, one of the top-end ones, actually.

He was also the registered owner of a charcoal gray 2010 Honda Accord, which was parked right now in the lot outside the ferry terminal in Anacortes, Washington.

Taylor Smith pulled his Chrysler 300 to a stop in the slot next to the Accord. He'd just gotten off the ferry and was in a bit of a hurry. He popped the Chrysler's trunk and quickly transferred luggage, his laptop, and other items to the smaller car. He then retrieved his briefcase from the passenger seat, opened it, took his wallet from his coat and placed it in a pocket of the briefcase, then took another wallet from the briefcase and slipped it into his coat pocket.

He closed and latched the briefcase, then carried it around to the driver's side of the Accord, tossed it into the passenger seat and climbed behind the wheel.

The only remarkable thing about Trevor Sanford was that until thirteen months ago, he hadn't existed. Now he drove his Accord out of the parking lot.

*

Joseph Mullen, director of security, sat in his well-appointed office on the nineteenth floor of the Lundgren Corporation building in downtown Seattle. It was late and it was Sunday. The building was all but empty. Only the truly dedicated workaholics and the hopelessly behind were in their offices tonight.

The director was not behind.

He was also not in Anacortes. He had not been to Anacortes in several years and no plans to go.

Now he sat reading weekly reports on several of the other operations security division was working: an attempt to prevent a union vote at one of their trucking subsidiaries in Portland; an investigation into how one of their competitors was suddenly able to undercut Lundgren's prices; and an attempt to sabotage a prospective merger between two of their other competitors.

The Japanese said it best: business was war.

Someone knocked on his office door.

"Enter," he said without looking up. He knew exactly who would be knocking on his door this late. "You have something to report?"

His assistant stopped just inside the doorway and cleared his throat. "Yes, sir."

"Well?" He finally looked up at the young man. "Report."

"We haven't been able to make contact with Christine Florek since 6:30 this evening. She hasn't reported in and all efforts on our part have failed. Her cell phone is out of service."

The director checked his watch. It was almost 9:00. The ferry would have docked in Anacortes almost an hour ago. "She was the specialist we sent to meet Taylor Smith?"

"Yes, sir."

"I'd say she was unsuccessful then," he said. And probably on the bottom of the Sound by now.

Smith was in the wind. The problem now was to determine how much information he had, how damaging it was, and what he planned to do with it.

"Sir?" his assistant asked, awaiting orders.

"Smith is running," the director said. "Notify our associates at all the usual international crossings and give them the identity package. This is a level one priority. We have to locate and neutralize him."

"I'll get it out right away." His assistant turned to leave.

"Jesse."

His assistant stopped and turned back. "Sir?"

"Attach a bonus to the person or team that neutralizes Mr. Smith. Say, $100,000."

"Yes, sir."

His assistant left the room, closing the door behind him.

The director turned his chair to face the office windows and its view of the glittering Seattle skyline. He had the uncomfortable feeling that things were beginning to slip away. He did not like that feeling. He had worked hard, stabbed many backs, to get where he was today. He would not lose it without a fight.

He pulled out his cell and punched in a number. When the agent on the other end answered, he did not waste time with small talk or pleasantries. "Smith is in the wind. Burn it. Burn it to the ground."

*

"Do you really think this is such a good idea?" Sonny asked.

"I'm open to better ones," Jason said. "Right now I don't see another way of doing it."

They were riding in Sonny's beat up pickup, which looked like it had lost a battle with a ball peen hammer, but ran like a NASCAR racer. Clearly, Sonny had invested his money on the engine and transmission rather than the body or interior.

Danny had left the house shortly after dinner to visit her mother at the hospital. Her plan was to spend the night in her own bed for a change, take her mother home in the morning, and make sure she was set up comfortably. When she was done with that, probably in the early afternoon, she would pick up Jason and Lisa and take them down to the station to swear out their statements.

He and Lisa had spent most of the evening talking and watching television. At 11:30, when Lisa had gone to bed, he had stayed on the couch on the pretext of watching a movie and organizing his notes for the stories about Lundgren. At 1:00, when she was sound asleep, he snuck out the front door, grabbed Melissa's 9mm and Danny's .32 auto from the Jetta's glove box, and was waiting at the end of the drive when Sonny pulled up.

"I'm a little spooked about going into this thing blind and at night," Sonny said. "We should at least do some recon first, you know what I mean? I'd like to see that ravine, or whatever it is, in daylight before I try to bring a boat into it at night."

"Me too," Jason said. "I just don't know how much time we have. They could be destroying evidence right now."

They were entering the city limits now. Shoreline Drive became Ferry Street and they cruised on deserted streets toward the harbor. "These guys will be armed, right?"

"Probably automatic weapons," Jason said. "But I don't think there are very many of them. Three are already in jail."

"It don't take a lot when they have automatic weapons."

"Surprise is our edge," Jason told him. "They don't know how we're getting on the island. They certainly won't expect us at night and they don't know about you."

"Still. Automatic weapons?"

Sonny had brought his own 9mm auto, as well as a pair of field glasses and a waterproof camera he'd used on the fishing boat. That meant they had three handguns, about fifty rounds of ammo, and Sonny's deer rifle to use against who knew how many bad guys with automatic weapons.

Jason was counting on getting in and out without a confrontation.

"I'm hoping there won't be any reason to use our guns. Get in quietly, take some photos, gather some evidence, and get out without them ever knowing we're there."

"You hope," Sonny said.

They turned right onto Harbor Way and Sonny hit the brakes.

"What the hell?"

It looked like a Fourth of July celebration at the marina. Emergency vehicles were clustered down by the docks, their colored strobes lighting up the night.

"Something's happening," Jason said.

"Ya think?"

Jason's cell phone rang in his coat pocket. The display said it was Danny, calling from her own cell, not the disposable one.

He answered it. "What's up?"

"Want to get on Deception Island? This is your chance. Get down to the marina right now."

Sonny had cut his lights and coasted to a stop just inside the marina parking lot.

"Actually," he told her. "We're here now. What's going on?"

"You're what?" Danny paused. "Whatever. We received a tip that the shooters from the Safeway are holed up in the caretaker's house. We need your dad's boat to help get our people over to the island."

"Okay. Done."

He told Sonny what Danny had told him and they drove up to the cluster of law enforcement vehicles.

Danny met them as they climbed out of the truck. She was suited up in a helmet and body armor and carried an assault rifle slung from her shoulder. She pulled Jason aside, not gently. "You were going to try and get on that island, weren't you?"

Jason didn't answer.

"I thought we'd agreed not to do that."

"You and Lisa agreed. I just stopped arguing."

"I can't believe you." She glared at him. "Those guys are heavily armed. You could have gotten yourself killed."

He knew that. "It's a risk I needed to take."

Danny was so mad, she couldn't find the words. "This isn't over."

The next thirty minutes were taken over by logistics and planning. The sheriff's department had two boats. They would take the lead, with the fourteen-person SWAT team split between the two. Jason and Sonny, as well another civilian boat, would each follow with a half dozen armed sheriff's deputies and state troopers each. They all loaded up, the boats pulled away from the docks and formed a single file for the trip down the channel toward the island.

The rain had begun to pick up and they were running with minimal lights. Sonny ran the wheel, with Jason beside him helping to keep an eye out for the other boats and any obstacles that might show up. Danny sat behind them, not talking. A radio bud in her ear provided all the operational information they would need.

The officers behind them were quiet. It was cold. It was wet. And it was clear this was dangerous.

"This is how D-Day must have felt," Sonny told Jason.

Jason nodded.

Within ten minutes, the procession of boats had rounded the headland and could see the lights of the caretaker's house on the west end of Deception Island. Jason raised the field glasses. He could just make out two boats tied at the dock below the house. He couldn't see any people. But that didn't mean anything.

The two sheriff's boats were to pull up to the dock first and unload the SWAT team. They would lead the assault. The sheriff's boats would then pull away and the two civilian boats would pull in to the dock and unload the backup officers.

The civilians were then to stay with the boats until it was time to take the officers back to the marina.

"I want to make this perfectly clear," Danny had told them before they'd left the marina. "If I or any other officer catches either of you anywhere besides on this boat, I will personally put you in handcuffs and escort you to jail. Is that understood?"

"Understood," Jason said.

"Yes, ma'am," Sonny had told her. "I'm not leaving the boat."

Ahead of them, the sheriff's boats had reached the dock. The SWAT team wasted no time. They were all off the boats in seconds and scrambling up the stairs toward the gated fence at the top. One of the officers already had a pair of bolt cutters out and ready to go.

The Sheriff's boats pulled away from the dock and circled around.

"Okay, Sonny," Danny said. "Let's go."

Sonny gunned the motor and brought the boat expertly into the dock. Danny and the other officers scrambled over the sides and followed the SWAT team up the stairs toward the house. When the officers had all left the boat, Sonny pulled the boat away from the dock and coasted back to wait with the other boats.

He glanced at Jason. "Just so you aren't tempted."

"Thanks," Jason said.

Then they waited.

And waited.

No gunfire cracked the darkness, no explosions. With the rain, the lapping of water on the hull, and their distance, Jason wasn't sure how much they'd be able to hear anyway, but it certainly didn't sound like a firefight. It didn't sound like much of a fight at all. Which, of course, was what the SWAT team wanted. Hit the bad guys with surprise and overwhelming force and defeat them before they could fight back.

Still, five minutes turned to fifteen and then thirty and they'd still heard nothing.

"This sucks," Jason said.

"Beats being cuffed and hauled off to jail."

"Just barely."

Almost a full hour after landing their load of officers, the ship-to-shore radio finally crackled to life. It was the lead sheriff's boat. "Okay folks. We've received the all clear. The SWAT team will be heading out first, so we go in just like we unloaded: sheriff's boats first, then the civilian."

Sonny acknowledged the order.

The two sheriff's boats surged toward the dock. Almost at the same time, Jason could see the SWAT team members starting down the wooden stairs from the caretaker's house. Their body language looked much more relaxed than when they went in, but no one seemed upbeat, or celebratory.

Jason pulled out his cell to call Danny. No service. No bars at all.

It figured.

"What happened up there?"

Sonny shook his head. "No telling. We're just going to have to wait to find out."

"Yeah, and it sucks."

Sonny smiled.

The sheriff's boats loaded the SWAT team members, then pulled away from the dock, heading back toward the marina. This time, they cruised with all their running lights.

"Our turn," Sonny said and maneuvered the boat up to the dock. Jason jumped on to the dock and tied the mooring lines. Only a few officers had begun to trickle down to the dock at this point. Apparently, they had investigative work to do after the SWAT team was no longer needed.

Jason cornered a sheriff's deputy he thought he recognized. "What happened up there?"

The deputy eyed him suspiciously. "Who are you?"

"The guy they tried to kill at the Safeway."

"That was you?" The deputy's eyes widened. "Okay. Well, you don't have to worry about it anymore. They were all dead when we got here."

"All dead?"

The deputy nodded, suddenly looking much older than his thirty-something years. "Every one of them."

"What happened?"

"That's all I can tell you," he said. "I probably shouldn't have told you that much."

The Deputy shook his head, climbed into the boat and sat down to wait for the ride back to the marina.

Jason looked at Sonny, who just shrugged and shook his head.

Over the next half hour more sheriff's deputies trickled down from the caretaker's house as their services were no longer needed in the investigation. Soon, the other civilian boat filled and pulled away from the dock, heading back to the marina. Jason and Sonny continued to wait. There had been no sign of Danny yet and very few of the state troopers had returned to the boat.

The deputies who had gathered in the boat were quiet, subdued. Some seemed to be trying to catch some sleep. No one was willing to give Jason any more information.

Finally, fifteen minutes later, Jason spotted Danny descending the stairs from the house. He was out on the dock to meet her.

"What happened up there?"

Danny looked exhausted. "Let's get these guys back to the marina. I'll tell you on the way."

Jason waited while she climbed on board, then untied the lines and climbed in himself. Sonny opened the throttle and pulled away from the dock. Like the other boats before them, he turned on all their running lights.

Danny waited for Jason to stow the tie-up ropes, then followed him into the wheel house. The other deputies ignored them.

"They were all dead when we got there," Danny told them. "Four males, including the caretaker. All shot at close range. Most of them head shots."

"Executions?"

Danny shrugged. She looked terribly tired. It had been an awful few days for everyone. "More like an ambush. They were all gathered around the table in the dining room. Like they were in a meeting that went bad. None of them even got off a shot."

"Any of the dead our Mr. Smith?"

"Doesn't look like it."

"Lundgren's cleaning up loose ends."

"That was my thought," Danny said. "We don't have exact time of death yet, of course, but we think they were already dead when the tip came in."

"A parting gift. You can almost hear the shredders working at Lundgren headquarters right now."

Danny nodded. "The state troopers are working the case. They don't expect to have ballistic results for a couple of days, but there were three MP5s on the scene. The odds are pretty good one of them fired the shots at the Safeway Friday night."

"And put a bow on it."

"Yeah, it's pretty neat, isn't it? Case closed."

Jason turned and looked back at the lights of Deception Island receding into the darkness behind them. There was still something on that island. Something bad enough to kill all these people to keep it a secret. And he intended to drag it kicking and screaming into the light of day.

*

Fifteen minutes later, Sonny guided the boat around the breakwater and into the Port Salish harbor, heading toward the marina docks. Almost immediately, Jason's cell phone began chirping that he had missed calls. He pulled the phone from his pocket, glanced at the display, and groaned. Three missed calls and four texts. Every one of them was from Lisa.

"Crap."

Sonny looked over. "Bad news?"

"Lisa's been trying to get a hold of me," he said.

"Me, too." Danny was also looking at her phone. She typed something and hit the send key. "I told her you're okay and with me."

"Thanks."

"You owe me one."

He too typed out a quick text, telling Lisa that he'd had to help Danny with something that took them out of cell service.

And seconds later, he received a reply.

You could have left a damn note.

Sorry.

He looked at Danny. "It might be better if you took me back, rather than Sonny."

"Just don't expect me to lie for you."

He shook his head. He wouldn't have asked.

Sonny maneuvered the boat into its berth and shut down the engines. Slowly, wearily, the officers climbed out, unloaded their equipment and trudged up the dock to their waiting vehicles. It was past 6:00 in the morning. It had been a long day for everyone.

Jason helped Sonny finish securing the boat, then thanked him and sent him home to his family.

Danny was waiting at her mother's Buick. Her Subaru had been totaled in the accident.

She held out her hand as he approached.

"What?" Jason asked.

"The guns. Now."

He handed over both pistols. She unloaded each, left the bolts open, and then climbed behind the wheel. Jason climbed into the passenger seat.

They drove for a few moments in silence.

"Listen," Danny finally said. "I understand what you're trying to do. Why you want to get on that island so bad. I really do."

"I just want the truth."

"I know. So do I, but there are many ways to get to the truth and some are better than others. You know what I mean?"

He did.

"For one thing, those guys all had automatic weapons, machine guns. You could have gotten both of your asses shot off."

"But they were already dead."

"You didn't know that, did you?"

No. He hadn't known that. "I don't want this whole thing to get swept under the rug."

"Neither do I, believe me."

They were well out of town by this time and Danny slowed down as they approached the driveway for the safe house. "Tell you what. If you can just keep it together for a little while, I'll see if I can get permission from the state troopers for you to visit the island as a member of the press. There's no guarantee. They may say no, but it's worth a shot, isn't it?"

"It is." They rolled to a stop beside the Jetta. Lights were on in both the house's living room and kitchen. "Thank you. All I want is a chance to get up there and look around."

"I'll let you know tomorrow when I pick you up. We still have to swear out our statements, remember?"

He nodded.

The front door opened and Lisa stood in the doorway, back lit by the living room lights. Her arms were crossed under her breasts.

"Well, I guess I'd better go face the music." Jason unlatched his door and released his seat belt.

Danny stopped him with a touch on his arm. "Try to see this from her point of view, Jason. She almost watched you get killed the other day. It makes her very vulnerable."

He nodded again.

She was about to say something else, but thought better of it. "See you tomorrow."

"Tomorrow," Jason agreed and climbed out of the car.

Danny backed away from the house, turned around, and headed back to the highway.

Jason walked up to Lisa, still standing in the doorway. "I'm sorry. I shouldn't have scared you like that. I wasn't thinking."

For a second or two she didn't reply. Nor did she move from the doorway to let him in.

"Can we go inside? It's cold out."

Lisa turned and went inside. Jason followed, closing the door behind him.

"You're soaked," Lisa said. "I'll get you some dry clothes."

She disappeared into the bedroom and returned with a dry shirt, jeans, and a pair of socks. Jason stripped off his wet clothes and put on the dry ones. Lisa curled up on one end of the couch, her arms once again folded under her breasts.

Jason tossed his wet clothes over the back of an armchair, then went to sit beside her. Lisa didn't move away from him, but wasn't exactly welcoming him either.

A log collapsed in the woodstove with a muffled thud.

"So how badly did I screw things up tonight?"

Lisa shrugged.

"I never intended to hurt you. I never would."

She wouldn't look at him. Didn't respond.

"You have to believe that."

She wiped at her eyes. "That's the problem."

"I don't understand."

Lisa took a deep breath, trying to fight back tears, with only partial success. She wiped her eyes again. "You went to try and get on that island."

"Lisa..."

"Don't b.s. me, Jason. I don't know if the plans changed, or you somehow talked Danny into covering for you, and I don't really care. But I know Danny didn't come out to pick you up. I would have heard her car on the gravel."

He hadn't thought of that.

"We'd talked about this. We'd agreed it was too dangerous. But you went anyway. You risked your life despite everything we talked about."

All he could do was nod. Everything she said was true.

"I was so scared, especially when you wouldn't answer your cell. I thought they'd got you and I'd never see you again."

"I'm sorry. That's not what I wanted.""

"I know. I believe you. You didn't do this to hurt me." She turned to look at him. "You did it for the story. You're a reporter, Jason, and one of the best around. But in order to be as good a reporter as you are, the story always comes first."

"That's not true," he told her.

"Yes, it is, or you wouldn't have gone, would you? It's the story. The story is everything."

He didn't know what to say.

"I don't know if I can stand to be number two in your world."

Jason was at a loss. He sat there for a few moments, listening to Lisa softly cry, his gaze centered somewhere around his feet. Finally, he reached over and found her hand with his own. She returned his grasp.

"What are you going to do?" he finally asked.

She wiped her eyes again. "I—."

The front door swung open and a man in a dark overcoat spotted with rain stepped in. He was big and powerful and completely bald.

Jason started to his feet.

The man pointed a handgun at Jason's midsection. "Not a good idea."

Jason sank back down. Lisa clung to his side.

"We've never been formally introduced," the man said. "I'm Taylor Smith."

PART THREE

Deception Island

CHAPTER 18

"Please, don't hurt us," Lisa whispered.

"My dear Lisa," Smith said as he closed the door behind him. "It is Lisa, isn't it?"

She nodded stiffly. Her arms and legs were both crossed. She was wearing only the tank top and shorts she'd worn to bed. Not normally what she'd choose to entertain strangers.

"If I wanted to harm you, surely you would be dead right now, wouldn't you?"

Jason had to admit Smith had a point. They were alone, out in the middle of nowhere. No one would even hear the shot.

Shots.

"You should really keep your doors locked," Smith told them. "It's a dangerous world."

"What do you want?" Jason asked.

"Just to chat for a bit," Smith said as he took a seat in the vacant armchair and crossed his legs. The pistol never wavered from Jason's midsection. "So this is where you managed to hide from everybody? Brilliant. It would have taken us forever to find you here. Even the police didn't have a clue, though I don't think they were trying very hard."

"How did you find us?" Jason asked.

Mr. Smith smiled. "I followed you from the marina, of course."

Jason groaned. It hadn't even occurred to him to check for a tail. He doubted Danny had either, not after the events of the night. The threat seemed to have passed. He just hoped that mistake wouldn't cost them.

"Understand," Smith told them. "I've never had anything personally against any of you. In fact, I have grown to rather admire you. I've gone up against professionals who didn't show half the courage and resourcefulness you have."

"You shot me," Jason pointed out.

Smith shrugged. "I had a job to do. That meant stopping you any way we could. That's all it was, a professional decision."

"Sorry if I take it a little more personally than that."

Smith smiled.

"What about the woman you killed?" Lisa asked. "Was killing her a *business* decision?"

"The government calls it 'collateral damage.' Unfortunate, but it happens sometimes."

"And my dad?" Jason asked. "Was he collateral damage too?"

Smith thought about it for a few seconds. "I suppose you could say that. But I didn't come here to explain myself, or my actions."

"Then why *did* you come here?"

Smith smiled again. "To make you a proposition, of course."

Jason wasn't afraid anymore. He was skeptical. He was angry. But he wasn't afraid. "What kind of proposition could you make that would possibly hold any interest for me?"

"A legitimate question." Smith reached into a coat pocket with his left hand and pulled out a thumb drive. He tossed it to Jason.

"What's this?"

"All the information you'll need to nail Lundgren Corporation, its security division, and its director of security to the wall. Names, dates, memos, recorded conversations. Everything you need."

Jason looked at the drive in his hand, then back up at Smith. "And you're just giving it all to me? A present?"

"Like I said, I never had anything personally against you. It was my job. Now the circumstances have changed. I and my employers have had something of a falling out. People in my position aren't offered a golden parachute. We're just pushed out of the plane."

Jason had seen Lundgren's retirement plan earlier tonight. Four men with bullets through their heads.

"So this is your revenge?"

"Not at all. It's my life insurance policy," he smiled. "With the information on that drive, I'm hoping that you and law enforcement will keep my former employers busy enough that they have neither the time nor money to hunt me."

"But doesn't this prove you are as guilty as they are?" Lisa asked.

He shrugged. "By this time tomorrow, I will be out of the country. My hope is that the legal eagles will be satisfied with frying the bigger fish."

"What's to keep me from making a phone call and having you picked up at the border?" Jason asked.

"Nothing, except the knowledge that you'll never get past the password on the files. And I won't give you the password until I'm safely out of the country." Mr. Smith looked at him. "That is my proposition. You get the information you need; I get a new life. Take it or leave it."

Jason tried to come up with an angle, but couldn't find one. Mr. Smith's deal was pretty cut and dried. If Jason wanted the information, he let Smith go. If he wanted to nail Smith as well as his bosses, Smith wasn't going to do anything to help him.

"When will you send me the password?"

Smith smiled. "Via text message. Noon tomorrow."

Jason looked at Lisa. She shrugged. The decision was his.

"Do we have a deal, Mr. Reynolds?"

Jason hesitated, then nodded. "We have a deal."

"Very good," Mr. Smith stood and headed toward the door. "It's been a pleasure, but I have a train to catch, so to speak."

"This deal doesn't mean I won't be looking for you."

Smith stopped at the door and turned back to Jason. "I would expect nothing less."

And he walked out the door.

*

Naturally, the first thing Jason did once Smith left—other than lock the door—was to get out his laptop and plug in the thumb drive. The only file on the device was a zipped folder entitled: "Ejector." When he tried to open it, the computer asked for a password. Rather than risk some kind of meltdown, he canceled the request.

"I guess we have to wait."

"Do you think he'll actually send you the password?" Lisa asked. She had put on sweats as soon as the door had shut behind Smith.

He thought about it for a moment. "Yeah, I think he will. He wants Lundgren to be so tied up in their own problems they forget about him. That won't happen without the password. I think we'll get it right when he said we would."

Lisa nodded. She looked exhausted.

"We should try and get some sleep."

It was nearing 8:40. It was already daylight outside.

"I can sleep out here, if you want."

Lisa shook her head, grabbed his good hand, and led him back to the bedroom.

*

Jason slept, but not well. He kept having variations of the same dream. He was visiting Lisa. He parked in his usual spot and walked across the parking lot, only to find the apartment complex had turned into a maze and he could not find her apartment. Not only could he not find her apartment, he couldn't find any familiar landmarks or faces. He wandered and wandered without getting anywhere, without finding Lisa.

Finally, at 10:20, he gave up and climbed out of bed.

Lisa slept on, as if she had not a care in the world. Or like she'd been up for almost twenty-four hours.

He went into the kitchen and started a pot of coffee, then showered and did his best to change the dressings on his wounds. The wounds themselves were ugly and inflamed and still hurt like crazy, but seemed to be healing.

More important, he was regaining his strength.

By now it was approaching 11:00. He still had an hour before Smith was supposed to send him the password. Another hour and a half before Danny was due to pick them up to file their statements. He poured himself a cup of coffee and strolled into the living room.

It was chilly in the house. Last night's fire had long ago burned itself out, but he hesitated to start a new one when they would be leaving in a couple of hours. Outside the living room window, yesterday's rain had morphed into a thick misty fog, bordering on a drizzle. Moisture dripped steadily from the eaves and beaded thick on the Volkswagen parked in front of the house.

The fog was so thick the cedars at the far edge of the parking area were shapeless dark masses.

He turned from the window and sat down on the couch in front of his laptop.

The thumb drive was still plugged in to the USB port where he'd left it.

He resisted the urge to look at the file again. It wouldn't do any good until he had the password and a superstitious part of him didn't want to risk messing with it too much. He wouldn't doubt Smith had set the file up with some sort of fail safe.

Instead, he opened the word processing program and began writing up his notes on everything that had happened since he'd arrived on the island. It took a little while to get used to working around the stiffness in his right hand, but soon the words were flowing as fast as he could hit the keys. It was a story, a hell of a story, and he was the only one who could tell it.

Sometime later—he was too far into the zone to accurately judge time—the toilet flushed down the hall. Lisa was awake. A few seconds later, she appeared at the end of the couch in her tank and shorts, her hair mussed and her eyes swollen with sleep. Or lack of sleep. She squinted down at him like he was a curious, exotic insect.

"There's coffee in the kitchen."

"Did you sleep at all?"

He shrugged. "A couple of hours. I'm fine."

Lisa shook her head and went into the kitchen after coffee.

Jason checked the time. Fifteen minutes.

He finished the thought he'd started in his notes, saved his work, and shut the application down. He did not want to be working on anything when Lisa came back out. If she wanted to talk, he wanted to be ready.

Lisa stepped out of the kitchen, a mug of coffee clutched like a religious icon before her, walked over and curled up on the couch beside him. Jason was always amazed that she could sit comfortably like that, sometimes for hours, her butt directly on top of her ankles. If he'd sat like that for more than a minute or two, he'd be crippled.

"How long until the big show?" Lisa asked as she sipped her coffee.

"Five minutes."

She sipped her coffee again, and ran fingers through her hair, finally tucking the locks behind both ears.

"I should go home today," she told him. "I can't afford to miss any more class. I don't remember the last time I even looked at my thesis."

"You've been distracted."

"That's a nice way of putting it."

Lisa sipped her coffee, then shivered. "You didn't build a fire this morning?"

"I didn't think it'd be a good idea," he told her. "Not with us leaving in a couple of hours."

"It's still cold."

He checked his cell phone again in case he'd missed a message. He hadn't, but it was still two minutes before noon.

"Anything?"

"Not yet," he shook his head.

She sipped her coffee.

"I'm probably going to need to spend a couple more days up here," he said. "I still need to take care of my dad's finances and close down the house. Plus, whatever Danny and her colleagues need me to do."

"And then there's that island."

"And then there's that island."

Lisa sipped her coffee.

He decided a different subject would be nice.

"Do you want me to call you when I get back to the city?"

"You'd better call me before then." Lisa peered at him over the rim of her mug. "It's the only way I'll know you're not dead."

"Lisa..."

"Sorry," she shook her head. "That wasn't fair."

His cell phone chirped. A text message.

Jason didn't recognize the originating number, but he hadn't expected to.

"Is that it?" Lisa asked, peering over.

"Let's see."

He accepted and opened the message.

As promised. The password IS case sensitive and one word: PairofGrinsFallCones.

Jason opened the file labeled "Ejector" on the thumb drive, then carefully entered the password. The file immediately unzipped and displayed a series of some two dozen files across the screen. Most of them were print files in MS Word format, but roughly a third were audio files.

The very first file was one of those audio files, labeled "Meeting 10-17-2013, 09:00, Joseph Mullen, Director of Security, Lundgren Corporation."

"We're in," Jason said.

"Look at all those files...."

Jason opened the first audio file.

It was somewhat difficult to hear. Jason stopped the playback, turned the speakers on his laptop up to full volume and re-started the file. It was still muffled a little; he guessed that Smith had concealed the recorder in a pocket during the meeting, but now the words could be heard and understood.

*

A clipped, baritone spoke first. "Have a seat."

Rustling, as if someone were rubbing fabric over the microphone.

"We have a situation developing in Port Salish, on Ebey Island. Are you familiar with the area?"

"I've heard of it, of course. It's where Lundgren started out."

"It's a little island out in the San Juans and, yes, it's where Lundgren was headquartered until 1965. The Lundgren family still maintains a house there. All of which is immaterial. Someone has started poking their nose into something that's none of their business. I've received reports that the subject began making inquiries in Friday Harbor a week ago. Now it seems he's moved to Port Salish."

"The subject's name?"

"Gregory Takashi. The dossier has all the background information you'll need."

"Very good."

"Take your team to Port Salish at once and convince Mr. Takashi that it's in everyone's best interest that he discontinue his inquiries. Particularly his."

"Priority?"

"One, Mr. Smith. Priority one. Do whatever you have to do, but make this Takashi character go away."

"Anything else I should know about?"

"Port Salish is the boonies. Requisition any equipment you think your people may need before you go because it's unlikely you'll find anything out there."

"Yes, sir."

"Any questions?"

"May I inquire as to the subject this Takashi is so interested in? It's useful if we know what to push him away from."

"Anything having to do with a place called Deception Island. That's as much as you need to know."

"Very good. I'll get my people on it."

"Don't disappoint me Mr. Smith. Make Takashi go away."

"We will, sir."

The file ended.

*

"Oh. My. God."

Jason looked up at Lisa. Her eyes were wide, her expression stunned.

"He really did it," she said. "He really gave you everything?"

Jason was fairly stunned himself. "It looks that way."

His cell chirped again about another message. *We good?*

Jason replied. *We're good.*

*

Several hundred miles away, the man formally known as Taylor Smith stood at the waterfront railing as a gentle snow swirled around him. The flakes were fat and picturesque, falling steadily, but with virtually no wind behind them. Four inches already covered the ground and the weather report forecast another three before the current system moved out of the area. It was cold, but he was dressed for it, so he wasn't uncomfortable. Because of the weather, there were almost no sightseers this morning. The only people around were those whose jobs required them to be here and they were too busy to pay much attention to him.

His disposable cell phone signaled an incoming text.

We're good.

"Give them hell," he whispered, closed the cell phone and let it fall into the murky water below.

He turned away from the harbor, shoved his hands into his overcoat pockets, and began to walk.

*

Jason and Lisa spent most of the next thirty minutes skimming through the files and documents on the flash drive. One thing quickly became very clear. Taylor Smith had carefully documented every interaction he had with the director of security, either by saving a copy of the print document, or by recording the actual meeting or phone conversation. It was a thorough record.

"Wow," Lisa said at one point. "He really didn't trust his boss, did he?"

"No, he didn't. I think, though, if you're in his business long enough, you wouldn't trust anyone," Jason told her. "Just think about what he named the file. 'Ejector,' like a pilot's ejection seat. From the beginning this was about saving his own butt."

"But why work for a place that breeds this kind of paranoia?"

"I don't know," he said. "People work unpleasant jobs all the time."

She shook her head. "That's not what I mean. Did he do this for every job he was given? Or was there something special about this one?"

She'd raised an interesting question. He doubted they would ever know the answer to it.

Most of the files were print documents in MS Word format. By far the majority of those were brief summaries of strategy and actions, a kind of daily report Smith emailed to the director. Others were requisitions for various weapons and surveillance equipment, or memos requesting assistance from other teams.

Four of the files were actually file folders, labeled "PP/GT," "PP/LR," "PP/JR," and "PP/DH." The first one turned out to be probably the most thorough background check Jason had ever come across. The subject was Takashi. Lundgren had everything from his home address to his cell phone number, to his girlfriend's class schedule, to his father's law firm's credit rating, to his mother's club memberships. It was an incredibly detailed profile of his life.

The second dossier was just as thorough a profile of Jason's father. The third was about Jason himself. The fourth, Danny.

The audio files, mostly phone calls, only seemed to occur when a serious problem arose, either something Smith didn't feel comfortable deciding himself, or something his boss was unhappy about the decision he did make.

One particular audio file caught Jason's attention. It was dated the Friday before his father's body was found.

He ordered it to play.

*

The first voice they heard was Smith's.

"Sorry to call you so late, sir," Smith said. "But we have a situation I thought you should know about."

"What situation?"

"The Takashi kid and Reynolds got on the island."

"They what? How did you let them get on the island?"

"I don't know. They found another access point."

"Goddamn it, Smith! Your job was to keep this from happening!"

"That isn't the situation I'm talking about."

"There's another one?"

"Yes, sir. We caught them, but Baxter opened fire and killed the Takashi kid."

The director paused for a moment as this sunk in. "What about the old man? The guide?"

"He got off the island, but we intercepted him at the marina. He's injured, but alive. That's the situation. He's a witness. What do we do with him?"

The director didn't hesitate. "Fishing is a dangerous sport. There are accidents. Fatal ones."

"Very good. We'll take care of it within the hour."

"What about the kid's body?"

"We've already disposed of it."

"Good."

The director abruptly hung up.

*

Jason felt as if he'd been kicked in the stomach. He sat there for a few moments, struggling to catch his breath as he tried to process what he'd just heard. He'd been right all along. His dad had been murdered. His dad had witnessed Lundgren's thugs shoot Greg Takashi and they'd killed him to keep him quiet.

Now he had the proof. Indisputable proof. He had the killers, in their own words and voices, making the decision to kill.

Now everyone had to listen. They had to believe. Now his father would get justice.

Lisa stirred beside him.

He looked over to find her blinking away tears. "It's everything you need, isn't it? They have to admit it wasn't an accident now."

Jason nodded.

Lisa gave him a fierce, triumphant hug. Jason returned the hug with all the strength his good arm could muster. It felt so good, holding her, feeling her warmth, the warm smell of her hair.

They separated, both wiping their eyes.

"You did it," Lisa told him. "You've won. You're going to nail Lundgren and their thugs."

"It was a team effort." He shook his head. "*I* didn't win. *We* did."

Lisa smiled, then shrugged. "Okay. I'll take some credit. At least you won't have to sneak onto that island anymore."

"No, we should have no trouble getting a search warrant now."

Lisa bounced up in her seat. "We need to call Danny. She needs to know about this."

"Wait. I need to do something first."

"What?"

He'd already begun hitting keys on his computer. "I need to make a couple of copies, just in case."

"In case what?"

"Things don't go as well as we're expecting."

*

"I'm not a cripple, you know," Alice Teale said as Danny set a tray with a bowl of tomato soup, grilled cheese sandwich, and cup of tea on the night stand. "I have a broken arm and a broken nose, that's all. I can feed myself."

Danny smiled down at her mother. One of the unfortunate side effects of a broken nose was that both of her eyes were black. She looked like a boxer who'd lost a brutal match.

"Eat your lunch," Danny told her. "Graciously."

Her mother smiled. "Thank you so much, dear, for making me lunch."

"You're welcome."

Her mother reached over with her good hand, grabbed half of the cheese sandwich and took a bite.

Like a shark.

"Is there anything else I can do for you?" Danny asked. "I'm going to have to take Jason and Lisa down to the station to swear out their statements. It will probably take most of the afternoon."

"I'll be fine." Her mother took another bite of her sandwich. "Do what you need to do."

"I'll stop by later to fix dinner."

"Honestly, you don't need to do that."

"Mom, I want to help. At least for a couple of days."

Danny's cell rang. The display said it was Jason, which was a surprise. They were already supposed to hook up in a few minutes.

"It's Jason," she told her mother. "I'd better see what he wants."

Her mother nodded.

She accepted the call. "Hey, what's up?"

"What are you doing?"

"Right now? I'm trying to convince my dear mother that it's okay to take it easy for a couple of days after a car accident."

Her mother stuck her tongue out.

Jason laughed. "Tough sell, is it?"

"You have no idea. She's worse than you."

Her mother laughed. "Maybe her mother thinks someone's overreacting."

Danny shot Alice an annoyed look, before turning her back and walking to the other side of the room. "What do you need? I'm planning to pick you up in about thirty minutes, remember?"

"I remember," he told her. "But something has come up. I didn't think it could wait."

"What's that?"

"The smoking gun."

"The what? What are you talking about?"

"Danny, I have in my possession enough hard evidence to convict Lundgren and their employees for every crime they've committed."

"Okay," Danny paused. "What kind of evidence?"

"Print documents mostly, voice recordings. Danny, I've got the conversation when the director of security ordered Smith to kill my dad."

Danny began to feel some of the excitement clearly running through Jason. "Is it genuine?"

"I think so." She could almost hear him grinning. "Taylor Smith gave it to me."

"He what? When? What are you talking about?"

"It's a long story, too long for the phone. I just thought you might want to look this stuff over before we pass it on to the rest of the task force."

Of course she would. "I'll be there as soon as I can. Ten to fifteen minutes."

They disconnected.

Danny turned back to her mother. "Something's come up. I need to go."

Her mother smiled. "I've been telling you all day I'll be fine."

"I know you will, but let me do this for you. It makes me feel better."

"Honey," her mother said, suddenly serious. "It wasn't your fault that that woman ran into me. It was her decision." She emphasized each point with a wave of her soup spoon, like a conductor used his baton. "I appreciate your wanting to help and I am grateful. But I don't want you doing it because you feel guilty. You have nothing to feel guilty about. Okay?"

Danny leaned down to kiss her mother on the cheek. "I'll be back to fix you dinner."

"Be careful."

*

Jason punched in a text and sent it to Sonny. *Out of the house by 2. Thanks. We owe you.*

Lisa was straightening up in the kitchen. He could hear plates clattering as she put them away and the muffled thump of cabinet doors. She'd already made the bed, gathered their things from the bathroom and wiped it down. Jason had been relegated to stuffing dirty clothes into their suitcases and double-checking rooms for things they might have missed the first time through. It hadn't been hard. They'd consciously tried to minimize their footprint while they'd stayed here.

"What should we do with the food in the refrigerator?" Lisa called from the kitchen. "It's going to spoil."

"Leave it," Jason suggested. "I'll let Sonny know. Maybe his family can use it."

Sonny replied to his text. *Danger over?*

Seems to be.

"What should we do with the garbage?" Lisa asked from the kitchen.

"I'll ask," Jason said.

He keyed in another text. *There's food in the fridge. You're welcome to it. Also, what should we do with trash?*

Sonny's reply was quicker this time. *Leave the trash. I'll deal w it.*

K. Thanks again. We owe you.

*

"Taylor Smith was actually here, in this house?"

Lisa nodded. "Scared the shit out of me. I thought he was going to kill us."

"He probably thought about it," Danny told her.

Lisa had nothing to say about that.

They were gathered under the covered porch at the front of the house. Jason and Lisa had just finished loading their things into the Volkswagen when Danny pulled in. The plan was to follow Danny down to the police station to swear out their statements and never come back to the safe house. They didn't think they'd need to.

"So why would he give all this stuff to you? If it's evidence against Lundgren, and it's as good as you say it is, doesn't it implicate him just as badly?"

"It does," Jason told her. "Every inch of it. But I think Lundgren tried to do to him what they did to those shooters on Deception Island. This is his insurance policy."

Lisa looked from Jason to Danny. "What happened on Deception Island? Are you talking about last night?"

Jason had never had a chance to tell her.

Danny shot him a look, then turned to Lisa. "We received a tip that the guys who did the Safeway shooting were hiding in the caretaker's place on Deception

Island. That's why I needed Jason last night. We needed his dad's boat to help get enough officers over to the island."

Lisa gave Jason a look that made him want to crawl under the car.

Danny touched her arm. "They never left the boat. I made sure of it."

"*They?*"

"Jason and Sonny."

"You roped Sonny into this?"

Jason pointed to his right arm. "I couldn't run the boat and man the dock, not with one arm. I needed help."

"He's right. The boat was full of deputies and state troopers, it was raining and pitch black. It wasn't a one-man job."

Lisa glared at him. "So what happened?"

"They were all dead when we got there," Danny said. "Every one of them, including the caretaker. All shot."

Lisa caught her breath, then turned and punched Jason on the good arm.

"What was that for?"

"Wanting to sneak out on to that island by yourself. These people are killers."

"I guess I deserved that."

Danny took a deep breath. "Well, let's take a look at what you've got."

*

Danny summed up all their feelings about the files in one word. "Wow."

They were seated on the couch in the living room, Danny in the middle, in front of the laptop, with Jason and Lisa to either side, watching as she browsed through the entries. It was like being at a birthday party, anticipating her reaction to each new discovery.

After fifteen minutes of letting her make her way at her own pace, Jason finally suggested she listen to the audio file regarding Takashi's death. And his father's. "Try this one."

"Okay." Danny opened the file and sat back in stunned silence as Smith and his boss discussed covering up one murder and the commission of a second.

Jason could still hardly believe what he was hearing.

"Think that will be enough to get a judge to issue a search warrant?"

Danny nodded. "I think that will be enough to issue an arrest warrant. Several of them."

Jason's cell signaled an incoming call.

"Who is that?" Lisa asked.

"I have no idea." He fished the phone out of his pocket and checked the display. "It's Sonny. Wonder what he wants?"

"Probably to see if we're still here."

Danny ignored them. She had moved on to another file.

Jason accepted the call. "What's up?"

"Were you expecting company today?"

"What?"

"There are two black SUVs blocking the drive."

Jason's stomach fell. "Shit."

"What?" Danny looked up at him.

"Somebody's blocked the drive," he told her. "Black SUVs. Were you followed?"

"I wasn't watching." She closed the laptop, stood, and drew her pistol from the holster on her waistband.

Jason got back on the phone. "Sonny?"

"What do you want me to do?"

"Call 911. Report an officer needs assistance, shots fired, everything you can. Get the cavalry out here."

"Got it."

They disconnected.

"Make sure all the doors are locked," Danny told them as she moved toward the living room window. Lisa scurried off to check the back door. Jason quickly locked the front, then hurried back to the laptop, detached the flash drive, and slipped it into his sock.

Lisa returned from the back. "Everything's locked."

"Good," Danny said. "Now which one of you is the better shot?" She pulled the little .32 from her ankle holster.

Lisa shook her head.

"Left-handed," Jason said. "But I can make them think about it."

"That might be enough."

Just then, he saw the first shadowy figure emerge from the trees and slip through the fog to hide behind the Jetta. He was carrying a submachine gun.

CHAPTER 19

"Stay low and away from the windows," Danny told them.

No one argued. They hugged the floor well below the line of sight of the windows.

"What do we do?" Lisa asked, her voice high and tight.

"Get in the kitchen. And stay low."

Again, no one argued. Danny seemed to know what she was doing.

At least someone did.

"Go!" she urged them. "Get in the kitchen!"

Lisa didn't need to be told again. Like a lizard, she scrambled across the floor on her belly and disappeared through the kitchen doorway. It was an athletic maneuver Jason couldn't hope to duplicate, not with his right arm in a sling.

Besides, he had something else he needed to do.

He crouched as low as he could, darted over to the coffee table and grabbed his laptop.

His whole life was on it.

Someone shouted outside.

Jason slipped the laptop under his injured right arm, grabbed his briefcase, and, still crouching as low as he could, sprinted for the kitchen.

"Jason!" Danny yelled.

A string of flat reports sounded outside. The living room window shattered and a flock of angry sparrows darted past his head to slam into the wall above the couch. Splinters flew everywhere.

"Damn it! I said stay down!" Danny yelled.

Jason slid on his knees through the kitchen doorway.

Danny fired three quick shots through the window, then dove after Jason. The fog lit up with another burst of automatic gunfire. Slugs slammed into the wall above the couch and the couch itself. Pieces of upholstery and stuffing spit into the air.

Lisa was curled in a fetal position at the base of the sink, her hands covering her head. Jason scrambled over to her, let the laptop and briefcase slide to the floor. "You okay?"

She cringed at his touch, then shook her head.

Jason looked over to Danny who sat on the floor across the room with her back against one of the cabinets. Glass sparkled in her hair and a thin trickle of blood ran down from her right temple.

"You're bleeding," Jason said. "You okay?"

"Just glass," she said. "You guys?"

"Fine," Jason told her. "Scared shitless, but fine."

Danny pulled the clip from her pistol to check the remaining ammunition, then replaced it.

"So, what's our plan?"

"Hold out until help gets here," Danny said. "Other than that...." She shrugged.

It didn't seem like much of a plan, but Jason couldn't think of anything better. Defensively, the kitchen was a pretty good place to make a stand. The only door opened into the living room, the only window was a smallish one above the sink, and there were plenty of cabinets and appliances around to help stop bullets. The outside walls were also whole logs, much thicker than a normal house, which offered them even more protection.

Of course, Lundgren's goons had them terribly outgunned. Their submachine guns could pump out slugs about a hundred times faster than his and Danny's pistols. If their attackers decided to rush them, they wouldn't stand much of a chance.

Jason hoped it wouldn't come to that.

"I'm sorry guys," Danny said. "I guess I led them right to us."

Jason shook his head. "We all thought it was over."

"Who are they?" Lisa asked. "Why are they doing this?"

"Lundgren's extermination squad," Danny told her. "We're the last loose ends. They kill us and Lundgren doesn't have anything to worry about."

"Oh, God...."

Jason grabbed Lisa's hand and gave it a squeeze. "Sonny called for help. It's on its way."

Lisa nodded, barely.

He strained to hear the wail of approaching sirens, but could hear nothing. Literally. The air was dead silent. No sirens, no distant television, no birds calling. He couldn't even hear anything from their attackers. Was it just a trick of the fog? Fog could do some weird things with sound, muffling the voice of someone in your yard, yet carrying a dog's bark for miles.

He wanted to hear emergency vehicles. Surely Sonny had called for help? Surely Danny's colleagues were on their way?

Unless Lundgren's hit squad had gotten to Sonny before he could make the call.

Jason pulled out his cell and punched in 911. Nothing. He didn't have service.

"What are they doing?" Lisa finally removed her hands from her head and looked up at them. "It's so quiet. Maybe they left."

It had been quiet for a long time. A very long time.

"No, I don't think so." Jason shook his head and returned the cell to his pocket. "They haven't gone anywhere."

"What are they doing?"

Danny turned her gaze from the doorway to Lisa. "Probably figuring out how to kill us without losing any of their own people. They know we're armed now; that changes things."

Jason agreed. "They were counting on surprising us. Now they're coming up with Plan 'B.'"

Where were those sirens?

Glass crashed in the back of the house, followed by a curious *pop*! The stench of gasoline flooded the air. Followed by the distinctive sound of fire. Black smoke began to drift into the kitchen.

"Crap!" Danny said and sat up straight, alert.

More glass shattered out in the living room. Again, an explosive *whump* was followed by the glow and roar of a fire.

Molotov cocktails. They'd firebombed the house.

"Oh, God," Lisa moaned. "We're going to burn to death."

Actually, Jason thought as he eyed the thickening layer of smoke churning below the ceiling, they'd probably suffocate long before the actual fire reached them. Most people did. Of course, he wasn't about to tell Lisa that. He squeezed her hand.

The smoke was building quickly. Black and churning with trapped heat, the layer was already building down to the counter tops, just above their heads. Soon they'd be swimming in it.

His lungs were beginning to protest. Beside him, Lisa coughed.

Panic began to nibble at the edges of his consciousness. They had to make a choice soon: stay in the house and die in the fire, or make a run for it and face those submachine guns.

Talk about a Catch-22.

Lisa coughed again, a deep, rasping cough.

Jason looked over at Danny. "Ideas?"

Danny was looking at something over his head. "Yeah, actually." She raised her pistol and aimed it at something behind and above him. "Cover your heads."

Jason and Lisa did as Danny fired two quick shots at the kitchen window above them. Jason heard the slugs hit the glass. Splinters fell into the kitchen sink.

"Damn it!"

"What?" Jason asked. The fire had grown loud enough that they had to raise their voices to be heard.

"It didn't break."

Jason looked up and saw that her shots had merely punched two holes in the glass, rather than shattering it.

Lisa began coughing again.

"Stay on the floor," he told her. "As low as you can get. Try to stay under the smoke."

Then his lungs too decided they'd had enough and he fell into a fit of coughing that left his throat and chest feeling scraped and raw.

Across the kitchen Danny frantically tore through the contents of the cabinets around her. Now she sat up with a six-inch cast iron skillet. "Cover your heads."

They did.

Danny heaved the skillet. Above and behind him, Jason heard the window shatter. A strong, warm breeze began to flow through the kitchen and out the window. The good news was that much of the smoke was sucked out on the breeze. The bad news was that the draft had kicked the fire into a new level of intensity.

Outside, Jason heard a sharp *crack*! Someone shouted. One of the submachine guns loosed a long string of shots. A second loosed a smaller, shorter burst. None of the slugs seemed to hit the house.

"Hear that?" Jason asked Danny.

She nodded. "Someone's out there. Someone on our side."

Maybe the cops had finally arrived. Maybe they'd come without their sirens.

Just in the nick of time, too. Jason could clearly see flames immediately outside the kitchen doorway. The heat felt like a blast furnace.

Another *crack!* It sounded like a high-powered rifle. A sniper rifle.

A short machine gun blast answered.

A man yelled something.

Then silence.

What was going on out there?

Lisa was coughing almost continuously now and the fire was so fierce and close it sounded like a jet engine. His own throat felt like he'd inhaled sawdust. Across the room, Danny too was coughing. They had to make a decision and they had to make it soon. Stay here and die or take their chances against Lundgren's guns.

He looked over at Danny. "We've got to get out of here."

She nodded, but made no move.

"Jason!" a voice called through the roar of the fire. "Jason!"

It was Sonny. Sonny was out there.

"Jason! Can you hear me?"

Jason pushed himself to his feet. It was harder than he'd expected and he had to steady himself on the counter against a sudden light-headedness. "Sonny!" He yelled through the broken kitchen window, as smoke poured past him. "Over here!"

Sonny appeared on the other side of the window. He was carrying a submachine gun, like the Lundgren thugs had been carrying. A hunting rifle was slung over his shoulder. "Get out of there! The whole house is going up!"

"Where are the other guys?"

"They're gone! Get out of there!"

Jason and Sonny used the butts of their guns to knock the remaining shards of glass from the window frame. Jason then helped Lisa, who was barely hanging on to consciousness, climb up on to the sink and through the window, where Sonny eased her to the ground and away from the burning building. Danny dove through the window next, landing in a rolling somersault and staggering off into the parking area.

Jason tossed his briefcase through the window and held his laptop safely against his chest as he awkwardly slid feet first through the window. He hit the porch, grabbed his briefcase and ran for the cars.

A portion of the house's roof collapsed behind him with a tremendous crash and blast of heat.

Jason stumbled to the ground beside the others, his entire body now wracked with horrible coughing.

"Your laptop?" Danny asked. Her face was smeared with soot and blood. "Really?"

"You wouldn't understand."

"You're right."

Lisa was on her hands and knees beside Danny's Buick, throwing up, or going through the motions anyway. Her stomach had been empty for a while. All her retching produced now was bile.

Sonny crouched beside her, holding her hair out of the line of fire.

Jason crawled over to Lisa. "How are you doing?"

Lisa groaned and shook her head.

"Oh, fuck," Sonny said and reached for the submachine gun.

Jason looked up. A figure emerged from the edge of the woods. He was dressed in black and carried an assault rifle aimed at them. As Jason reached for his pistol, two more figures emerged from the woods.

"Danny?" Jason said.

"Police!" one of the men yelled. "Drop your weapons! Now!"

"Drop your weapons!"

They did as they were told.

The cavalry had arrived.

*

Within a minute, the property around the burning house was flooded with police. Every agency was represented: the city police in their dark blue uniforms, the county sheriff's wearing brown on tan, and state police, in light blue. A sizable group wore plainclothes, and, of course, the SWAT team, in black, with body armor, helmets, and automatic weapons.

Sonny and Jason were quickly disarmed and placed in handcuffs. At first, it felt like an affront. They were the victims here, the ones who'd been attacked, the good guys. Then the rational part of his brain kicked in and told him it wasn't personal. It was protocol. The police would restrain everyone until the situation was stabilized and the facts could be sorted out.

He did, however, object when they turned their attention to Lisa. She had finally stopped retching, but had collapsed into a fetal position in the gravel.

"Hey, come on," he told the officer. "I really don't think she's much of a threat. Do you?"

The officer hesitated.

"He's right," Danny intervened. Her badge had saved her from her own set of handcuffs. "Post someone to keep an eye on her. That should be enough."

The officer looked skeptical, but put his cuffs away.

"Are EMT's on the way?" Danny asked.

The officer nodded. "As soon as we secure the scene."

They sat there for a good fifteen minutes while the police scoured the property for their assailants. Sonny and Jason sat leaning against the side of Danny's car, their hands secured behind their backs. Danny crouched beside Lisa at their feet, rubbing her back. Lisa didn't move.

A state trooper with an M-16 at the ready stood a few feet away, watching them.

Jason had no doubt whatsoever that he would blow them all away if anyone made a threatening move.

Beside him, Sonny was muttering something under his breath. He was probably complaining about being dragged into this. Jason couldn't blame him.

That was when he first noticed the bodies. There were two of them. One lay just behind the Jetta in a smear of bloody gravel. The other lay a few feet away from the first, closer to the woods. Two police officers were busy giving the second man first aid.

Two shots; two men down, one permanently.

Jason suddenly realized what Sonny was muttering to himself. He was saying "Oh, fuck. Oh, fuck." Over and over like some kind of twisted mantra.

"You were defending us," Jason told him. "It's justifiable."

"Shut up," their guard growled.

Jason did.

The all clear was given a few minutes later. The noise from the burning house, now fully engaged, was approaching the decibel level of a volcano. Flames and smoke punched a hole in the fog and stirred a breeze in the still air. The heat felt like an oven on Jason's face.

Another portion of roof collapsed into the fire, sending a torrent of sparks and cinders shooting into the sky.

The rumbling of heavy diesel engines sounded in the near distance. A few moments later, two fire engines ground out of the fog and parked a few feet behind the cars in the parking area. The truck doors burst open and firemen scrambled to deploy their hoses. The house was beyond saving. Their task would be to prevent the fire from spreading to the surrounding woods, save the nearby cars, and tend to the injured.

Shortly behind the fire trucks came two ambulances. They parked along the tree line opposite the house. The EMT's from the first ambulance hurried over to the wounded man lying on the ground and immediately began working on him. The other EMT's came over to examine Jason, Lisa, and Danny. Soon each had a portable tank connected to a mask pumping out pure oxygen.

It had to be one of the sweetest things Jason had ever experienced. He sat back and sucked in the life-giving gas until the police came to get his version of what had happened.

*

It took more than an hour for the police to satisfy themselves that they knew exactly what had happened at the vacation house. They'd questioned Jason and the others separately, then asked some pointed follow-up questions. Once they'd judged that they had all the information they could get, the officers gathered a few feet away and compared notes. Jason sat with Lisa and Sonny and watched the officers' discussion. He and Sonny were no longer handcuffed, though a uniformed deputy hovered nearby keeping an eye on them.

Lisa still sucked on one of the portable oxygen tanks. She was much better than she had been, but still pale and weak. She had refused the EMT's suggestion that she be checked out at the hospital.

None of the others felt they needed the oxygen anymore.

The house was now little more than a pile of smoking embers, surrounded by firefighters, hosing down hot spots.

The huddle of police officers finally broke up.

A tall, thin man in a sport coat walked over to them, trailed by Danny. "You're all free to go. We may need to contact you at some point, so don't leave the country or anything."

"I need to go to Seattle tonight," Lisa said. Her voice was raw and hoarse from the smoke. It hurt to hear her. "Can I still go?"

"Just make sure we have a phone number in case we need to reach you."

She nodded. "I hate this town."

The detective turned next to Sonny. "I'm afraid we'll have to hold on to your rifle for a while longer."

Sonny nodded.

"We think it's a pretty clearly justifiable, but we'll need to finish the investigation and run it by the district attorney. Until then, it's evidence."

"Take good care of her. My dad gave her to me."

"We will."

"What about the other shooters?" Jason asked.

"They're still at large," Danny told him. "But they're on foot and we've increased patrols in the area. We'll catch them."

"They're the same guys who took out the shooters on Deception Island?"

The detective glanced at Danny, then shook his head. "We haven't been able to establish that. Anything else?"

Jason shook his head.

The detective wished them well and walked back toward the rest of the investigators.

Danny looked at Jason and Lisa, then Sonny. "You guys ready to get out of here?"

*

Lisa insisted she was fine to drive.

She didn't seem fine. Her face was pale, her eyes bloodshot. Her voice was still hoarse and raspy and it was obviously painful to talk. But Jason didn't press the matter. Instinct told him that this was neither the time, nor the place. He buckled himself into the passenger seat and kept his mouth shut.

Sonny climbed into the back seat for the short ride to his truck where he'd left it up on Shoreline. He, too, didn't have much to say.

"You're still coming down to the station?" Danny leaned over to ask through his window. "We need to swear out our statements and I'd like to get some people who matter to look at those files Smith gave you."

"Yeah," he told her. "But I think we'll go by my dad's place first and get cleaned up."

They all looked like they'd been wrestling in campfire-scented charcoal briquettes.

"Don't be too long," Danny told him.

"We won't."

"Watch your back. We still haven't found the rest of those shooters."

Jason nodded.

None of them commented as they passed the two dark SUV's near the entrance to the driveway. They appeared to have been hurriedly pushed out of the way, probably by the fire trucks. One was canted partially on to its side in the ditch. The other had been knocked against a tree on the opposite side of the driveway. Both had police crime scene techs working on them.

"Truck's just to the left," Sonny told them. "On the shoulder."

Lisa turned the car that way.

Jason turned to look back at Sonny. "You okay?"

"Oh, sure. I just killed a couple of guys. I'm hunky-dory."

"If you hadn't, they would have killed us."

Sonny nodded, but didn't seem reassured. He found something fascinating outside his window.

Lisa pulled the Jetta to a stop beside the truck.

"See ya," Sonny said as he climbed out of the car.

"Thank you," Jason told him. "Seriously. For our lives."

Sonny waved weakly and climbed into his truck.

Lisa pulled back on to the highway and headed toward town.

They traveled in a utilitarian silence, broken only when Jason needed to give her directions. Twice they passed squad cars between the house and the edge of town, which was reassuring. The authorities were serious about looking for the shooters. Another car, a city police black-and-white, sat just inside the town line, eying the people in the passing cars. Interesting, Jason thought, since as far as he knew no one knew what the shooters looked like.

Several times as they passed through town, Jason turned and examined the traffic behind them, looking for a tail. He couldn't see anything suspicious.

Lisa kept her eyes on the road in front of her.

When they arrived at the house, Lisa parked behind Jason's car, which was still right where he'd left it Thursday night.

Thursday night? It seemed like it had been a lot longer than that.

They climbed out of the car, popped the trunk, and Jason began to unload his bags from the trunk. Lisa hovered nearby.

"I can get these," he told her. "Why don't you go in and get the shower warmed up?"

"Clean clothes," she croaked, pointing at her bag.

Listening to her made Jason want to wince.

He stepped aside.

She opened her suitcase, rummaged around among the contents before pulling out a pair of jeans, a fresh sweater, and underwear, and then closed the suitcase again. She turned and waited for him.

He needed to unlock the house.

"Oh. Sorry." He grabbed his suitcase with his good hand and led the way up to the front door, unlocked it, and let her in. Somewhat to his surprise, she had picked up both his briefcase and camera bag and carried them in. He decided to just go with it.

He found her fresh towels and showed her to the upstairs shower, then went back and carried in the rest of his bags. His briefcase, though undamaged by the fire, stunk of wood smoke, so he wet a cloth, added a dab of dish soap, and scrubbed down the exterior and then did it again with clear water. That seemed to help.

He dried it off with a dish towel, then opened it to make sure the contents were in decent shape. Of special concern were the Lundgren-related documents they'd collected and perhaps most important of all, his back-up of the flash drive. They were fine.

The only physical casualty of the fire was his laptop case. He simply wiped down the exterior of the laptop with the damp cloth, dried it, and booted it up to make sure nothing critical had been jarred loose in all the excitement. It seemed to be working.

The original flash drive in his sock was just fine. He returned it to his sock. It was as good a spot as any.

Upstairs, the shower shut down with a familiar thump of old pipes in the walls. Growing up it had been a familiar signal. Jeremy was done with his shower. It was his turn.

He hoped a nice hot shower would help Lisa feel better. He was more than aware that neither of them had touched each other since they'd escaped the burning house. Hell, they'd hardly spoken.

*

It took almost three hours to prepare and finalize their statements for the police. Each was paired with an officer who guided them as they wrote out their story on a legal pad. Once their accounts were typed up on the proper forms, each swore that the statements were true and signed them.

Now they were each officially part of the case file, officially witnesses.

Jason had been the most involved so his statement was the longest and most complex. Naturally, he was the last of the three to finish.

Lisa and Danny were sitting in Danny's office when he walked in. Both looked up as though he'd caught them doing something they shouldn't.

Danny managed a smile. "All done?"

"All done," Jason said, pulled out the other office chair and sat beside Lisa. "How you feeling?"

"Okay." She shrugged. "Tired."

Her voice still sounded like someone had taken a rasp to her vocal chords. He reached over to take her hand in his good one. She didn't resist. She even squeezed back.

"I made a few calls," Danny told him, ignoring the hand-holding. "We're going to meet with the task force at 6:00 to present the new evidence."

"We? Am I going to be involved too?" he asked. "Or am I just going to sit there while you present the evidence?"

Danny smiled. "I would never steal your thunder, Jason."

"It isn't you I'm worried about. It's those other guys around the table."

He had long ago lost any illusions about how the police viewed the press. His first assignment had been the police/crime beat and he'd quickly learned that most cops viewed reporters as annoying pests, occasionally useful, but usually just in the way.

Danny smiled fully now. "I'm sure they will be happy to hear from you."

"Good. Because I'm not going to be happy if they try to kick me to the side on this."

"They won't."

He already had a plan to prevent them from freezing him out, but he wasn't going to tell her about it. He didn't want her in the position of being pitted against her colleagues.

Lisa remained notably quiet during the conversation. Now she stirred. "I won't be there."

Jason turned to her. "You won't?"

She shook her head. "I'm catching the ferry at 7:00, remember?"

It was the longest speech he'd heard from her since their close call at the vacation house. It also obviously hurt. By the end, her voice had weakened to little more than a whisper.

"When are you planning to head down there?" Jason asked.

"Soon," was all she said.

"You want me to come down with you?"

She managed a sad-looking smile, but shook her head. "There isn't time."

She had a point.

"On other business," Danny stepped in. "There's been two developments. First, the second man Sonny shot didn't make it. He died on the operating table."

Sonny would take that hard. He was now responsible for two deaths. Justified, or not, he'd still taken two lives.

"Have they identified the men?"

"Both were employees of—you guessed it—Lundgren Corporation."

"Security division, no doubt."

"We haven't been able to determine that yet. Give us a little more time."

Jason had no doubt that was exactly what they would determine.

*

Lisa left for the ferry terminal a little before 5:30. She and Danny exchanged a hug, then she and Jason. Their hug lasted a bit longer. Both wished her a safe trip and that she start feeling better soon. She thanked them both.

"Call me when you get home?" Jason suggested.

She nodded, smiled sadly, and walked out the door.

*

Shortly before 6:00, the members of the task force began to gather in the conference room at the sheriff's substation. Danny and Jason were already there and prepared for their presentation. They had used the time since Lisa left to connect Jason's laptop to a large screen monitor and sound system so everyone would be able to see and hear the contents of Smith's "Ejector" files. Now they just waited for everyone to arrive.

Gradually, the others trickled in and took their places around the battered government-issue table. Jason didn't know a soul among them, though he did recognize a few faces from various encounters over the last week. Judging from the smell of wood smoke filling the room, most of the officers had spent the afternoon at the vacation house. It made sense. It had been a major crime. People had died.

Once everyone had settled into their seats, a middle-aged man with a gray walrus mustache and the air of command cleared his throat. "We all seem to be here. Why don't we get started so we can all get home sometime tonight."

Everyone seemed to like that idea.

He eyed Jason. "I'm Lt. Benjamin Cole of the San Juan County Sheriff's Department. I'm the director of this task force." He then quickly went around the table making introductions. He went so fast Jason never had a chance of remembering any of their names. All he came away with was the impression of investigators from the sheriff's office, the state police, and one lieutenant from the city police. A deputy district attorney sat next to the director.

When he was finished, Jason introduced himself. Everyone around the table nodded politely.

Lt. Cole, the task force director, turned his attention to Danny. "I believe you have something to show us, Sergeant."

Danny stood and gave the task force a brief account of how Jason came into possession of the files they were about to see.

"Excuse me," The Deputy DA interrupted. "Why would he give this information to you?"

"You'd have to ask him," Jason answered. "I can only speculate."

"Please speculate," the DA said.

"I believe he thought his former employers were out to kill him," Jason answered. "I think this was his way of buying himself some cover. A serious distraction, if you will."

The DA seemed satisfied.

"Okay," Lt. Cole said. "Let's see the dirt."

Danny looked to Jason, who clicked on the folder. The password screen popped up.

Jason waited.

Danny looked at him again, more intensely. "Jason?"

He just sat there.

"Is there a problem?" the Lieutenant asked.

"I don't know," Danny said and looked again at Jason, more than a little peeved. "This is the first I've heard of it."

"I believe this is where we begin to negotiate," Jason said. "I have something you want; you have something I want. Let's make a deal."

One of the detectives muttered something about "ultimatums." It wasn't flattering.

"Mr. Reynolds," the DA said. "You realize that if you have evidence relevant to this investigation and withhold it, you can and will be charged with obstructing justice."

"I don't think so," he shook his head. "The files are all on this flash drive. I have no problem turning it over to you right now. I'm sure your tech people will be able to hack the password. Eventually. Providing Mr. Smith didn't imbed a self-destruct code to prevent that. You know, a three-strikes-and-you're-out thing."

He let that sink in for a few moments.

Danny sunk back into her seat. "I'm going to kill you for this," she hissed.

"Sorry."

She made a frustrated sound.

Lt. Cole and the district attorney exchanged a few whispered remarks. The detectives around the table grumbled among themselves, but were largely ignored.

Finally, Lt. Cole asked the question. "What do you want?"

"Access," he said.

"Access?"

"My father is dead. There is evidence here that he was a victim of Lundgren's thugs. They've tried to kill me and my friends twice. I think I've earned access to this investigation."

"You're sitting here now," the DA said. "I don't see any other reporters in the room."

Jason smiled and shook his head. "That's not the kind of access I'm talking about. I want to be there if and when you search Deception Island, not just somewhere nearby, but actually, physically there as you conduct the search."

Lt. Cole scribbled something on his notepad. No one else around the table reacted at all to his request.

"Anything else?" The DA asked.

"I want the exclusive rights to the story for myself and my newspaper the *Seattle News*."

"Right off the bat, we will not allow you, or anyone else to write or publish anything that could compromise our investigation."

"Of course. And I wouldn't knowingly do that. I want you to nail these bastards. I just want your word—in writing—that I get to publish the story first."

"In writing?" The director repeated.

"In writing. But you don't have to get it notarized."

No one laughed.

Lt. Cole and the DA talked some more. This time, the lieutenant from the city police joined in, as did one of the state police investigators.

Danny elbowed him under the table. "I can't believe you pulled this."

He shrugged. "I didn't have a choice."

She just gave him a long look and shook her head.

Finally, Lt. Cole looked up at Jason. "We think we can accept your conditions."

Satisfied, Jason plugged the password into its proper place and opened the files.

CHAPTER 20

As he'd hoped, the contents of Taylor Smith's "Ejector" file raised as much interest and excitement among the members of the task force as it had in both himself and Danny. He spent nearly two hours playing and re-playing audio files, reloading print reports and dossiers as various members asked to see them, and furiously took notes. Finally, someone pointed out that hard copies would need to be made of all the print files to be entered into the various case files.

After they'd seen what they needed to see, the task force moved on to figuring out a strategy for approaching the principals. The DA was largely in charge of this portion and spent nearly as much time on his cell phone with his boss as talking to those around him.

Jason was left entirely out of this portion of the discussion. He might have been granted access to the investigation, but he still wasn't truly a part of it.

At 8:30, Danny finally turned to him. "There's no point in you sitting through all this. Why don't you head home and get some rest? I'll let you know if and when they ever decide on something."

Jason hesitated. The idea of rest was very appealing. It had been a very long day. But part of him still feared being frozen out of whatever was going to happen next.

"Don't worry," Danny told him. "I don't think they'd even consider forgetting your agreement now."

"You don't?"

"I wouldn't let them, anyway."

Jason relented, closed his laptop and started out of the room.

"Jason?"

He stopped and turned back to Danny.

She held out her hand, palm up. "The flash drive?"

"Oh. Yeah." He unplugged the drive and handed it to her, then wrote the password down in her notebook.

"I'll talk to you later," she told them. "Let you know what's going on."

"Thanks," he said and headed for his dad's house.

*

Jason's cell finally rang at a little after 9:30. It was Lisa; she had made it home. He hoped.

He accepted the call. "Hey, you make it home okay?"

"About ten minutes ago."

"How are you feeling?"

Her voice still sounded like something between a frog's croak and the squeak of a rusted hinge. It made him cringe.

"Tired. How'd your meeting go?"

"Good. I think so anyway. Hopefully, we'll be searching the island tomorrow."

"We?"

"Well, the cops will be doing the searching, of course. But I'll be there. I got them to promise me that."

"Good. Give the bastards hell."

Her words ended in a fit of coughing, brief, but painful.

"Sorry," she whispered.

"You probably shouldn't be talking anymore," he told her. "I'll let you go. Get some rest and I'll talk to you tomorrow."

"Thanks."

"And Lisa? I'm sorry."

A pause.

He thought he heard her sigh.

*

The brief conversation with Lisa left Jason feeling depressed and helpless. He was losing Lisa and he could do absolutely nothing about it. Even if he weren't several hours away, there was still nothing he could do, nothing he could say. It was all up to her, her decision alone. If he tried to talk to her now, he risked only making the situation worse.

Knowing that didn't make it any easier.

He found himself wandering from room to room, looking at the artifacts of his family. He needed to close up the house and do something with the contents. That meant keep them or sell them. He still had the auctioneer's card in his wallet. As recommended by his dear friend Taylor Smith. He needed to make some phone calls, get the process started. He need to start packing the items he wanted to keep. There were a lot of things he needed to do.

He didn't feel like doing any of it.

The doorbell rang and he nearly jumped out of his skin.

He wasn't expecting anyone.

Senses on alert, he eased up to the living room window immediately beside the door. The bell rang again, followed by a series of knocks. Impatient? He peeked out the window onto the front porch.

Danny.

He unlocked and opened the door.

"Hey," Danny smiled and held up a bag sporting the logo of Mary Lou's and the unmistakable scent of burgers and fries. "I figured you probably hadn't picked up anything to eat."

He hadn't. The scent of the hamburgers made his stomach growl.

He ushered her in, then quickly glanced out at the street. Danny's Buick was parked at the curb. Otherwise, nothing looked out of place.

"No one followed me," Danny told him. "I was careful."

Jason closed the door and locked it.

"I'm paranoid these days."

"It's not really paranoid when someone is actually trying to kill you."

He led Danny over to the table. As she removed the food from the bag and laid the burgers out in front of their chairs, he went to the refrigerator to find something for them to drink. The choices were somewhat limited.

"I have beer," he told her. "Other than that, it's pretty much water."

"Beer sounds great."

He opened two Coors and brought them back to the table.

Danny was sitting in front of her burger and fries, politely waiting for him to return before beginning. She accepted the bottle of beer from Jason, sipped it, and set it to the side.

Jason pulled out his chair and sat down across from her. "God, that smells wonderful."

"It does, doesn't it?" Danny said and popped a fry into her mouth.

Jason took a bite of his burger. It was the closest thing to heaven he thought he'd ever find. And not even ten dollars.

"So what did the brain trust finally decide?"

Danny smiled and held up a hand so he'd wait while she finished chewing.

"Sorry," he said. "I'm always doing that."

When she looked over at him in puzzlement, he elaborated. "Asking people direct questions right after they take a bite of food."

She nodded and finished chewing. "We're going to search Deception Island first thing in the morning. I thought I'd pick you up at 7:00. That work for you?"

"I'll be ready. No one tried to back out of the agreement?"

"Some grumbled, but I pointed out that you could just as easily have written this stuff up for the paper first, rather than bring it to us. That pretty much squashed the dissent."

"Sorry about ambushing you like that. I didn't want them to think you were in on it."

She waved his apology away.

"So, that's all they're going to do? Search the island?"

Danny shook her head. Again, she had just taken a bite of her burger. He had to wait until she finished chewing and swallowed before she could answer.

"They decided to wait until we searched the island to act. What we find will affect how we move forward."

"But they have enough to charge everyone with conspiracy, don't they?"

"Sure. Plenty," she said. "But it is much easier to prove conspiracy to commit murder if it's obvious a murder was committed. If we can find a body, it will make the case just that much stronger. Not to mention that if we can tie the killing to a specific person, we can use it as leverage. Maybe we can get someone to turn against the others."

That made sense.

He just hoped Lundgren's thugs had merely buried the body somewhere on the island, not dumped it in the Sound. If they'd done that, the body might never be found.

Maybe they'd been confident enough that they'd never considered a search a possibility.

"The state police are going to bring in some cadaver dogs from the mainland," Danny added. "But they won't be able to get there for a couple of hours. Our initial search is going to have to be the old-fashioned kind. Eyes on the ground."

The cadaver dogs could come in very handy, especially since he didn't think Mr. Takashi would be the only body they'd find up there. The tricky part could be convincing everyone to continue the search if they found Takashi's body relatively quickly.

He had a little bit of an idea of how he might be able to finesse that too.

Danny peered at him. "You have that look in your eyes again. What's going on in that brain of yours?"

"Just an idea," he shook his head. "Nothing important."

"Why do I not believe that?"

"Nothing that will embarrass you or jeopardize the case."

"Promise?"

"Cross my heart."

She seemed to accept that. "Have you talked to Lisa?"

"Yeah," he nodded. "Just for a little bit. Her throat is still bad, but she made it home safely."

Danny played with a French fry, dragging it back and forth through a puddle of ketchup. "She's had a tough time of it."

He nodded. "I know."

"It's tough enough for us to be almost killed, but it's part of the job, you know?"

He did.

"Lisa doesn't live in that world. Until now she hadn't even visited it. It's got to be a shock."

She was right. Until this week, Lisa hadn't had to deal with anything more dangerous than the academic backstabbing of the university. There, the politics were a minefield that could destroy one's career, but were seldom life-threatening.

Danny looked up at him. "She's going to need a little time to get used to this."

"If she can."

Danny nodded. "If she can."

That was the question, wasn't it? Whether she could get used to the idea that sometimes Jason's job, if he did it right, would place him and those around him in danger. And whether she could live with that danger.

*

At 8:00 Tuesday morning, Jason stood beside Danny on the edge of a group of about twenty officers gathered outside the caretaker's house on Deception Island. The house itself still held the seal the state police had placed over the door. It was an active crime scene, though it had nothing to do with why they were out here this morning.

The fog from yesterday was still hanging around, but the temperature had dropped into the mid-thirties overnight. It wasn't freezing, but it was close. Every officer there wore a heavy coat, knit cap, and gloves. Most of them sipped cooling coffee from paper cups and shuffled their feet to try and build up body heat. Jason had his own tall Starbucks, plus he'd put the hood of his sweatshirt up over his watch cap.

He was still cold.

But he wouldn't have given up this chance for the warmest tropical beach.

"I wouldn't be surprised if we get snow before the day's over," Danny said.

"Is that what the forecast says?"

"No." She shrugged. "But it feels like snow."

"It feels like ice. My feet are going numb."

She laughed.

"Gather round people!" someone yelled out and the conversations across the group quieted. "Let's get this thing started before we all freeze to death."

Several of the officers chuckled.

"Listen up. I've got some instructions for you."

The officers moved closer and grew quiet. They were as interested as anybody in getting this task finished and getting out of the cold.

Jason and Danny moved up with the others to easy hearing distance.

"Okay folks, listen up!" the man who had taken charge said. Jason recognized him as one of the detectives who'd been sitting at the table during yesterday's meeting. He couldn't, however, remember his name or which agency he worked for.

The final snatches of conversation within the group faded away.

"For those of you who haven't heard, we're looking for a DB today."

Someone in the group groaned.

"Yeah," he said. "This is why we make the big money."

A few laughed, but it was a strained laugh. It had been a trying week for everyone.

"This is going to be a grid search. If you've conducted a crime scene search, you know how this works. We'll form a line across the section at fixed intervals and walk forward, each person examining the ground in front and to either side of him or her. There is no prize for finishing first. It's more important that every square inch of the area is examined, that every piece of possible evidence is found and marked."

He turned to another man, who began handing something to the officers.

"Det. Solbane is handing out bundles of evidence flags. Should you find something that might be evidence, you will place one of these flags beside it to mark it for further examination."

Just like a crime scene, Jason thought. In reality, that was exactly what the island was: a crime scene. Greg Takashi had been shot and killed here, but he was only the most recent victim. Most of the police had no idea the number or extent of the crimes Jason believed had been committed here.

Would some evidence of those crimes be found?

"Now, a word about what we're looking for," the lead detective continued. "We believe the victim was killed somewhere on this island and the body hidden here. We have no idea how. It could have been buried, dumped in a patch of woods, or hidden in a pile of debris, so look for anything that looks out of place and fairly recent. The weather has been on the cool side, so we don't expect decomp to have progressed much, but pay attention to your nose. You might smell the body before you ever see it."

Danny shook her head. "There's no mistaking the smell of a decomposing body. You ever had the pleasure?"

Jason shook his head. "A cat died in the crawlspace under our house once."

"We also believe the primary crime scene is within our search area," the detective continued. "So keep an eye out for anything that might be out of the ordinary. The rain has probably destroyed any blood evidence, but there still could be brass, slugs, personal effects. So keep your eyes open and mark anything that looks out of place."

He checked his notebook to make sure he'd covered everything necessary.

"If there aren't any questions, let's get this thing started. We've got a lot of ground to cover."

*

Deception Island was a little over a mile long and shaped like an elongated water drop, with the wider part, maybe a half mile in width, at the western end. This was where Lundgren had built the caretaker's house and the complex of decaying warehouses and outbuildings the caretaker had been paid to watch over. The land to the east of the buildings rose in a series of gently rolling grassy hills, broken by the occasional oak or madrone and a few tangles of blackberry.

This part of the island would be relatively easy to search.

Harder to search would be the eastern portion of the island. Though it was narrower, scarcely a quarter mile wide for the most part, it was largely a single steep ridge rising as much as two hundred feet above the Sound, with deep ravines cut into the sides. It was also covered with the native forest of mixed cedar and hemlock. The dense shrubbery and ferns forming the understory of the forest could hide most anything from the casual observer.

All in all, the island formed some seven million square feet that needed to be searched.

They were doing it with scarcely twenty people in five yard intervals, walking at a speed of 2.5 feet per second. And the fog meant none of them could see anything more than twenty feet away ahead.

Also, from everything Jason had deduced, they were starting at the wrong end of the island.

*

It was just after 9:30 in the morning and they'd been searching for almost an hour and a half. It was still foggy and about as close to freezing as air could get without actually forming ice. Jason was particularly feeling the cold. He had tried to think of everything when he'd packed, but walking a grid search through shin-high wet grass was something he had not anticipated. Within minutes, his feet had been soaked, then they'd grown cold and stayed there.

They had just started their third grid, beginning from the crumbling remains of an old foundation and working east. So far there had been nothing found to generate any excitement.

It was a good definition of tedium.

"So," Danny said from her spot five yards to his right. "How's it working out?"

"How's what working out?"

"Your secret plan."

He looked over at her. "What secret plan?"

"The one you came up with when we were talking last night."

"Oh," he said. "That one. Well, it's early."

Danny stopped to bend down and examine something in the grass ahead of her. She quickly decided whatever she'd seen was insignificant and straightened up again. All her evidence flags still hung from her belt.

Jason carried all of his in his sling.

Almost two hours of searching and not a single piece of evidence.

"Can you tell me what the plan is yet?" Danny asked.

He shook his head. "Only if it works."

Someone shouted off to Jason's left, toward the center of the search line.

"Found something!" a young officer in a black watch cap called out. "It looks like someone's been digging here!"

The search line came to a sudden halt. Within seconds, people began to wander over to see the first find of the day. This, despite instructions to maintain the line's integrity. They were supposed to just mark any finds and keep going.

But then again, if they found the body early, they might be able to go home.

"I've got to see this," Jason told Danny. He was already feeling the excitement. "My plan may be working."

She shrugged and followed him.

Jason pushed his way through those gathered around the find. The officer who found it had been right. Someone had been digging here. What was left was an irregular oval of earth amid the expanse of grass, as though someone had dug a hole, then filled it in again. The surface was packed and weathered. It had been like this for a while, but not long enough for the grass to regrow.

"Well, someone's certainly dug here," one of the detectives said. "But it's a little small to hold a body."

"Maybe they buried him standing up," somebody said.

Chuckles spread through the gathered officers.

"Okay," the detective said. "False alarm. Let's get back to the search and find a body."

The searchers groaned, but began moving back toward their search positions.

"Aren't you even going to look at it?" Jason asked the detective.

He looked a little surprised by the question. "Probably, sooner or later. But our priority, as stated in the search warrant, is finding a dead body. I don't think it's in that hole."

"But there could be other things, the murder weapon, personal effects. We won't know until we look at it."

"Jason...," Danny whispered.

He ignored her. "Somebody dug that hole for a reason. I doubt they were planting a tree."

"Like I said, we'll get to it."

"How about if I take a look?"

The detective sighed heavily and peered at him. "Reynolds, isn't it?"

Jason nodded.

"I appreciate your enthusiasm, but I hardly think you're qualified to conduct a forensic excavation."

"Sgt. Hayden can make sure I don't ruin anything."

"Fine," the detective gave up. "Grab a shovel at the staging area and knock yourself out."

He turned on his heel and went to join the search line, which had already reassembled and was ten yards beyond the hole now.

"What was that all about?" Danny asked.

"My plan."

"Your plan? I don't get it."

But Jason was already headed back to the area in front of the caretaker's house where they'd received their briefing this morning, looking for a shovel. He didn't slow down to answer her.

Danny decided to stay beside the suspicious spot of ground until he returned. If evidence really was here, it was important to be able to prove no one had tampered with it. That, and she had no desire to follow him around the island like a puppy.

She sipped her coffee and waited.

It would be interesting to see how he planned to work a shovel one-handed.

*

Actually, working the shovel wouldn't be much of a problem. Anyone who's ever used one knows that most of the actual work is done with your feet (driving it into the ground) and your left hand (lifting and moving the debris). The right hand simply helps guide it and provide some leverage when needed.

Danny was impressed.

"So how do I do a forensic excavation?" he asked her. "As opposed to simply digging a hole?"

"Basically, you go slower and more carefully," she told him. "You don't want to destroy anything while you're trying to discover it."

He nodded. "Makes sense."

"Take it slow, one shovelful at a time. If you think you've found something substantial, we stop and finish the excavation by hand."

He thought he could do that.

"Mind telling me what we're looking for?" she asked. "It might help if I had some idea. Especially since you won't tell me about your plan."

He smiled. "My plan worked perfectly. We're digging here, aren't we?"

She just looked at him.

Jason slid the shovel into the dirt, lifted it and dumped it off to the side. Fortunately, since the area had recently been disturbed, it yielded easily to his shovel. This was a good thing, because though he truly did most of the work with his left hand and feet, it would have been much more difficult had the earth been packed.

Also on the plus side was that the physical labor generated body heat. His feet were still cold, but for the first time all morning he was generally comfortable.

"Well, what are we looking for?" Danny repeated.

"The same thing Takashi was looking for; something big enough and bad enough for Lundgren to kill to keep secret."

"Okay...."

He removed another shovel's worth of dirt from the hole and dropped it on the growing pile to the side. So far, they'd revealed nothing but dirt and a few small rocks.

He looked up at her. "We know that Lundgren's thugs killed Takashi somewhere on this island, right?"

She nodded. "That's why we're here. To look for his body."

"And they'll find it. Eventually." He pointed to the forested ridge at the east end of the island, well beyond the line of searchers. "Up there somewhere."

Danny frowned. "Up there?"

"Remember, I'd gotten my dad's chart and figured out how they'd gotten on the island?"

"I remember something about that."

"Well, the spot my dad marked was a ravine on the southeast corner of the island. If, as we believe and the 'Ejector' file seems to confirm, Takashi was killed while he and my dad were fleeing from Lundgren's thugs, that's where they would be headed. I think they were about to go into the woods. Lundgren's people panicked, thinking they'd lose them in the trees, and opened fire."

"And you didn't tell us this because...?"

"If I had, you wouldn't have searched this area," he told her. "And we wouldn't we digging here right now."

She looked at him. "That was your plan? To get us to search this area?"

"That was the plan."

"You knew this hole would be here?"

"I thought it might."

"Why?"

"Because Takashi dug it. It was what he was doing when Lundgren's thugs caught him."

*

"Okay," Danny said. "We agree that Takashi might have dug the original hole. That still doesn't explain what he was looking for. Or what we're looking for."

Jason emptied another shovel full of dirt on to the growing pile beside the hole and leaned on the shovel. Their hole was now about a foot deep and about two feet in diameter. So far, they hadn't uncovered anything interesting.

"Takashi was researching the internment of the Japanese during WWII for his Master's thesis, right?"

Danny nodded.

"Following his trail, we learned that Lundgren contracted with the government to evacuate the Japanese-Americans from the San Juan Islands and transport them to a camp in Tacoma. To help with that process, they established a temporary holding facility here on Deception Island. Several men from Port Salish, including my grandfather and two of the Morgans, were hired as guards at the camp."

"Okay."

"Well, as Lisa found out in the archives of the local paper, the whole thing was pretty big news around here, with numerous articles, editorials, and photo spreads for several weeks." He slid the shovel into the dirt again. "Then all coverage suddenly stops."

"I remember," Danny said. "But couldn't that just mean they'd shipped the prisoners to Tacoma and shut down the camp?"

"Sure, it's possible." Jason dumped another load of dirt on to the pile. "But that's not how the newspaper business works, especially the local paper in a quiet little town. It was big news. There should have been stories about the process of loading up the prisoners, photos of the ship, that sort of thing. Then they'd follow it with stories and photos of the process of shutting the camp down. They did nothing of the kind."

Danny had squatted down to look through the latest load of dirt. She caught Jason's eye and shook her head. "So, why wouldn't they cover it?"

"Because it never happened," he told her. "And someone with a lot of power and a lot of money persuaded them to make the whole thing go away."

Danny straightened up and brushed the soil off her gloves. "What are you thinking?"

"I'm probably thinking the same thing Takashi was thinking and trying to prove," he told her. "That Lundgren Corporation saw a higher profit margin in never actually transporting their prisoners, but pretending they had and billing the government."

"God...." Danny peered down at the growing hole. "So you're thinking...."

Jason nodded. "They killed them all, men, women, and children, and then covered it up. That's what the leases were for, to keep people quiet."

Danny was still staring into the hole, as though it held the secrets of the universe.

"I think we're standing on top of a mass grave."

*

Fifteen minutes later, Jason's shovel hit something solid.

He stopped and looked up at Danny. "I think we've got something."

"A rock?" Danny asked.

"I don't think so. It didn't feel that hard." It was solid, but not as solid as basalt.

He set the shovel aside and reached down into the hole, scooping out the dirt with his good hand. Danny crouched at the edge of the hole, watching. Within a few seconds, something appeared amid the earth at the bottom of the hole, something large and dirty white.

"Jesus," Danny whispered quietly.

He removed a few more scoops of soil and the shape of the object became clear. It was a skull. A human skull. They had uncovered it from the eye sockets to the cranium. A bullet hole was clearly visible just above the eyes.

"You better stop," Danny told him. "Let the crime scene people do the rest."

Jason climbed out of the hole. He stood there, gazing down at the artifact they'd just uncovered. Danny stood quietly beside him.

"I don't think that's Greg Takashi," he said.

"No, I don't think so," Danny agreed.

The skull was clearly too old to be Takashi's.

Danny raised her radio to her mouth. "This is Sgt. Hayden. I'm at the hole the search turned up this morning. We've found human remains. You'd better get some crime scene people over here."

*

With the help of the state police cadaver dogs, who finally showed up at lunch time, the search team found the partially decomposed remains of a young Asian man about twenty yards inside the tree line on the eastern part of the island. It was 4:30 in the afternoon. It quickly became apparent that the young man had been shot twice with a medium caliber round, probably 9mm, and then dragged off the trail and hastily concealed under loose brush and leaf debris.

Though positive identification would still have to be made by the Medical Examiner, no one present had much doubt who the body was.

Perhaps the most encouraging detail of the find was the fact that one of the slugs that had killed young Mr. Takashi had not exited his body. Which meant they would have ballistic evidence, just as soon as the ME recovered it.

Normally, that would be enough to make the day a success. Finding a dead body was never exactly celebrated, but there was a certain satisfaction.

But this day was anything but normal because of what they were uncovering on the west end of the island.

By the time it had grown too dark to safely work any longer, the crime scene people had uncovered ten skeletonized bodies, all of them showing some sign of gunshot wounds. Two of the skeletons appeared to be children.

With no end in sight.

The search team had returned after finding Takashi's body and formed a loose ring around the growing scar in the earth where the techs worked to uncover the remains. They stood and watched, quietly sipping their coffee, saying nothing. The entire scene was strangely, eerily quiet.

Jason and Danny also stood nearby, watching the progress of the excavation. They, also, had very little to say.

As it grew dark, the leader of the excavation team called the lead detective over.

"Look, it's decision time," he told the detective. "I see no sign that we're getting close to the end, but we're running out of daylight. Either we call it a day and come back at first light, or we're going to need to bring in some flood lights. It's your call."

"Okay." The detective said and rubbed a hand over his brow. "By the time we could get lights out here and set up, half the night would be gone anyway. Why don't you secure the site and start fresh tomorrow?"

The crime scene tech began directing his fellow techs on securing the site for the night.

The detective spotted Jason and walked over. "Something else, isn't it?"

Jason nodded.

"You knew these bodies were going to be here?"

"No," he shook his head. "I had my suspicions, but I wasn't sure."

The detective nodded. "So do you have any suspicions as to how many bodies we're looking at here?"

Jason glanced at Danny. She nodded.

He turned back to the detective. "If it's what I think it is, about two hundred."

"Two hundred?"

"Give or take a few."

CHAPTER 21

Cell phone service was sketchy at best on Deception Island. For Jason, whose service provider didn't operate at all in San Juan County, it was nonexistent. He would occasionally get one bar if he was in the right location, at the right altitude, and facing the right direction, but in practical terms, he was cut off from the rest of the world.

It was nearly 8:00 before he, Danny, and the other officers finally returned to the marina at Port Salish. Each was cold and tired, and not just from the long day hiking across the island. Finding the remains of so many murder victims had cast a pall over everyone. No one chatted much on the boat as they headed back to town. No one joked. No one wanted to think about the implications for their little community of what they'd just found.

Almost as soon as the boat pulled into the dock, Jason's cell phone chirped that he had unread messages.

Three of the messages were from Lisa, two texts and one voice mail. The first one was a text, sent at 6:05pm, shortly after she would have arrived home from class.

How's the search going?

"Anything important?" Danny asked.

"Lisa," he told her. "She wanted to know how the search is going."

"Tell her to watch the news tomorrow. It will be interesting. I guarantee it."

As the saying went, the shit would hit the fan tomorrow. Now that they had Takashi's body, nothing would hold law enforcement back.

Miles would probably appreciate a heads-up, too.

He punched in the code to access his voice mail.

A moment later, Lisa's voice was playing in his ear, still hoarse, but stronger than it had been the day before. "Hey. I hope you're okay. Do you get cell service on that island? Well, I hope you're okay. I'll try again a little later."

The phone call had come in at 6:37.

He turned to the final text. It had been sent at 7:25.

Going to bed. Hope all is well. I'll try again tomorrow.

Her last text had been sent almost a half hour ago, which meant she was probably asleep by now. He wanted to at least let her know he was fine, but didn't want to wake her.

He'd call her first thing in the morning.

"Come on," Danny said, climbing out of the boat. "It's going to be another long day tomorrow. Let's get something to eat and call it a night."

Jason pocketed his phone and followed her.

*

Mr. Joseph Mullen, Director of Security for Lundgren Corporation, arrived at his office on the nineteenth floor of the Lundgren Building in Seattle at precisely 7:30 Wednesday morning, just as he had every other weekday for the past twenty years. He was a workaholic and an unrepentant one. His wife, the former Miss Eva Lundgren, had long ago learned to accept the fact that she would seldom see him before 8:00 at night. Working longer and harder than everyone else was how he'd climbed to his present position and held on to it. Others might have more talent, or be smarter than he, but no one would ever outwork him.

He was also notorious for demanding the same from those who worked for him.

"Good morning, sir," Jesse, his assistant, said as Mullen passed his desk. "Your messages and the briefing are on your desk."

Mullen nodded in acknowledgment, though it would have been more newsworthy had his messages and briefing not been on his desk first thing in the morning. One of Jesse's duties was to come in early and go through all the daily reports from their teams in the field, assembling the critical information into a digest Mullen could go over when he arrived.

"Any word from X-ray?" he asked.

X-ray was the team he'd sent to Port Salish to clean up Smith's mess.

"No, sir. Nothing yet."

"Nothing?"

Jesse shook his head.

Mullen's team leaders never forgot their daily reports. Ever. It was part of the reason why they were team leaders.

No report usually meant someone was either incapacitated or in jail. Either way, it wasn't good news.

"Anyone tried to contact them?"

"There's been no response yet, sir."

Mullen walked into his office and closed the door behind him. He removed his overcoat and hung it in the closet, then walked over to the sideboard and poured himself a cup of the Celebes-grown coffee he preferred. Jesse, of course, had brewed a pot to be ready when he walked in. Another one of his duties.

Mullen sipped his coffee, walked over to his desk and sat down.

The daily briefing was centered on this blotter. His message slips were arranged to his right, with the highest priority messages on top.

He started up his computer and turned to the briefing.

The office door burst open and a half dozen men in cheap suits strode in.

"What the hell?" Mullen surged to his feet. "You can't just walk in here!"

No one walked into Joseph Mullen's office without knocking. Not even Leo Lundgren himself.

"Actually, we can," one of the men said.

"Joseph Mullen?" another said. "We have a warrant for your arrest."

"That's preposterous." He couldn't believe what he was hearing. "On what charge?"

"How about conspiracy to commit murder, to start with?"

Mullen stood in shock as his hands were pulled behind his back and handcuffs snapped around his wrists. As he was led from the room, other officers began dismantling his computer and going through his files.

*

No one asked Joseph Mullen whether he felt alone and humiliated as they led him out of the building. To tell the truth, the arresting officers, detectives from the Seattle barracks of the Washington State Police, didn't give a flip how he felt. They were merely serving an arrest warrant out of San Juan County. Just doing their job.

It isn't clear whether the truth would have made Mullen feel any better anyway. For at the same time as the arrest warrant was served on him and search warrants served to seize his office computer, his assistant's office computer, any and all digital communication devices, and any documents referring or related to Port Salish, Gregory Takashi, Lee Reynolds, Jason Reynolds, Danielle Hayden, Taylor Smith, and/or any operations taking place in Port Salish, Washington, similar warrants were served on Lundgren Corporation's accounting department, operations department, executive department, legal department and the security division at large.

All in all, with police officers and evidence techs seizing computers and digital communication devices and going through files, business at Lundgren Corporation came to a screeching halt.

*

At the same time as the forces of the state police descended upon the office of the Lundgren Corporation in Seattle, a dozen detectives and deputies from the San Juan County Sheriff's Department and the Port Salish City Police walked into the main branch of Evergreen Bank. Without too much fuss, Martin Haislip, III and his father, Martin Haislip, II were both taken into custody on charges of conspiracy to commit murder, obstruction of justice, tampering with witnesses, theft by deception, and fraud. The junior Haislip openly wept while he was led out of the building in handcuffs. His father managed to maintain a semblance of dignity.

At the same time as the Haislips were being arrested, search warrants were served on the remaining bank officers for any and all documents relating to the perpetual leases, the dispositions of all properties the bank handled for Japanese internees during the war years, all communications between the bank and Lundgren Corporation, and any financial transactions between the companies.

Needless to say, Evergreen Bank was also closed for business for the day.

*

At 8:00 Wednesday morning, the San Juan County district attorney's office issued subpoenas to Pacific Wireless, the contracted wireless carrier for all Lundgren Corporation's company-issued smart phones, requesting the telephone and text records for all transactions by Leo Lundgren, the CEO of Lundgren Corporation; Richard Ward, the chief operating officer; Joseph Mullen, the director of security; Jesse Young, his administrative assistant; Taylor Smith, security team manager; and Todd Baxter, Benjamin Jackson, Thomas Anderson, and Melissa Devereux, all security operatives. The subpoenas covered the four weeks ending the day before.

*

At 9:00 Wednesday morning, Ben Jackson was escorted from his cell in the San Juan County jail in Friday Harbor and shown into an interview room. Jeremy Hall, the attorney Lundgren had provided for him was already in the room, a legal pad on the scarred table in front of him, ready for notes.

He stood when Jackson entered the room and the two men shook hands. "How are you doing? The food's not too bad, I hope."

Jackson shook his head. "Nothing I can't handle. What's this all about? My arraignment?"

He was supposed to have been arraigned two days ago, but the routine procedure had been postponed at the last minute. There had been no explanation for the postponement.

"Not a clue," Hall shook his head. "The DA requested this meeting, but I have no idea what he wants."

Jackson sat down in the chair beside his attorney. "Maybe a plea offer?"

The attorney shrugged. "It's possible."

They sat in relative silence for the next ten minutes until the door opened and Assistant District Attorney David Sherman swept in, accompanied by a serious-looking woman in a business suit. Both carried heavy briefcases, which they set on the floor before sitting down. ADA Sherman took the chair opposite Hall, while his companion took the chair opposite Jackson.

"This is District Attorney Andrea Meade," ADA Sherman said. "She asked for this meeting."

Hall nodded politely at the district attorney, who returned it without a smile.

"What can we do for you, counselor?" Hall asked.

The ADA bent down and drew a form from his briefcase. "We're formally notifying you that we're amending the charges against your client." He slid the form across to Hall. "To include two counts of conspiracy to commit murder, two counts of obstruction of justice, and two counts of tampering with evidence."

Hall took the form and looked over it. "Where did this come from?"

"We have received new evidence," the DA spoke for the first time. "And there's more."

Hall looked up at her. "Do tell."

"Yesterday afternoon," she said. "The body of Gregory Takashi was found on Deception Island. As we speak, the bullet that killed him is at the state crime lab for ballistic testing. We expect to have the results by this evening. When we do, we will be filing first-degree murder charges."

"You wouldn't be talking to us if you didn't have something to offer," Hall said.

"I'm making the same offer to you and each of your colleagues," DA Meade said. "The first one to come clean, and agree to testify against the others gets the deal. Everyone else takes their chances with the jury. The clock is ticking."

"And what is the nature of the deal?" Hall asked. "What's in it for us?"

"How about the possibility of getting out of prison in time to see your grandkids graduate?"

"You've got to be kidding," Jackson said.

"Not in the slightest," she shook her head. "Ask your attorney what the sentencing guidelines are for two counts of murder conspiracy."

"We'll need some time to discuss this," Hall told her. "I'd also like to see the evidence against my client."

"Of course. I'll have copies sent to you," DA Meade rose to her feet. "But remember, it's first come, first served on this deal, so don't discuss it too long."

She picked her briefcase off the floor and headed toward the door.

The ADA followed her. At the door, he stopped and turned back toward the two men still at the table. "Oh, a piece of friendly advice, Mr. Jackson. You might consider replacing your attorney."

"Excuse me?" Hall objected.

ADA Sherman smiled.

"Why should I?" Jackson asked.

"Because as many charges will be filed against Lundgren Corporation and its officers as against its employees. I don't think having an attorney who gets paid by your bosses will necessarily be in your best interests."

Jackson turned to look at his attorney.

*

An arrest warrant was also issued for one Taylor Smith, charging him with three counts of conspiracy to commit murder, multiple counts of obstruction, assault and tampering with evidence. The warrant was immediately forwarded to the Seattle office of the FBI, since the district attorney's office had credible evidence that the subject had fled the state.

At this point, that was all they could do.

*

Jason knew nothing of the particulars of the task force's operations that morning. He didn't go on any of them. Instead, he pulled his car into the parking lot at the city marina just before 6:00 Wednesday morning and parked at the edge of the group of official vehicles. He grabbed his camera, then locked the car and headed down toward the boat basin.

The crime scene people had called in reinforcements. Several vehicles he passed as he walked bore the emblems of the Skagit County Sheriff, Island County Sheriff, and even the Skagit County Medical Examiner. They must have come in last night. The first ferry didn't arrive for another hour.

The plan, he knew, was to already be on the island and working by then.

As he walked across the lot, he pulled out his cell phone and keyed in the message he'd decided to send Lisa: *Sorry I missed you. Working out of cell service. Going well. Watch the news today. Lundgren's going down.*

He sent the message, hoping it wouldn't wake her. She usually got up at 6:30 to get ready for school, but he didn't think he could wait that long to send it. By 6:30 he would probably be well on his way out to the island and out of cell range. If the message did wake her, hopefully it wouldn't cost her too much sleep.

The fog of the last two days had disappeared overnight. A heavy overcast now blotted out the stars, turning the morning as dark as a cave. Dawn was still an hour away and there wasn't so much as a glow in the east. The only light came from the electric globes scattered along the docks and the officers' flashlights.

It was still cold. Jason wore the same hat, sweatshirt and gloves he'd worn yesterday. And like yesterday, his feet were already growing cold.

Danny had been assigned as liaison to one of the warrant teams in Seattle, so he was on his own.

He walked down the ramp to where the techs were busy loading equipment on to the sheriff's boats. There were as many techs this morning as there had been searchers the day before. Maybe two dozen. They were obviously not messing around with this.

Good.

He spotted the leader of the tech crew from yesterday off to the side, talking with the supervising detective, Ridley Walker.

"Good morning," Jason said as he walked up to them. He shook each of their hands. "Mind if I tag along again today?"

The tech shrugged and looked to the detective.

"I don't see why not," Walker said. "We wouldn't be here at all if you hadn't started digging that hole."

Jason smiled. "I was hoping you were going to feel that way."

The detective pointed at Jason's camera. "That for us or your story?"

Jason shrugged. "My story. I figured you'd have your own photographers who'd do a much better job than I can."

The tech smiled. "You're probably right about that."

"But I think people need to see this. They need to see this for exactly what it is."

The other men nodded.

*

With the expanded workforce, progress was quicker than it had been the day before. By the time they broke for lunch, they had unearthed some thirty more remains. There still was no end in sight. At this point no one could even say how large the mass grave actually was, only that it was big. None of the remains had been removed. The medical examiner's people had decided that it was more important that they document the entire site as they'd found it.

At lunch, they lined up for Styrofoam cups of coffee, vegetable-beef soup, and cold sandwiches.

Jason managed to sit next to one of the medical examiner's men and introduced himself. They shook hands. The man said his name was Matt Kelly, assistant medical examiner.

"You're the one who found this mess," the man said.

Jason shrugged. "I just pointed everyone in the right direction."

Kelly smiled and sipped his coffee.

"You mind answering a question for me?"

"Will I be reading my name in the paper?"

Jason shrugged. "It's up to you. I could do it either way, a direct quote or on background. I'm mainly looking for information."

"What's the question?"

"I was wondering what the odds are of identifying those people." Jason nodded toward the earth-colored scar behind them. Curiously, almost every single person there had chosen to eat lunch with his back to the site.

"Well, it depends on how old the remains are."

"I believe they were killed in the spring of 1942," Jason told him. "I might be able to narrow it down to within a couple of weeks, but the spring of 1942."

Kelly shook his head. "It's going to be tough. The easiest identification tool is dental records, but after sixty years, they've probably all been lost or destroyed. And that's providing we know which records to look for."

"What about DNA?" Jason asked.

"It's possible we could recover DNA, but it's expensive. Very expensive. As much as twenty-five hundred apiece. With this many victims...."

Jason nodded.

"Even if we had enough money in the budget to do DNA testing on all of the remains, it might not do anybody any good," Kelly told him. "It's not like on the TV forensics shows. DNA's not a magic bullet. You have to have someone to compare it to, otherwise it's just a series of meaningless numbers."

"Maybe I could help with that," Jason said. The front page of the *Seattle News* was read by thousands of readers in the Everett-Seattle-Tacoma-Olympia metroplex, the Pacific Northwest, and the nation. In short, he had reach.

He'd written ninety percent of the article last night after returning home and had turned out what he believed to be a slam-bang exposé of corporate greed leading to mass murder. More greed and a large portion of racism had led an entire community to cover up the crime for seventy years. It would be big.

He just needed some good photos and strategic quotes to give it maximum impact.

It probably wouldn't win him many friends in Port Salish.

Of course, he still needed the permission of the task force leadership to run it. A deal was a deal. He had given his word.

"I need to talk to one of the task force supervisors," he told the tech.

Unfortunately, they were all busy supervising the raids, not the excavations.

He looked at his cell phone. No service.

"Good luck," the tech said.

*

As usual, as soon as the boat carrying Jason and a half dozen forensic techs rounded the breakwater and entered the harbor at 7:30 that night, his phone chirped that he had messages. Judging by the sudden activity around him, so did most of the weary techs. It was like a dance; everyone had their cell out and was bent over the ethereal white light of a smart phone display. It seemed no one had coverage on Deception Island.

He pulled his phone from his pocket.

Today he only had two missed texts and one missed call. An improvement from yesterday, mostly because Lisa now knew he was out of cell service during the day.

Sure enough, the first text was from Lisa and had come in nearly two hours ago at 5:30, probably sent as soon as she'd gotten home from classes. He opened the message.

Saw the news. Wow! We got them! Call me when you can.

Well, no, they really didn't have them yet. There had been arrests, but they wouldn't really "have" them until someone was convicted and in prison.

The boat's engine throttled back. Jason looked up as the boat coasted expertly into the dock and came to a stop. Again, like a well-choreographed dance, everybody on the boat stood at once and began gathering belongings for the trudge up to the parking lot and their vehicles.

To a man, they were tired and cold and more than a little depressed by what they'd seen all day. The drizzle had thickened with nightfall, still not enough to be considered real rain, but enough to make everything wet. And it was cold. Jason's feet felt like lumps of Play-Doh at the end of his legs.

He decided he would wait until he got back to the house to call Lisa. He would be in a better mood and able to enjoy the conversation more after a hot shower.

He climbed out on to the dock and started toward his car. As he walked, he turned to the second text message. It was from Danny and had come in about thirty minutes after Lisa's.

He opened it.

Call me when you get a chance. I'll be up late.

Just like Danny: short and simple.

He found her number and punched it in. She answered on the second ring. "Hey. You back in civilization?"

"Not until I've had a hot meal and shower. We just got back to the marina. How was the raid?"

"Satisfying. But we're neck deep in documents now. It will take a month to go through everything. At least."

He could only imagine.

"Are you home now?"

"No," she told him. "We didn't get finished in time to catch the ferry. I'm sitting in a motel. We'll be back in the morning. Along with a U-Haul full of Lundgren documents."

He laughed. "Sounds like you'll be busy for a while."

She groaned.

"Listen, I wonder if I can get you to do a favor for me?"

"What's that?" Danny asked.

"Call someone and get me permission to run the story about Deception Island. I'm getting nervous about leaks. It's already been two days and you know everyone in town is asking questions."

"I could make a couple of calls for you. Does it have to be tonight? It's getting late."

"The deadline for tomorrow's paper is one in the morning. Besides, I don't think anyone connected with this is getting much sleep right now. Do you?"

She admitted the truth in that. "Okay. Let me make a couple of calls. I'll give you a buzz when I find out something."

"Thanks."

Jason disconnected and checked his final message, a voice mail from Miles. He didn't even bother to listen to it; he knew exactly what it would say: where's the story? No thank you for the tip about the Lundgren bust. No nothing. He shoved his phone into a coat pocket.

He had just reached his car and unlocked the door, when someone in a heavy coat and a knit cap approached him. "Excuse me?"

Jason looked at the middle-aged man hidden under the coat, hat and gloves. He looked nearly as cold and miserable as Jason felt. "Yes?"

"I'm Jonathan Hoffman, a reporter for *The Ebey Island Press*," the man said. "Could you tell me what's going on out on Deception Island?"

"Sorry," Jason shook his head. "I'm not authorized to talk about it."

The reporter looked disappointed, but resigned. No doubt he'd heard the same response more than a few times over the last day or two.

"Hey," Jason stopped. "You want a story?"

"Yeah. Of course."

"Write about Sonny Adams. He single-handedly defeated the gunmen out on Shoreline Drive the other day. He saved us all. Write about that."

*

Jason picked up a burger and fries from a fast food place on the way home, then left them on the kitchen table while he headed upstairs to shower some warmth back into his body. On the way, he noticed the message light flashing on the answering machine. There were two messages. Both were from the reporter he'd met at the dock. He erased them.

Fifteen minutes later, refreshed by a shower, Jason returned to the dining room and his cooling burger. As he began to eat, he checked his cell phone again. Danny still hadn't called. Was she having trouble getting a hold of someone? Or having trouble convincing them to make a decision?

If it came down to it, there was really no legal way to prevent him from running the story. The press was still free and as long as he revealed nothing that could put someone's life in danger, they would have no choice in the matter.

There was even a bit of a gray area regarding that.

But he had given his word. He would rather they gave him the okay first.

He finished his cheeseburger without really tasting it, lingered a bit longer on the fries, and opened his laptop. He pulled the memory card from his camera and quickly uploaded the photos he'd taken at the grave site. Only some of them would be good enough to use, but he'd let Miles and his people make that decision. He would submit them as an attachment to the main story.

He checked his phone again, though obviously he would have noticed if Danny had called. He was, after all, sitting right there.

Finally, he could stand it no longer. He punched in a text and sent it to her.

Anything?

The reply came a few seconds later. *They're talking it over. DA, etc. Patience.*

He smiled. *Deadline. Editor.*

Lol.

Jason set his cell aside, thought about it for a few seconds, then grabbed the cordless phone from its cradle and dialed Lisa's number. She answered on the second ring, sounding guarded. Naturally. She wouldn't know the number showing up on her phone.

"Hi," he said. "It's me, Jason. You still awake?"

"Yeah. You just get back?"

Her voice sounded better. It was still hoarse, but not as bad as the other day. He no longer wanted to wince every time she spoke.

"Pretty much. How are you feeling? You sound better."

"I am. I basically didn't talk all day. That helped."

"Good."

"Been coughing up some nasty crap, too."

That was probably as helpful as anything. Get the irritants out of there. It had probably helped more than not speaking.

"So, did you find what you thought you would on that island?"

He briefed her about what they had uncovered and what still remained to be done. He also told her about the article he was hoping to have published tomorrow.

When Lisa spoke again, her voice was muted, strained. "What's wrong with people? How could they do something like that?"

"I don't know," Jason said. "I honestly don't have an answer to that."

"They'll pay for this, though. Right?"

In truth, he didn't think anyone would do any jail time, or even go to trial for the mass murder. After all, it had happened more than seventy years ago. Most of the people who had ordered and carried out the killings were dead now, or so old as to be as good as. His emphasis now was just getting the truth out in public. As public as he could get it.

He wasn't going to tell her that, though.

His cell phone buzzed.

"Hang on," he told Lisa. "Someone's on my cell."

It was a text from Danny. *They said go ahead.*

He returned to Lisa. "I'd better go. I have an article to finish tonight."

"Tomorrow's paper?"

"I'm hoping."

CHAPTER 22

Jason's story not only made the front page of Thursday's paper, a coup for every reporter, but filled the entire page under a banner headline reading: "Mass Grave in San Juan County." A full color photograph, one Jason had submitted, ran with the story, featuring two grim forensic technicians working amid a tangle of half-buried skeletons. It was a powerful, disturbing photo and Jason imagined there had been a spirited debate among the editors about whether it was too graphic for the front page.

Personally, he thought it suited the story perfectly. It was a disturbing story; it deserved a disturbing photo.

The first text message came in just after 6:00 as he was leaving a convenience store with coffee and a copy of the paper. It was from Danny. She was, no doubt, on her way to catch the ferry back to the island. Her and the U-Haul full of Lundgren documents.

He didn't envy her job for the next few days.

He opened the text.

Damn! You are good. Everybody loves it.

Thanks. Was all he could think of in reply.

BTW there are a half dozen TV vans waiting for the ferry.

He groaned. *Figures.*

Fair warning.

The marina would be a zoo when they returned at the end of the day.

*

The next text came in just as he was pulling into the parking lot at the marina. He parked amid the assortment of official vehicles, left the engine and heater running, and checked his cell phone's display. Lisa.

He accepted the text.

OMG! Loved it. Made me cry and want to throw up at the same time.

Jason smiled. Again, the only thing he could think to say in reply was: *Thanks.*

*

They were still stripping the tarps off the work area when Jason heard the first one. The sun had been up barely twenty minutes and it was weak at best. The sky was still covered by a thick overcast that continued to spit a cold, steady drizzle that threatened to become snow, but never quite did. All the techs were bundled up in heavy coats, knit caps, gloves, and boots. Their breath formed white clouds of vapor around their heads as they worked.

Now all heads turned skyward as the familiar throbbing chop grew louder and closer. A few seconds later, the first helicopter appeared.

"Smile," someone said. "You're on TV."

Within an hour, three helicopters, all bearing the markings of television stations were circling over the island like seagulls, jockeying for the best shots, the best position. They were mildly annoying, but really didn't interfere with the work.

"How long do you figure this will go on?" Det. Solbane asked Jason.

Jason shrugged. "An hour, probably less. Fuel is expensive and there really isn't anything terribly interesting to photograph. They'll shoot some film and go away."

"Let's hope so."

"The bigger challenge is going to be the marina when we get back," Jason told him. "It's going to be a zoo. Every TV station and newspaper in the region is going to have a reporter there wanting an interview. "

"Wonderful."

"Tell everyone to just keep walking. Refuse to comment and get out of there as soon as possible. Maybe the task force could hold a news conference, give them something to put on the air," Jason told him. "That's all they really want. Something to put on the air."

"I think someone's working on that."

Someone should have been working on a press conference as soon as they'd given him permission to run the story. It didn't take a brain surgeon to realize this thing was going to draw press attention. Mass graves weren't found in a sleepy little corner of the United States every day. The key was how the authorities handled it.

He watched the helicopters circle idly overhead.

*

By the time they closed the site down for the night on Thursday, they had uncovered more than one hundred skeletons. So far, none of the uncovered bodies had been moved, nor had any attempt been made to identify them, or even establish conclusive causes of death. Since the area was being treated as a crime scene, it was important that the bodies be analyzed in relation to all the others so a sequence of events could be recreated. Numerous photos were taken of the skeletons where they lay, from every possible angle and from close, medium, and long range. Other techs drew up sketches of the grave layout and every skeleton's location.

They were creating a detailed map of the mass grave.

It meant leaving the uncovered skeletons in place while excavations continued on the rest of the grave. In many instances—possibly even most—the techs could clearly see more bones below the surface ones, but would not be able to approach them until the removal began.

Two anthropologists from the University of Washington had joined the team today. Their experience with organizing and directing large-scale archaeological excavations would greatly help the crime scene people.

Jason thought it was a brilliant idea. It was a huge and extremely complex crime scene. The authorities needed to bring in as many skilled people as possible.

Near the end of the day, Jason managed to get Det. Solbane alone. "How's it going?"

The detective shrugged. He looked exhausted. "As well as expected. At least the damn news choppers have gone."

As Jason had predicted, they'd only hung around for an hour or so before heading back to base.

"How much longer do they think it's going to take to finish this?"

"We should have the full extent of the grave uncovered by the end of the week," he said. "If the weather holds. Excavating the remains will probably take two or three weeks after that."

Jason nodded.

"That's provided we don't have any more crimes that pull away manpower. We've got pretty much every available person working on it now."

Jason understood. Resources were strained now trying to handle the situation, and there were too many things out of their control. Other crimes were only one of them. There was also the weather. So far, the drizzle was continuing, but not growing heavier. If that changed and real rain arrived, the grave would become a mud pit. In that case, the work might have to stop altogether until it dried out.

"I'm going to have to head back to Seattle," he told the detective. "I hope I'll be able to check in with you now and then, see how the investigation's going."

"I think we can work something out," Solbane said. "It was an interesting article in the paper this morning."

Jason smiled. "Thanks."

"Though you jumped to some conclusions the evidence doesn't support yet."

"I know." Jason held his smile. "But it will."

*

Jason didn't know it until later, but his story had been picked up by the Associated Press Wire Service. The story of the mass grave in San Juan County appeared whole or in part in well over a hundred newspapers across the country. Naturally, it was picked up by the regional papers in Portland, Eugene, Spokane, and Boise, but it also appeared in papers from the *L.A. Times* to the *Chicago Tribune*, the *Boston Herald* to the *Miami Herald* and the *Rocky Mountain News*. And it wasn't only the larger newspapers either. Smaller papers in towns from Huntsville, Alabama, to Helena, Montana and Des Moines, Iowa carried it too.

It was also carried by the *Guardian* newspaper in London, a daily in Sydney, Australia, and a dozen newspapers in Japan.

Within a few hours of publication, the story was the lead on CNN and all three major television networks. By mid-afternoon, it was the most viewed news story on the web.

In short, it was big.

Jason first got an inkling of just how big the story had become when he returned to the marina at the end of the day and collected his missed cell messages. There were ten. The key one was a text from Miles, sent at 11:35 that morning.

CNN wants to set up an interview. What do you want me to tell them?

Jason didn't have a clue what he wanted Miles to tell them.

He'd also received a text from Debbie, sent a few minutes after Miles'. *Congratulations! People are talking Pulitzer around here. And CNN wants to interview you. You're famous.*

Jason could only shake his head.

He looked up as the boat approached the dock and spotted the cluster of satellite vans waiting for them in the parking lot.

*

Thursday evening, after more than two days of refusing to comment about the arrests or the mass grave, Lundgren Corporation finally issued an official statement to the press. It read:

"It is Lundgren corporate policy to withhold comment on any ongoing investigation."

They had nothing else to say.

*

"They're probably sitting in some conference room right now, trying desperately to figure out how to spin this," Jason said.

"Good luck with that," Danny said. "And I mean that in the worst possible way."

It was Friday evening and they had met at Mary Lou's for dinner. The drizzle of the last few days had finally given way to real rain. It poured straight down from the layer of cloud hidden in the darkness without a lick of wind to move it around. It felt like a cold, heavy shower.

They stood in the entryway of the busy restaurant, along with a dozen others, waiting for a table to open up.

"Did they shut down the dig today?" Jason asked her.

Danny shook her head. "I haven't heard."

Jason hadn't gone out to the site this morning. There wasn't much more he could do out there and he had to deal with his dad's estate. So he'd spent all day doing that. He'd picked up his dad's mail at the post office, including the copies of the death certificate he'd ordered last week. He'd then closed all his father's bank accounts, notified the insurance company and Social Security Administration of the death, gathered the urn with his dad's ashes from the funeral home, and paid whatever outstanding bills he could find.

Last of all, he had called the auctioneer Taylor Smith had recommended and arranged to sell the pickup and the contents of the house at auction.

It had been an exhausting day. But it had to be done.

Tomorrow morning he was planning to return to Seattle. At least until new developments in the case warranted returning.

For her part, Danny had spent the day, along with several other members of the task force, going through the documents they'd seized from Lundgren until—as she'd put it—her eyes crossed.

The hostess called their name and escorted them to a table. It wasn't a window table, or even a booth against a wall, but at this point anything was fine. Jason was tired and hungry. He hadn't come here for the ambiance.

He nodded politely at the folks at the next table and settled into his chair. Danny sat down across from him.

"Wow," he said. "The place is hopping tonight."

Danny agreed. "Lots of strange faces. Media in town?"

"Probably."

Jason opened his menu; Danny didn't.

"You going to order the same thing you always do?" he asked.

"If it works, don't fix it."

Jason smiled, shook his head, and turned to the menu. This was going to be tough. The very air inside the restaurant seemed to drip with the aromas of fried onion and bacon. It made him want to eat everything.

"Hey, Danny." Amber was their waitress again. She looked at Jason. "I'm sorry. I don't remember your name."

He told her his name.

"That's right," she said like it had been on the tip of her tongue.

Jason smiled and forced himself to make a decision about dinner.

"You guys are busy tonight," Danny said.

"It's been crazy all day. It's got to be all the reporters in town. Can you believe what they found out on Deception Island?"

Jason and Danny exchanged a look. Yes, they believed it.

"Sorry, that was stupid. I mean, things like that don't happen around here. I mean, it's Port Salish. Nothing ever happens here."

Jason looked up at her. "Except drive-by shootings?"

She blushed. "I'll be quiet now."

They told Amber what they wanted for dinner and she swept away again to submit their order to the kitchen and get their drinks.

"How can she be so cheery about it?" Jason asked. "It's mass murder."

"I don't know. I guess it's her job to be cheery."

Jason could only shake his head.

A minute later, Amber re-appeared with their drinks, but only spent a few seconds with them before she had to attend to another table.

"So, ballistics came back," Danny said. "The slug taken from Takashi's body was a positive match to the Glock 23 we impounded from Todd Baxter. The DA has filed murder charges against him."

"He didn't take the deal?"

She shook her head. "The deal was never for the shooter. The deal was to get the details on the conspiracy. And guess who took it?"

He shook his head.

"Melissa Devereux, the one who put my mom in the hospital. I guess she was Taylor Smith's number two."

"And what does she get in return?"

"I imagine it depends on the quality of the information," Danny said. "But a reduced sentence of some sort."

Jason nodded. He knew it was standard practice and it always helped to have the testimony of an insider, but he also felt they probably had enough evidence to convict them without trading away any jail time. He almost felt cheated.

"How do you feel about that?" he asked her.

Danny shrugged. "It's how the system works."

"Even if it means she walks on what she did to your mother?"

"Oh, she'll still do time," she said. "Prison time is prison time; it doesn't have to be specifically for assaulting my mom."

Amber brought their burgers and set them on the table in front of them, along with a caddy of condiments. Danny had ordered her usual Fajita burger. Jason was living dangerously and ordered a Napa burger, drizzled with wine sauce and topped with tomatoes, avocado, and alfalfa sprouts. It smelled fabulous.

He took a bite. It tasted as good as it smelled.

"Good?" Danny asked with a smile.

"Oh yeah."

For a few minutes, they concentrated on their food, eating like people who had worked hard all day without refueling.

As he ate, Jason suddenly realized that for being as busy as the restaurant was, it wasn't as loud as you'd expect. With this many people in a closed room, just talking, there should be a certain amount of ambient noise.

It was as if a pall hung over the crowd.

"So, other than Amber," Jason said, "how is the news going over in town?"

Danny shrugged. "I think most people are having a hard time processing it."

"Hell of a shock, learning someone committed mass murder in your back yard."

"Even harder once you realize that the killers were your grandparents."

Jason nodded.

"What about the mayor? City Council? Any official statements?"

"Not yet," Danny shook her head. "But what can they say?"

Jason didn't have a clue. Even if the town and its residents were completely innocent of wrongdoing in the mass killings—which he didn't think was the case—something like this was a public relations nightmare. "Visit Port Salish, home of the biggest American mass murder since the Indian Wars."

It wasn't exactly a selling point.

A group of one man and three women rose from a table at the window to Jason's right. He hadn't noticed them before, but now, as they wove their way between the tables toward the cashier, he recognized one of the women. Sonya Devray, a reporter for the Seattle CBS affiliate.

Their eyes met. She waved and detoured over to the table. "Reynolds, right? Congratulations on your story. I hear people are talking Pulitzer."

"It's just talk," Jason said. "But, thanks."

He introduced her to Danny. The two women exchanged polite greetings.

"What are the odds I could get you to do an on-screen interview? The story behind the story?"

He smiled. "Not very good. I'm heading back to Seattle tomorrow."

She returned his smile. "It was worth a shot."

"You have to try."

Sonya congratulated him again and left to join her colleagues at the cashier.

"Wow," Danny said. "I'm eating with a celebrity. Who'd a thought?"

"Whatever."

"Change of subject." Danny had finished her burger and was dragging a French fry through a pool of ketchup on her plate. "Have you talked to Lisa?"

"Not today," Jason told her. "But yeah, I have."

"How's she doing?"

"She's getting better. I don't think of chalkboards every time she talks anymore."

"Good." She looked up at him. "But that wasn't what I was asking about."

The elephant in the room had raised its leathery head.

"We haven't talked about it."

*

Saturday morning, Jason caught the 7:00 ferry to Anacortes and drove straight to the *Seattle News* offices. He walked into the newsroom at 10:00 to a subdued, if heroic welcome by the light weekend staff. He accepted the congratulations with as much humility as he could muster.

Jason met briefly with Miles, who immediately wanted to know what Jason planned to do as a follow up to Thursday's story. Good old Miles. Not even a congratulations. Just what's next?

Fortunately, Jason had anticipated the question and already had a story sketched out detailing the process that led to the discovery of the mass grave. Miles only thought for a minute before giving him the go-ahead.

"It's 10:25," Miles told him, looking significantly at his watch. "I want to see a first draft by the end of business today."

"5:00?"

"5:00," Miles said. "The spotlight is on us. I want plenty of time to go over it. That a problem?"

"Not at all."

It should only take a few hours to develop the final product.

Jason got to his feet. "I'll get on it."

"You still want to do that CNN interview?"

Jason hesitated. "What do you think?"

"It could be a good career move. It would certainly raise your profile nationally. And the paper's."

"Okay. Let's do it."

"I'll make the call. Now get to work."

Jason smiled and headed to his desk.

*

At 6:00, Jason submitted the final revision to Miles, leaned back in his desk chair and pulled out his cell phone. He typed in a text message and sent it to Lisa.

In town. Mind if I come over?

The reply came within a minute.

Sure.

He shut down his computer.

*

At 6:45, Jason climbed up the steps to Lisa's apartment and knocked on her door. He had a key, but, under the circumstances, didn't feel comfortable letting himself in. A certain amount of formality was called for. At least until the air was cleared.

The rain that had hit Port Salish yesterday was lingering over Seattle. Everything was soaking wet and runoff gurgled steadily in the gutters of the apartment building, pattering against the shrubs in the planters to either side of Lisa's door. It did seem to be warmer than it had on the island. That was something.

He turned up the collar of his coat and knocked again.

This was weird. He felt as nervous as a high school kid on his first date.

The door swung open and Lisa stood there, smiling shyly, softly back lit by the living room lights. Somehow, she could make faded jeans and a UW sweatshirt look elegant.

He stepped forward and they hugged.

He found himself looking for Hector, expecting his greeting. But Hector wasn't there.

"You're drenched," she said as she closed and locked the door behind him. "Why didn't you just come in?"

"I don't know."

She took his coat and went to get him a towel.

Jason wandered into the living room and sat down on the sofa. A stack of books lay on the coffee table. One lay open and beside it, a notebook was open to a blank page. A half-finished cup of tea and Lisa's laptop stood off to one side.

"Have you eaten?" he asked. "I thought maybe we could go get some dinner."

She returned to the room with a towel and handed it to him. "It's nasty out. Maybe we could order a pizza."

Pizza sounded good to him.

"I like the beard." She settled down beside him on the couch. "It looks good on you."

"Thanks." It had been almost a week now since he'd stopped shaving. It was just now getting thick enough to look like a real beard.

Lisa gently touched his injured arm. "You're not wearing your sling."

He smiled and shook his head. "It's feeling better. The doctor said if I didn't start using it, I was going to lose my range of motion."

Lisa nodded. Her hand drifted down his arm to trace the heavy scab covering the wound on his hand. It was sore, but healing well. If nothing else, he was going to have some interesting scars to show his kids.

She clasped his hand. He returned the pressure.

Their eyes met. For a few moments, they gazed at each other. Lisa's eyes were shining. His own vision was blurred.

"We need to talk," she said.

"I know."

CHAPTER 23

The man dressed for the day in a white cotton shirt, khaki shorts, and sandals. Though it was technically autumn, the forecast called for temperatures in the mid-eighties today, the same as it had been yesterday and would probably be tomorrow. This close to the equator, there were no real seasons, only rain or sunshine.

He shared the elevator to the lobby with a young couple who were clearly on their honeymoon. They were so wrapped in each other and so full of absolute joy it formed an aura around them. Enjoy it, he mentally told them, as long as you can. The real world will rear its ugly head soon enough.

At the lobby, the honeymooners ignored him and strolled toward the street door.

He turned and headed for the terrace.

"*Pardonez, monsieur,*" the hotel concierge stopped him. "*Le journal Americain que vous voulez. C'est arrivée.*"

He handed a neatly folded newspaper to the man.

"*Merci,*" the man said. "*C'etait tres rapide.*"

"*Mon plaisir, monsieur.*"

The man carried the paper out on to the terrace, found a vacant table and ordered an espresso and croissant from the waiter. Only then did he open his copy of the *Seattle News* and begin to read. The headline on the front page read: "A Deadly Cover-Up."

As he read, a smile formed on Taylor Smith's face. "Well done, Mr. Reynolds," he murmured. "Well done."

Note from the Author

Thank you very much for taking a chance and reading a novel by me, an author you've probably never heard of before. I truly hope you enjoyed my work. If you did enjoy it, I'd like to ask one more favor: help me spread the word. Word-of-mouth is by far the best advertising, so tell your friends and family about it. Write a brief review and post it on Amazon, Goodreads, or Shelfari. Mention it on your blog, on Facebook and Twitter, in your book club. Suggest your local library add it to their shelves. Anything will help. And thank you again.

About The Author

James Boyle has previously published three urban fantasy novels: *Ni'il: The Awakening*, *Ni'il: The War Within*, and *Ni'il: Waking Turtle*. He is a graduate of the University of Oregon and an organizer for the South Coast Writers Conference. He writes a blog on writing and the writing life at www.alifewellwritten.wordpress.com. He lives and works in Gold Beach, on the south coast of Oregon.

CPSIA information can be obtained
at www.ICGtesting.com
Printed in the USA
FSOW01n1336040216
16574FS

9 781457 537264